POSTAL™

CREATED BY MATT HAWKINS

VOLUME 1

PUBLISHED BY TOP COW PRODUCTIONS, INC.
LOS ANGELES

POSTAL

CREATED BY MATT HAWKINS

BRYAN HILL
MATT HAWKINS
WRITERS

ISAAC GOODHART
ARTIST

FOR THIS EDITION COVER ART [
LINDA SEJIC

ORIGINAL EDITIONS EDITED B●
BETSY GONIA

BETSY GONIA
COLORIST & EDITOR

BOOK DESIGN & LAYOUT BY
TRICIA RAMOS

TROY PETERI
LETTERER

Top Cow Productions, Inc.

●Silvestri - *CEO* • Matt Hawkins - *President and COO*

●Gonia - *Managing Editor* • Elena Salcedo - *Operations Manager*

●Cady - *Editorial Assistant* • Vincent Valentine - *Production Assistant*

To find the comic shop
nearest you, call:
1-888-COMICBOOK   for ●

OMICS, INC.
– Chief Operating Officer
ief Financial Officer
– President
Chief Executive Officer
Vice-President
– Publisher
Director of Sales
– Director of Digital Sales
ector of PR & Marketing
irector of Operations
stone – Senior Accounts Manager
ccounts Manager
rector
– Production Manager
e – Print Manager
– Marketing Production Designer
– Content Manager
Production Artist
Production Artist
oduction Artist
Production Artist
– Sales Assistant
– Administrative Assistant

POSTAL VOLUME 1 TRADE PAPERBACK.

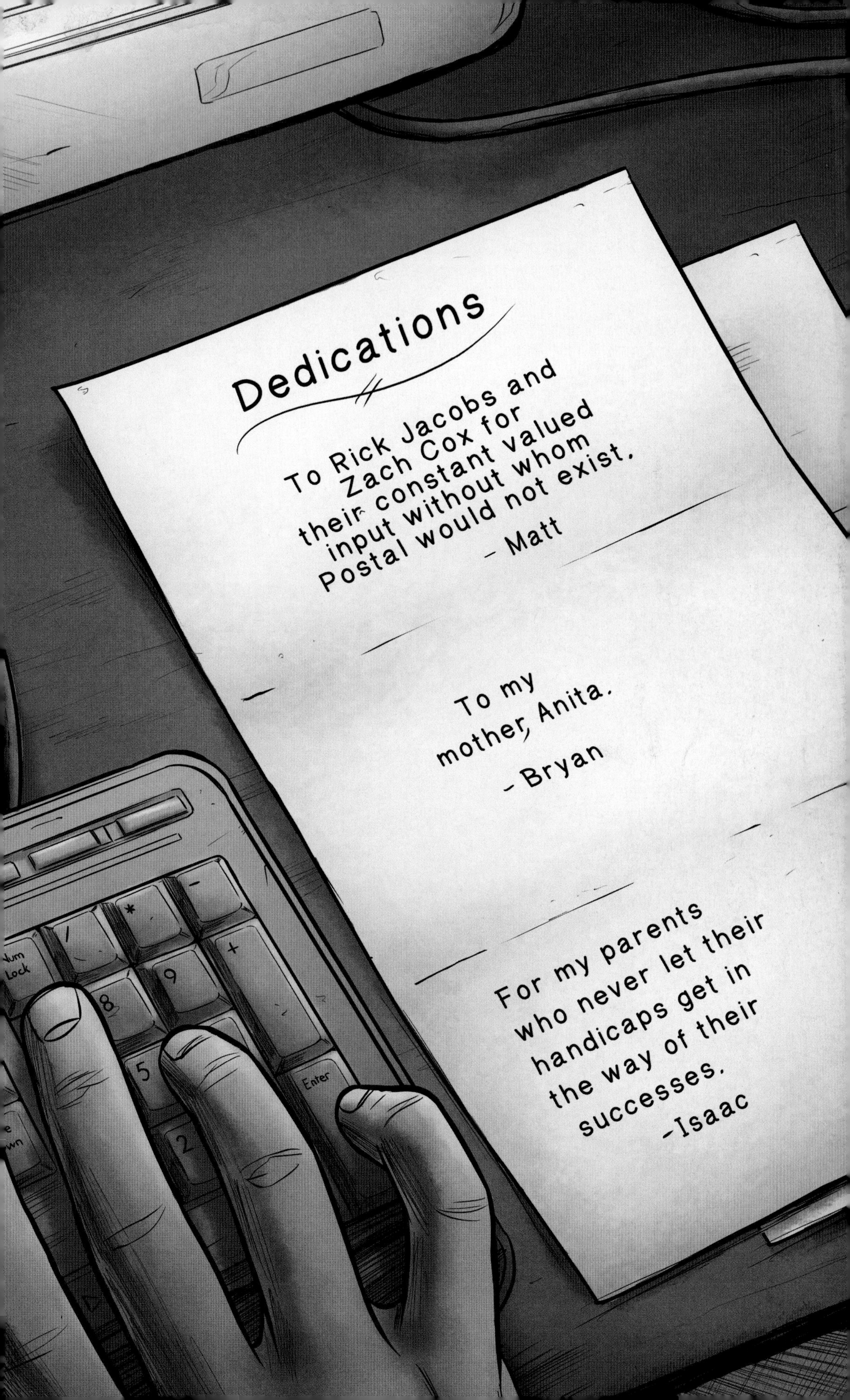
Dedications
To Rick Jacobs and Zach Cox for their constant valued input without whom Postal would not exist.
- Matt
To my mother, Anita.
- Bryan
For my parents who never let their handicaps get in the way of their successes.
-Isaac

Chapter 1

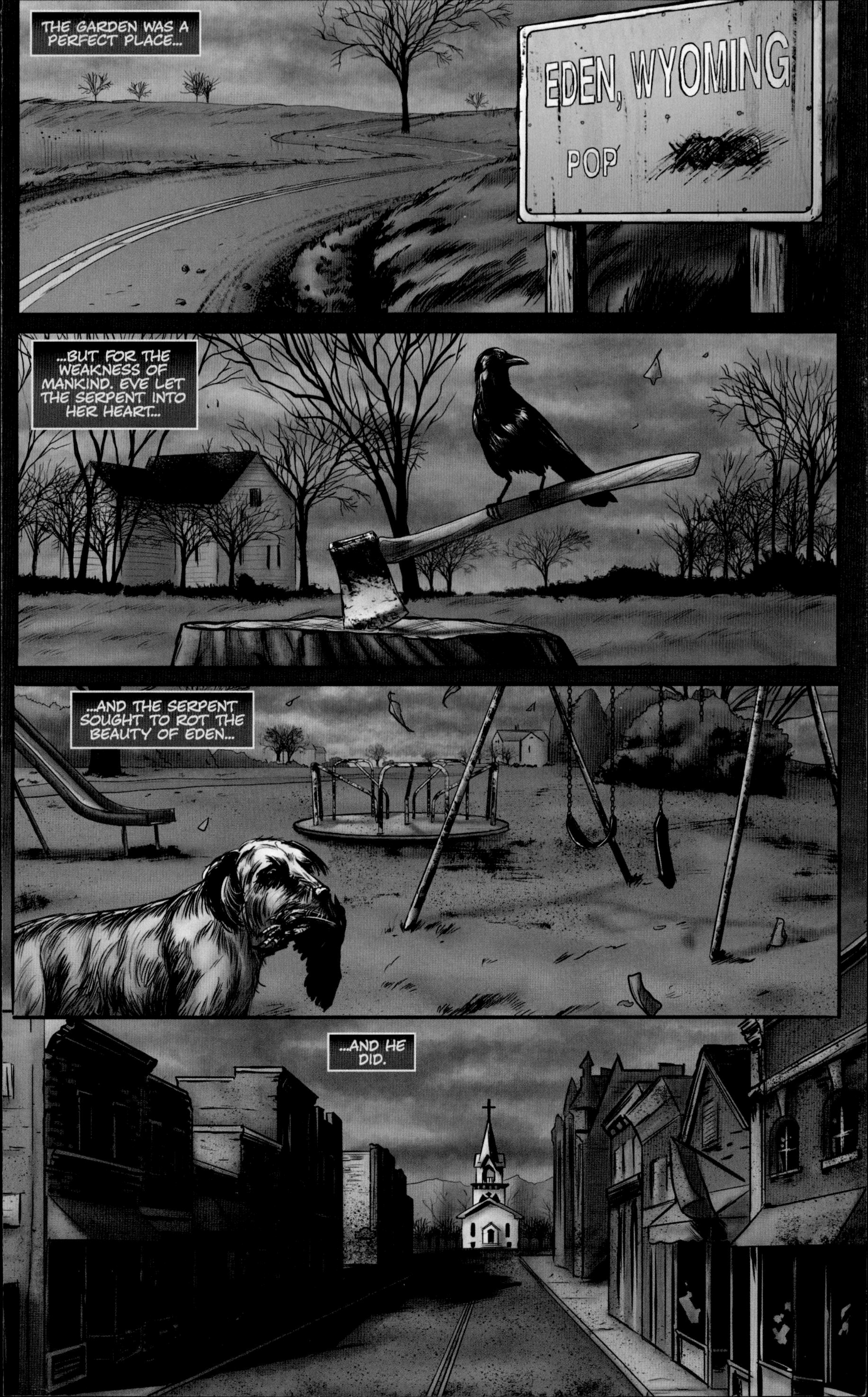
THE GARDEN WAS A PERFECT PLACE...
EDEN, WYOMING
POP
...BUT FOR THE WEAKNESS OF MANKIND. EVE LET THE SERPENT INTO HER HEART...
...AND THE SERPENT SOUGHT TO ROT THE BEAUTY OF EDEN...
...AND HE DID.

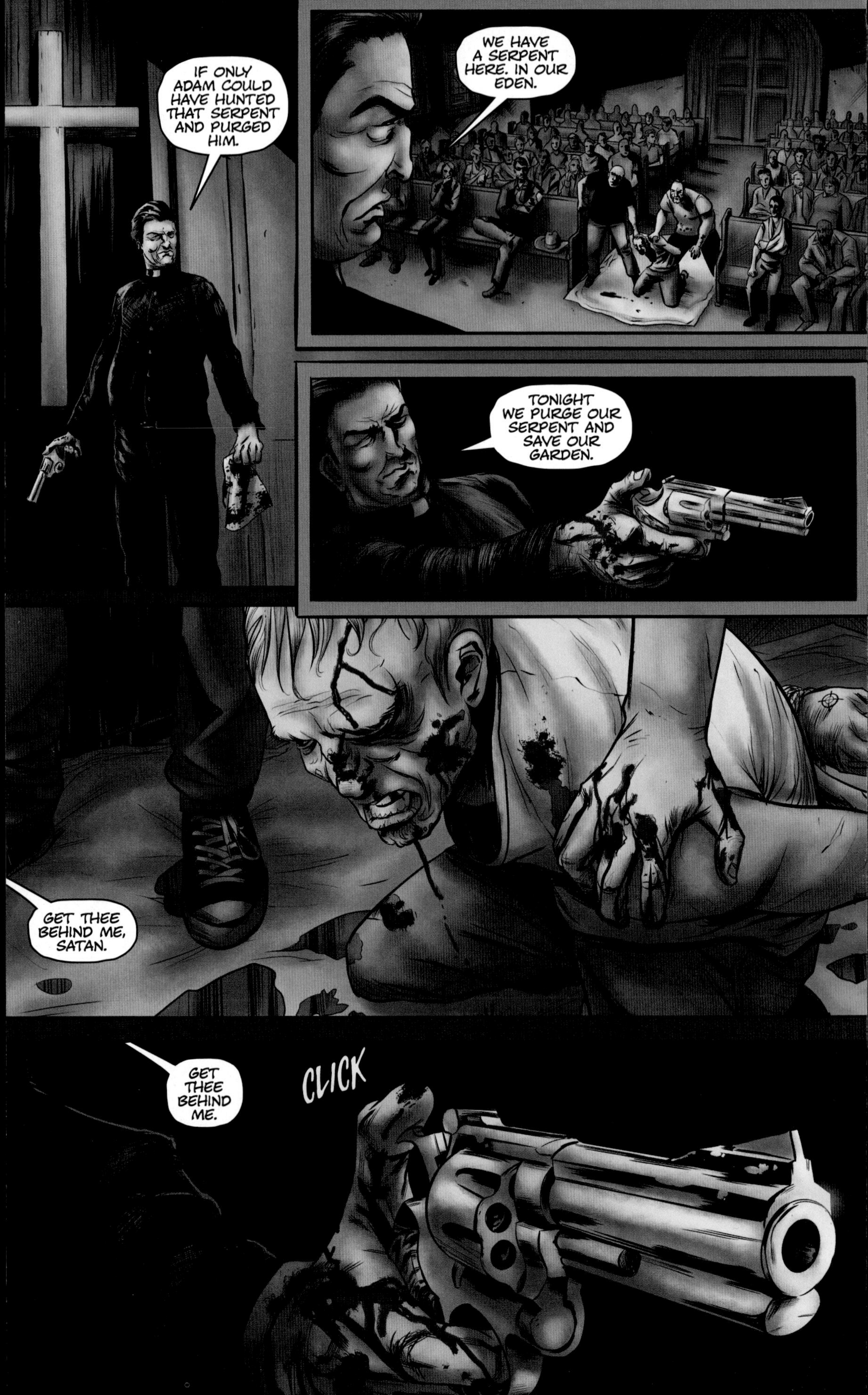
IF ONLY ADAM COULD HAVE HUNTED THAT SERPENT AND PURGED HIM.
WE HAVE A SERPENT HERE. IN OUR EDEN.
TONIGHT WE PURGE OUR SERPENT AND SAVE OUR GARDEN.
GET THEE BEHIND ME, SATAN.
GET THEE BEHIND ME.
CLICK

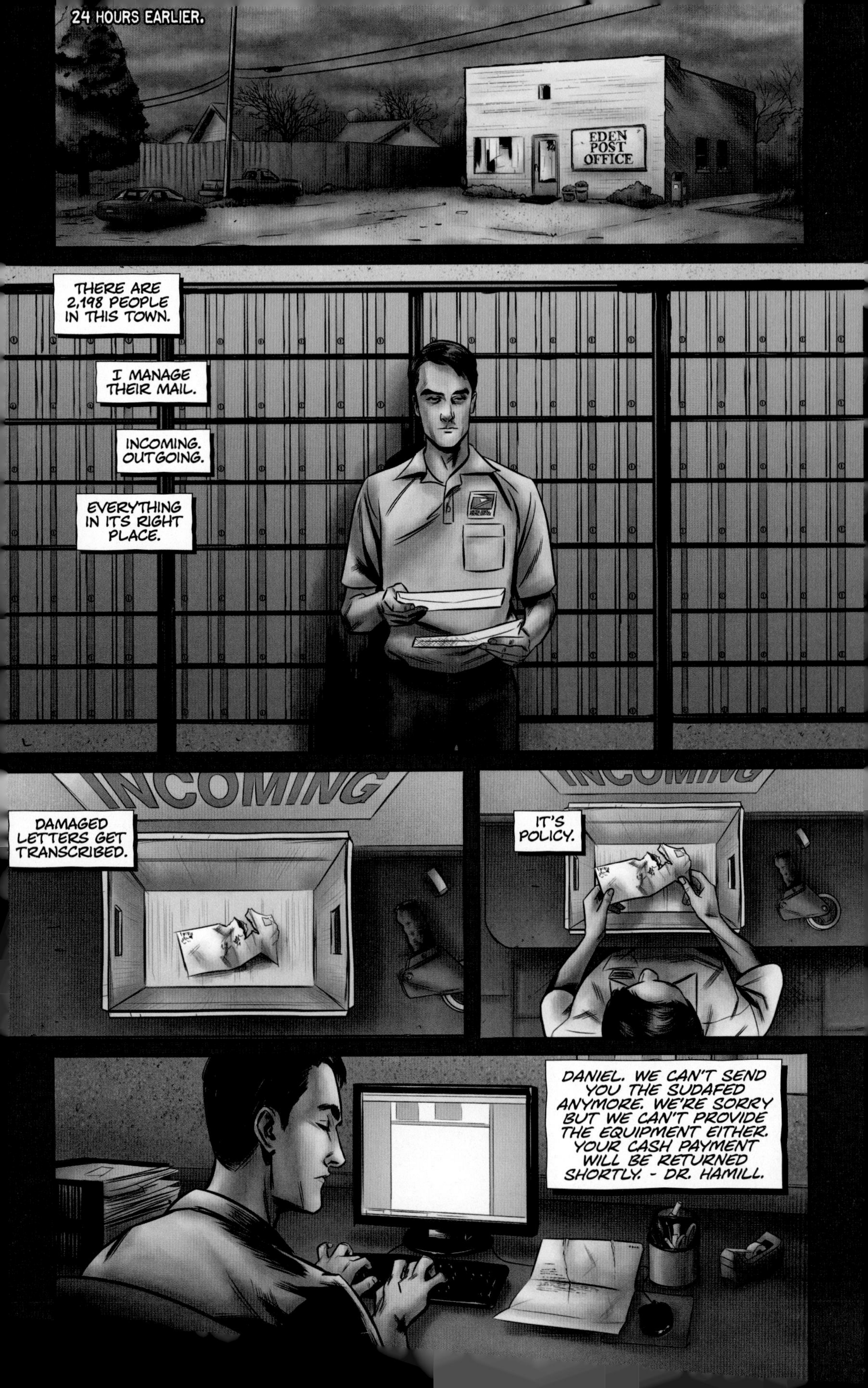
24 HOURS EARLIER.
EDEN POST OFFICE
THERE ARE 2,198 PEOPLE IN THIS TOWN.
I MANAGE THEIR MAIL.
INCOMING. OUTGOING.
EVERYTHING IN ITS RIGHT PLACE.
INCOMING
DAMAGED LETTERS GET TRANSCRIBED.
INCOMING
IT'S POLICY.
DANIEL. WE CAN'T SEND YOU THE SUDAFED ANYMORE. WE'RE SORRY BUT WE CAN'T PROVIDE THE EQUIPMENT EITHER. YOUR CASH PAYMENT WILL BE RETURNED SHORTLY. - DR. HAMILL.

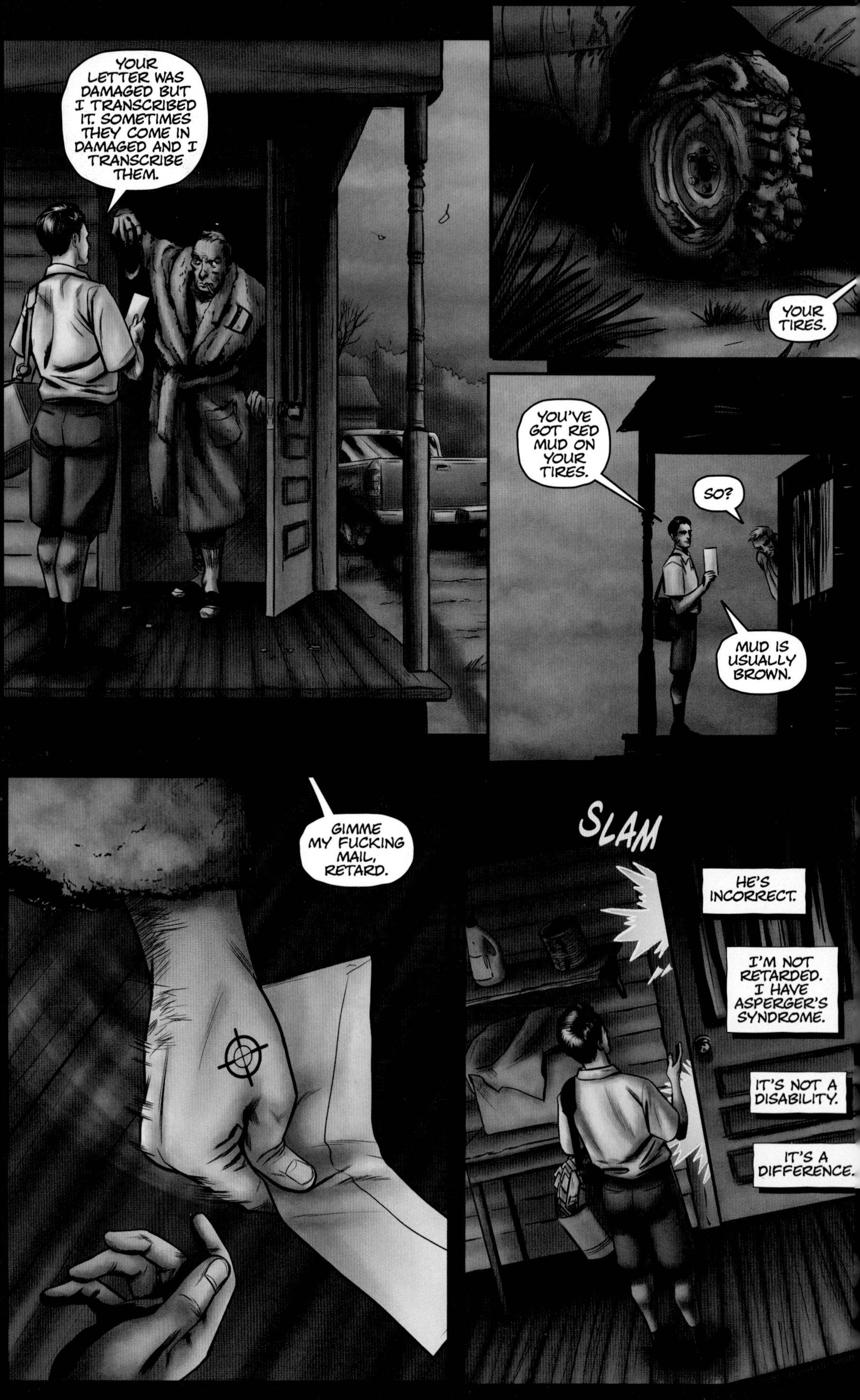
YOUR LETTER WAS DAMAGED BUT I TRANSCRIBED IT. SOMETIMES THEY COME IN DAMAGED AND I TRANSCRIBE THEM.
YOUR TIRES.
YOU'VE GOT RED MUD ON YOUR TIRES.
SO?
MUD IS USUALLY BROWN.
GIMME MY FUCKING MAIL, RETARD.
SLAM
HE'S INCORRECT.
I'M NOT RETARDED. I HAVE ASPERGER'S SYNDROME.
IT'S NOT A DISABILITY.
IT'S A DIFFERENCE.

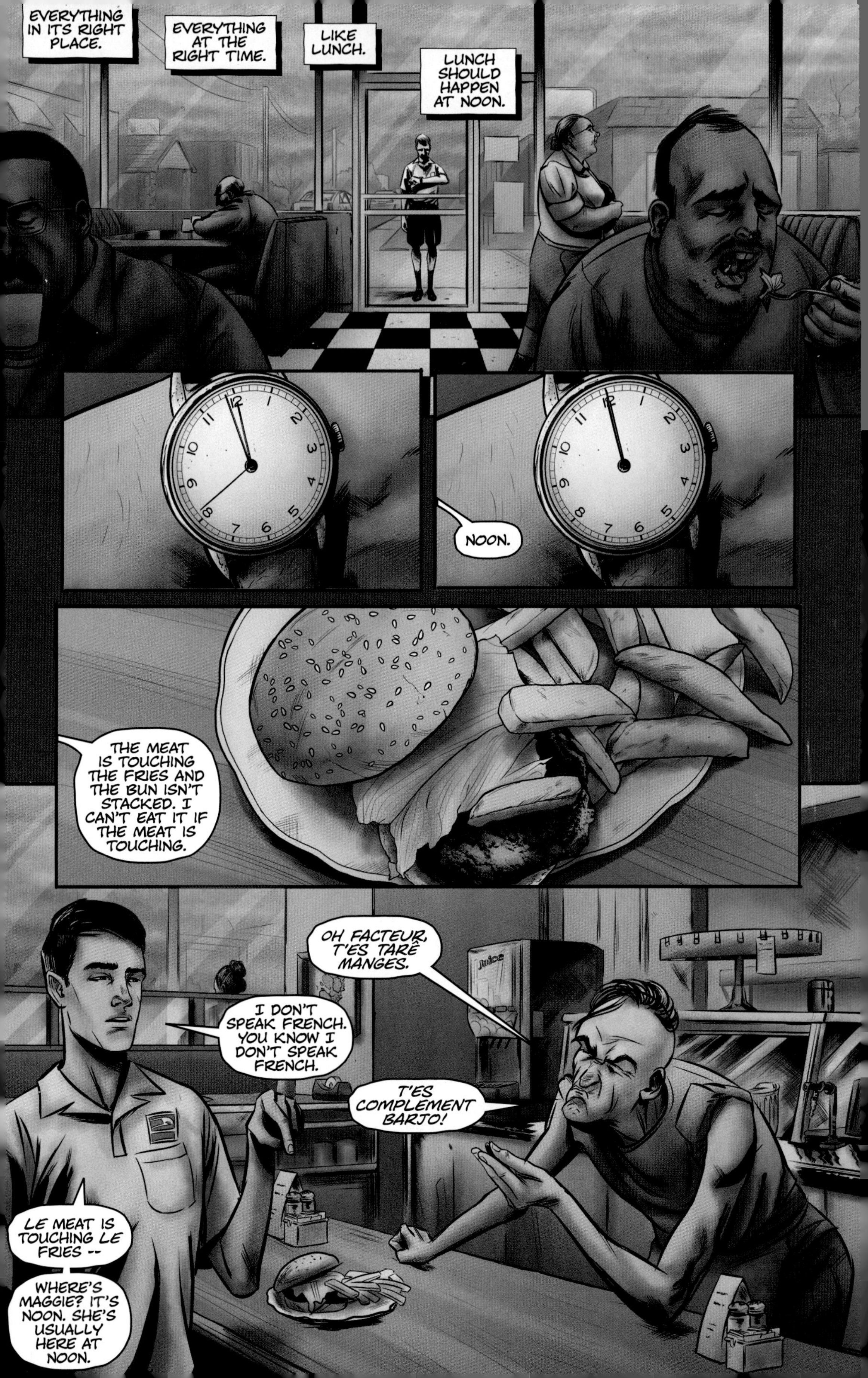
EVERYTHING IN ITS RIGHT PLACE.
EVERYTHING AT THE RIGHT TIME.
LIKE LUNCH.
LUNCH SHOULD HAPPEN AT NOON.
NOON.
THE MEAT IS TOUCHING THE FRIES AND THE BUN ISN'T STACKED. I CAN'T EAT IT IF THE MEAT IS TOUCHING.
OH FACTEUR, T'ES TARÉ MANGES.
I DON'T SPEAK FRENCH. YOU KNOW I DON'T SPEAK FRENCH.
T'ES COMPLEMENT BARJO!
LE MEAT IS TOUCHING LE FRIES --
WHERE'S MAGGIE? IT'S NOON. SHE'S USUALLY HERE AT NOON.

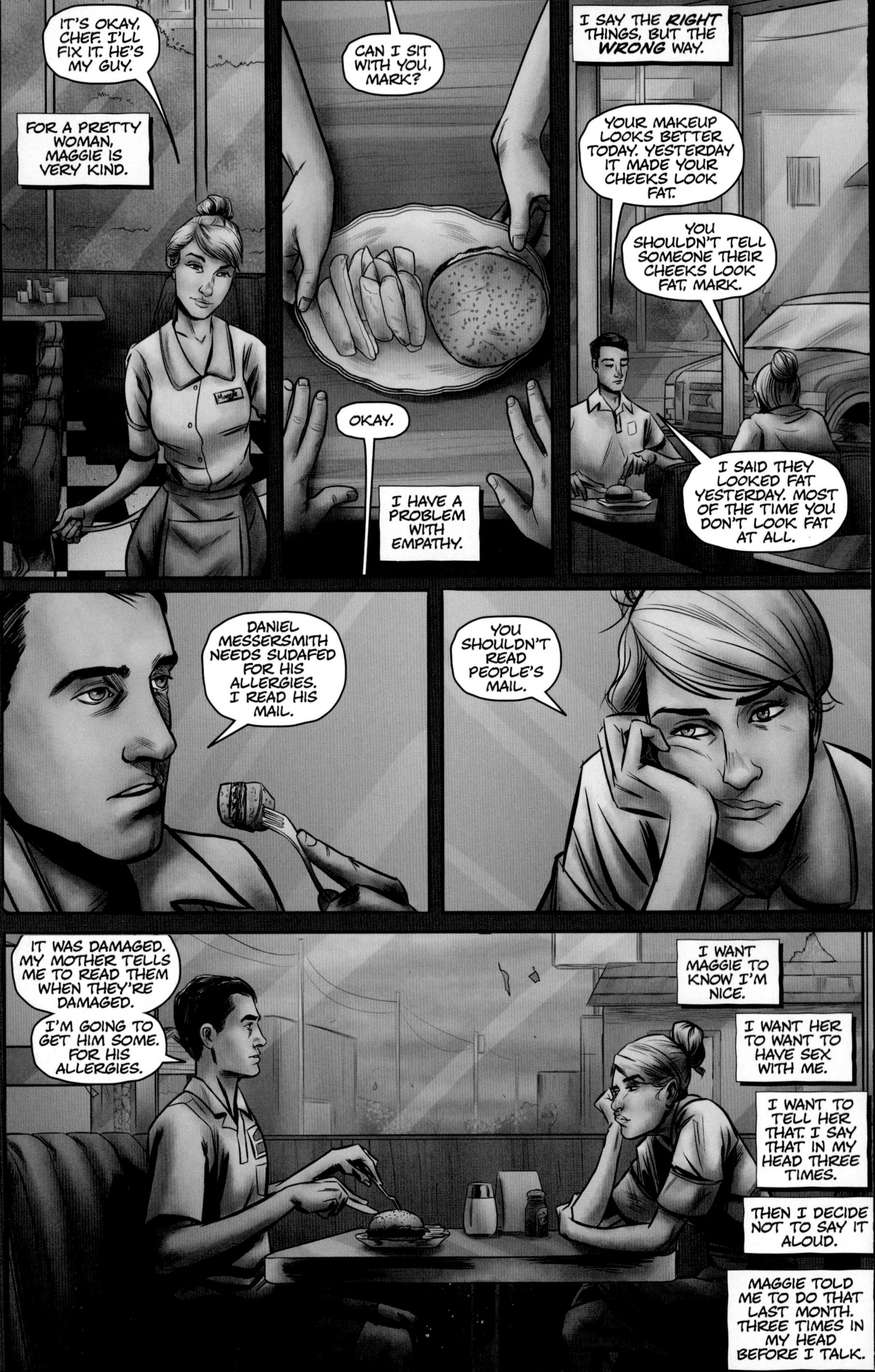
IT'S OKAY, CHEF. I'LL FIX IT. HE'S MY GUY.
FOR A PRETTY WOMAN, MAGGIE IS VERY KIND.
CAN I SIT WITH YOU, MARK?
OKAY.
I HAVE A PROBLEM WITH EMPATHY.
I SAY THE RIGHT THINGS, BUT THE WRONG WAY.
YOUR MAKEUP LOOKS BETTER TODAY. YESTERDAY IT MADE YOUR CHEEKS LOOK FAT.
YOU SHOULDN'T TELL SOMEONE THEIR CHEEKS LOOK FAT, MARK.
I SAID THEY LOOKED FAT YESTERDAY. MOST OF THE TIME YOU DON'T LOOK FAT AT ALL.
DANIEL MESSERSMITH NEEDS SUDAFED FOR HIS ALLERGIES. I READ HIS MAIL.
YOU SHOULDN'T READ PEOPLE'S MAIL.
IT WAS DAMAGED. MY MOTHER TELLS ME TO READ THEM WHEN THEY'RE DAMAGED.
I'M GOING TO GET HIM SOME. FOR HIS ALLERGIES.
I WANT MAGGIE TO KNOW I'M NICE.
I WANT HER TO WANT TO HAVE SEX WITH ME.
I WANT TO TELL HER THAT. I SAY THAT IN MY HEAD THREE TIMES.
THEN I DECIDE NOT TO SAY IT ALOUD.
MAGGIE TOLD ME TO DO THAT LAST MONTH. THREE TIMES IN MY HEAD BEFORE I TALK.

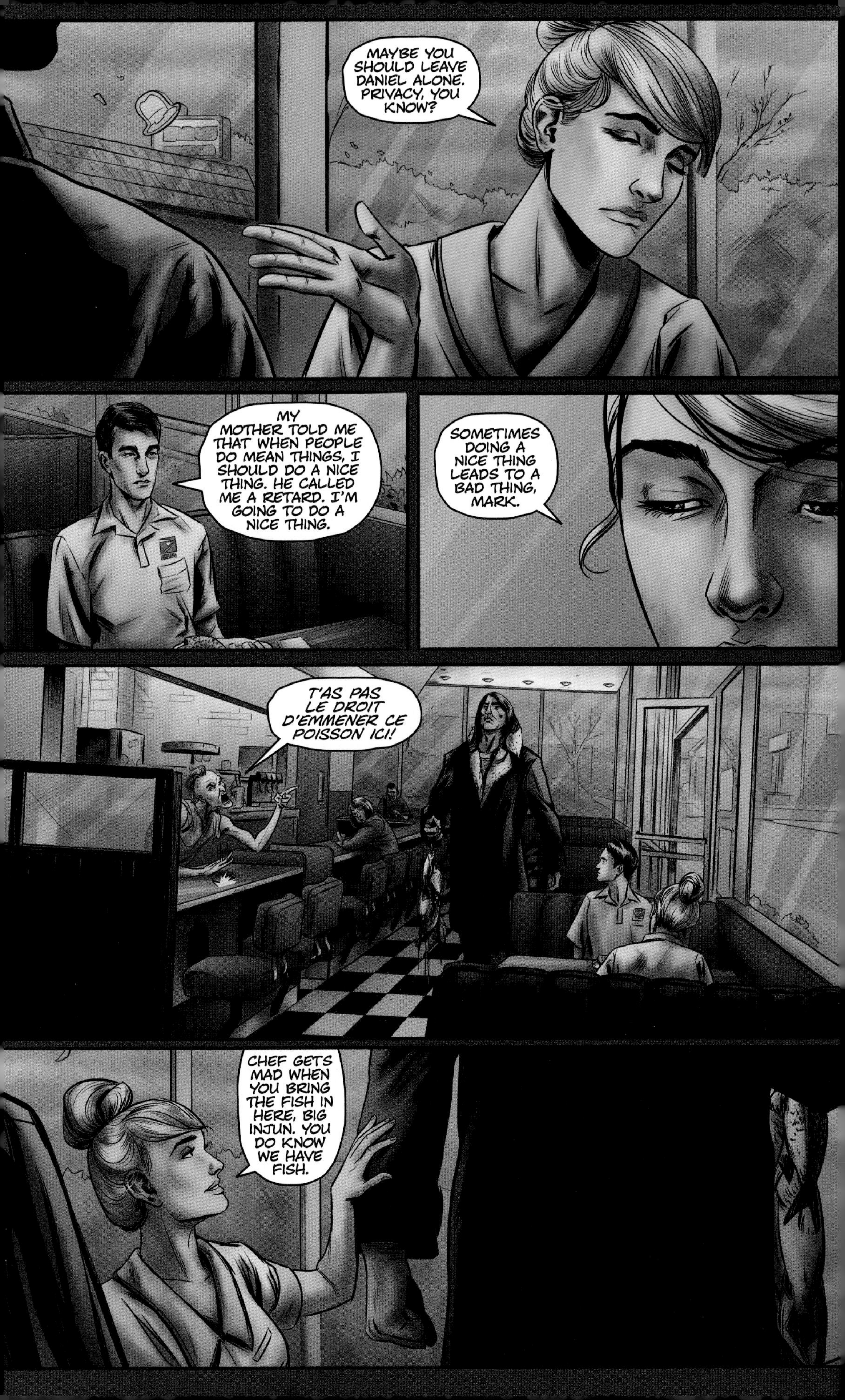
MAYBE YOU SHOULD LEAVE DANIEL ALONE. PRIVACY, YOU KNOW?
MY MOTHER TOLD ME THAT WHEN PEOPLE DO MEAN THINGS, I SHOULD DO A NICE THING. HE CALLED ME A RETARD. I'M GOING TO DO A NICE THING.
SOMETIMES DOING A NICE THING LEADS TO A BAD THING, MARK.
T'AS PAS LE DROIT D'EMMENER CE POISSON ICI!
CHEF GETS MAD WHEN YOU BRING THE FISH IN HERE, BIG INJUN. YOU DO KNOW WE HAVE FISH.

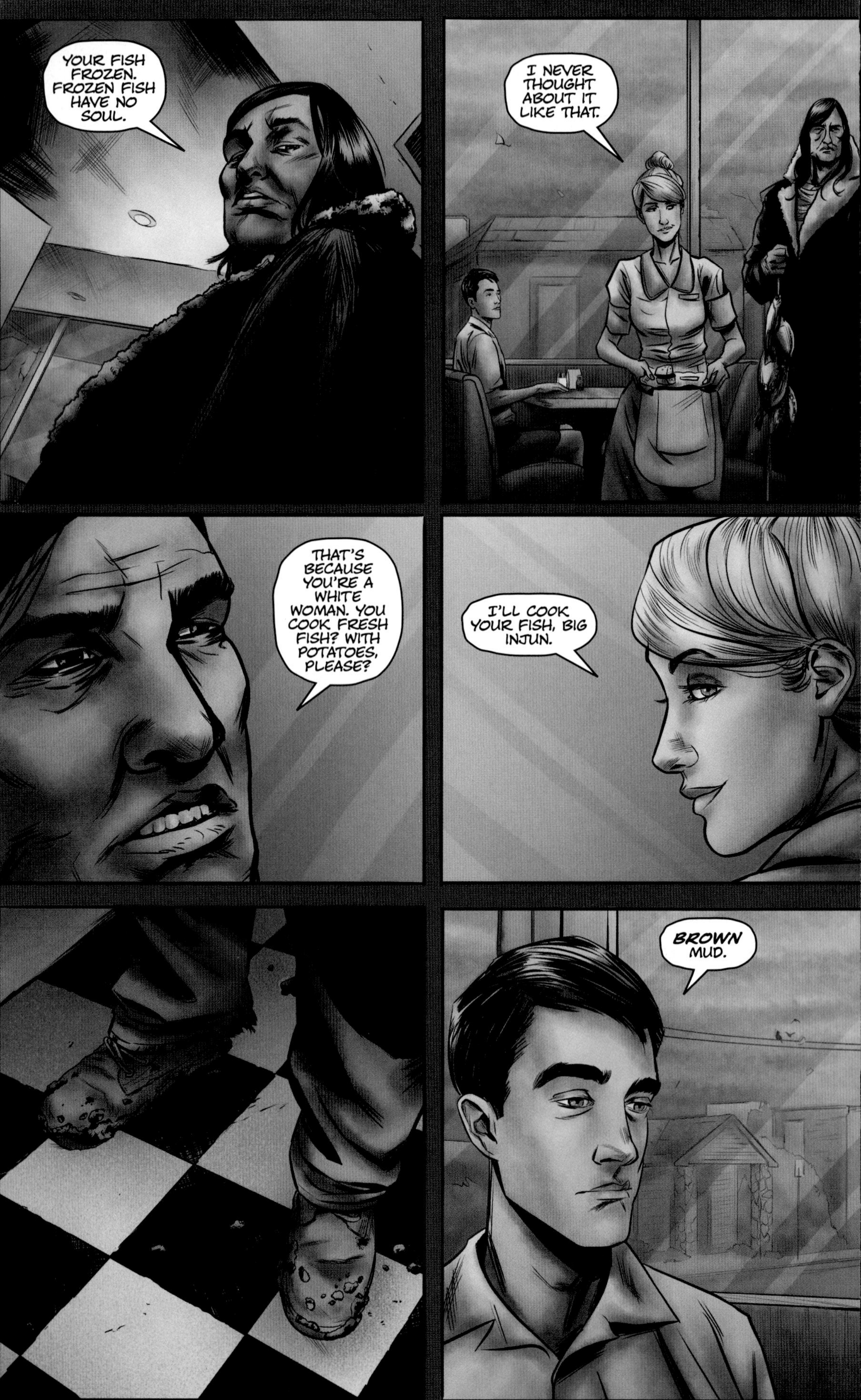
YOUR FISH FROZEN. FROZEN FISH HAVE NO SOUL.
I NEVER THOUGHT ABOUT IT LIKE THAT.
THAT'S BECAUSE YOU'RE A WHITE WOMAN. YOU COOK FRESH FISH? WITH POTATOES, PLEASE?
I'LL COOK YOUR FISH, BIG INJUN.
BROWN MUD.

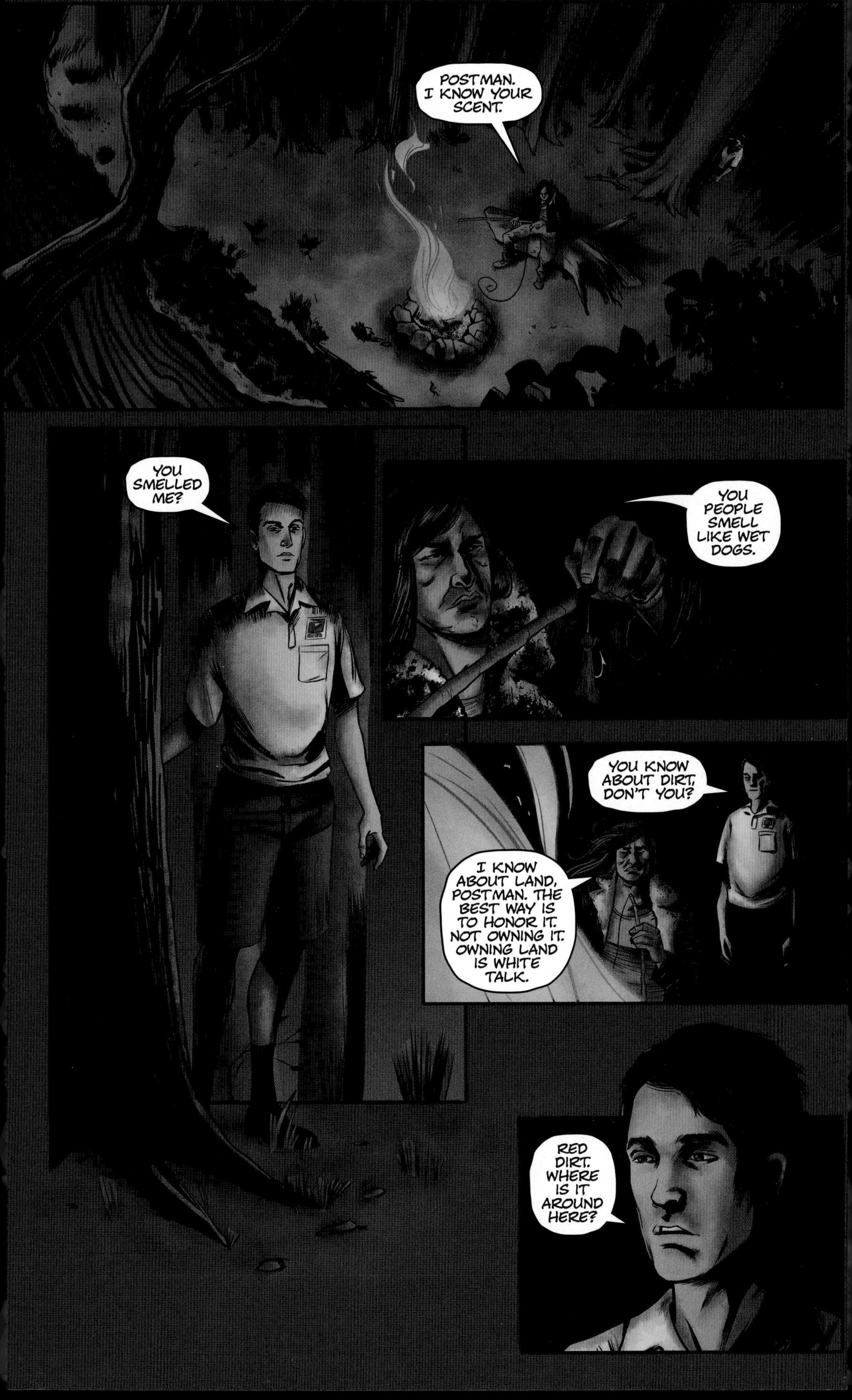
POSTMAN. I KNOW YOUR SCENT.
YOU SMELLED ME?
YOU PEOPLE SMELL LIKE WET DOGS.
YOU KNOW ABOUT DIRT, DON'T YOU?
I KNOW ABOUT LAND, POSTMAN. THE BEST WAY IS TO HONOR IT. NOT OWNING IT. OWNING LAND IS WHITE TALK.
RED DIRT. WHERE IS IT AROUND HERE?

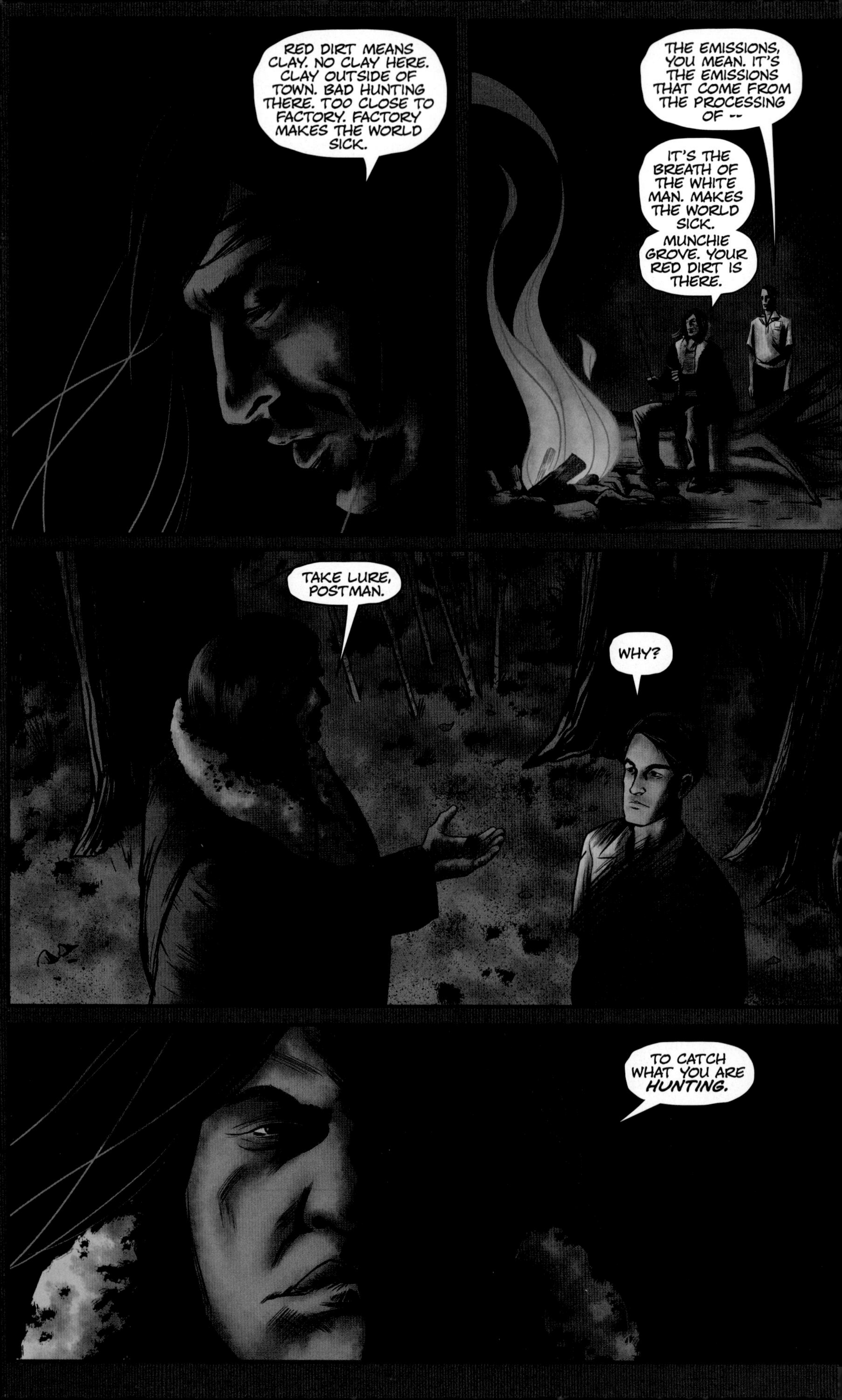
RED DIRT MEANS CLAY. NO CLAY HERE. CLAY OUTSIDE OF TOWN. BAD HUNTING THERE. TOO CLOSE TO FACTORY. FACTORY MAKES THE WORLD SICK.
THE EMISSIONS, YOU MEAN. IT'S THE EMISSIONS THAT COME FROM THE PROCESSING OF --
IT'S THE BREATH OF THE WHITE MAN. MAKES THE WORLD SICK.
MUNCHIE GROVE. YOUR RED DIRT IS THERE.
TAKE LURE, POSTMAN.
WHY?
TO CATCH WHAT YOU ARE *HUNTING.*

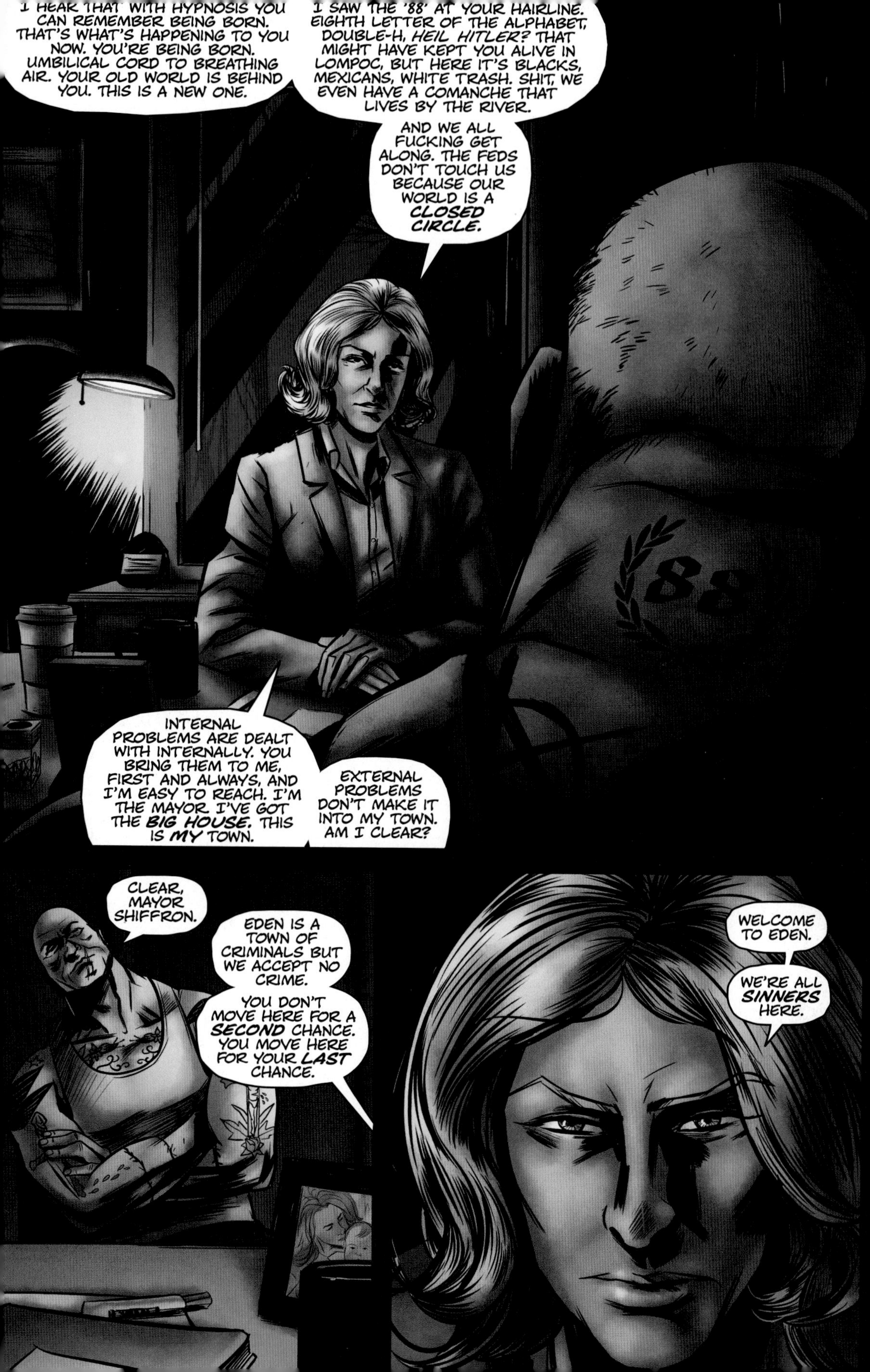
I HEAR THAT WITH HYPNOSIS YOU CAN REMEMBER BEING BORN. THAT'S WHAT'S HAPPENING TO YOU NOW. YOU'RE BEING BORN. UMBILICAL CORD TO BREATHING AIR. YOUR OLD WORLD IS BEHIND YOU. THIS IS A NEW ONE.
I SAW THE '88' AT YOUR HAIRLINE. EIGHTH LETTER OF THE ALPHABET, DOUBLE-H, HEIL HITLER? THAT MIGHT HAVE KEPT YOU ALIVE IN LOMPOC, BUT HERE IT'S BLACKS, MEXICANS, WHITE TRASH. SHIT, WE EVEN HAVE A COMANCHE THAT LIVES BY THE RIVER.
AND WE ALL FUCKING GET ALONG. THE FEDS DON'T TOUCH US BECAUSE OUR WORLD IS A CLOSED CIRCLE.
88
INTERNAL PROBLEMS ARE DEALT WITH INTERNALLY. YOU BRING THEM TO ME, FIRST AND ALWAYS, AND I'M EASY TO REACH. I'M THE MAYOR. I'VE GOT THE BIG HOUSE. THIS IS MY TOWN.
EXTERNAL PROBLEMS DON'T MAKE IT INTO MY TOWN. AM I CLEAR?
CLEAR, MAYOR SHIFFRON.
EDEN IS A TOWN OF CRIMINALS BUT WE ACCEPT NO CRIME.
YOU DON'T MOVE HERE FOR A SECOND CHANCE. YOU MOVE HERE FOR YOUR LAST CHANCE.
WELCOME TO EDEN.
WE'RE ALL SINNERS HERE.

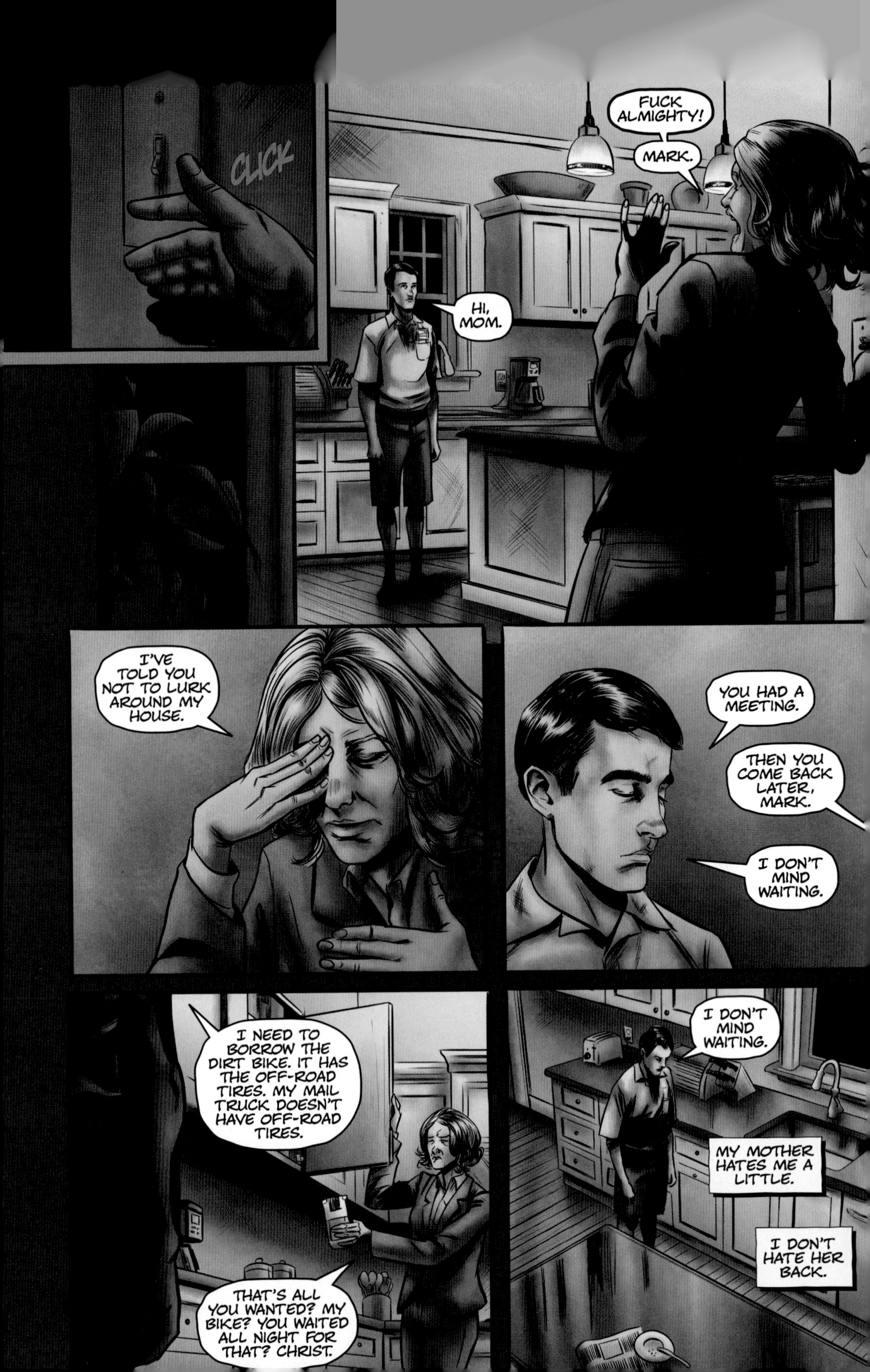
CLICK
FUCK ALMIGHTY!
MARK.
HI, MOM.
I'VE TOLD YOU NOT TO LURK AROUND MY HOUSE.
YOU HAD A MEETING.
THEN YOU COME BACK LATER, MARK.
I DON'T MIND WAITING.
I NEED TO BORROW THE DIRT BIKE. IT HAS THE OFF-ROAD TIRES. MY MAIL TRUCK DOESN'T HAVE OFF-ROAD TIRES.
THAT'S ALL YOU WANTED? MY BIKE? YOU WAITED ALL NIGHT FOR THAT? CHRIST.
I DON'T MIND WAITING.
MY MOTHER HATES ME A LITTLE.
I DON'T HATE HER BACK.

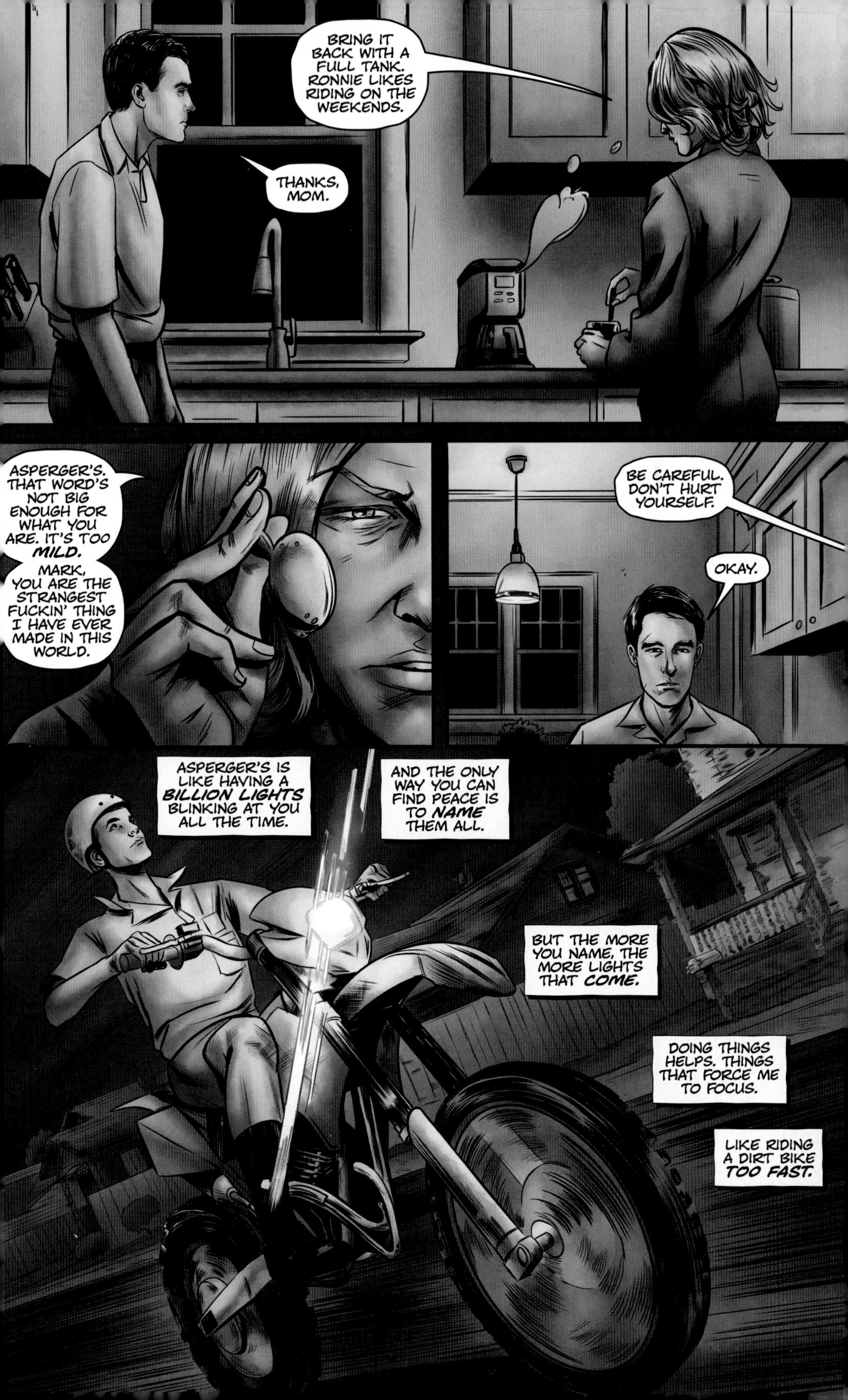
BRING IT BACK WITH A FULL TANK. RONNIE LIKES RIDING ON THE WEEKENDS.
THANKS, MOM.
ASPERGER'S. THAT WORD'S NOT BIG ENOUGH FOR WHAT YOU ARE. IT'S TOO MILD.
MARK, YOU ARE THE STRANGEST FUCKIN' THING I HAVE EVER MADE IN THIS WORLD.
BE CAREFUL. DON'T HURT YOURSELF.
OKAY.
ASPERGER'S IS LIKE HAVING A BILLION LIGHTS BLINKING AT YOU ALL THE TIME.
AND THE ONLY WAY YOU CAN FIND PEACE IS TO NAME THEM ALL.
BUT THE MORE YOU NAME, THE MORE LIGHTS THAT COME.
DOING THINGS HELPS. THINGS THAT FORCE ME TO FOCUS.
LIKE RIDING A DIRT BIKE TOO FAST.

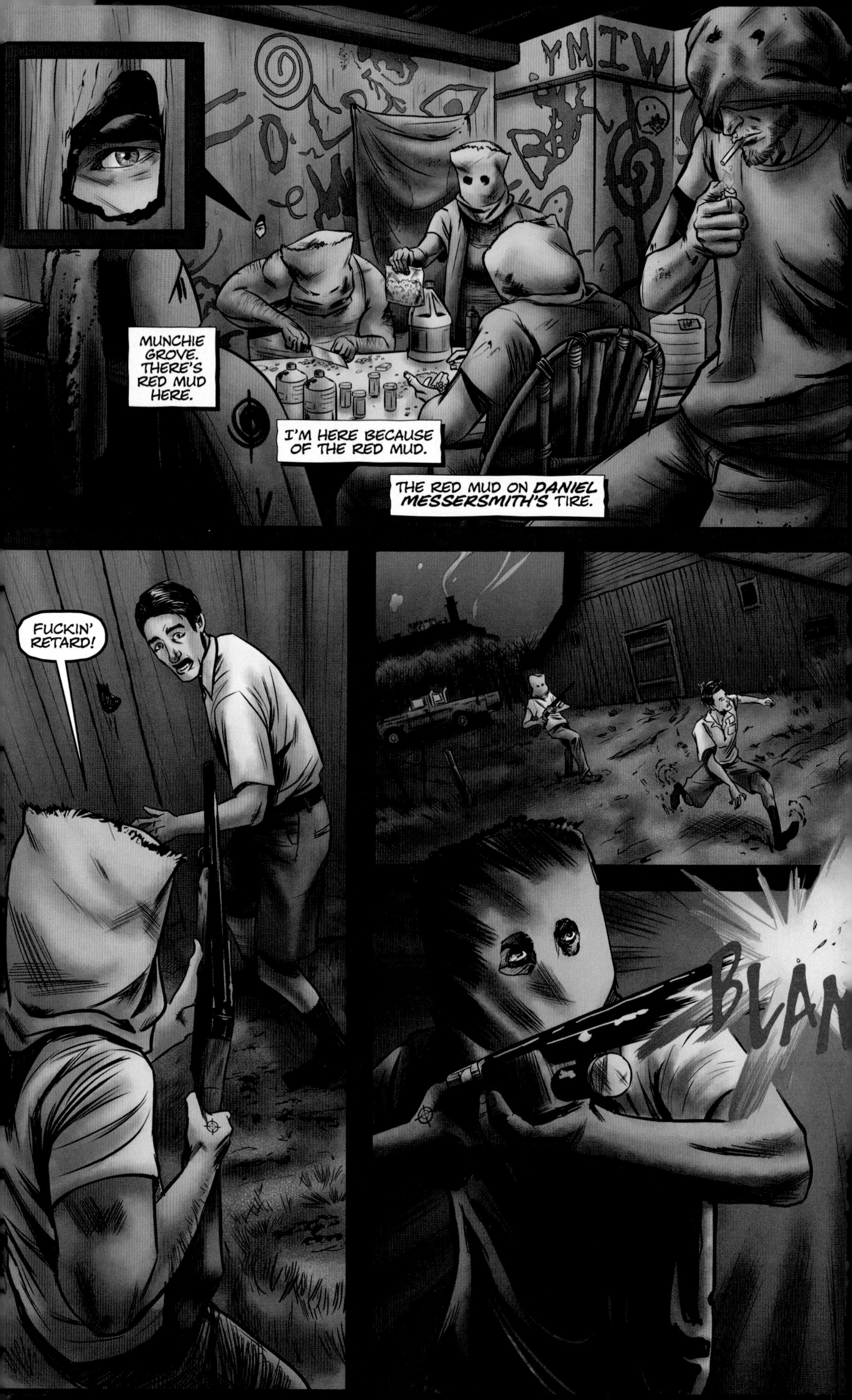

MUNCHIE GROVE. THERE'S RED MUD HERE.
I'M HERE BECAUSE OF THE RED MUD.
THE RED MUD ON DANIEL MESSERSMITH'S TIRE.
FUCKIN' RETARD!
BLAM

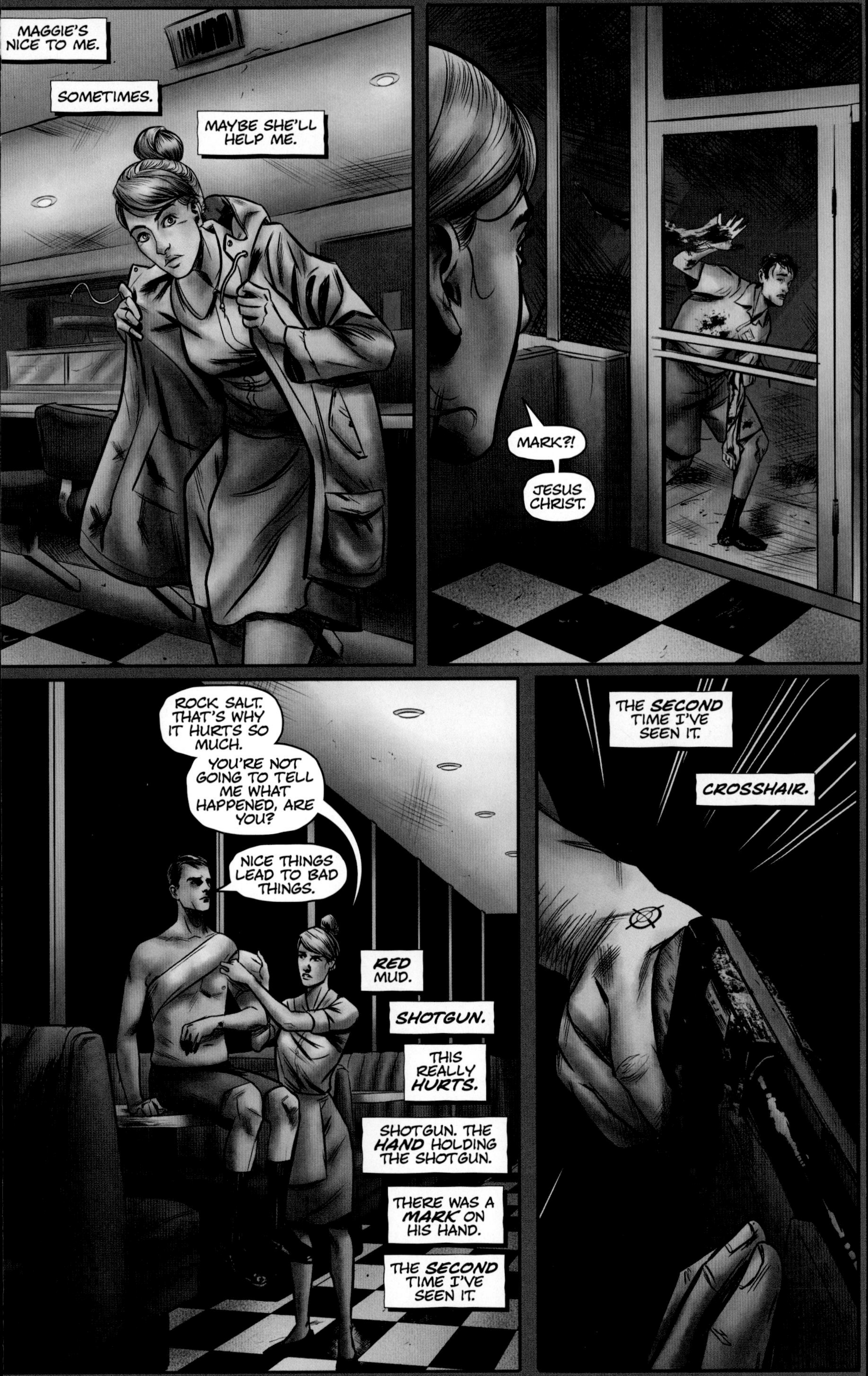
MAGGIE'S NICE TO ME.
SOMETIMES.
MAYBE SHE'LL HELP ME.
MARK?!
JESUS CHRIST.
ROCK SALT. THAT'S WHY IT HURTS SO MUCH.
YOU'RE NOT GOING TO TELL ME WHAT HAPPENED, ARE YOU?
NICE THINGS LEAD TO BAD THINGS.
RED MUD.
SHOTGUN.
THIS REALLY HURTS.
SHOTGUN. THE HAND HOLDING THE SHOTGUN.
THERE WAS A MARK ON HIS HAND.
THE SECOND TIME I'VE SEEN IT.
THE SECOND TIME I'VE SEEN IT.
CROSSHAIR.

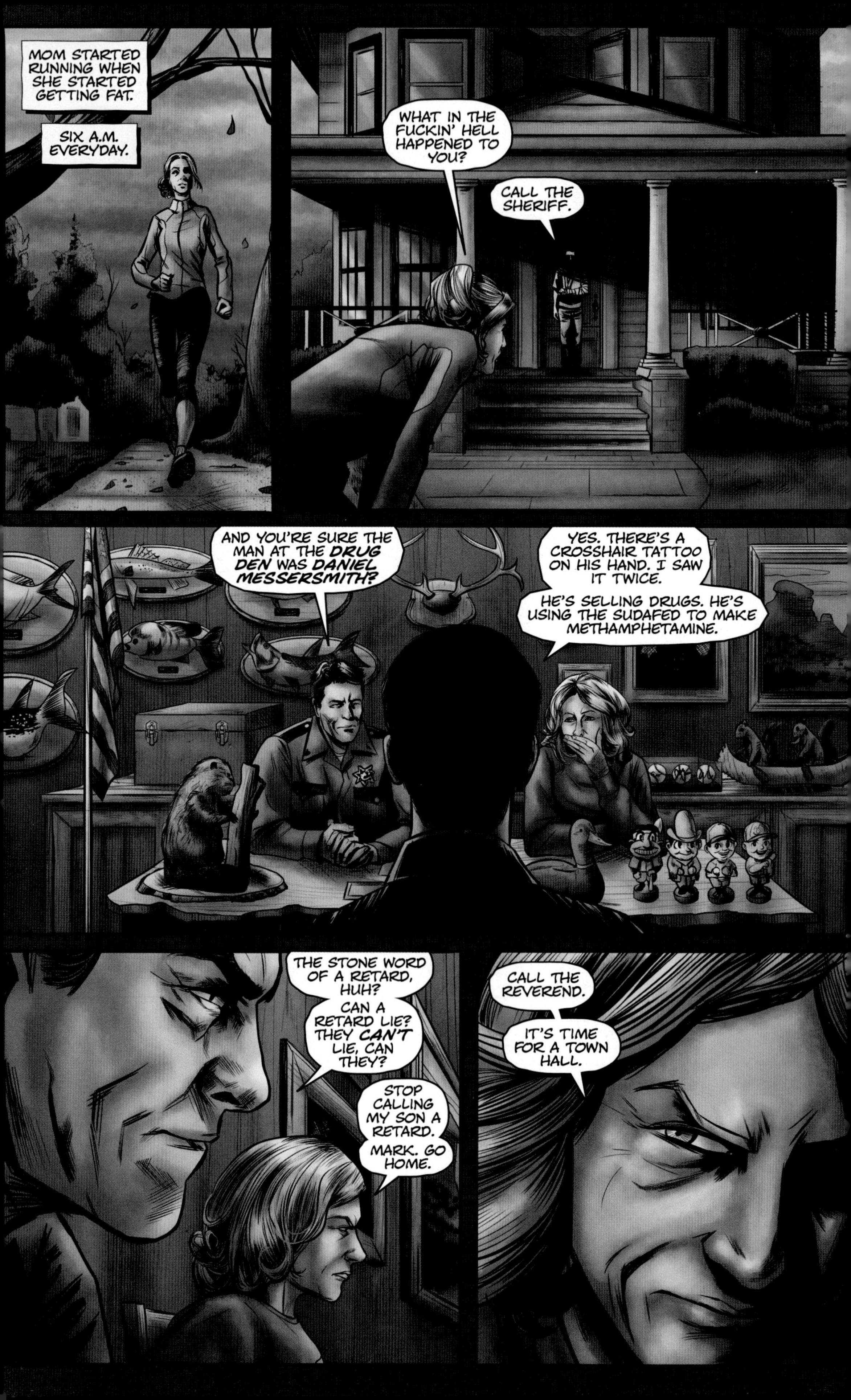

MOM STARTED RUNNING WHEN SHE STARTED GETTING FAT.
SIX A.M. EVERYDAY.
WHAT IN THE FUCKIN' HELL HAPPENED TO YOU?
CALL THE SHERIFF.
AND YOU'RE SURE THE MAN AT THE DRUG DEN WAS DANIEL MESSERSMITH?
YES. THERE'S A CROSSHAIR TATTOO ON HIS HAND. I SAW IT TWICE.
HE'S SELLING DRUGS. HE'S USING THE SUDAFED TO MAKE METHAMPHETAMINE.
THE STONE WORD OF A RETARD, HUH?
CAN A RETARD LIE? THEY CAN'T LIE, CAN THEY?
STOP CALLING MY SON A RETARD.
MARK. GO HOME.
CALL THE REVEREND.
IT'S TIME FOR A TOWN HALL.

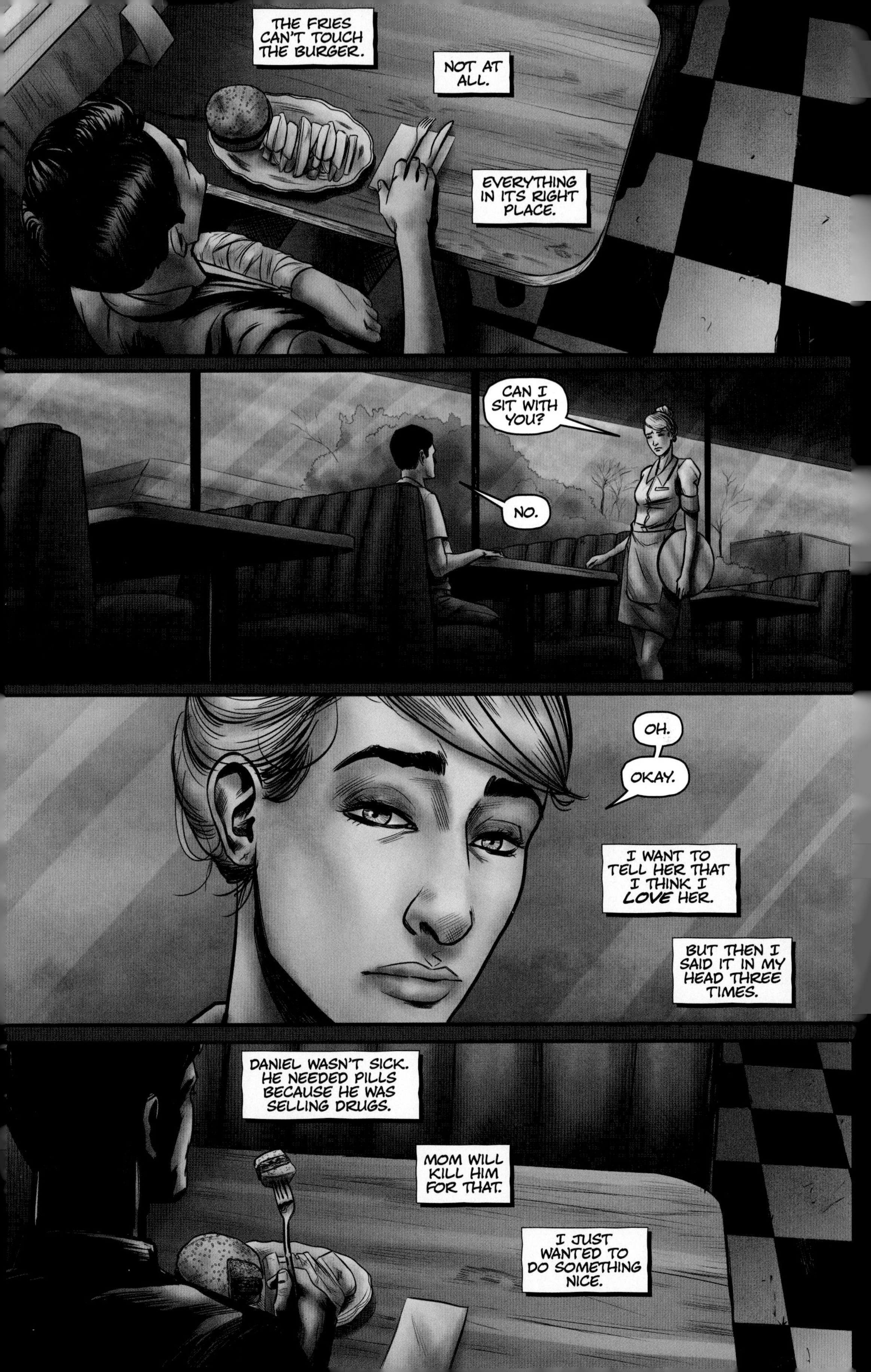
THE FRIES CAN'T TOUCH THE BURGER.
NOT AT ALL.
EVERYTHING IN ITS RIGHT PLACE.
CAN I SIT WITH YOU?
NO.
OH.
OKAY.
I WANT TO TELL HER THAT I THINK I LOVE HER.
BUT THEN I SAID IT IN MY HEAD THREE TIMES.
DANIEL WASN'T SICK. HE NEEDED PILLS BECAUSE HE WAS SELLING DRUGS.
MOM WILL KILL HIM FOR THAT.
I JUST WANTED TO DO SOMETHING NICE.

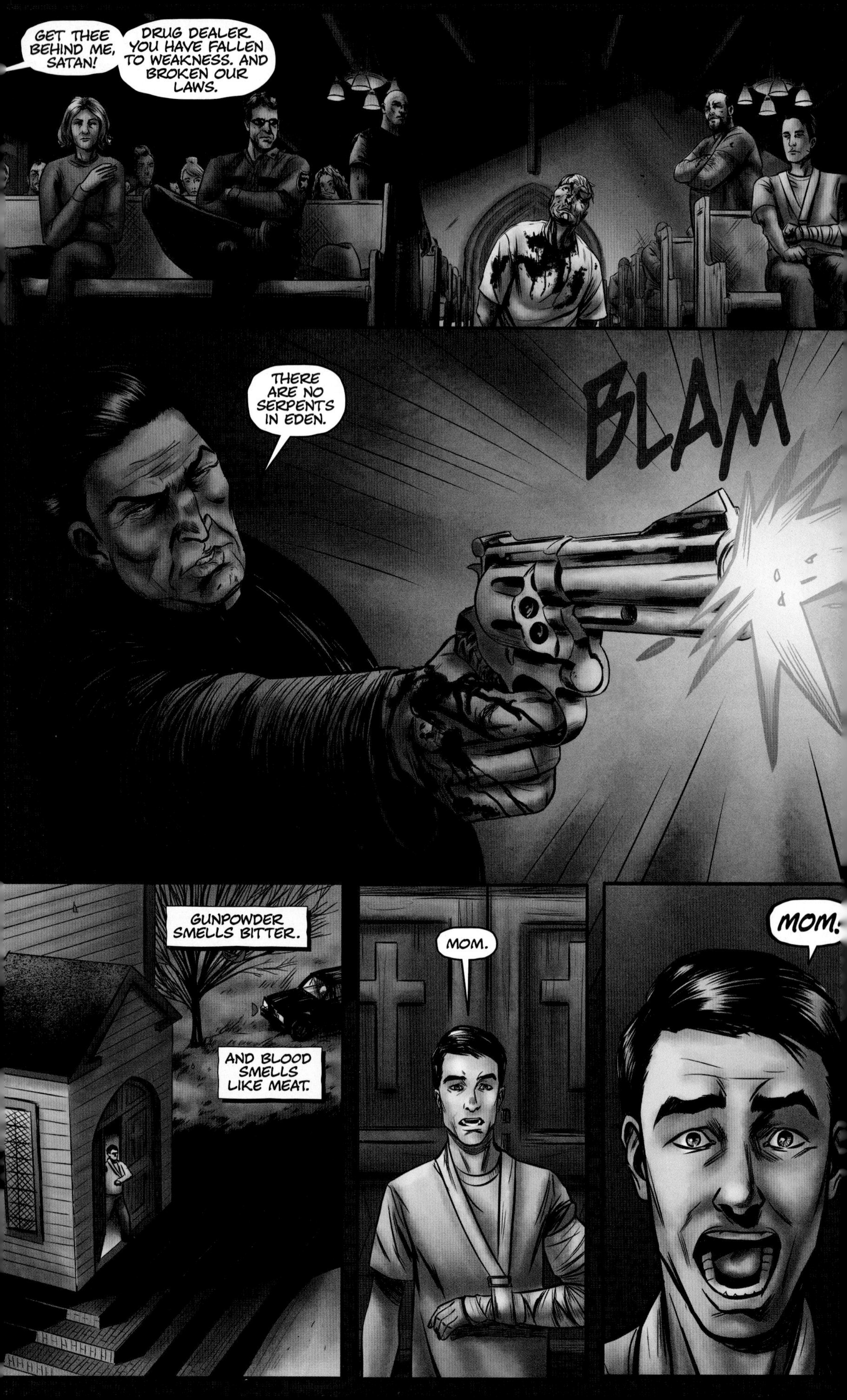

GET THEE BEHIND ME, SATAN!
DRUG DEALER YOU HAVE FALLEN TO WEAKNESS. AND BROKEN OUR LAWS.
THERE ARE NO SERPENTS IN EDEN.
BLAM
GUNPOWDER SMELLS BITTER.
AND BLOOD SMELLS LIKE MEAT.
MOM.
MOM!

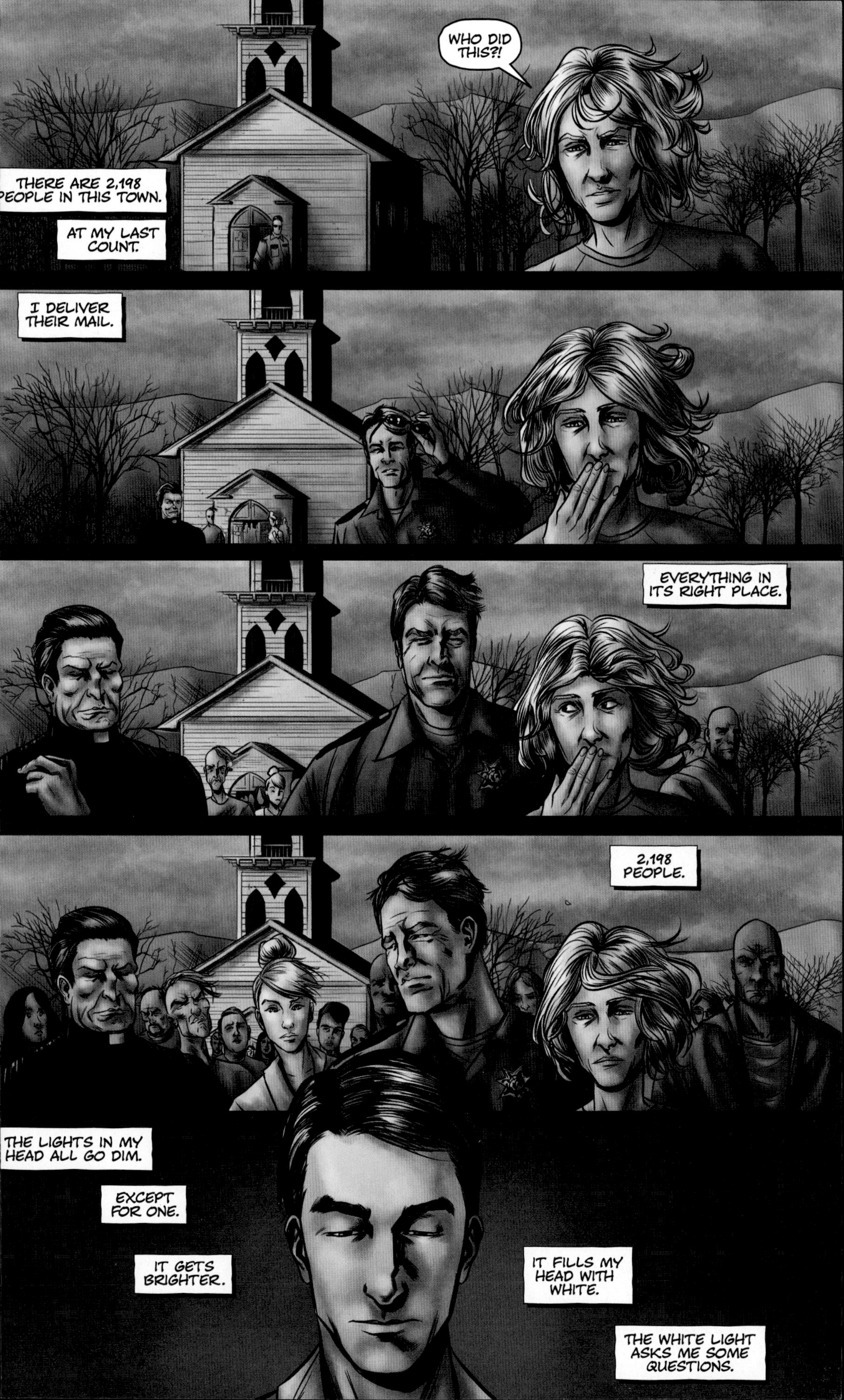
WHO DID THIS?!
THERE ARE 2,198 PEOPLE IN THIS TOWN.
AT MY LAST COUNT.
I DELIVER THEIR MAIL.
EVERYTHING IN ITS RIGHT PLACE.
2,198 PEOPLE.
THE LIGHTS IN MY HEAD ALL GO DIM.
EXCEPT FOR ONE.
IT GETS BRIGHTER.
IT FILLS MY HEAD WITH WHITE.
THE WHITE LIGHT ASKS ME SOME QUESTIONS.

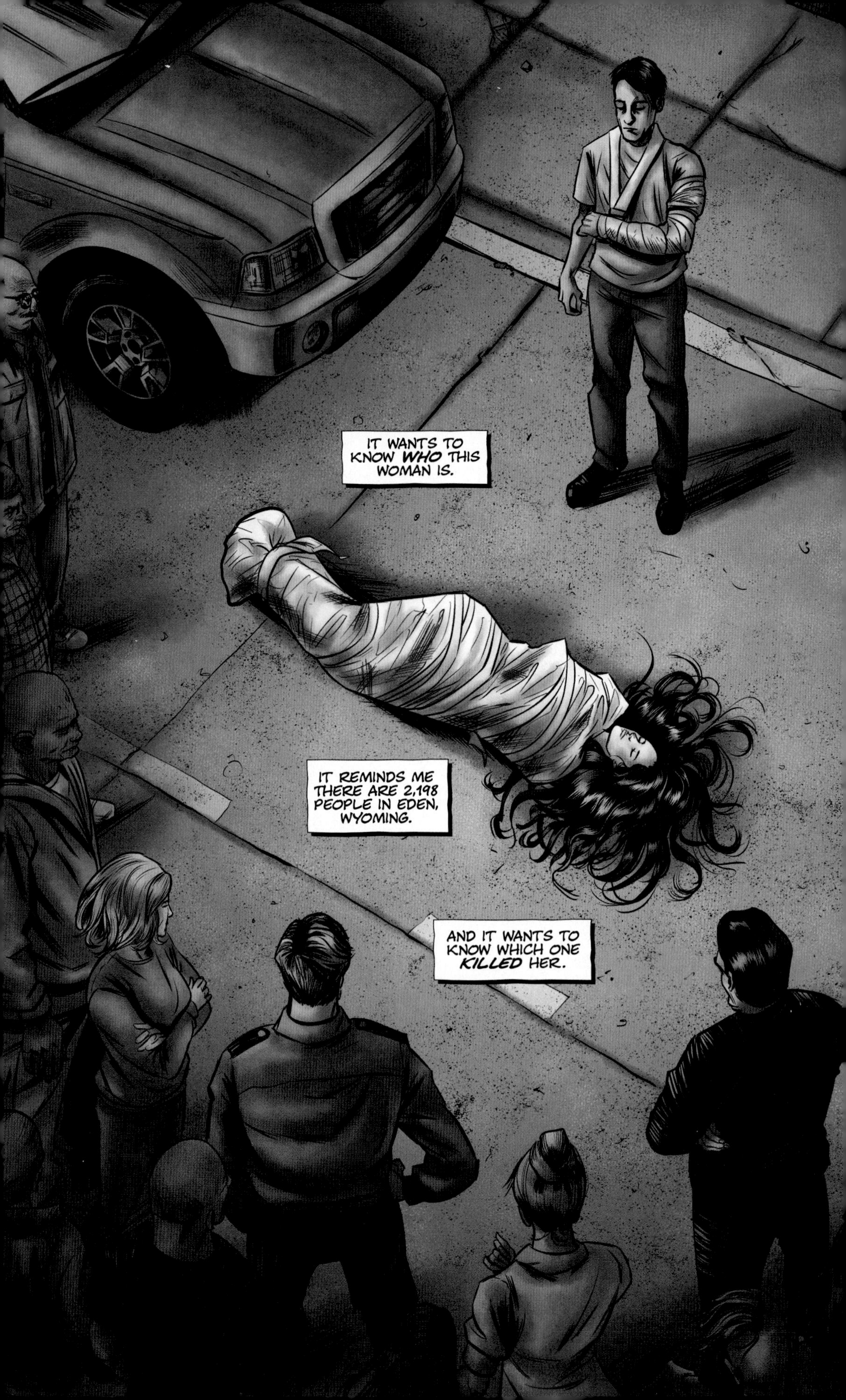
IT WANTS TO KNOW WHO THIS WOMAN IS.
IT REMINDS ME THERE ARE 2,198 PEOPLE IN EDEN, WYOMING.
AND IT WANTS TO KNOW WHICH ONE KILLED HER.

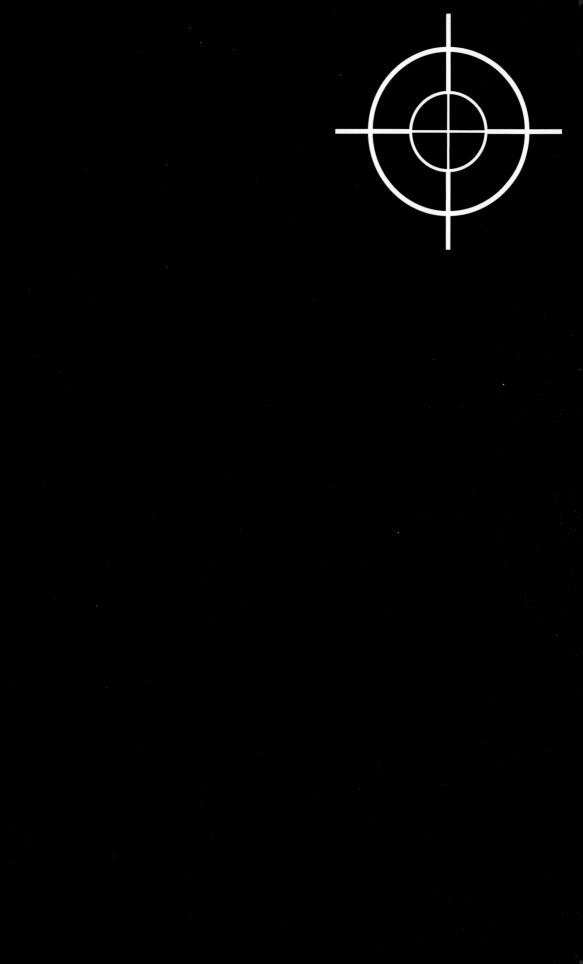

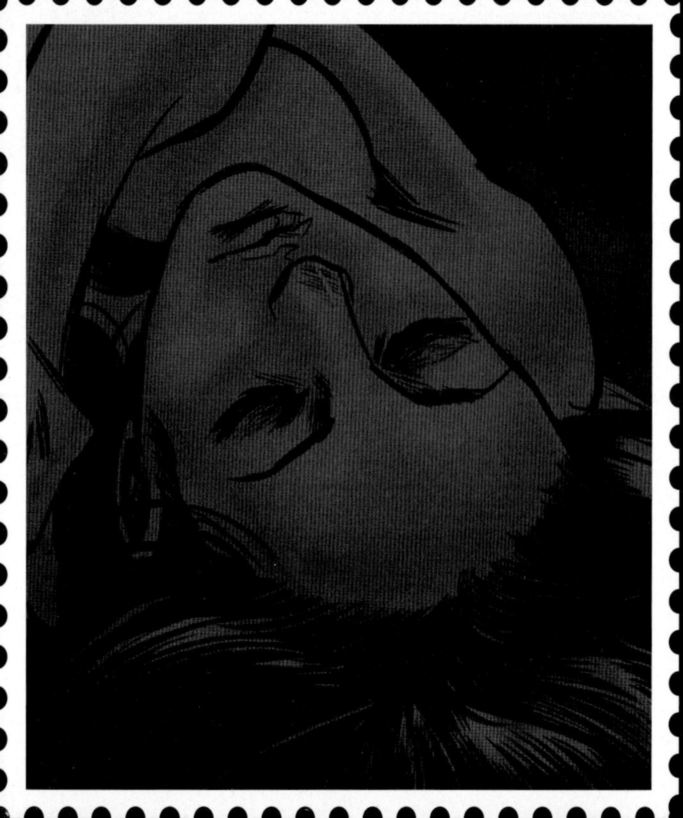

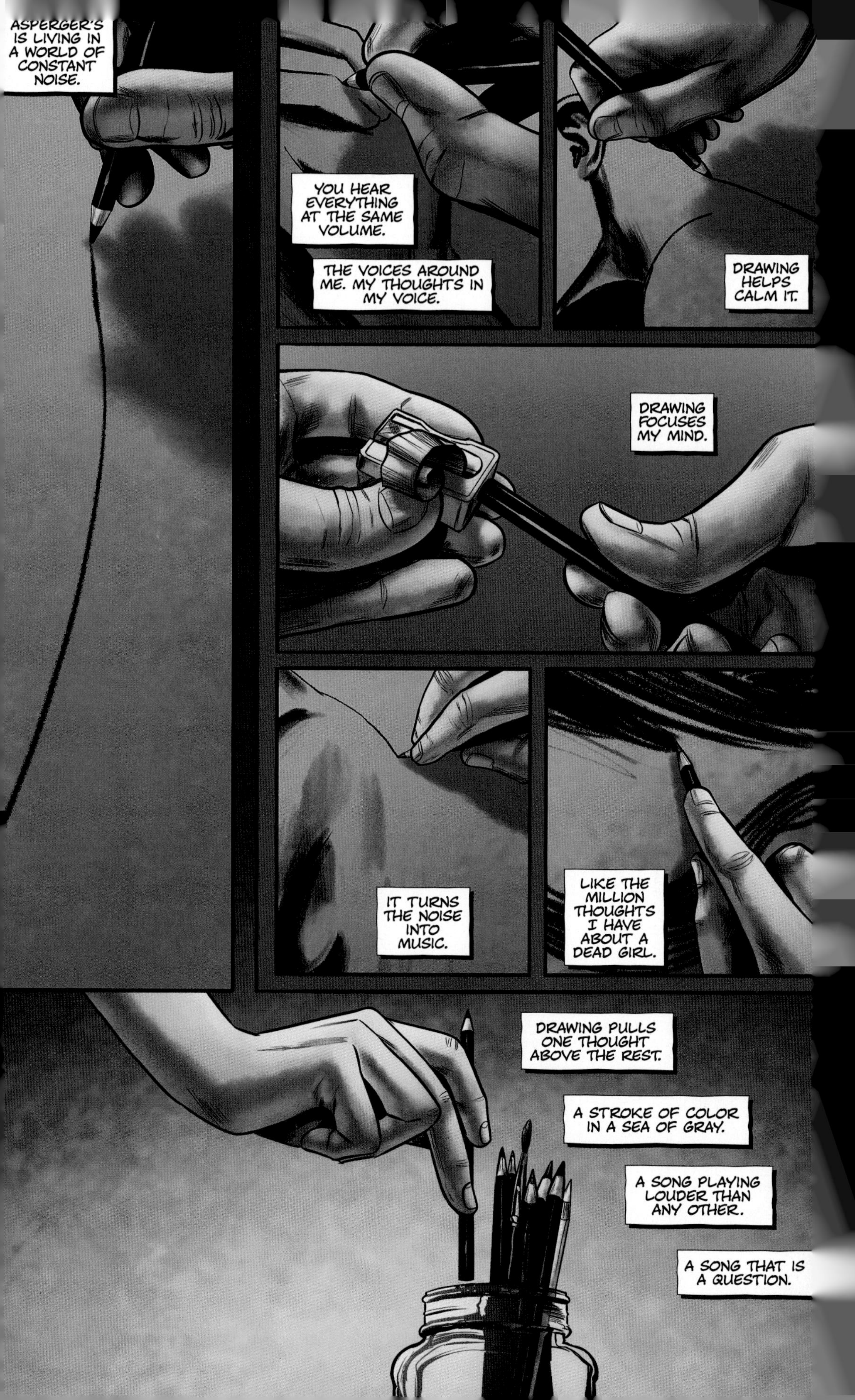
ASPERGER'S IS LIVING IN A WORLD OF CONSTANT NOISE.
YOU HEAR EVERYTHING AT THE SAME VOLUME.
THE VOICES AROUND ME. MY THOUGHTS IN MY VOICE.
DRAWING HELPS CALM IT.
DRAWING FOCUSES MY MIND.
IT TURNS THE NOISE INTO MUSIC.
LIKE THE MILLION THOUGHTS I HAVE ABOUT A DEAD GIRL.
DRAWING PULLS ONE THOUGHT ABOVE THE REST.
A STROKE OF COLOR IN A SEA OF GRAY.
A SONG PLAYING LOUDER THAN ANY OTHER.
A SONG THAT IS A QUESTION.

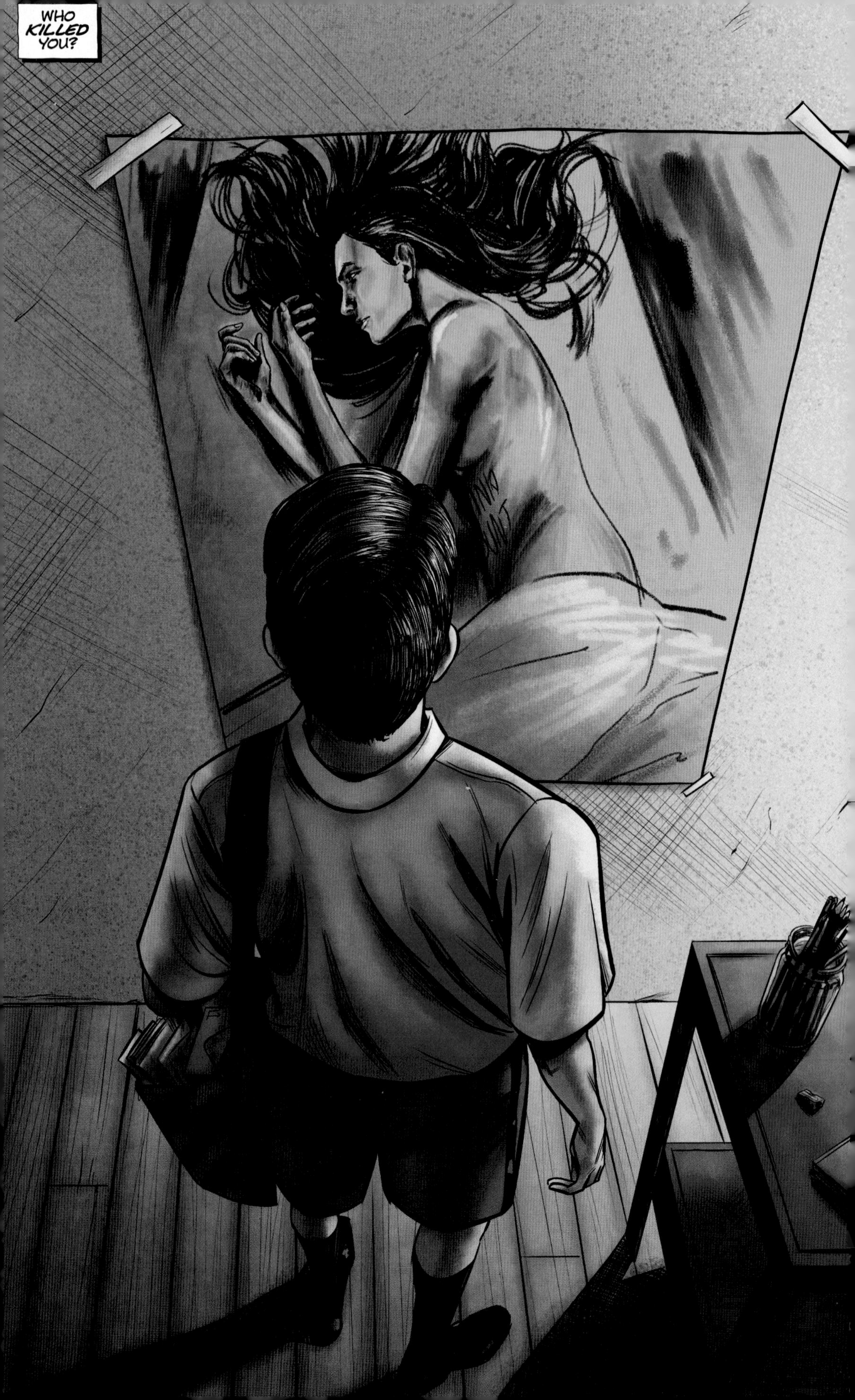
WHO KILLED YOU?

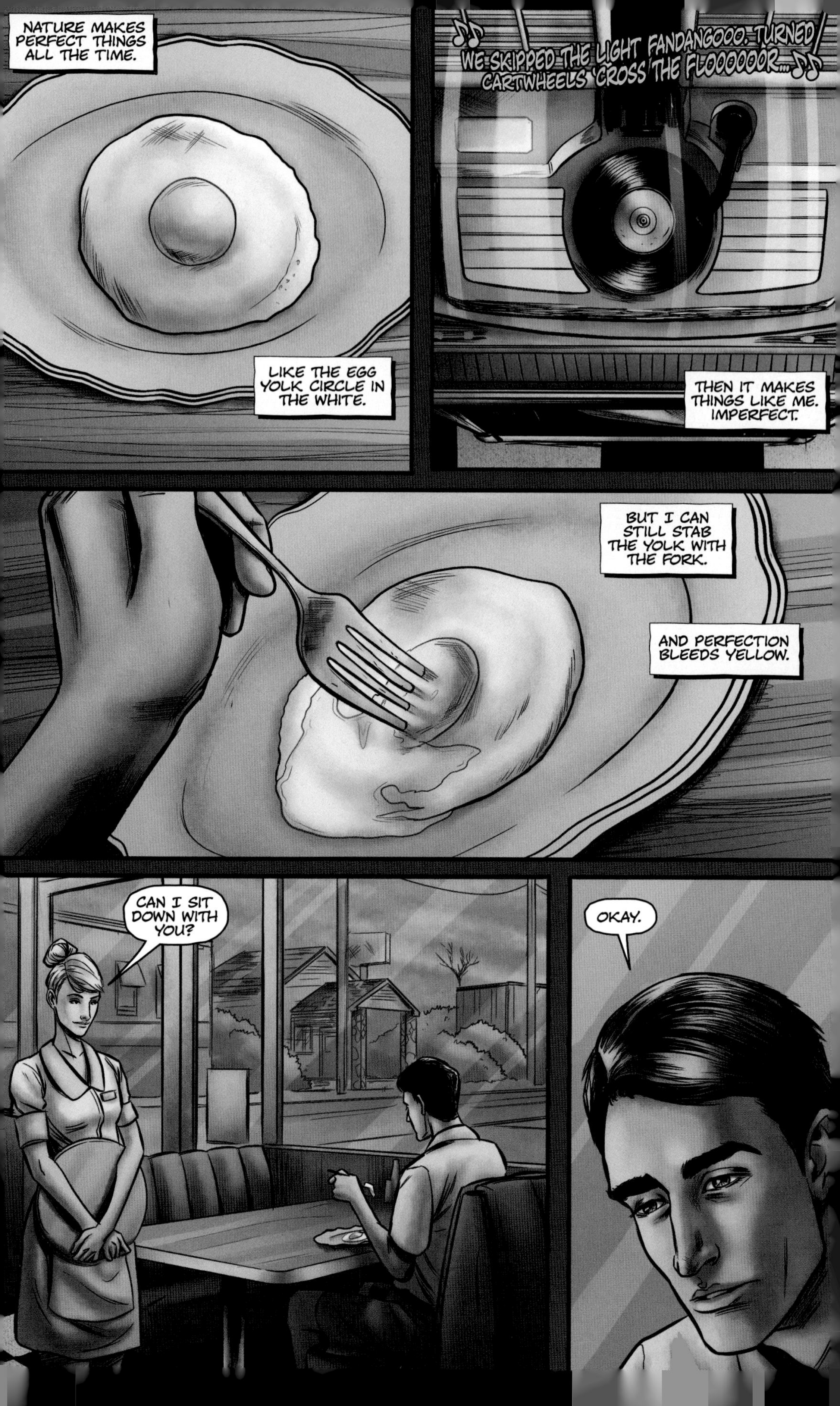
NATURE MAKES PERFECT THINGS ALL THE TIME.
LIKE THE EGG YOLK CIRCLE IN THE WHITE.
♪♪ WE SKIPPED THE LIGHT FANDANGOOO. TURNED CARTWHEELS 'CROSS THE FLOOOOOR... ♪♪
THEN IT MAKES THINGS LIKE ME. IMPERFECT.
BUT I CAN STILL STAB THE YOLK WITH THE FORK.
AND PERFECTION BLEEDS YELLOW.
CAN I SIT DOWN WITH YOU?
OKAY.

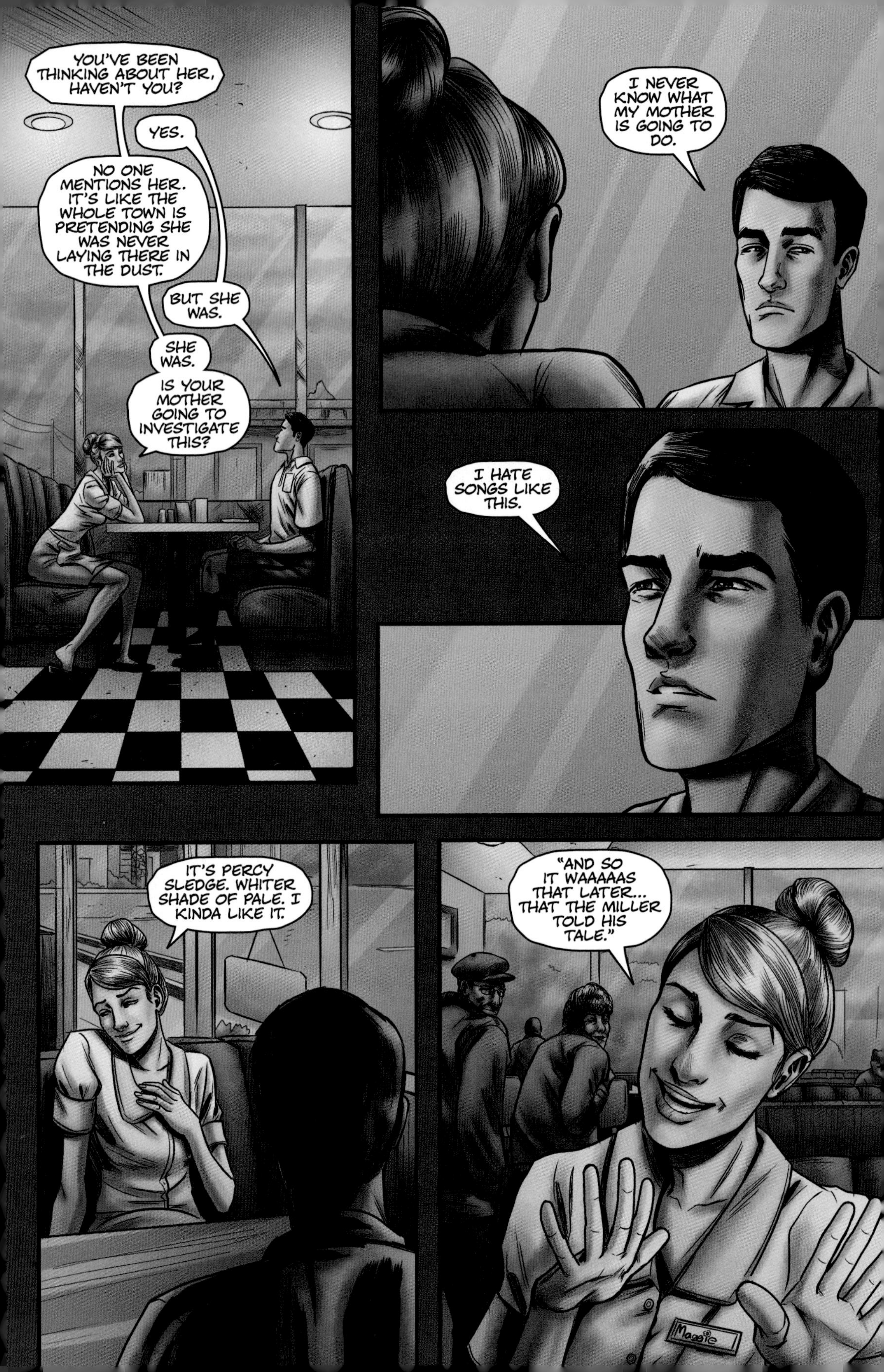
YOU'VE BEEN THINKING ABOUT HER, HAVEN'T YOU?
YES.
NO ONE MENTIONS HER. IT'S LIKE THE WHOLE TOWN IS PRETENDING SHE WAS NEVER LAYING THERE IN THE DUST.
BUT SHE WAS.
SHE WAS.
IS YOUR MOTHER GOING TO INVESTIGATE THIS?
I NEVER KNOW WHAT MY MOTHER IS GOING TO DO.
I HATE SONGS LIKE THIS.
IT'S PERCY SLEDGE. WHITER SHADE OF PALE. I KINDA LIKE IT.
"AND SO IT WAAAAAS THAT LATER... THAT THE MILLER TOLD HIS TALE."
Maggie

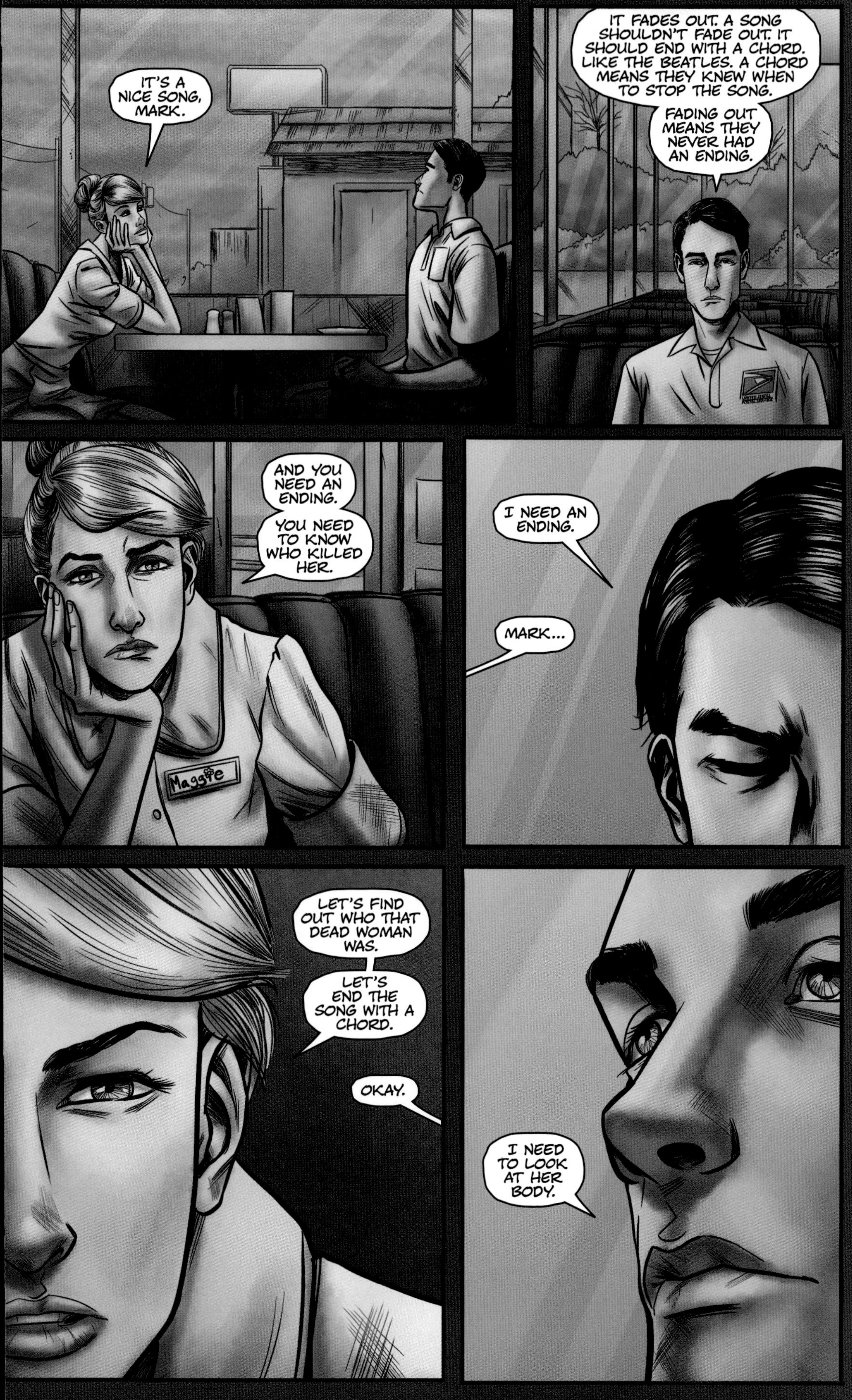

IT'S A NICE SONG, MARK.
IT FADES OUT. A SONG SHOULDN'T FADE OUT. IT SHOULD END WITH A CHORD. LIKE THE BEATLES. A CHORD MEANS THEY KNEW WHEN TO STOP THE SONG.
FADING OUT MEANS THEY NEVER HAD AN ENDING.
AND YOU NEED AN ENDING.
YOU NEED TO KNOW WHO KILLED HER.
Maggie
I NEED AN ENDING.
MARK...
LET'S FIND OUT WHO THAT DEAD WOMAN WAS.
LET'S END THE SONG WITH A CHORD.
OKAY.
I NEED TO LOOK AT HER BODY.

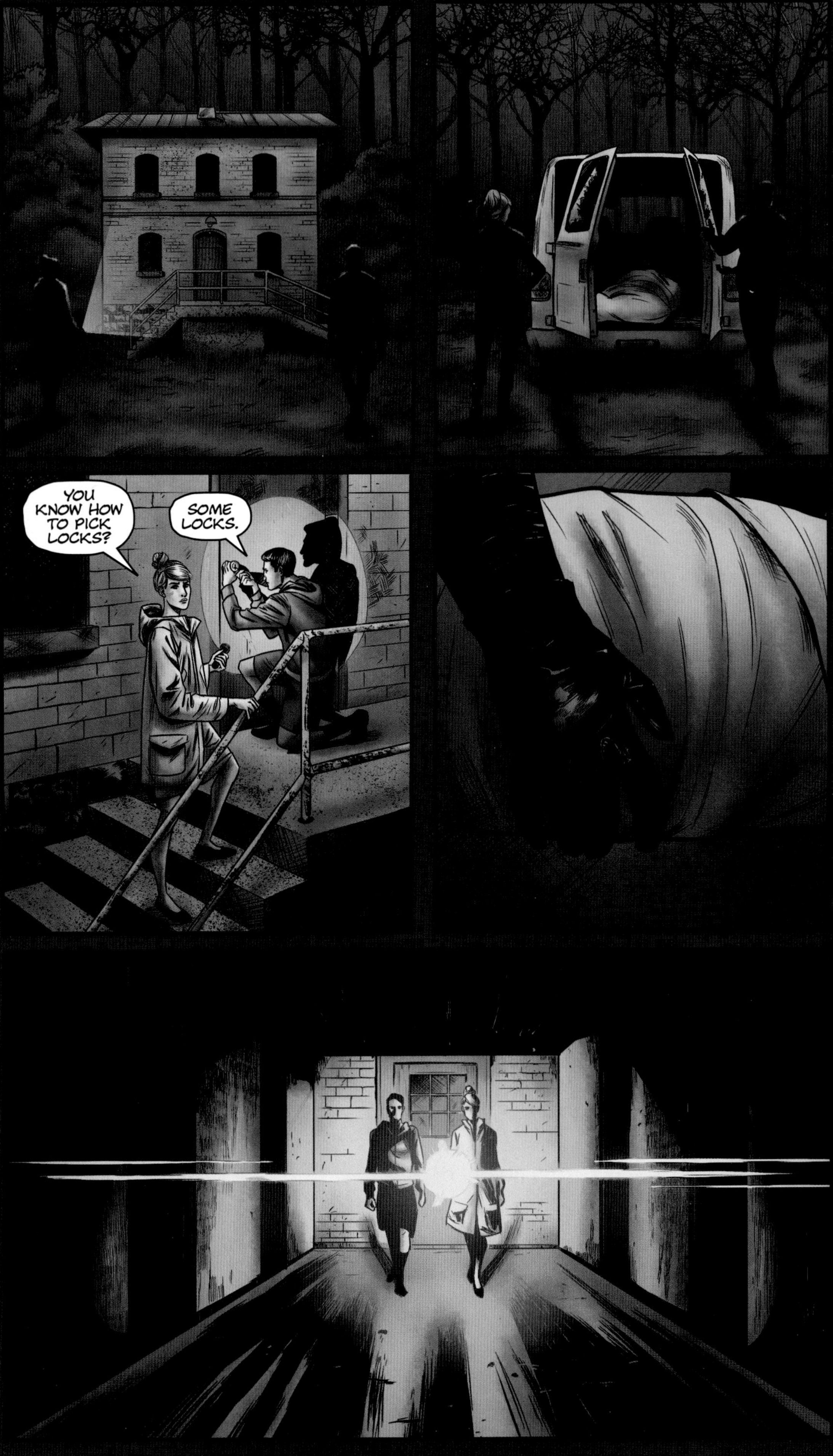
YOU KNOW HOW TO PICK LOCKS?
SOME LOCKS.

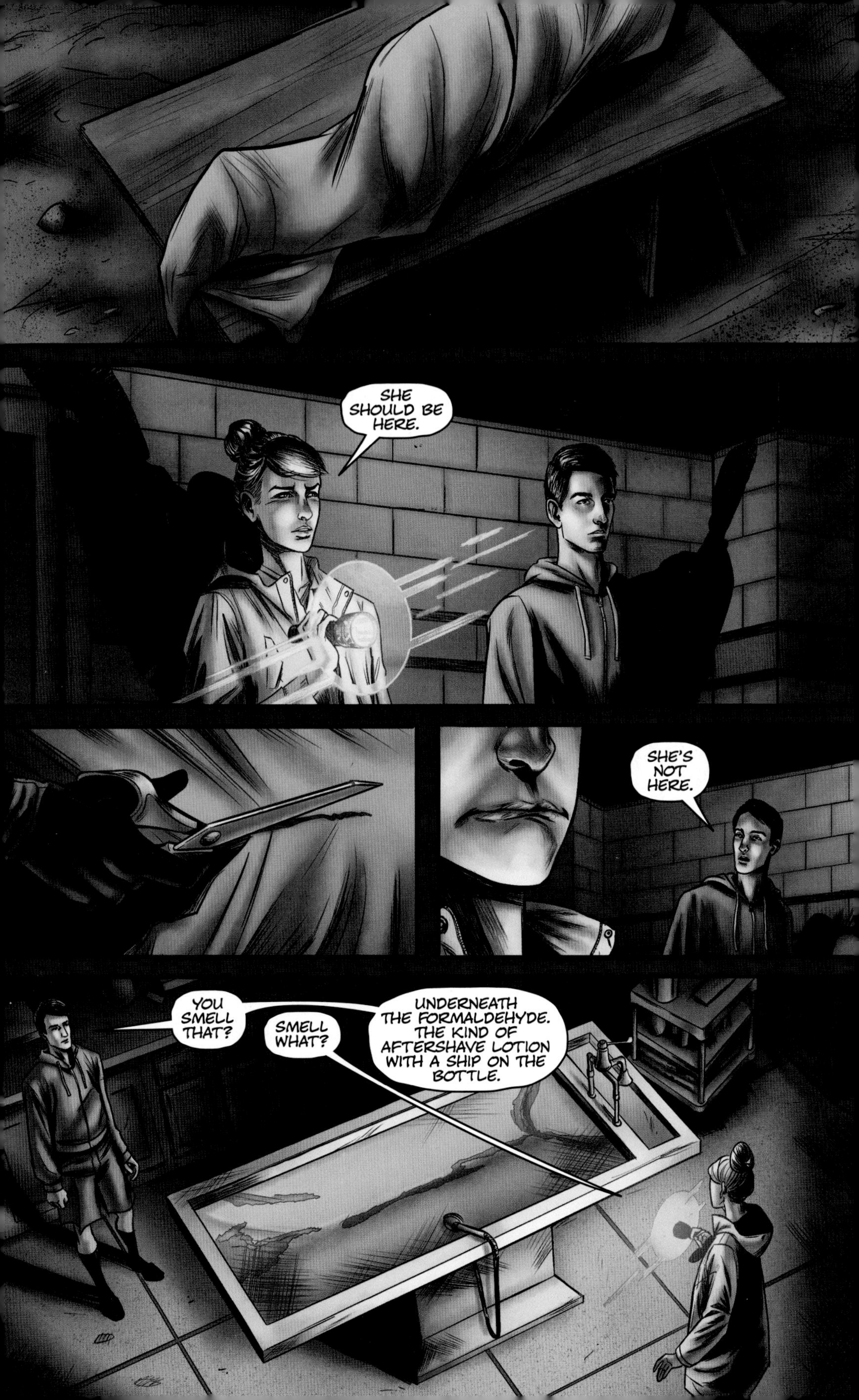
SHE SHOULD BE HERE.
SHE'S NOT HERE.
YOU SMELL THAT?
SMELL WHAT?
UNDERNEATH THE FORMALDEHYDE. THE KIND OF AFTERSHAVE LOTION WITH A SHIP ON THE BOTTLE.

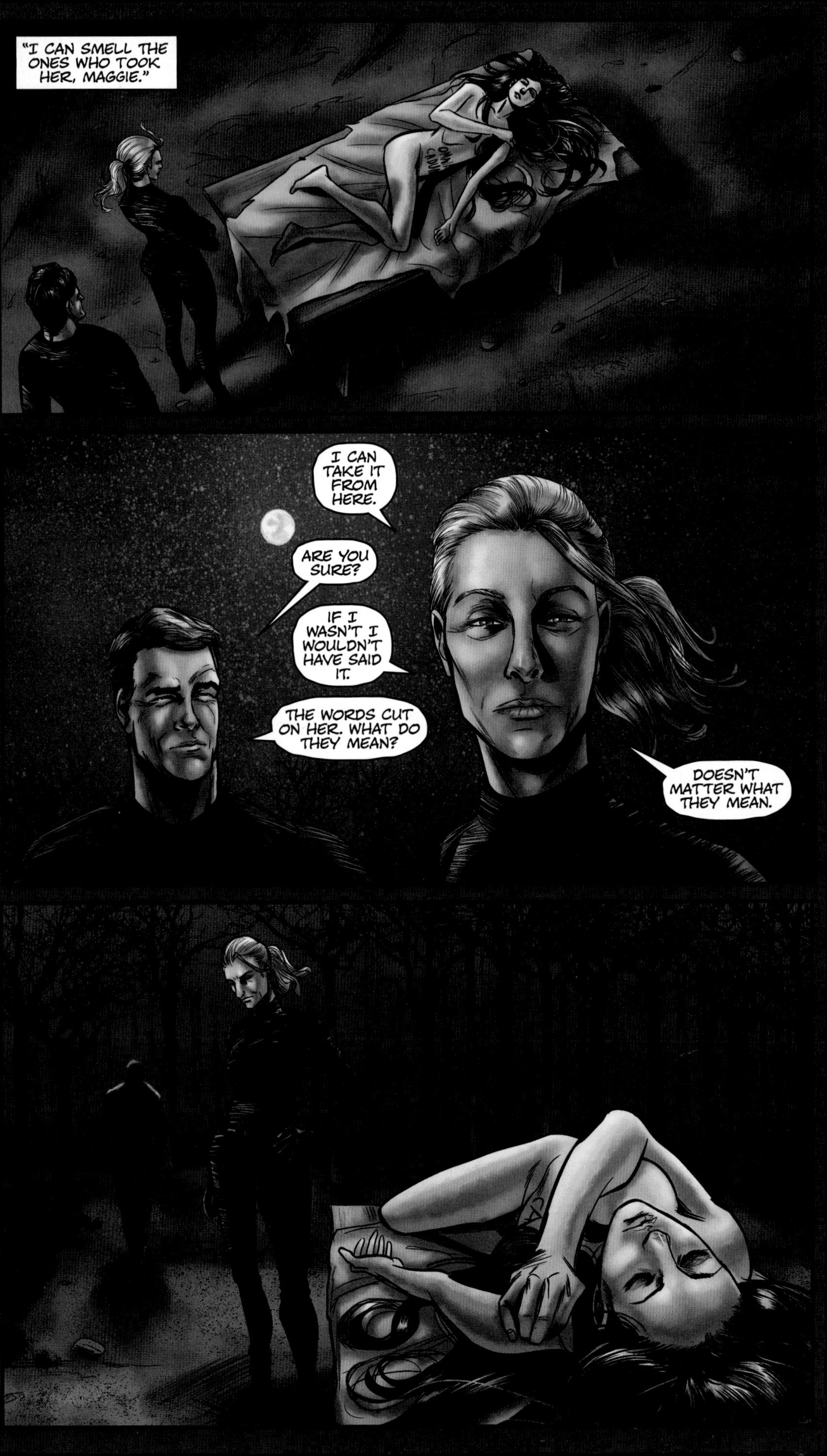
"I CAN SMELL THE ONES WHO TOOK HER, MAGGIE."
I CAN TAKE IT FROM HERE.
ARE YOU SURE?
IF I WASN'T I WOULDN'T HAVE SAID IT.
THE WORDS CUT ON HER. WHAT DO THEY MEAN?
DOESN'T MATTER WHAT THEY MEAN.

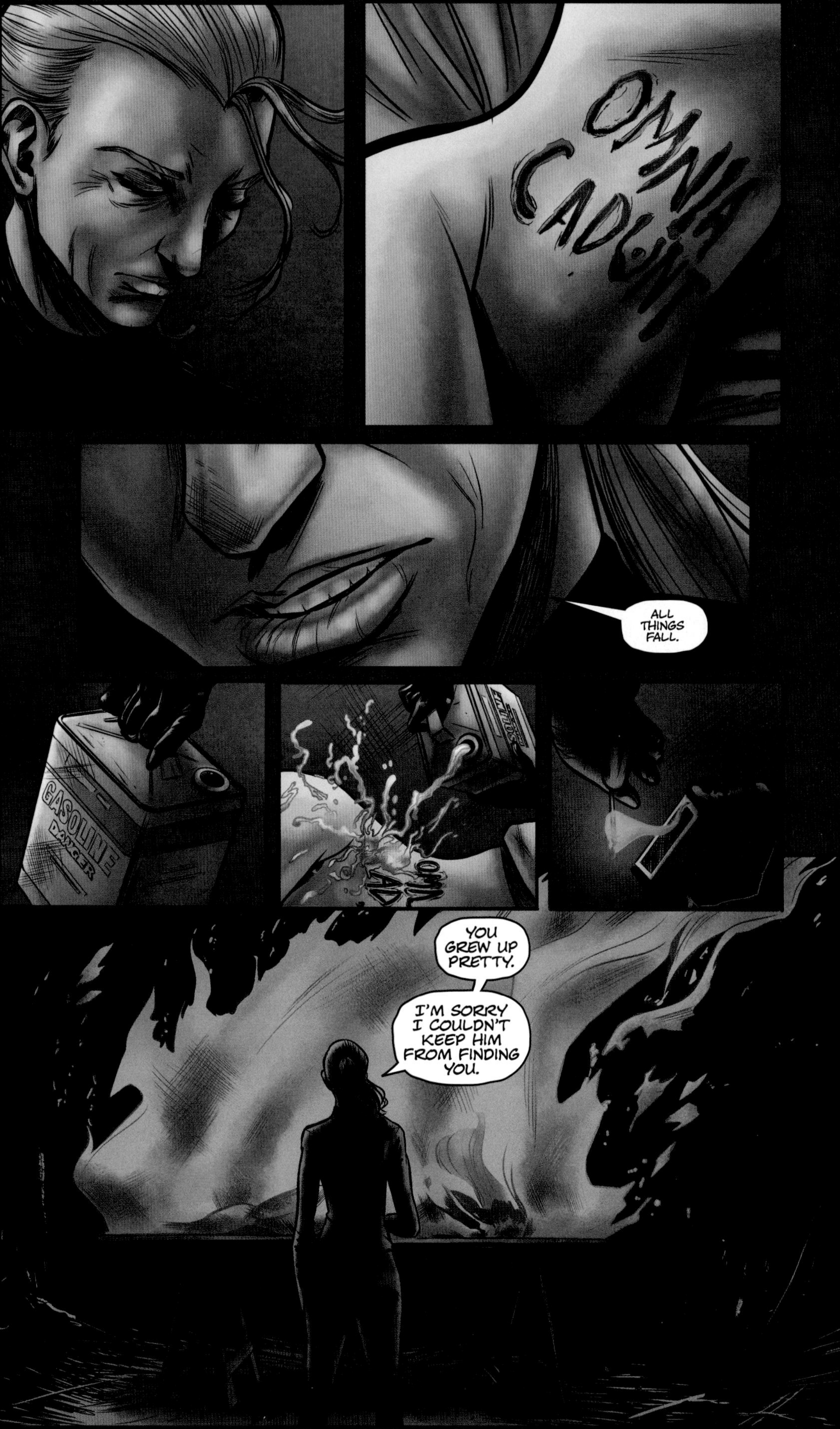
OMNIA CADUNT
ALL THINGS FALL.
GASOLINE
DANGER
YOU GREW UP PRETTY.
I'M SORRY I COULDN'T KEEP HIM FROM FINDING YOU.

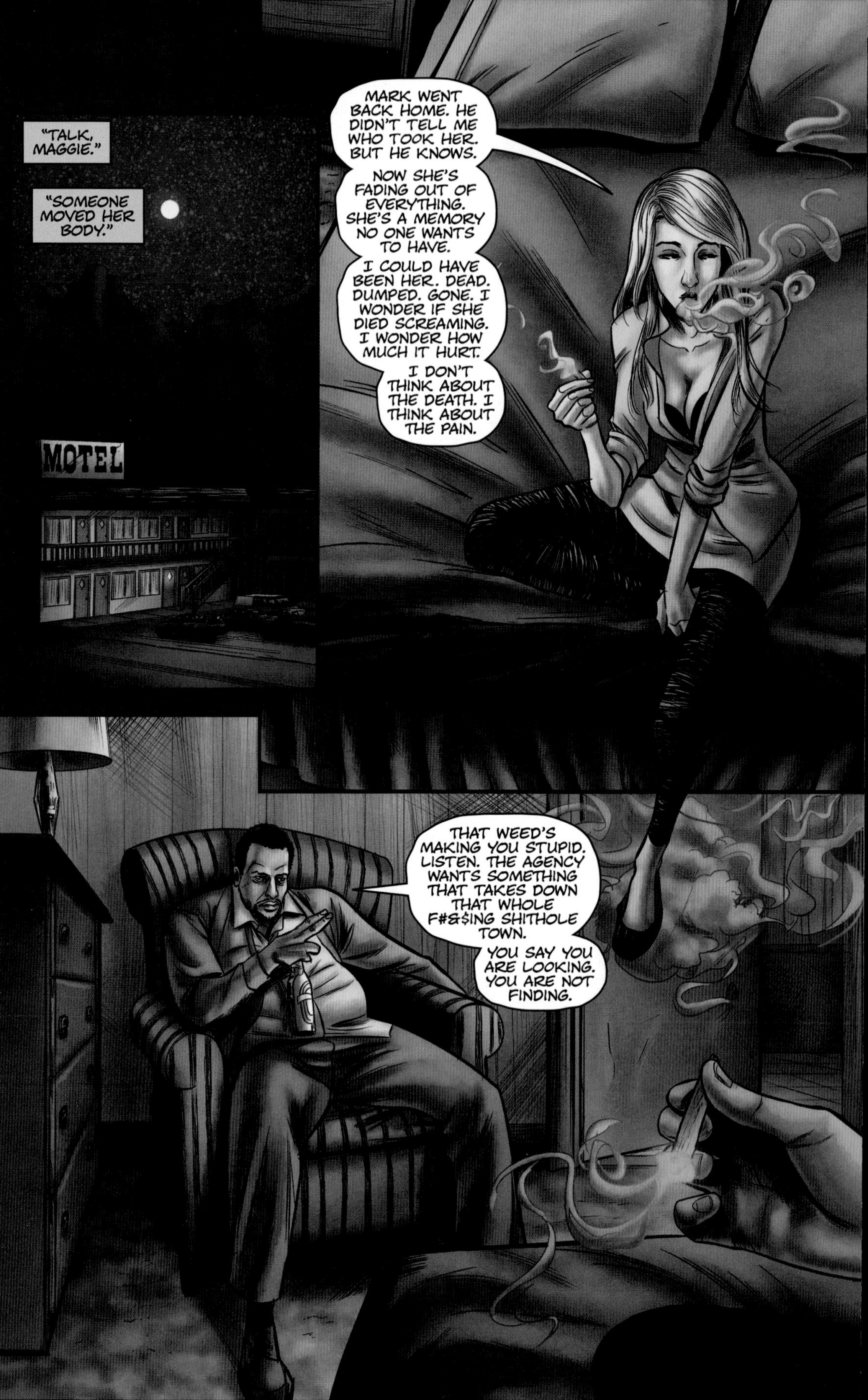
"TALK, MAGGIE."
"SOMEONE MOVED HER BODY."
MOTEL
MARK WENT BACK HOME. HE DIDN'T TELL ME WHO TOOK HER. BUT HE KNOWS.
NOW SHE'S FADING OUT OF EVERYTHING. SHE'S A MEMORY NO ONE WANTS TO HAVE.
I COULD HAVE BEEN HER. DEAD. DUMPED. GONE. I WONDER IF SHE DIED SCREAMING. I WONDER HOW MUCH IT HURT.
I DON'T THINK ABOUT THE DEATH. I THINK ABOUT THE PAIN.
THAT WEED'S MAKING YOU STUPID. LISTEN. THE AGENCY WANTS SOMETHING THAT TAKES DOWN THAT WHOLE F#&$ING SHITHOLE TOWN.
YOU SAY YOU ARE LOOKING. YOU ARE NOT FINDING.

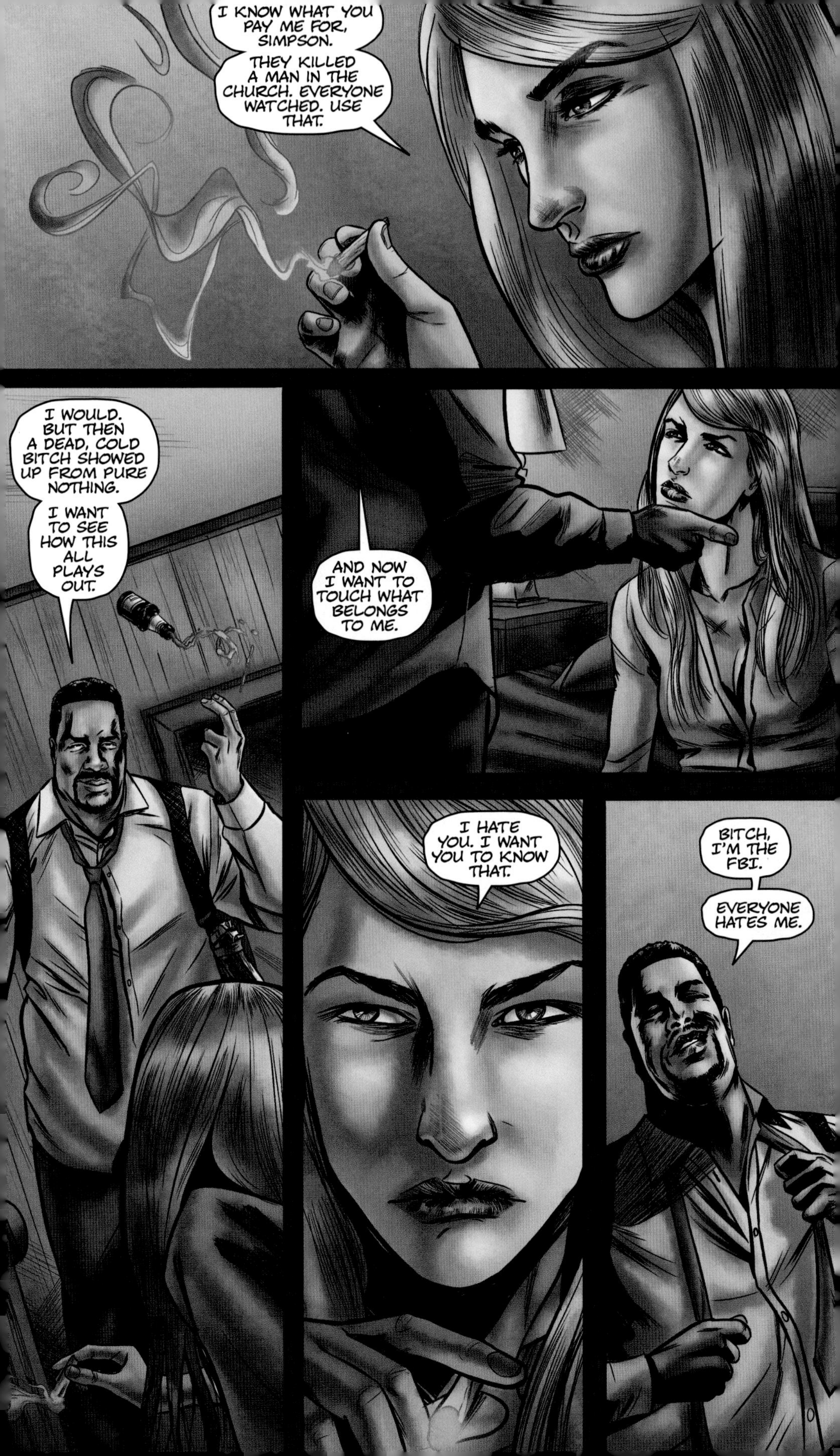
I KNOW WHAT YOU PAY ME FOR, SIMPSON.
THEY KILLED A MAN IN THE CHURCH. EVERYONE WATCHED. USE THAT.
I WOULD. BUT THEN A DEAD, COLD BITCH SHOWED UP FROM PURE NOTHING.
I WANT TO SEE HOW THIS ALL PLAYS OUT.
AND NOW I WANT TO TOUCH WHAT BELONGS TO ME.
I HATE YOU. I WANT YOU TO KNOW THAT.
BITCH, I'M THE FBI.
EVERYONE HATES ME.

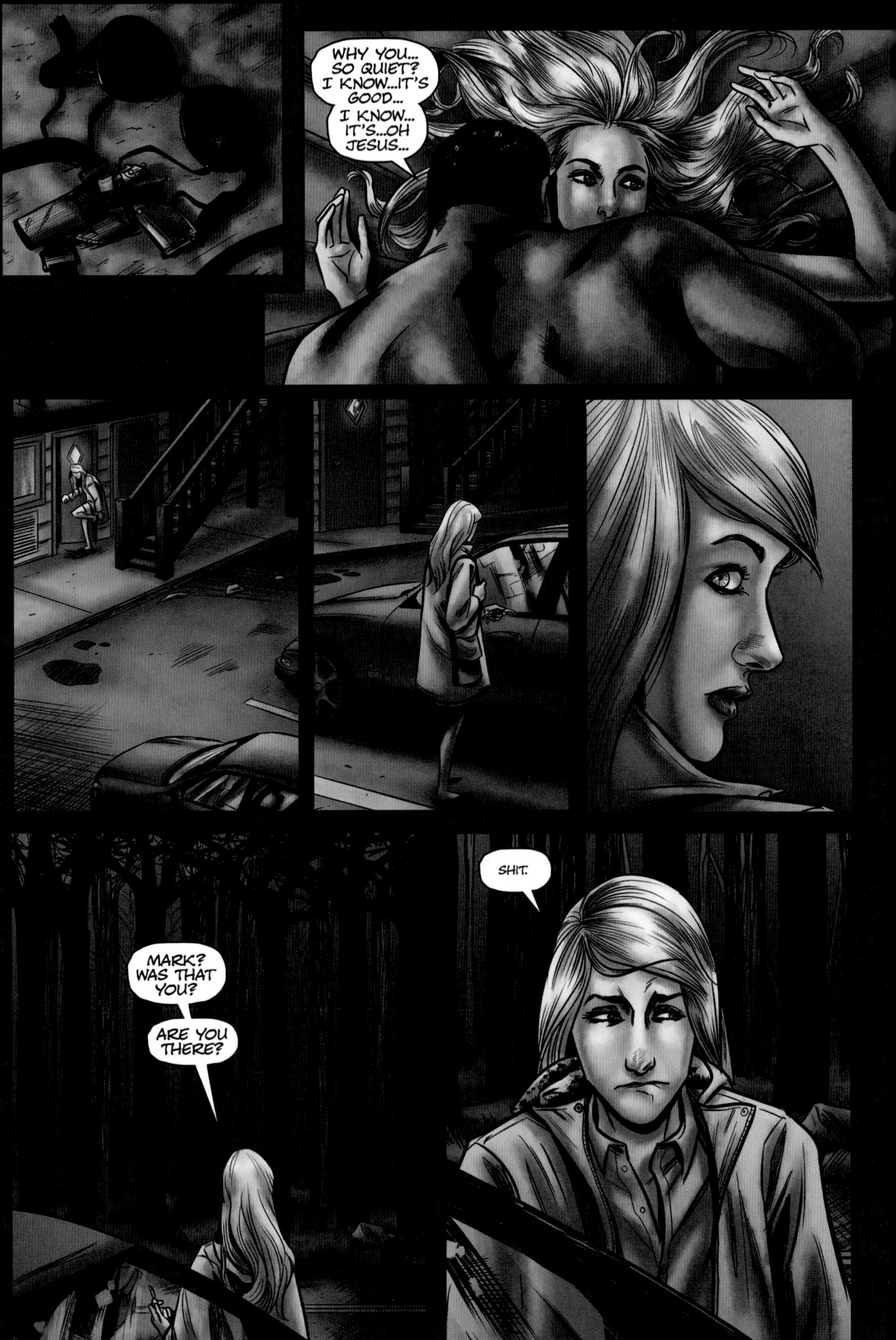
WHY YOU... SO QUIET? I KNOW...IT'S GOOD... I KNOW... IT'S...OH JESUS...
SHIT.
MARK? WAS THAT YOU?
ARE YOU THERE?

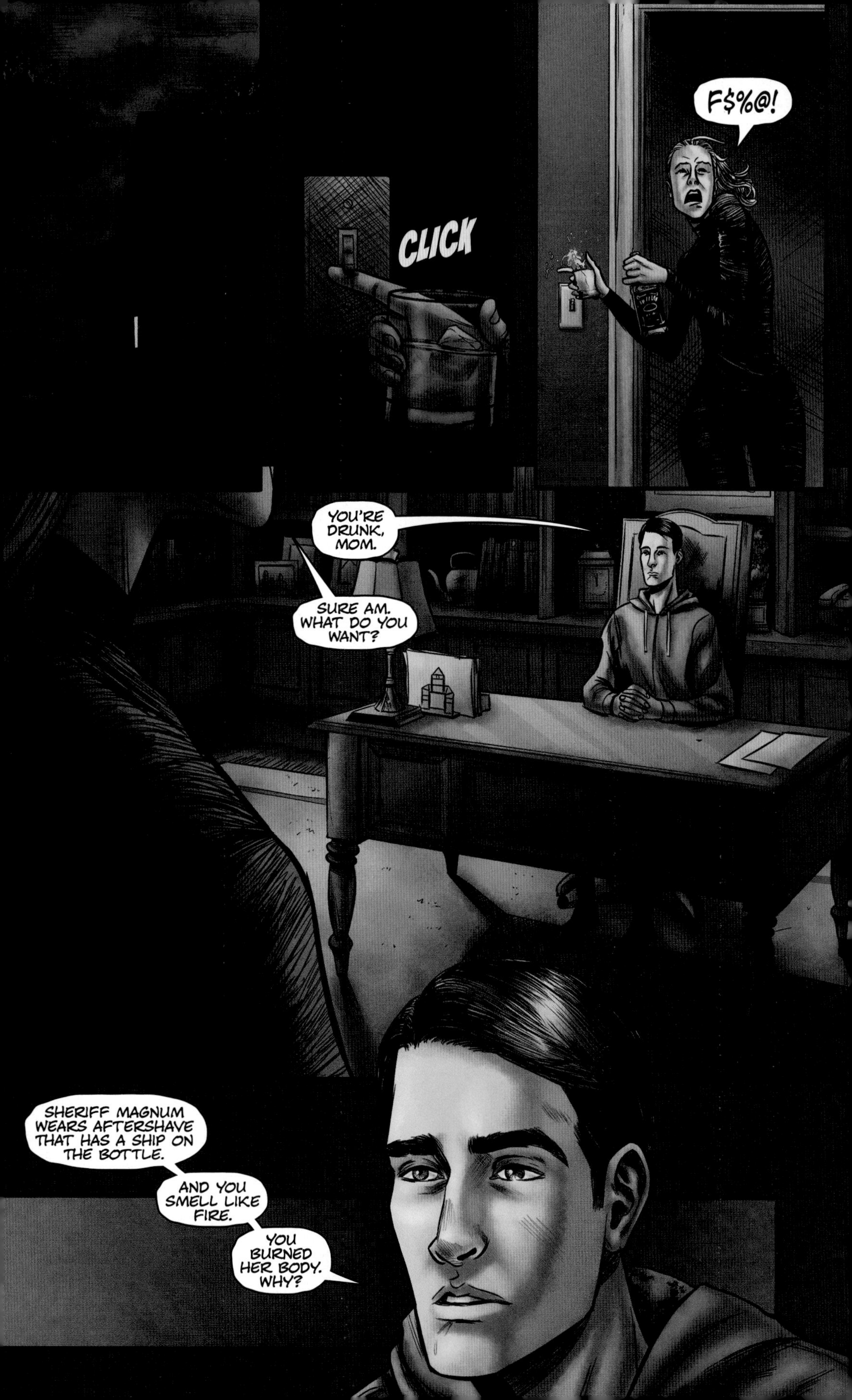
CLICK
F$%@!
YOU'RE DRUNK, MOM.
SURE AM. WHAT DO YOU WANT?
SHERIFF MAGNUM WEARS AFTERSHAVE THAT HAS A SHIP ON THE BOTTLE.
AND YOU SMELL LIKE FIRE.
YOU BURNED HER BODY. WHY?

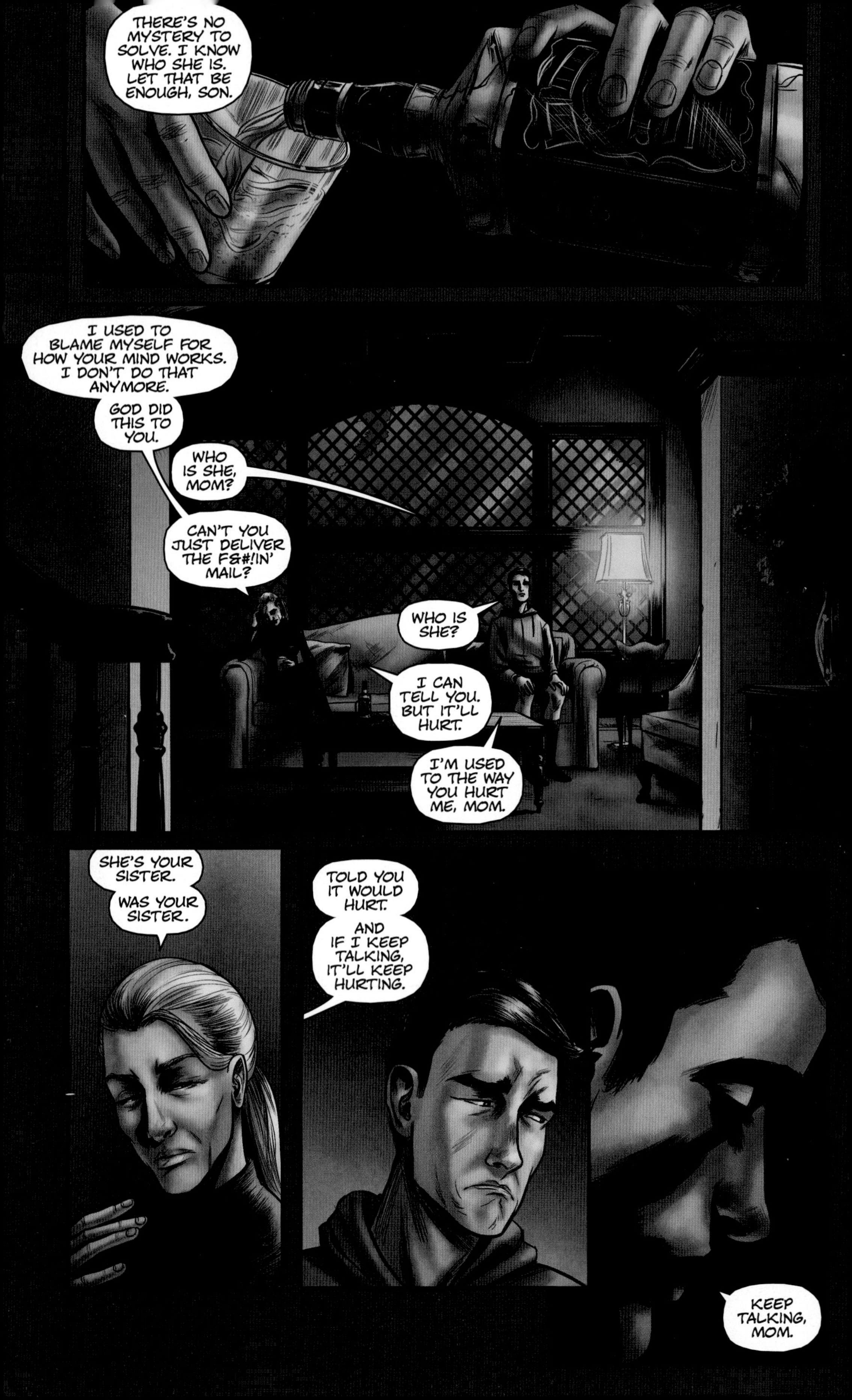
THERE'S NO MYSTERY TO SOLVE. I KNOW WHO SHE IS. LET THAT BE ENOUGH, SON.
I USED TO BLAME MYSELF FOR HOW YOUR MIND WORKS. I DON'T DO THAT ANYMORE.
GOD DID THIS TO YOU.
WHO IS SHE, MOM?
CAN'T YOU JUST DELIVER THE F&#!IN' MAIL?
WHO IS SHE?
I CAN TELL YOU. BUT IT'LL HURT.
I'M USED TO THE WAY YOU HURT ME, MOM.
SHE'S YOUR SISTER.
WAS YOUR SISTER.
TOLD YOU IT WOULD HURT.
AND IF I KEEP TALKING, IT'LL KEEP HURTING.
KEEP TALKING, MOM.

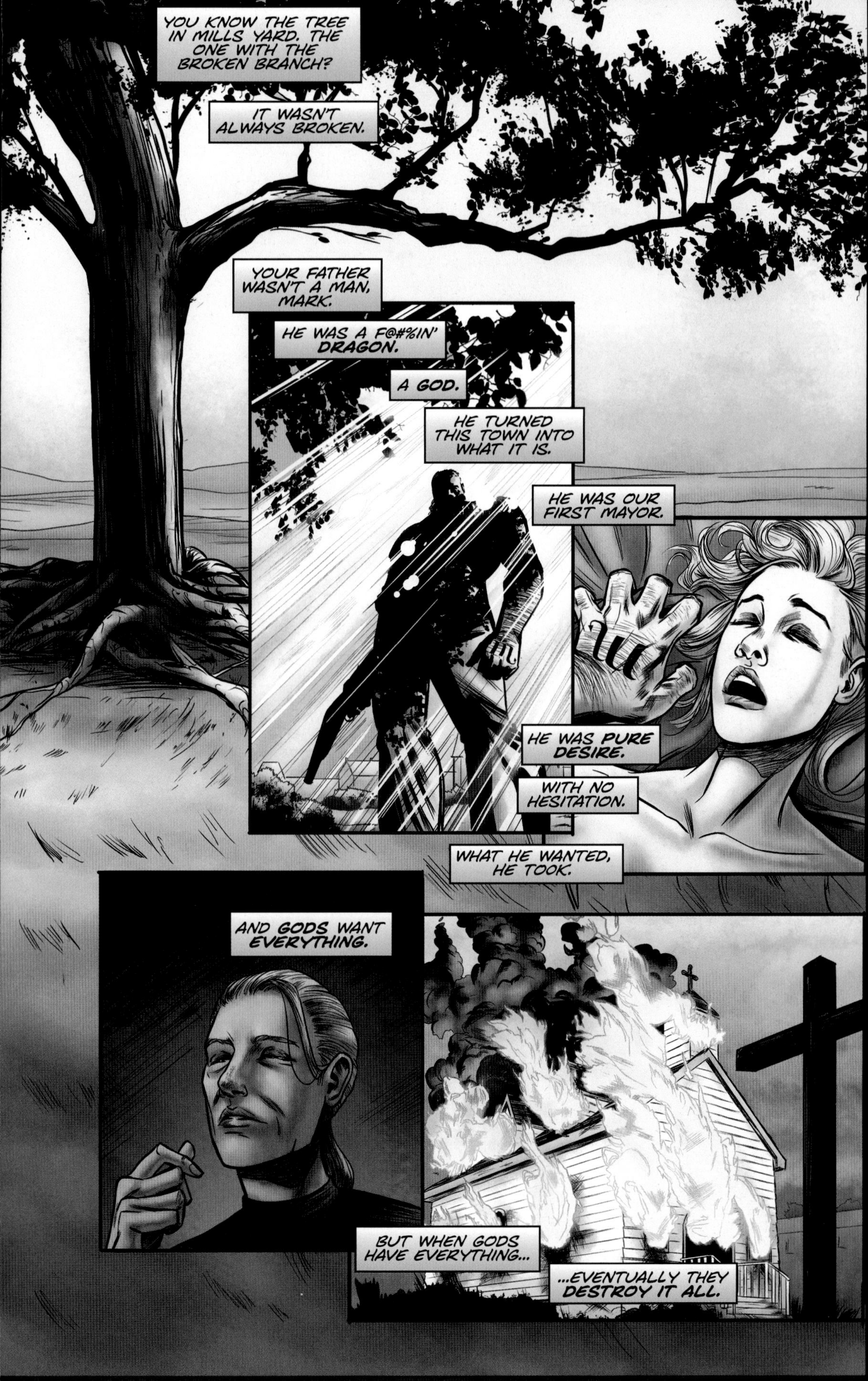
YOU KNOW THE TREE IN MILLS YARD. THE ONE WITH THE BROKEN BRANCH?
IT WASN'T ALWAYS BROKEN.
YOUR FATHER WASN'T A MAN, MARK.
HE WAS A F@#%IN' DRAGON.
A GOD.
HE TURNED THIS TOWN INTO WHAT IT IS.
HE WAS OUR FIRST MAYOR.
HE WAS PURE DESIRE.
WITH NO HESITATION.
WHAT HE WANTED, HE TOOK.
AND GODS WANT EVERYTHING.
BUT WHEN GODS HAVE EVERYTHING...
...EVENTUALLY THEY DESTROY IT ALL.

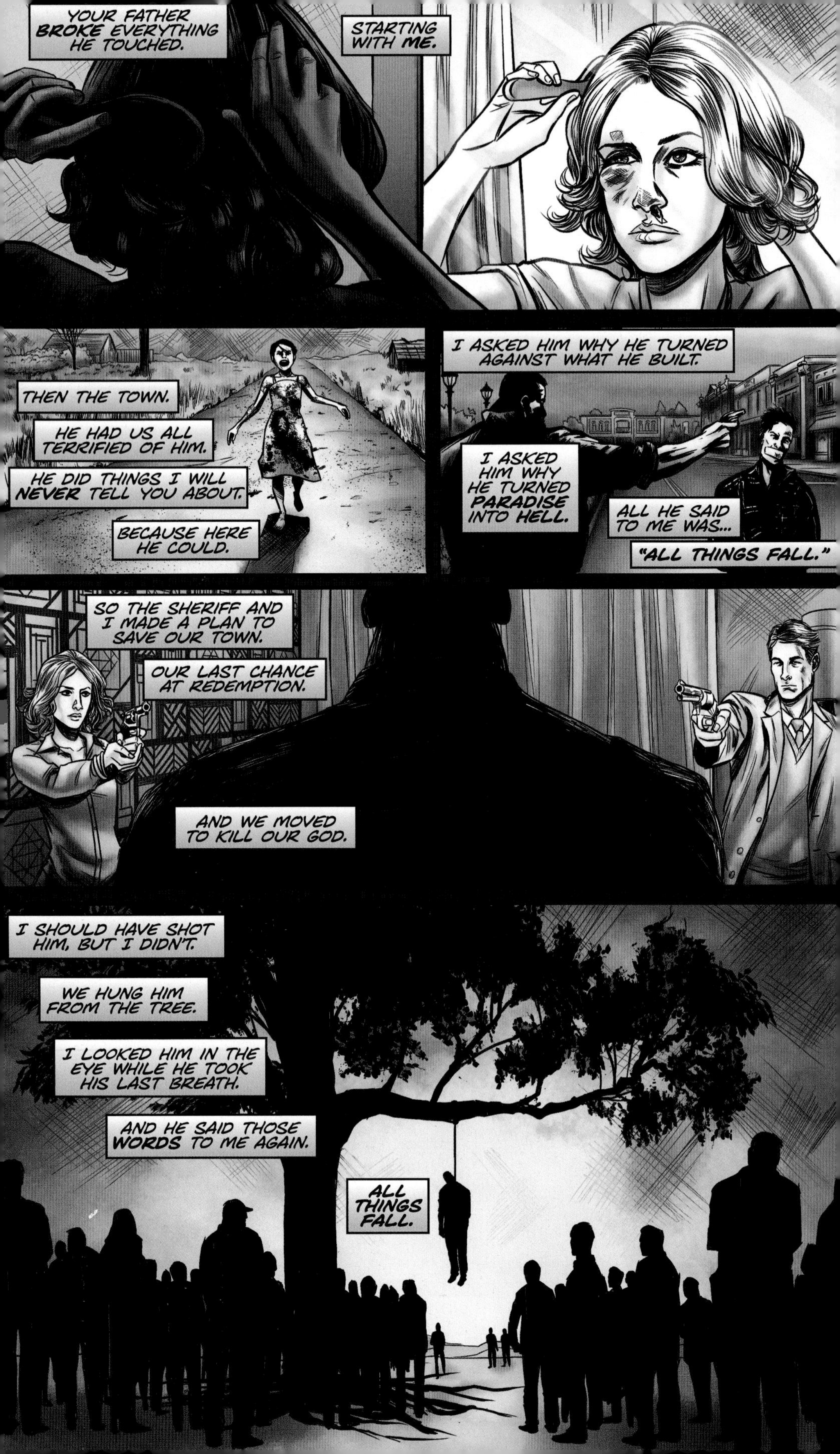
YOUR FATHER BROKE EVERYTHING HE TOUCHED.
STARTING WITH ME.
THEN THE TOWN.
HE HAD US ALL TERRIFIED OF HIM.
HE DID THINGS I WILL NEVER TELL YOU ABOUT.
BECAUSE HERE HE COULD.
I ASKED HIM WHY HE TURNED AGAINST WHAT HE BUILT.
I ASKED HIM WHY HE TURNED PARADISE INTO HELL.
ALL HE SAID TO ME WAS...
"ALL THINGS FALL."
SO THE SHERIFF AND I MADE A PLAN TO SAVE OUR TOWN.
OUR LAST CHANCE AT REDEMPTION.
AND WE MOVED TO KILL OUR GOD.
I SHOULD HAVE SHOT HIM, BUT I DIDN'T.
WE HUNG HIM FROM THE TREE.
I LOOKED HIM IN THE EYE WHILE HE TOOK HIS LAST BREATH.
AND HE SAID THOSE WORDS TO ME AGAIN.
ALL THINGS FALL.

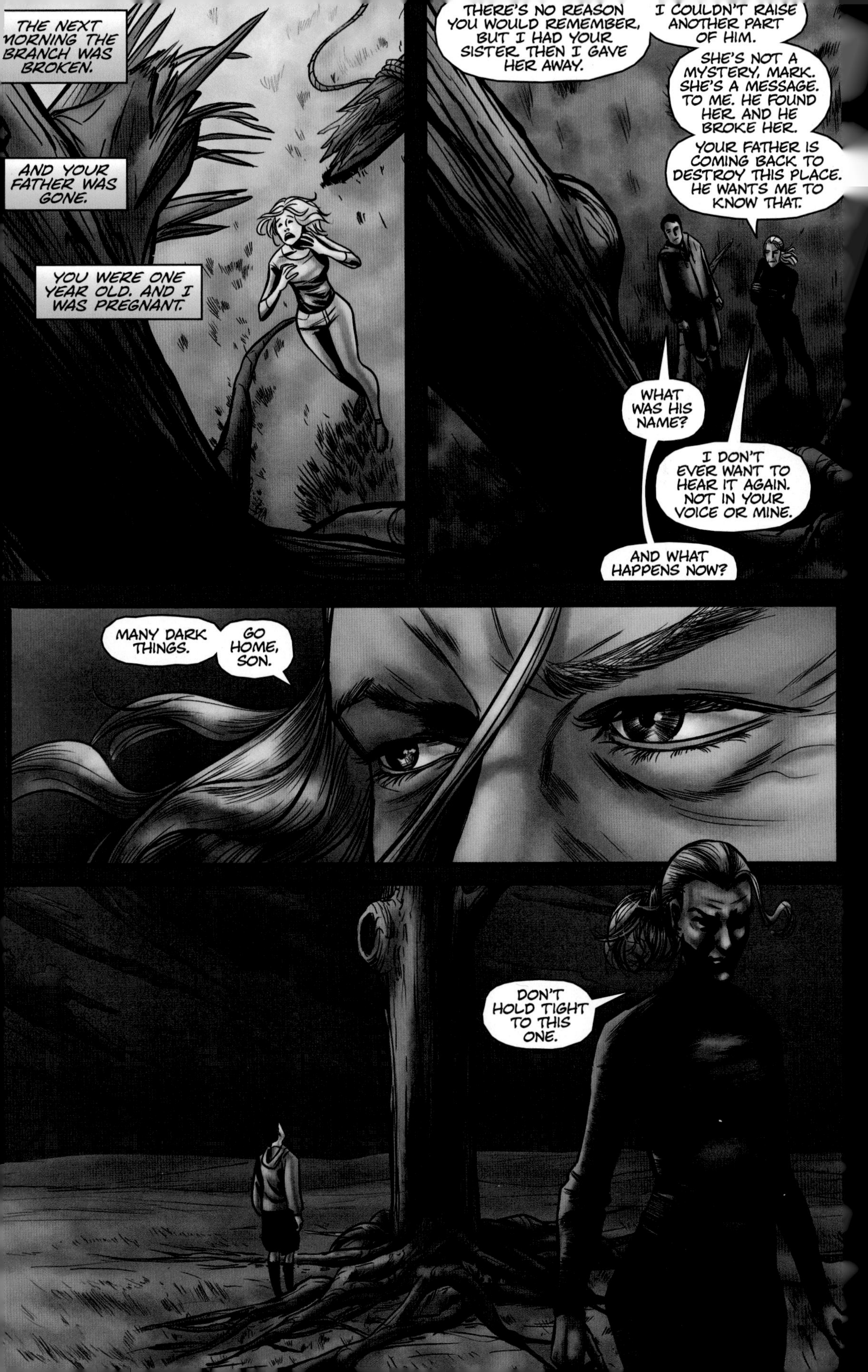
THE NEXT MORNING THE BRANCH WAS BROKEN.
AND YOUR FATHER WAS GONE.
YOU WERE ONE YEAR OLD. AND I WAS PREGNANT.
THERE'S NO REASON YOU WOULD REMEMBER, BUT I HAD YOUR SISTER. THEN I GAVE HER AWAY.
I COULDN'T RAISE ANOTHER PART OF HIM.
SHE'S NOT A MYSTERY, MARK. SHE'S A MESSAGE. TO ME. HE FOUND HER AND HE BROKE HER.
YOUR FATHER IS COMING BACK TO DESTROY THIS PLACE. HE WANTS ME TO KNOW THAT.
WHAT WAS HIS NAME?
I DON'T EVER WANT TO HEAR IT AGAIN. NOT IN YOUR VOICE OR MINE.
AND WHAT HAPPENS NOW?
MANY DARK THINGS.
GO HOME, SON.
DON'T HOLD TIGHT TO THIS ONE.

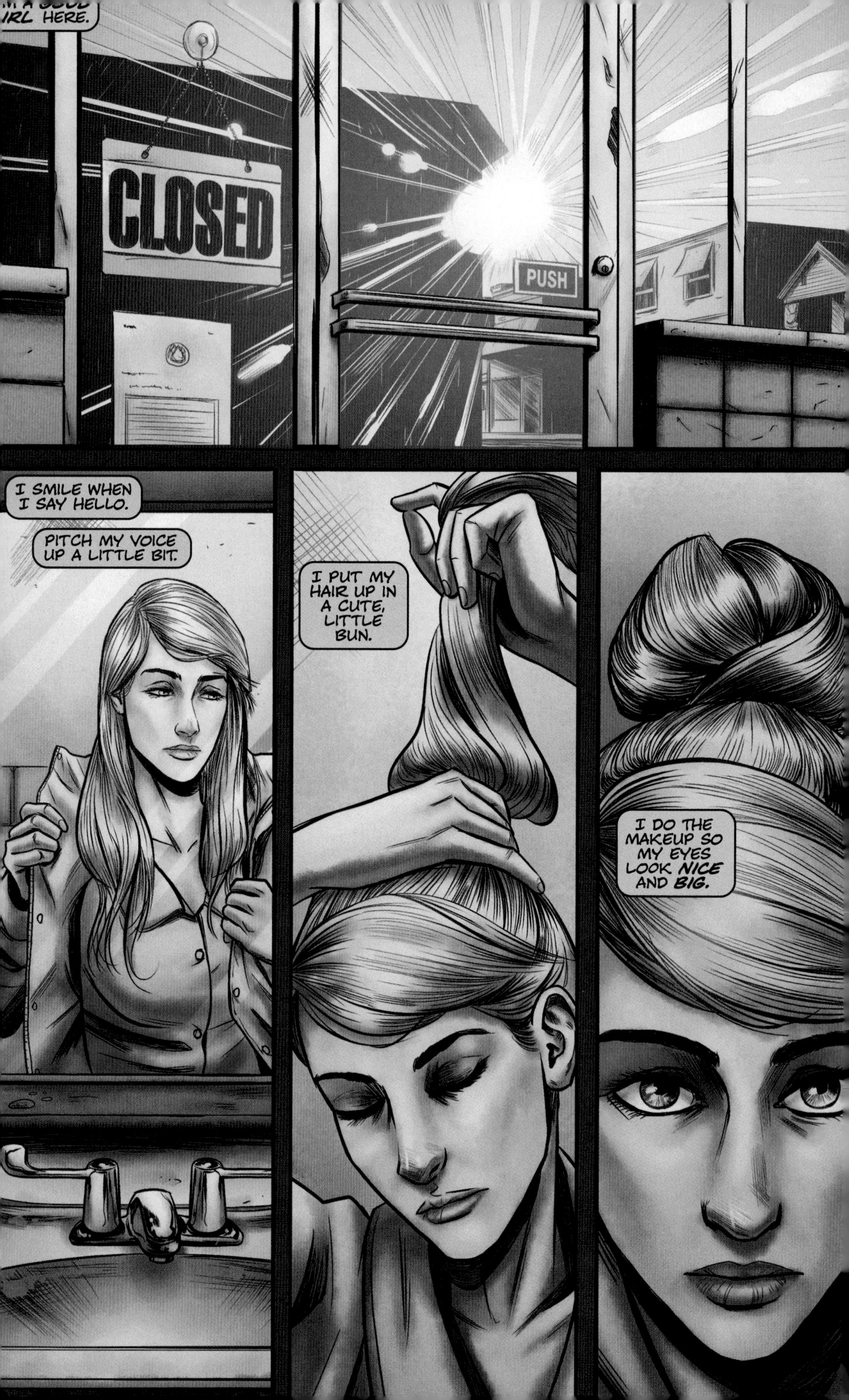
CLOSED
PUSH
I SMILE WHEN I SAY HELLO.
PITCH MY VOICE UP A LITTLE BIT.
I PUT MY HAIR UP IN A CUTE, LITTLE BUN.
I DO THE MAKEUP SO MY EYES LOOK NICE AND BIG.

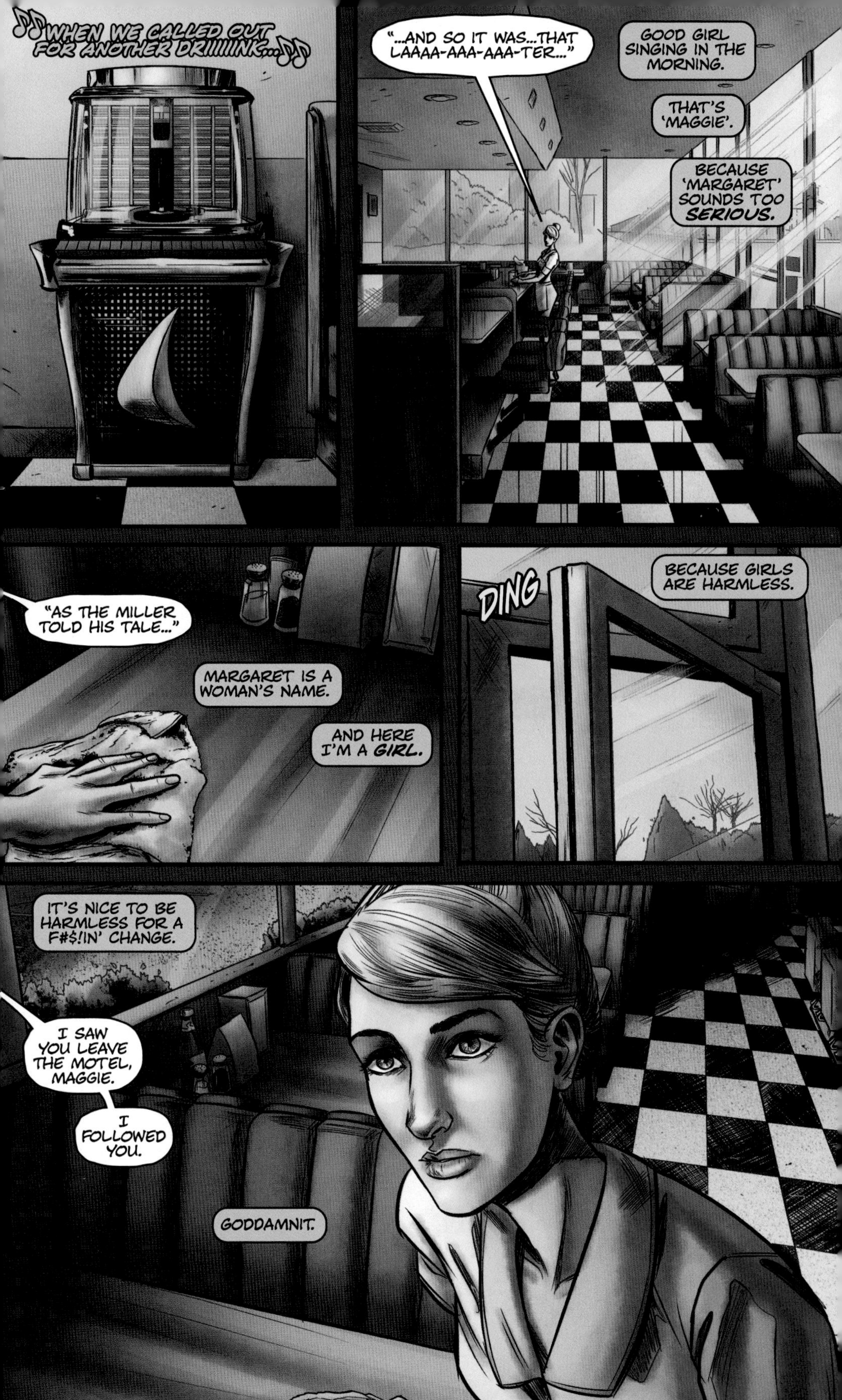
♪♪WHEN WE CALLED OUT FOR ANOTHER DRIIIIINK...♪♪
"...AND SO IT WAS...THAT LAAAA-AAA-AAA-TER..."
GOOD GIRL SINGING IN THE MORNING.
THAT'S 'MAGGIE'.
BECAUSE 'MARGARET' SOUNDS TOO SERIOUS.
"AS THE MILLER TOLD HIS TALE..."
MARGARET IS A WOMAN'S NAME.
AND HERE I'M A GIRL.
DING
BECAUSE GIRLS ARE HARMLESS.
IT'S NICE TO BE HARMLESS FOR A F#$!IN' CHANGE.
I SAW YOU LEAVE THE MOTEL, MAGGIE.
I FOLLOWED YOU.
GODDAMNIT.
Maggie

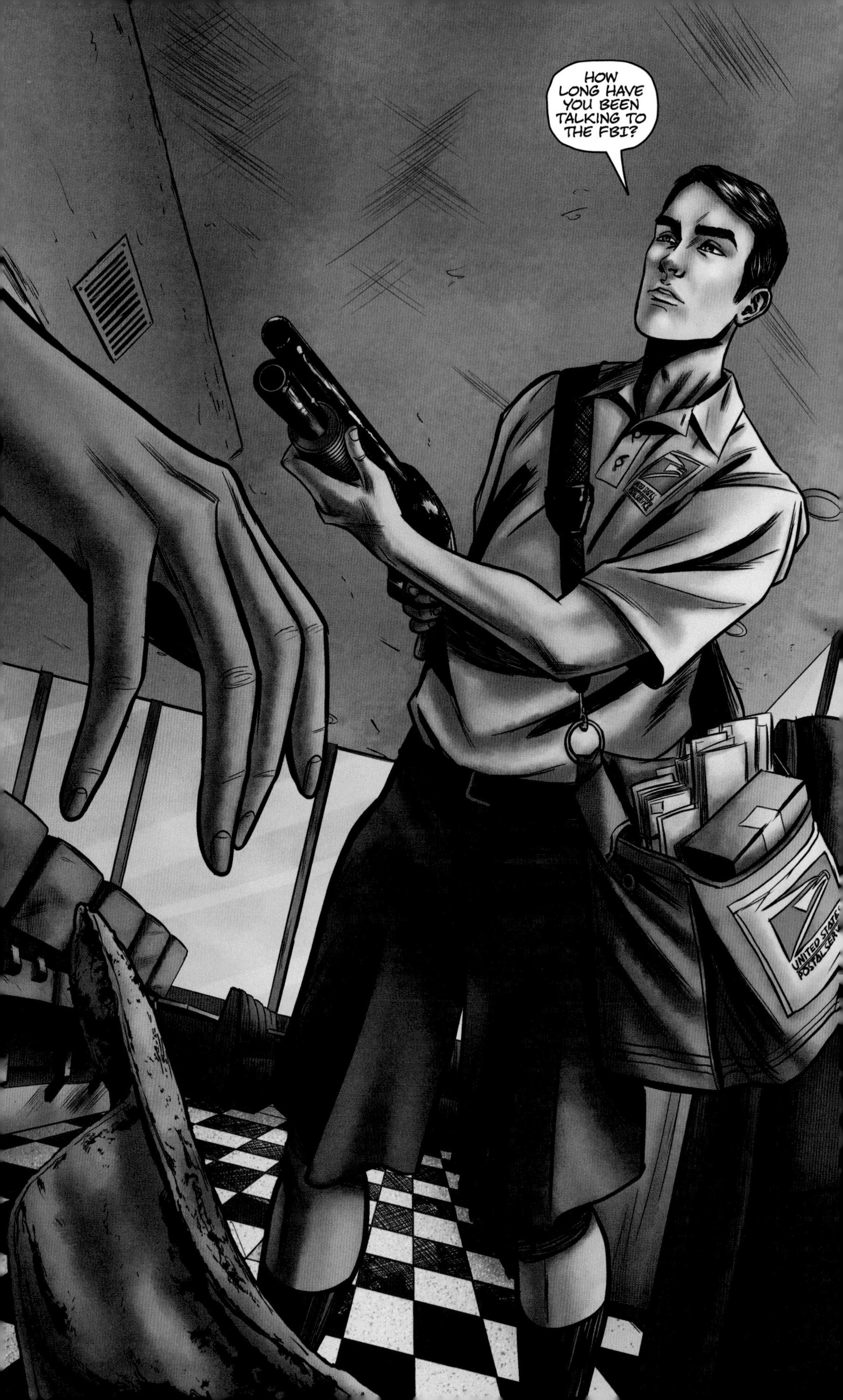
HOW LONG HAVE YOU BEEN TALKING TO THE FBI?
UNITED STATES POSTAL SERVICE

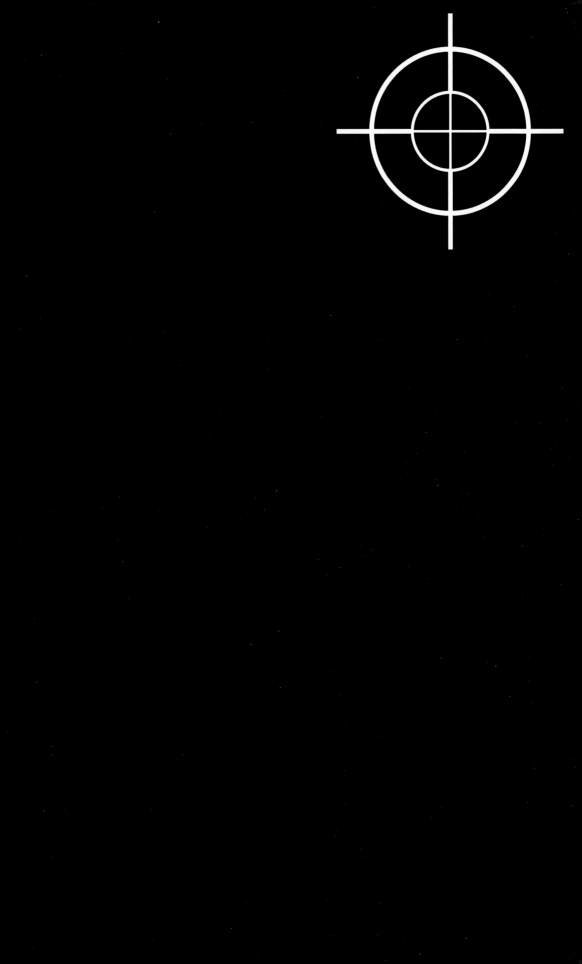

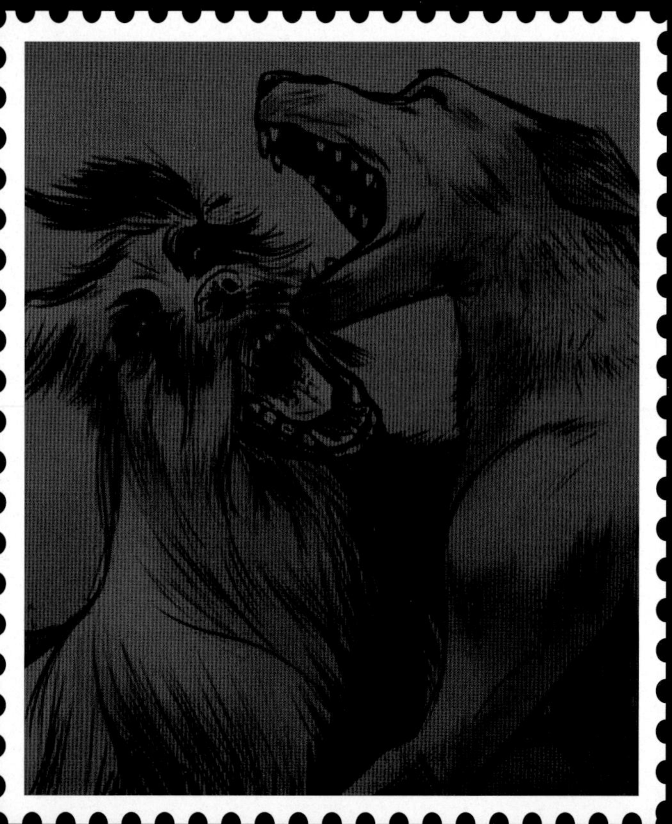

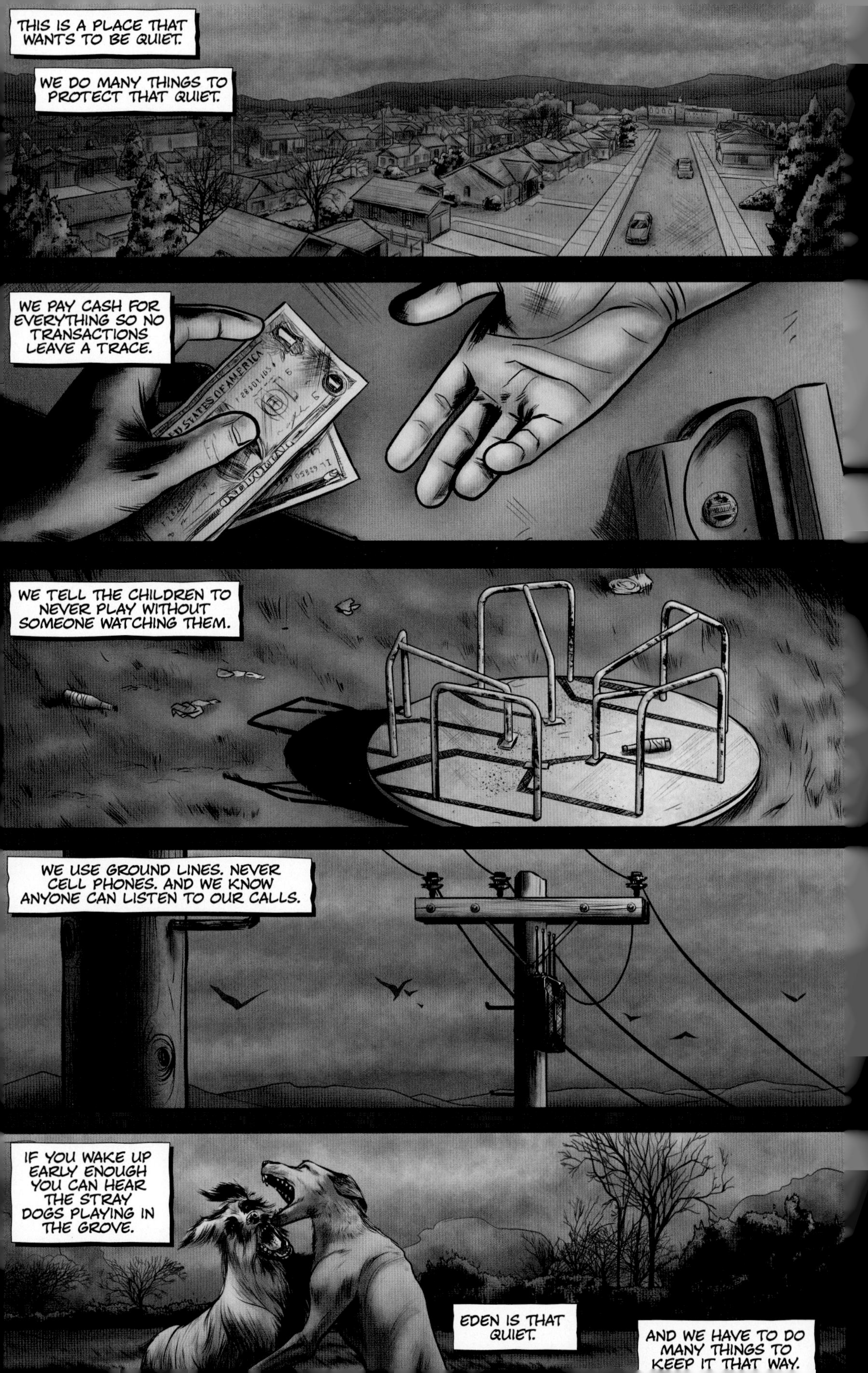
THIS IS A PLACE THAT WANTS TO BE QUIET.
WE DO MANY THINGS TO PROTECT THAT QUIET.
WE PAY CASH FOR EVERYTHING SO NO TRANSACTIONS LEAVE A TRACE.
WE TELL THE CHILDREN TO NEVER PLAY WITHOUT SOMEONE WATCHING THEM.
WE USE GROUND LINES. NEVER CELL PHONES. AND WE KNOW ANYONE CAN LISTEN TO OUR CALLS.
IF YOU WAKE UP EARLY ENOUGH YOU CAN HEAR THE STRAY DOGS PLAYING IN THE GROVE.
EDEN IS THAT QUIET.
AND WE HAVE TO DO MANY THINGS TO KEEP IT THAT WAY.

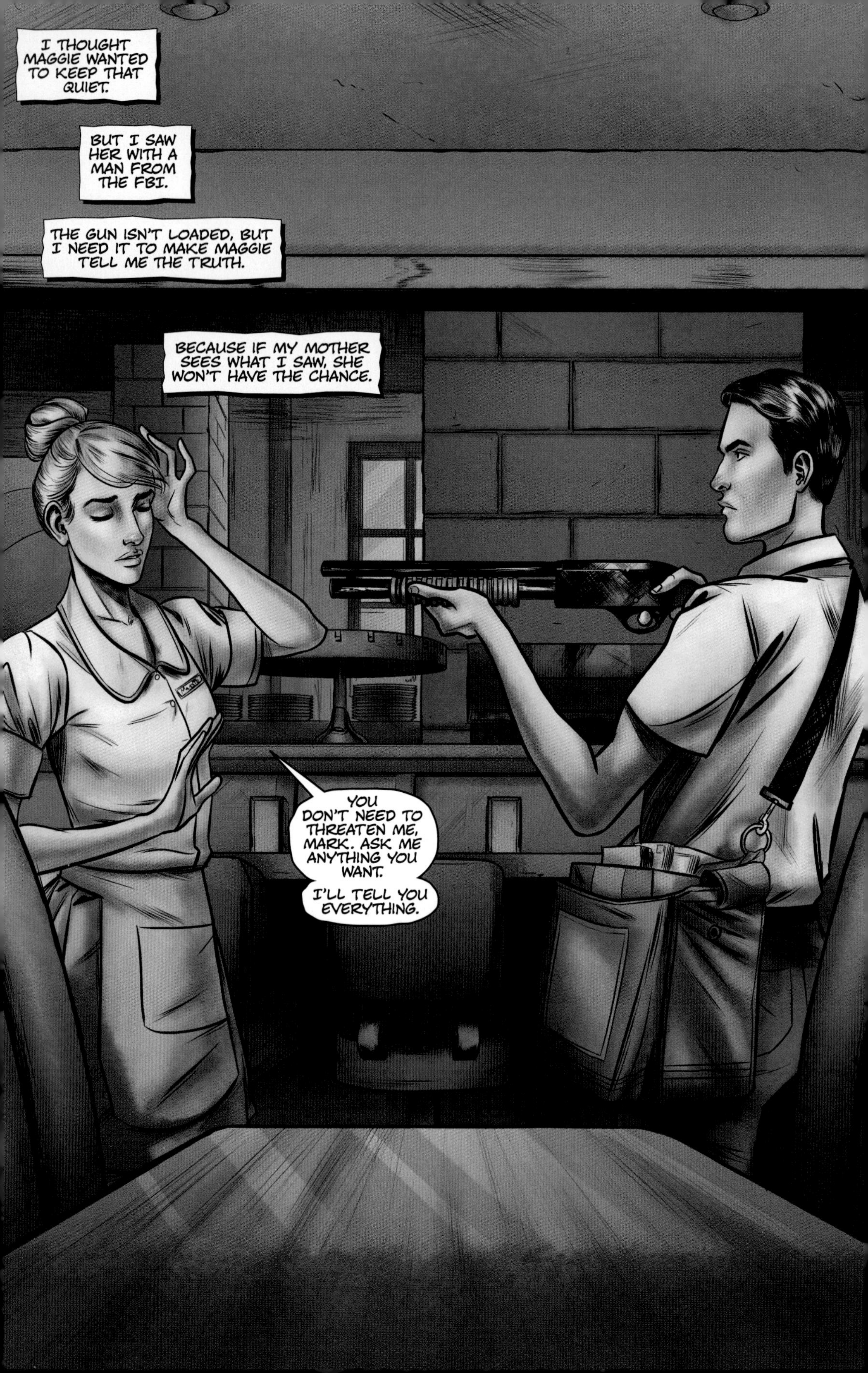
I THOUGHT MAGGIE WANTED TO KEEP THAT QUIET.
BUT I SAW HER WITH A MAN FROM THE FBI.
THE GUN ISN'T LOADED, BUT I NEED IT TO MAKE MAGGIE TELL ME THE TRUTH.
BECAUSE IF MY MOTHER SEES WHAT I SAW, SHE WON'T HAVE THE CHANCE.
YOU DON'T NEED TO THREATEN ME, MARK. ASK ME ANYTHING YOU WANT.
I'LL TELL YOU EVERYTHING.

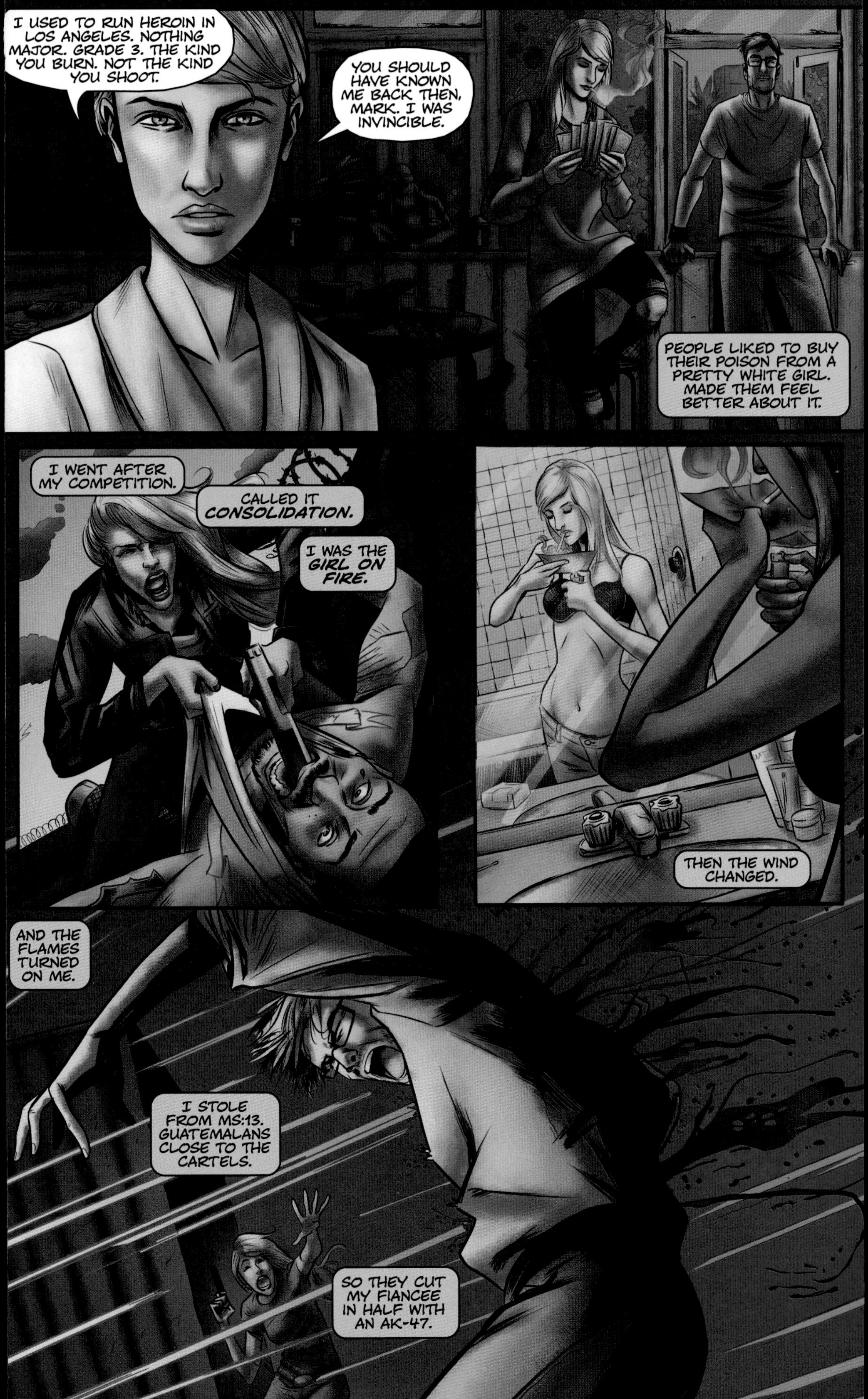
I USED TO RUN HEROIN IN LOS ANGELES. NOTHING MAJOR. GRADE 3. THE KIND YOU BURN. NOT THE KIND YOU SHOOT.
YOU SHOULD HAVE KNOWN ME BACK THEN, MARK. I WAS INVINCIBLE.
PEOPLE LIKED TO BUY THEIR POISON FROM A PRETTY WHITE GIRL. MADE THEM FEEL BETTER ABOUT IT.
I WENT AFTER MY COMPETITION.
CALLED IT CONSOLIDATION.
I WAS THE GIRL ON FIRE.
THEN THE WIND CHANGED.
AND THE FLAMES TURNED ON ME.
I STOLE FROM MS:13. GUATEMALANS CLOSE TO THE CARTELS.
SO THEY CUT MY FIANCEE IN HALF WITH AN AK-47.

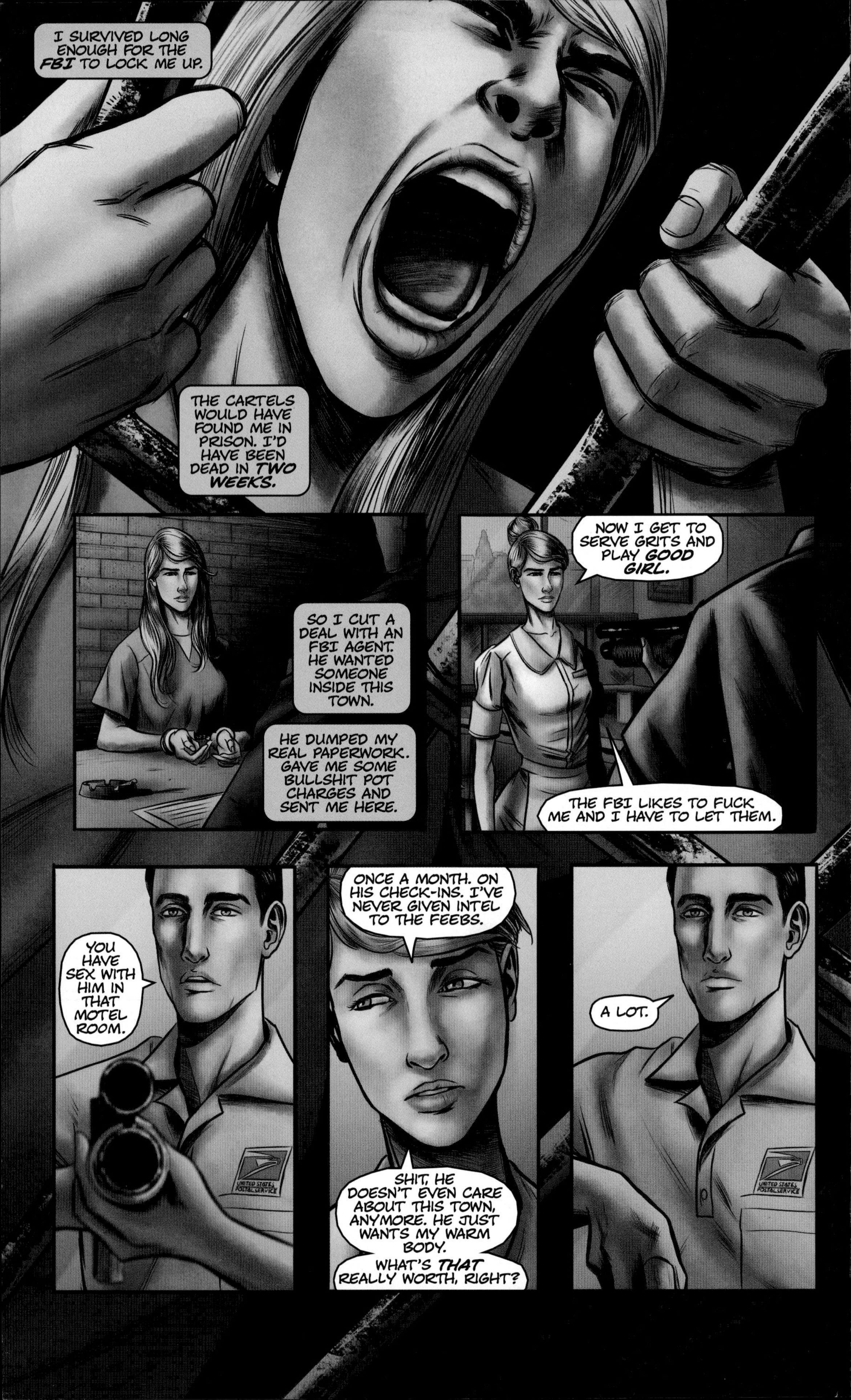
I SURVIVED LONG ENOUGH FOR THE FBI TO LOCK ME UP.
THE CARTELS WOULD HAVE FOUND ME IN PRISON. I'D HAVE BEEN DEAD IN TWO WEEKS.
SO I CUT A DEAL WITH AN FBI AGENT. HE WANTED SOMEONE INSIDE THIS TOWN.
HE DUMPED MY REAL PAPERWORK. GAVE ME SOME BULLSHIT POT CHARGES AND SENT ME HERE.
NOW I GET TO SERVE GRITS AND PLAY GOOD GIRL.
THE FBI LIKES TO FUCK ME AND I HAVE TO LET THEM.
YOU HAVE SEX WITH HIM IN THAT MOTEL ROOM.
ONCE A MONTH. ON HIS CHECK-INS. I'VE NEVER GIVEN INTEL TO THE FEEBS.
SHIT, HE DOESN'T EVEN CARE ABOUT THIS TOWN, ANYMORE. HE JUST WANTS MY WARM BODY.
WHAT'S THAT REALLY WORTH, RIGHT?
A LOT.

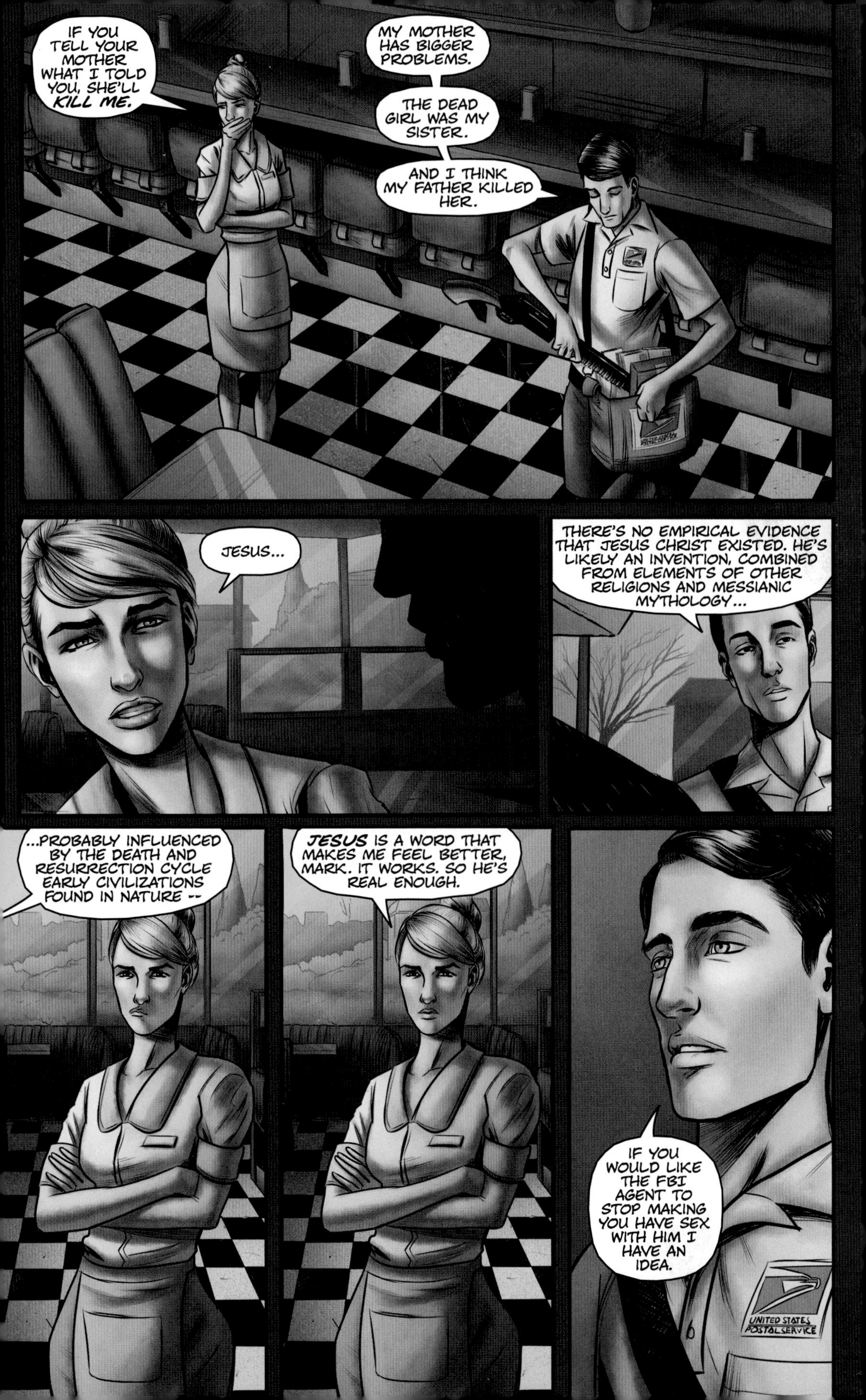
IF YOU TELL YOUR MOTHER WHAT I TOLD YOU, SHE'LL KILL ME.
MY MOTHER HAS BIGGER PROBLEMS.
THE DEAD GIRL WAS MY SISTER.
AND I THINK MY FATHER KILLED HER.
JESUS...
THERE'S NO EMPIRICAL EVIDENCE THAT JESUS CHRIST EXISTED. HE'S LIKELY AN INVENTION, COMBINED FROM ELEMENTS OF OTHER RELIGIONS AND MESSIANIC MYTHOLOGY...
...PROBABLY INFLUENCED BY THE DEATH AND RESURRECTION CYCLE EARLY CIVILIZATIONS FOUND IN NATURE --
JESUS IS A WORD THAT MAKES ME FEEL BETTER, MARK. IT WORKS. SO HE'S REAL ENOUGH.
IF YOU WOULD LIKE THE FBI AGENT TO STOP MAKING YOU HAVE SEX WITH HIM I HAVE AN IDEA.
UNITED STATES POSTAL SERVICE

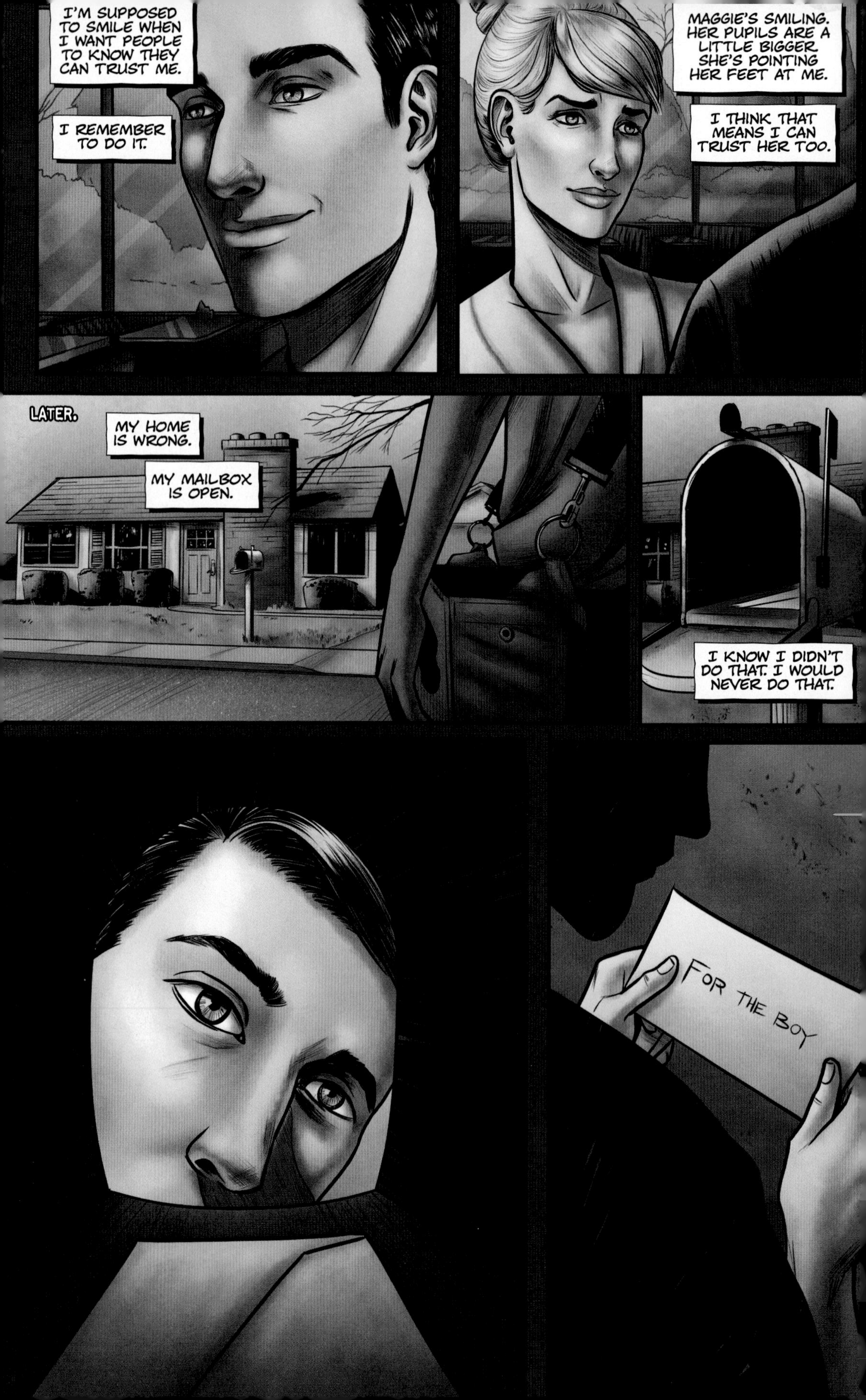
I'M SUPPOSED TO SMILE WHEN I WANT PEOPLE TO KNOW THEY CAN TRUST ME.
I REMEMBER TO DO IT.
MAGGIE'S SMILING. HER PUPILS ARE A LITTLE BIGGER. SHE'S POINTING HER FEET AT ME.
I THINK THAT MEANS I CAN TRUST HER TOO.
LATER.
MY HOME IS WRONG.
MY MAILBOX IS OPEN.
I KNOW I DIDN'T DO THAT. I WOULD NEVER DO THAT.
FOR THE BOY

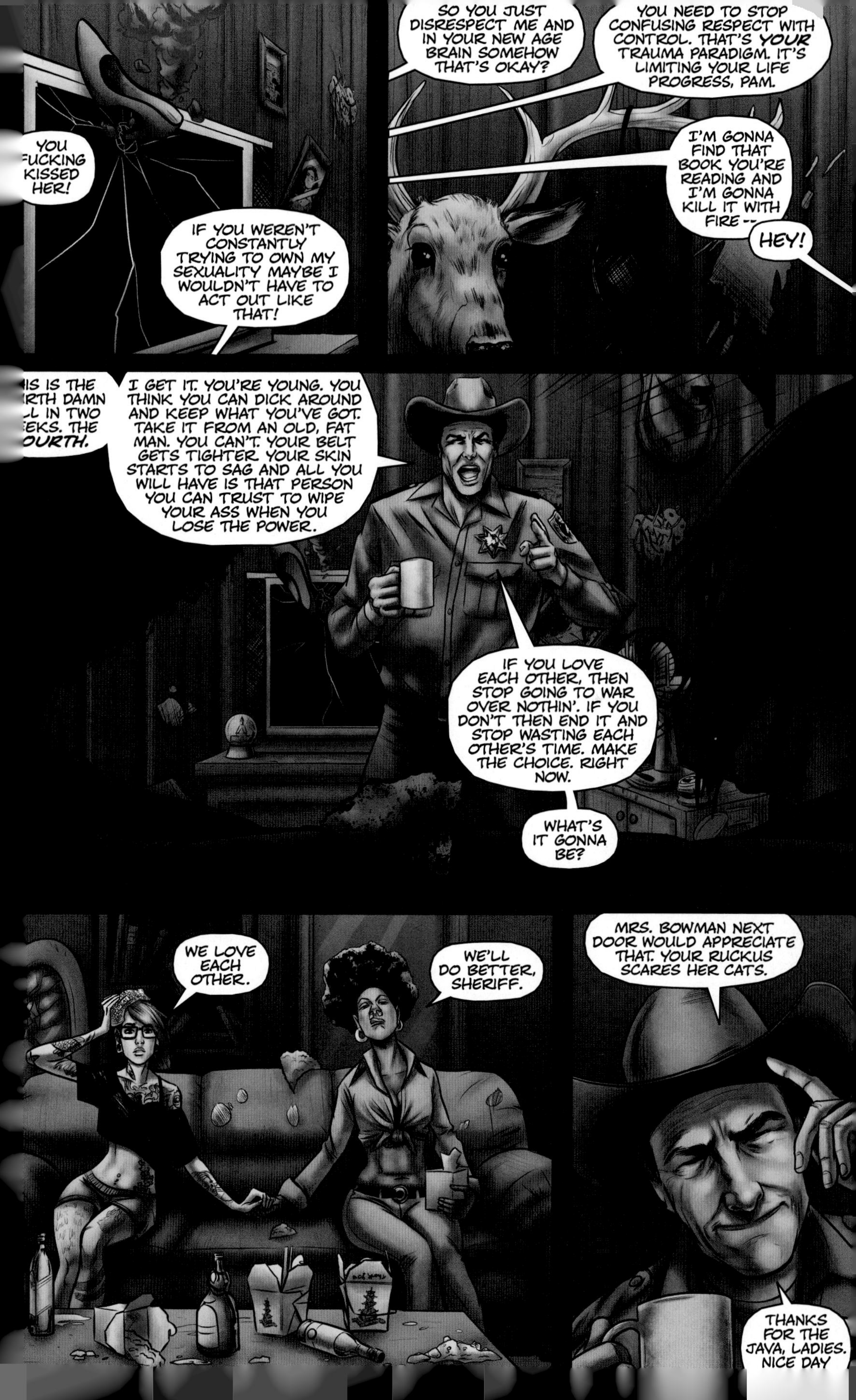

YOU FUCKING KISSED HER!
IF YOU WEREN'T CONSTANTLY TRYING TO OWN MY SEXUALITY MAYBE I WOULDN'T HAVE TO ACT OUT LIKE THAT!
SO YOU JUST DISRESPECT ME AND IN YOUR NEW AGE BRAIN SOMEHOW THAT'S OKAY?
YOU NEED TO STOP CONFUSING RESPECT WITH CONTROL. THAT'S *YOUR* TRAUMA PARADIGM. IT'S LIMITING YOUR LIFE PROGRESS, PAM.
I'M GONNA FIND THAT BOOK YOU'RE READING AND I'M GONNA KILL IT WITH FIRE --
HEY!
IS IS THE RTH DAMN L IN TWO EKS. THE *OURTH.*
I GET IT. YOU'RE YOUNG. YOU THINK YOU CAN DICK AROUND AND KEEP WHAT YOU'VE GOT. TAKE IT FROM AN OLD, FAT MAN. YOU CAN'T. YOUR BELT GETS TIGHTER. YOUR SKIN STARTS TO SAG AND ALL YOU WILL HAVE IS THAT PERSON YOU CAN TRUST TO WIPE YOUR ASS WHEN YOU LOSE THE POWER.
IF YOU LOVE EACH OTHER, THEN STOP GOING TO WAR OVER NOTHIN'. IF YOU DON'T THEN END IT AND STOP WASTING EACH OTHER'S TIME. MAKE THE CHOICE. RIGHT NOW.
WHAT'S IT GONNA BE?
WE LOVE EACH OTHER.
WE'LL DO BETTER, SHERIFF.
MRS. BOWMAN NEXT DOOR WOULD APPRECIATE THAT. YOUR RUCKUS SCARES HER CATS.
THANKS FOR THE JAVA, LADIES. NICE DAY

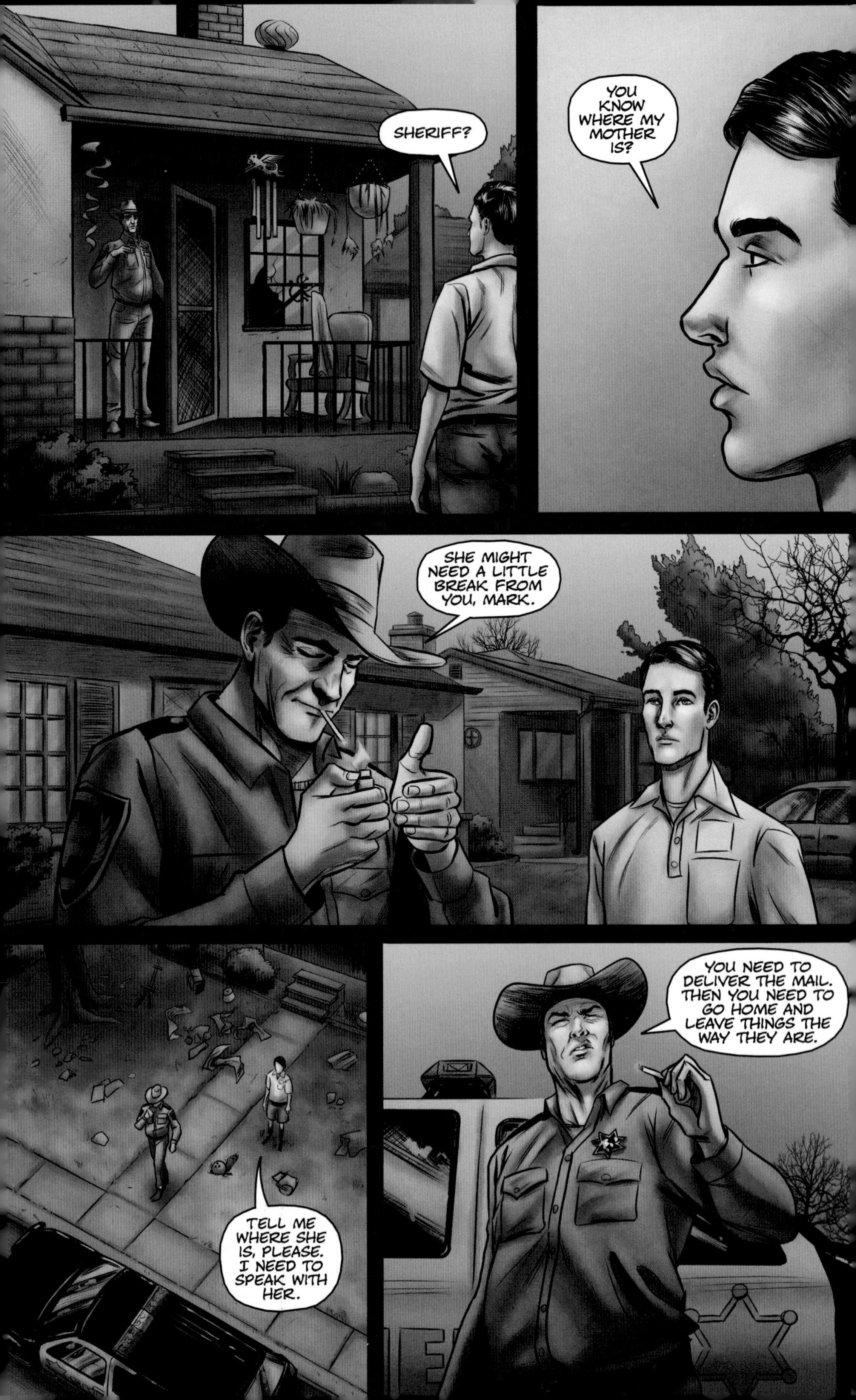
SHERIFF?
YOU KNOW WHERE MY MOTHER IS?
SHE MIGHT NEED A LITTLE BREAK FROM YOU, MARK.
TELL ME WHERE SHE IS, PLEASE. I NEED TO SPEAK WITH HER.
YOU NEED TO DELIVER THE MAIL. THEN YOU NEED TO GO HOME AND LEAVE THINGS THE WAY THEY ARE.

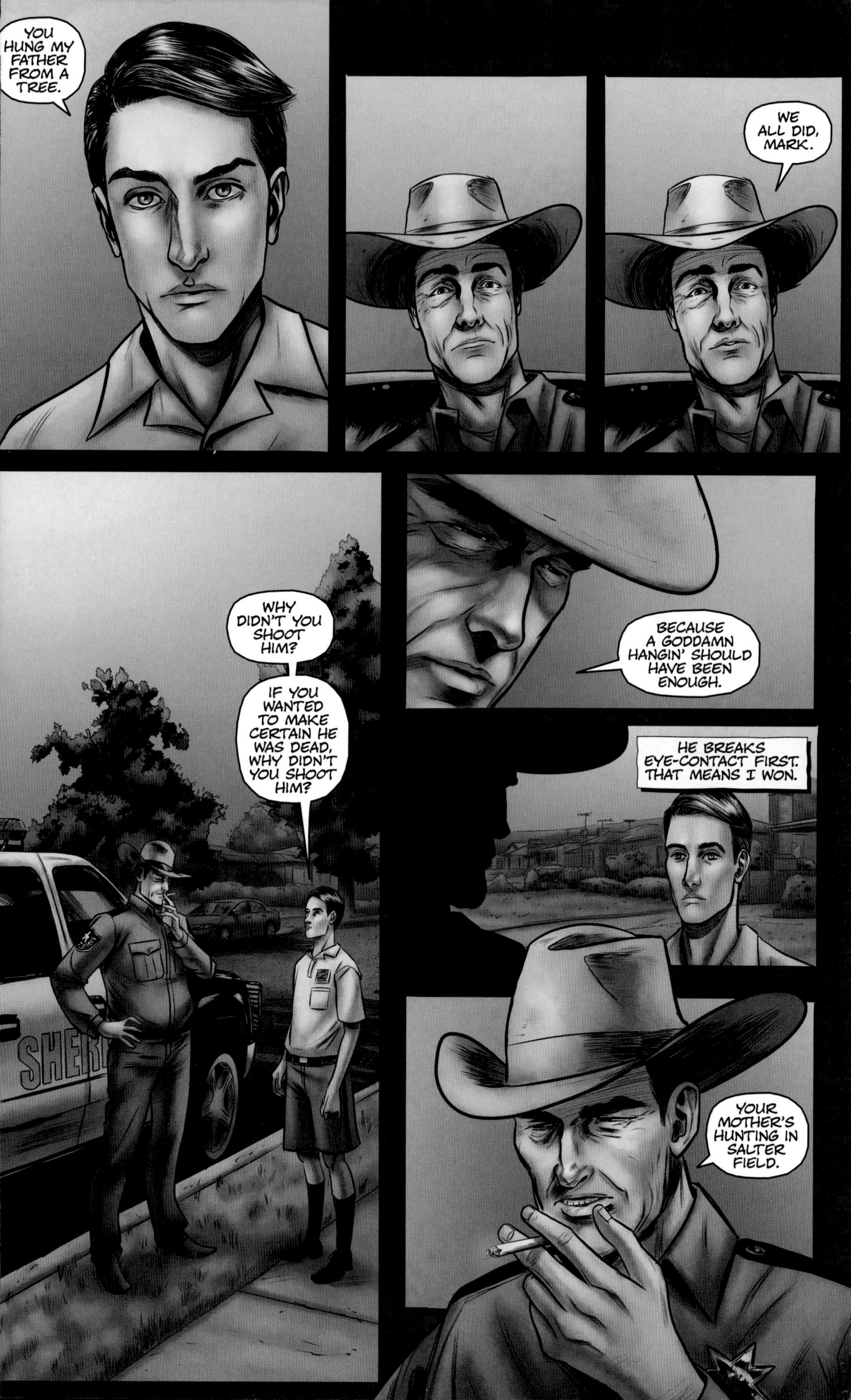
YOU HUNG MY FATHER FROM A TREE.
WE ALL DID, MARK.
WHY DIDN'T YOU SHOOT HIM?
IF YOU WANTED TO MAKE CERTAIN HE WAS DEAD, WHY DIDN'T YOU SHOOT HIM?
SHER
BECAUSE A GODDAMN HANGIN' SHOULD HAVE BEEN ENOUGH.
HE BREAKS EYE-CONTACT FIRST. THAT MEANS I WON.
YOUR MOTHER'S HUNTING IN SALTER FIELD.

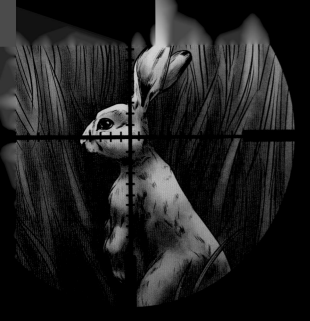

DEAD BANG, BUGS.

BLAM

YOU DIDN'T SHOOT IT.

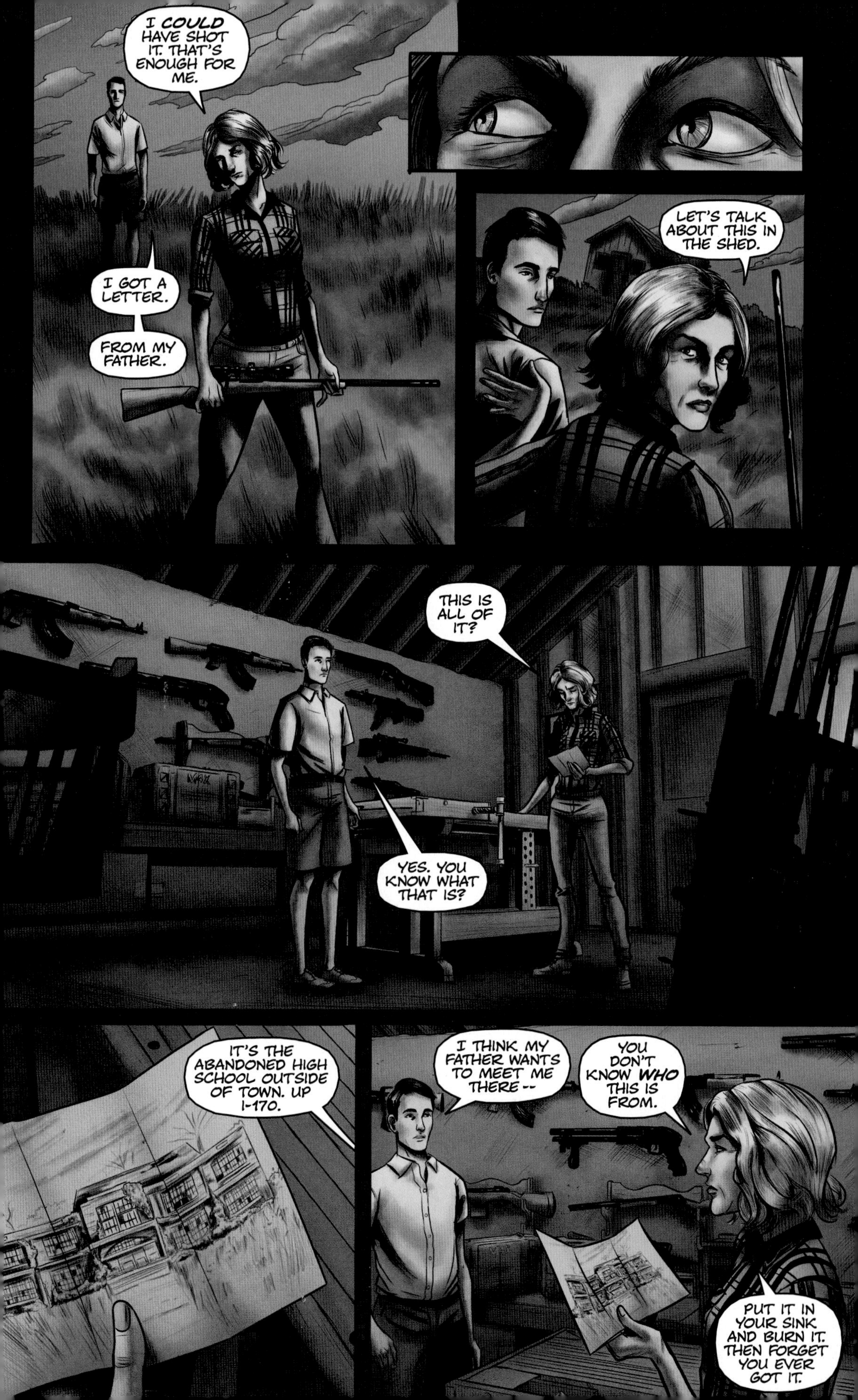
I COULD HAVE SHOT IT. THAT'S ENOUGH FOR ME.
I GOT A LETTER.
FROM MY FATHER.
LET'S TALK ABOUT THIS IN THE SHED.
THIS IS ALL OF IT?
YES. YOU KNOW WHAT THAT IS?
IT'S THE ABANDONED HIGH SCHOOL OUTSIDE OF TOWN. UP I-170.
I THINK MY FATHER WANTS TO MEET ME THERE --
YOU DON'T KNOW WHO THIS IS FROM.
PUT IT IN YOUR SINK AND BURN IT. THEN FORGET YOU EVER GOT IT.

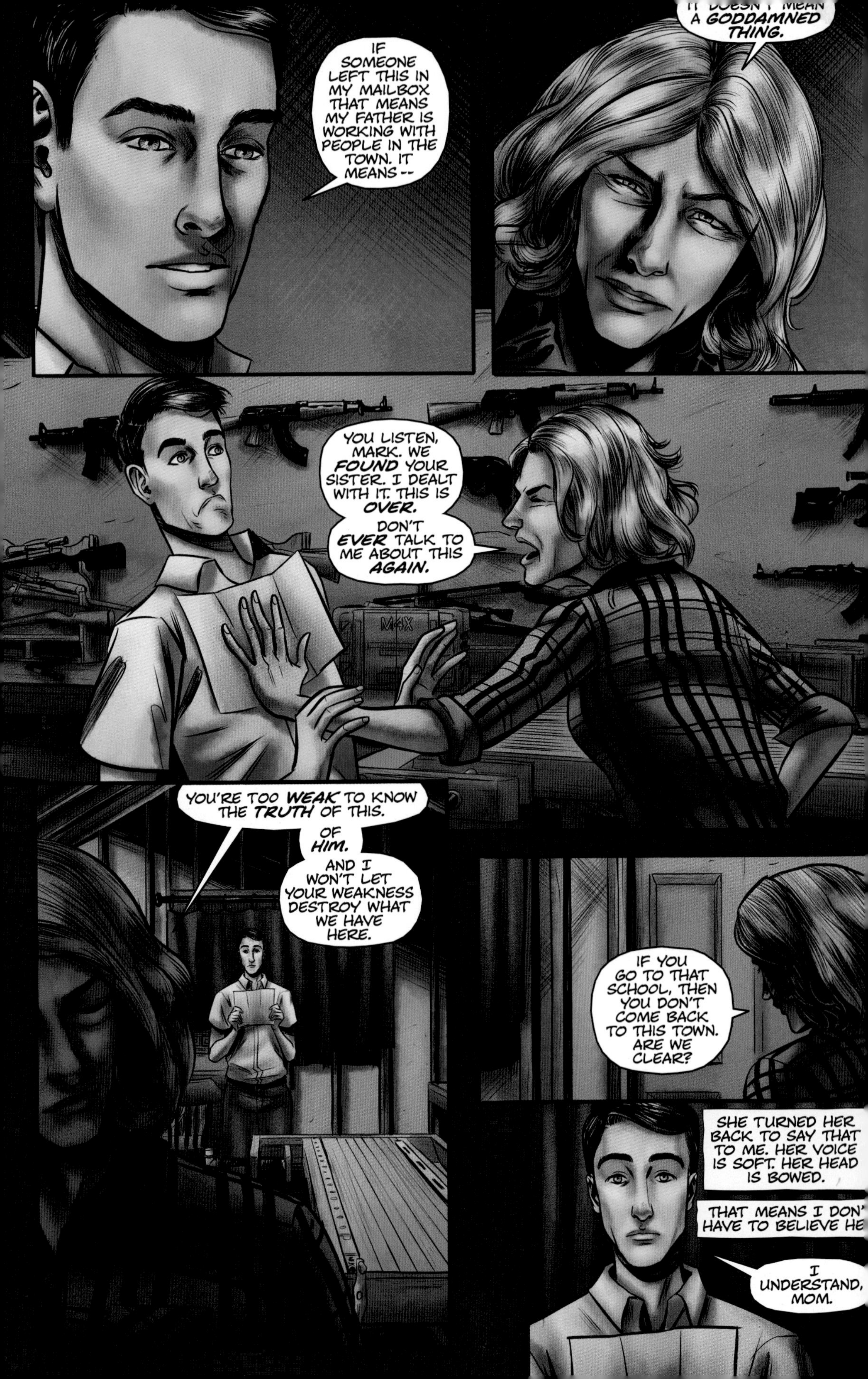
IF SOMEONE LEFT THIS IN MY MAILBOX THAT MEANS MY FATHER IS WORKING WITH PEOPLE IN THE TOWN. IT MEANS --
A GODDAMNED THING.
YOU LISTEN, MARK. WE FOUND YOUR SISTER. I DEALT WITH IT. THIS IS OVER.
DON'T EVER TALK TO ME ABOUT THIS AGAIN.
M4X
YOU'RE TOO WEAK TO KNOW THE TRUTH OF THIS.
OF HIM.
AND I WON'T LET YOUR WEAKNESS DESTROY WHAT WE HAVE HERE.
IF YOU GO TO THAT SCHOOL, THEN YOU DON'T COME BACK TO THIS TOWN. ARE WE CLEAR?
SHE TURNED HER BACK TO SAY THAT TO ME. HER VOICE IS SOFT. HER HEAD IS BOWED.
THAT MEANS I DON' HAVE TO BELIEVE HE
I UNDERSTAND, MOM.

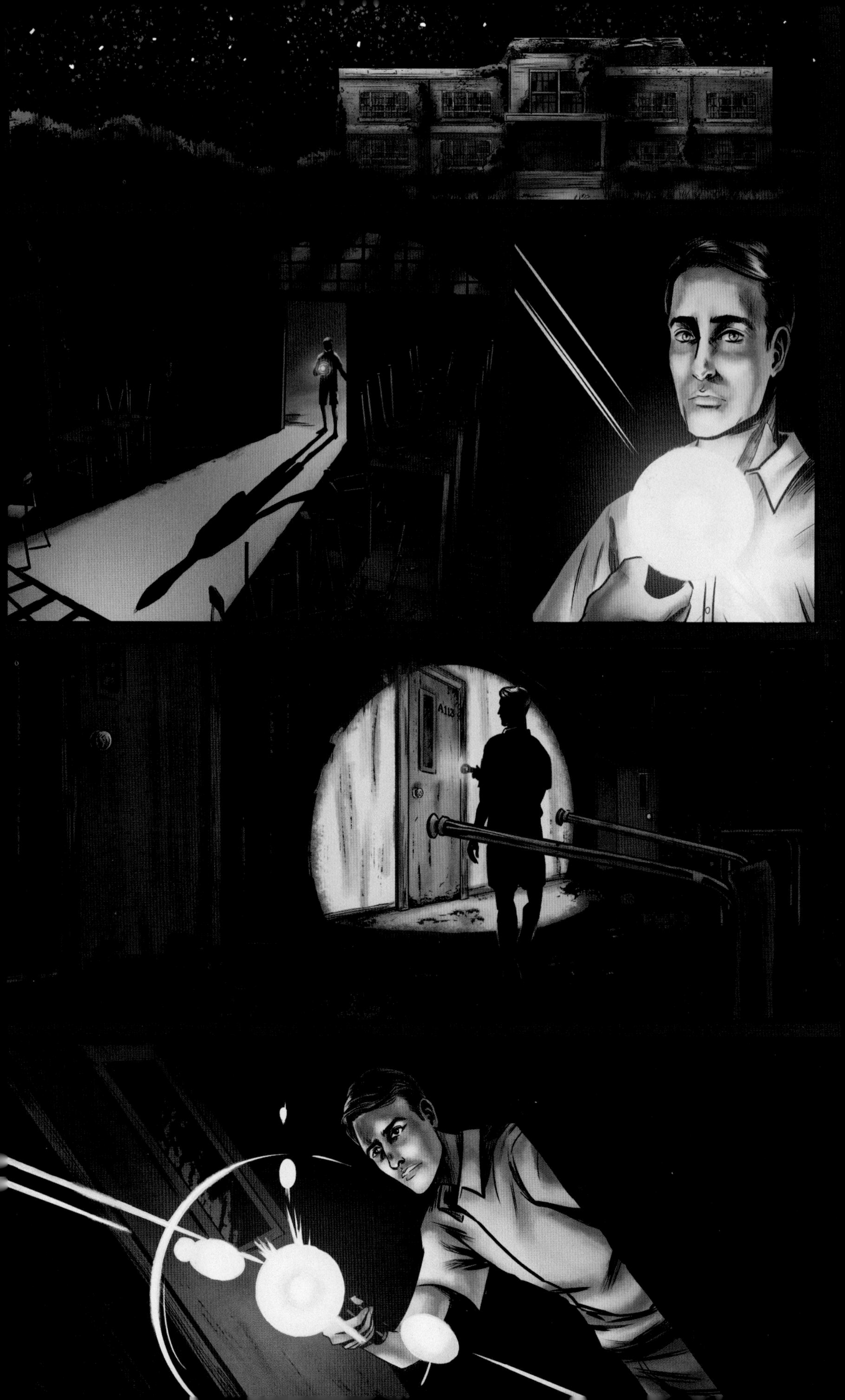
A113

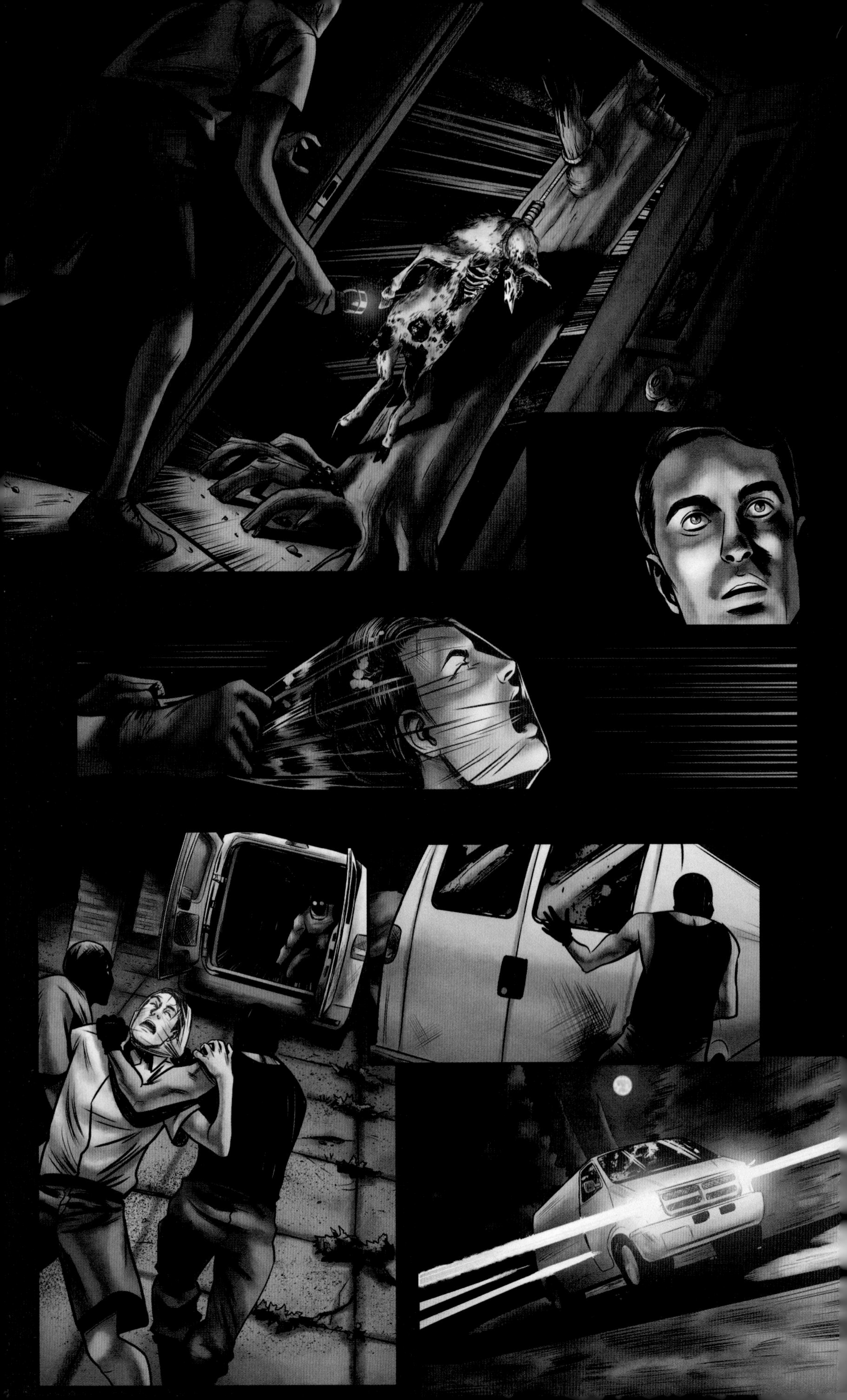

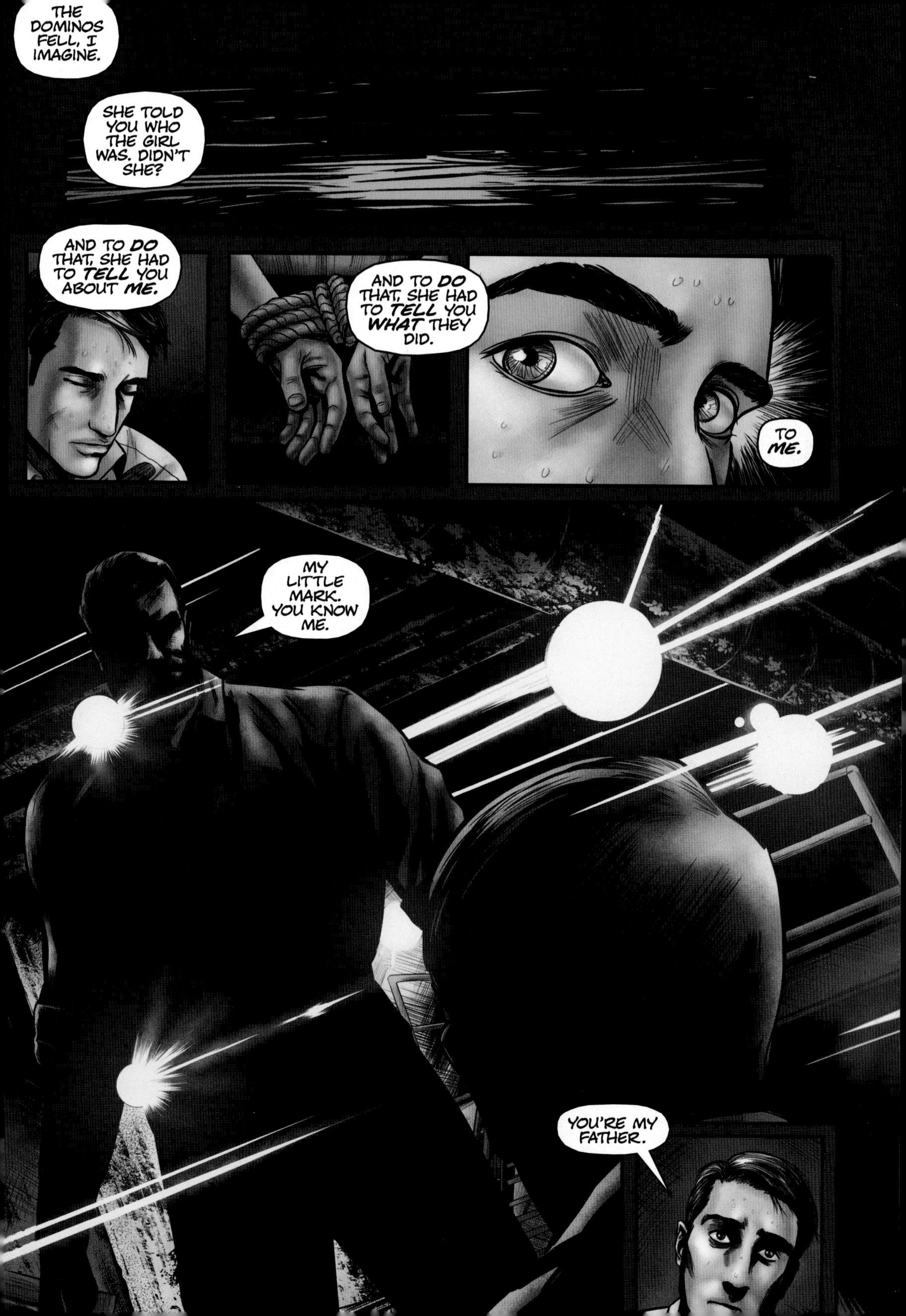
THE DOMINOS FELL, I IMAGINE.
SHE TOLD YOU WHO THE GIRL WAS. DIDN'T SHE?
AND TO DO THAT, SHE HAD TO TELL YOU ABOUT ME.
AND TO DO THAT, SHE HAD TO TELL YOU WHAT THEY DID.
TO ME.
MY LITTLE MARK. YOU KNOW ME.
YOU'RE MY FATHER.

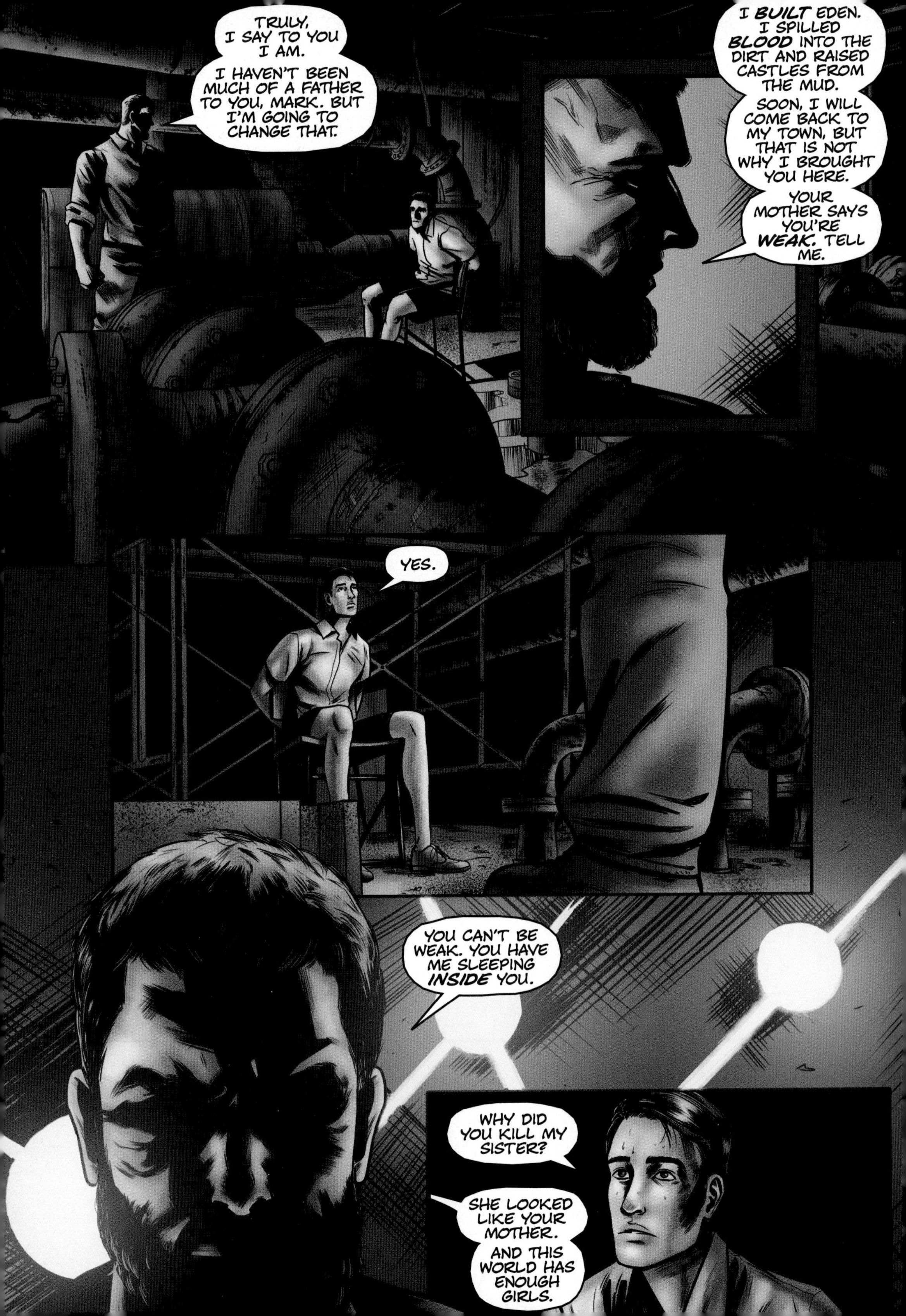
TRULY, I SAY TO YOU I AM.
I HAVEN'T BEEN MUCH OF A FATHER TO YOU, MARK. BUT I'M GOING TO CHANGE THAT.
I **BUILT** EDEN. I SPILLED **BLOOD** INTO THE DIRT AND RAISED CASTLES FROM THE MUD.
SOON, I WILL COME BACK TO MY TOWN, BUT THAT IS NOT WHY I BROUGHT YOU HERE.
YOUR MOTHER SAYS YOU'RE **WEAK.** TELL ME.
YES.
YOU CAN'T BE WEAK. YOU HAVE ME SLEEPING **INSIDE** YOU.
WHY DID YOU KILL MY SISTER?
SHE LOOKED LIKE YOUR MOTHER.
AND THIS WORLD HAS ENOUGH GIRLS.

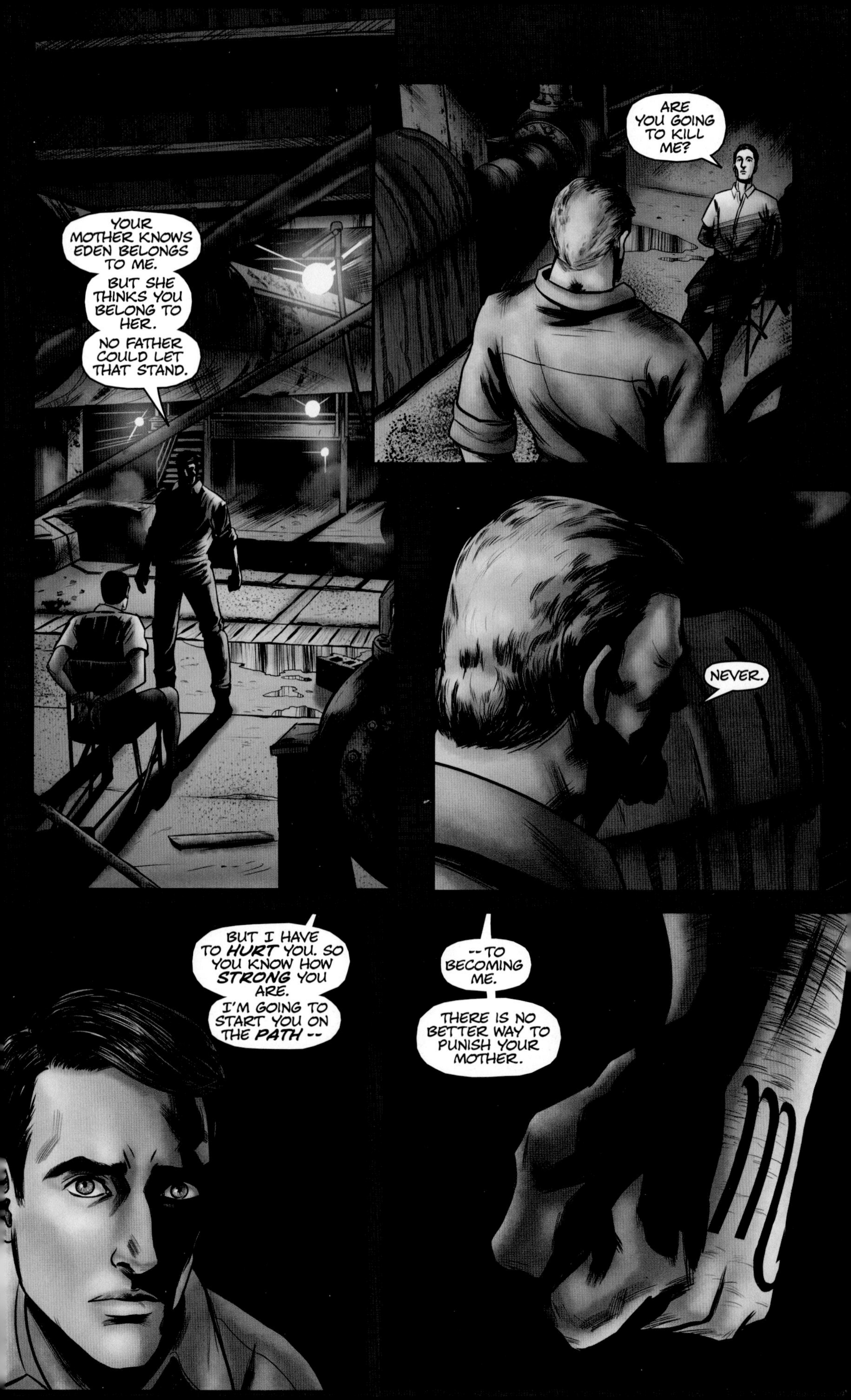
YOUR MOTHER KNOWS EDEN BELONGS TO ME.
BUT SHE THINKS YOU BELONG TO HER.
NO FATHER COULD LET THAT STAND.
ARE YOU GOING TO KILL ME?
NEVER.
BUT I HAVE TO HURT YOU. SO YOU KNOW HOW STRONG YOU ARE.
I'M GOING TO START YOU ON THE PATH --
--TO BECOMING ME.
THERE IS NO BETTER WAY TO PUNISH YOUR MOTHER.

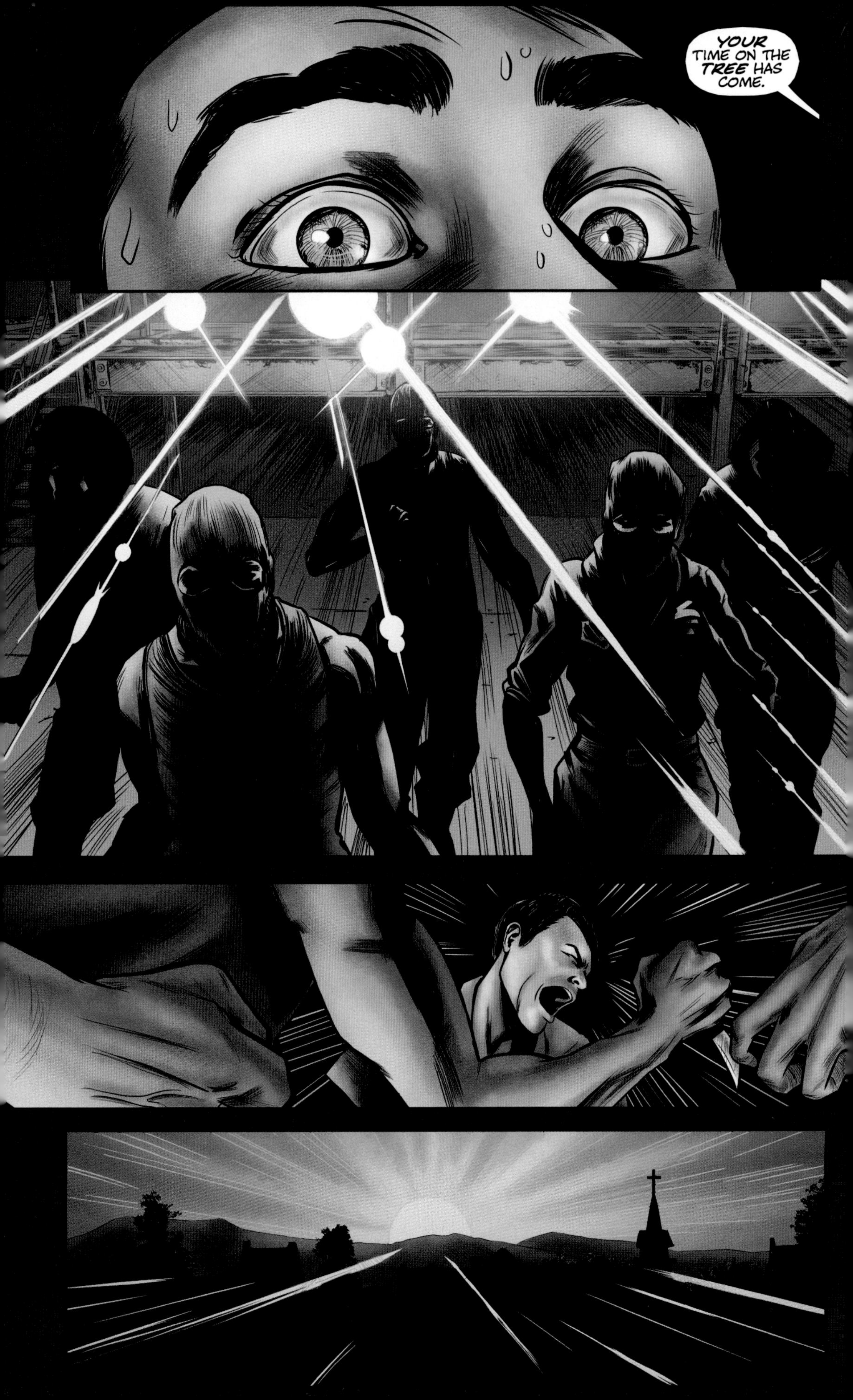
YOUR TIME ON THE TREE HAS COME.

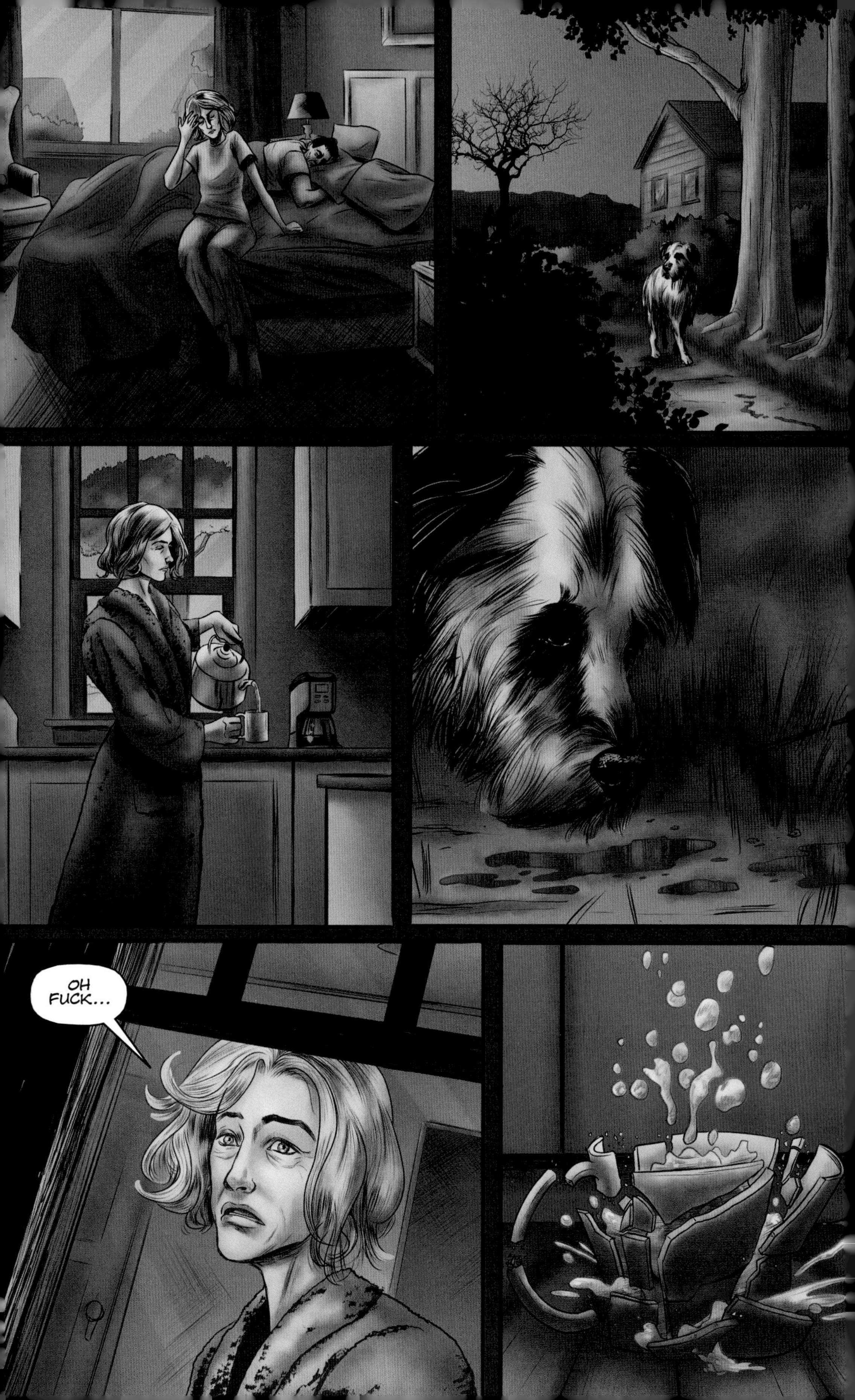
OH FUCK...

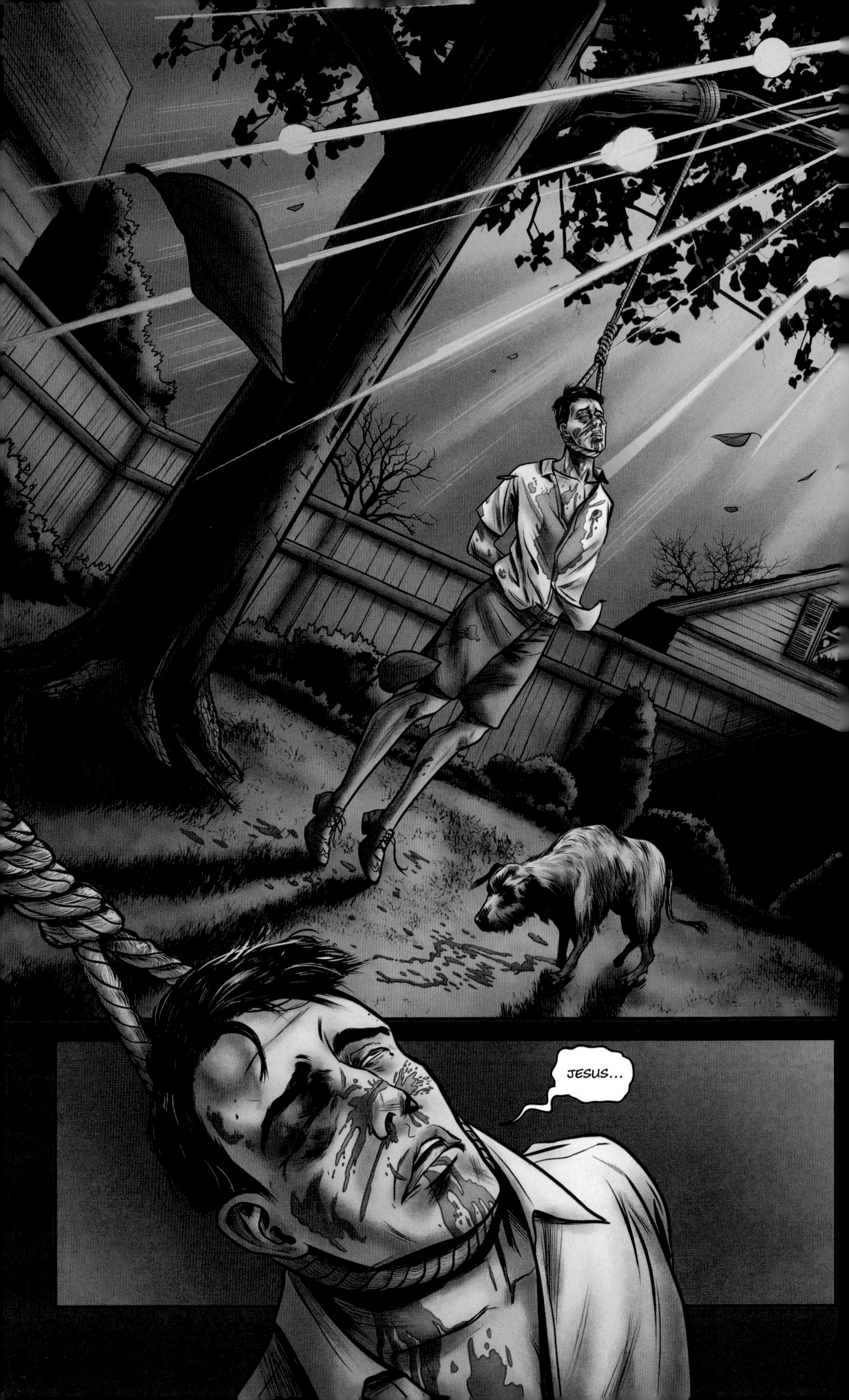
JESUS...

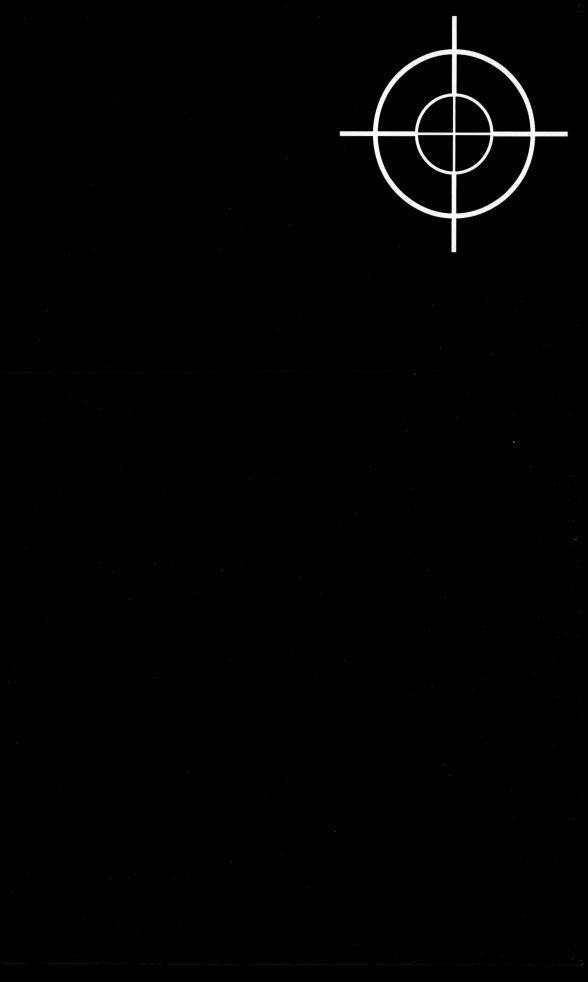

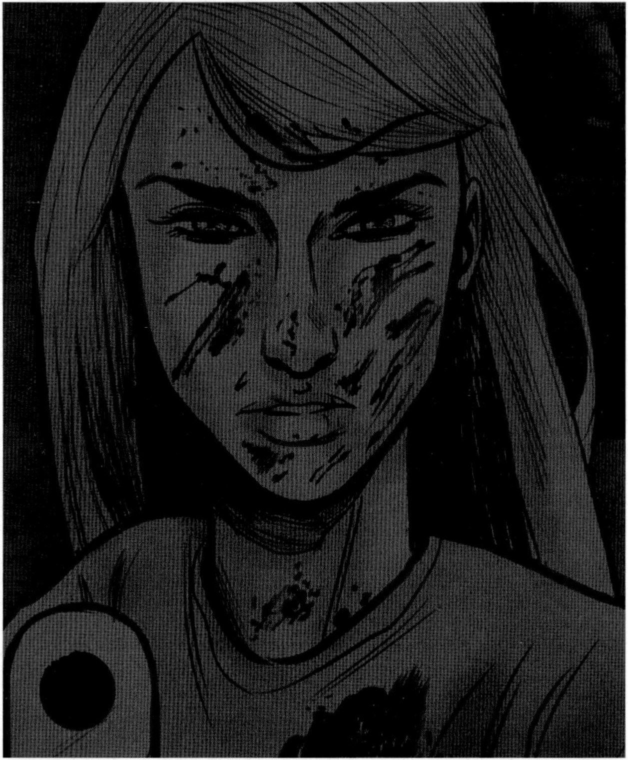

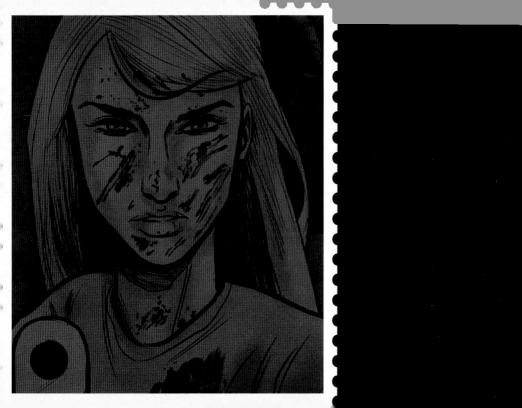

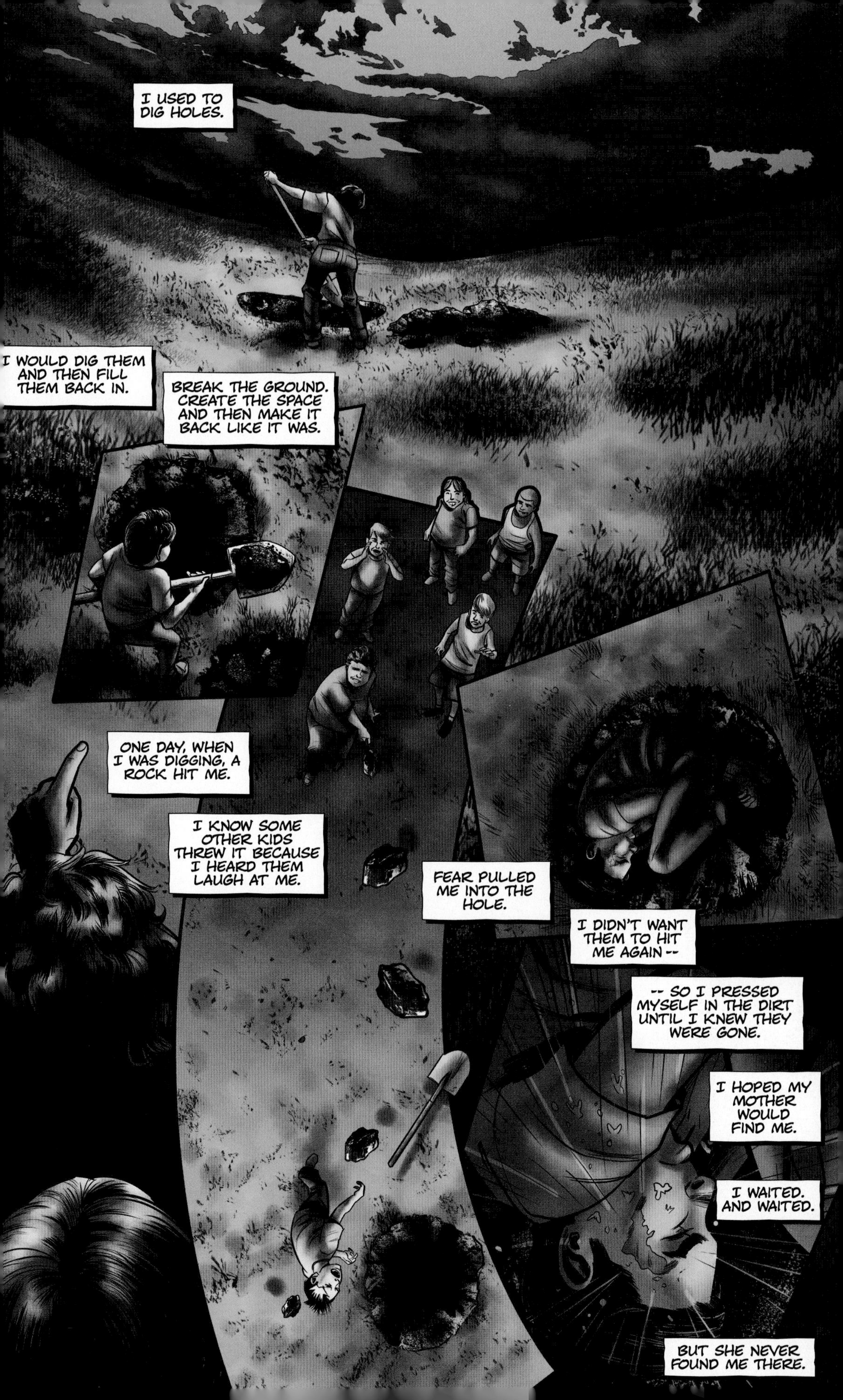
I USED TO DIG HOLES.
I WOULD DIG THEM AND THEN FILL THEM BACK IN.
BREAK THE GROUND. CREATE THE SPACE AND THEN MAKE IT BACK LIKE IT WAS.
ONE DAY, WHEN I WAS DIGGING, A ROCK HIT ME.
I KNOW SOME OTHER KIDS THREW IT BECAUSE I HEARD THEM LAUGH AT ME.
FEAR PULLED ME INTO THE HOLE.
I DIDN'T WANT THEM TO HIT ME AGAIN --
-- SO I PRESSED MYSELF IN THE DIRT UNTIL I KNEW THEY WERE GONE.
I HOPED MY MOTHER WOULD FIND ME.
I WAITED. AND WAITED.
BUT SHE NEVER FOUND ME THERE.

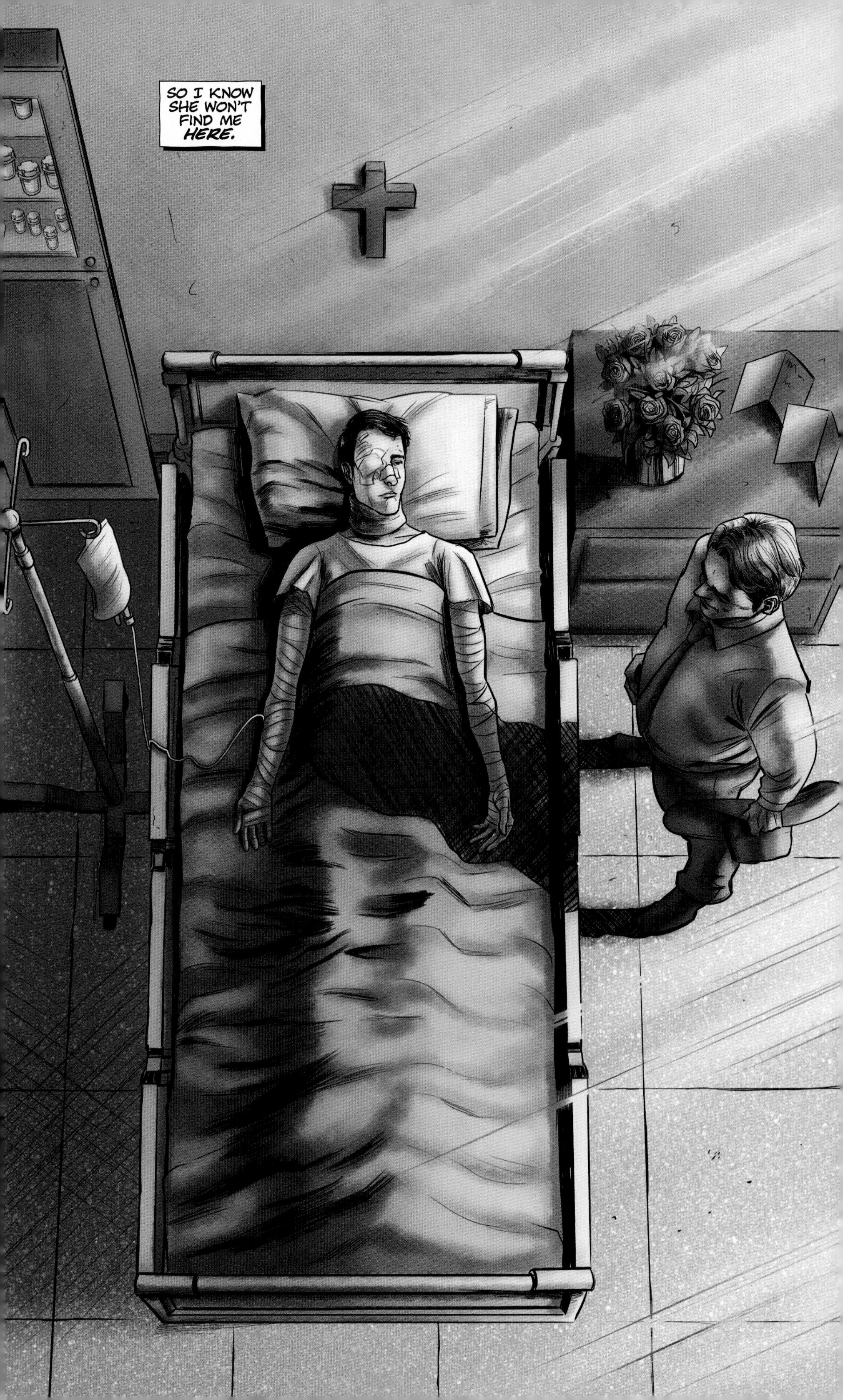
SO I KNOW SHE WON'T FIND ME *HERE.*

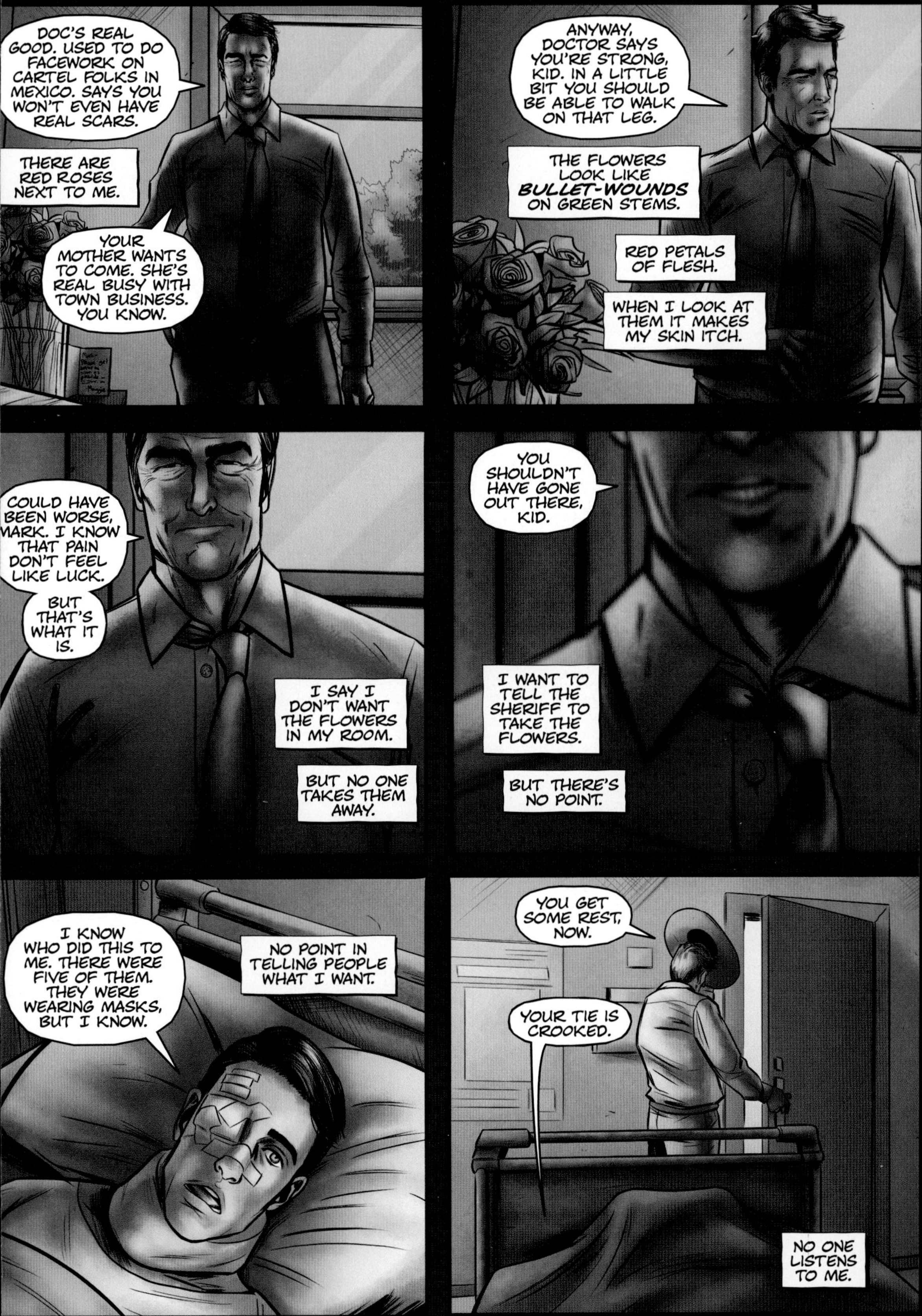
DOC'S REAL GOOD. USED TO DO FACEWORK ON CARTEL FOLKS IN MEXICO. SAYS YOU WON'T EVEN HAVE REAL SCARS.
THERE ARE RED ROSES NEXT TO ME.
YOUR MOTHER WANTS TO COME. SHE'S REAL BUSY WITH TOWN BUSINESS. YOU KNOW.
ANYWAY, DOCTOR SAYS YOU'RE STRONG, KID. IN A LITTLE BIT YOU SHOULD BE ABLE TO WALK ON THAT LEG.
THE FLOWERS LOOK LIKE ***BULLET-WOUNDS*** ON GREEN STEMS.
RED PETALS OF FLESH.
WHEN I LOOK AT THEM IT MAKES MY SKIN ITCH.
COULD HAVE BEEN WORSE, MARK. I KNOW THAT PAIN DON'T FEEL LIKE LUCK.
BUT THAT'S WHAT IT IS.
I SAY I DON'T WANT THE FLOWERS IN MY ROOM.
BUT NO ONE TAKES THEM AWAY.
YOU SHOULDN'T HAVE GONE OUT THERE, KID.
I WANT TO TELL THE SHERIFF TO TAKE THE FLOWERS.
BUT THERE'S NO POINT.
I KNOW WHO DID THIS TO ME. THERE WERE FIVE OF THEM. THEY WERE WEARING MASKS, BUT I KNOW.
NO POINT IN TELLING PEOPLE WHAT I WANT.
YOU GET SOME REST, NOW.
YOUR TIE IS CROOKED.
NO ONE LISTENS TO ME.

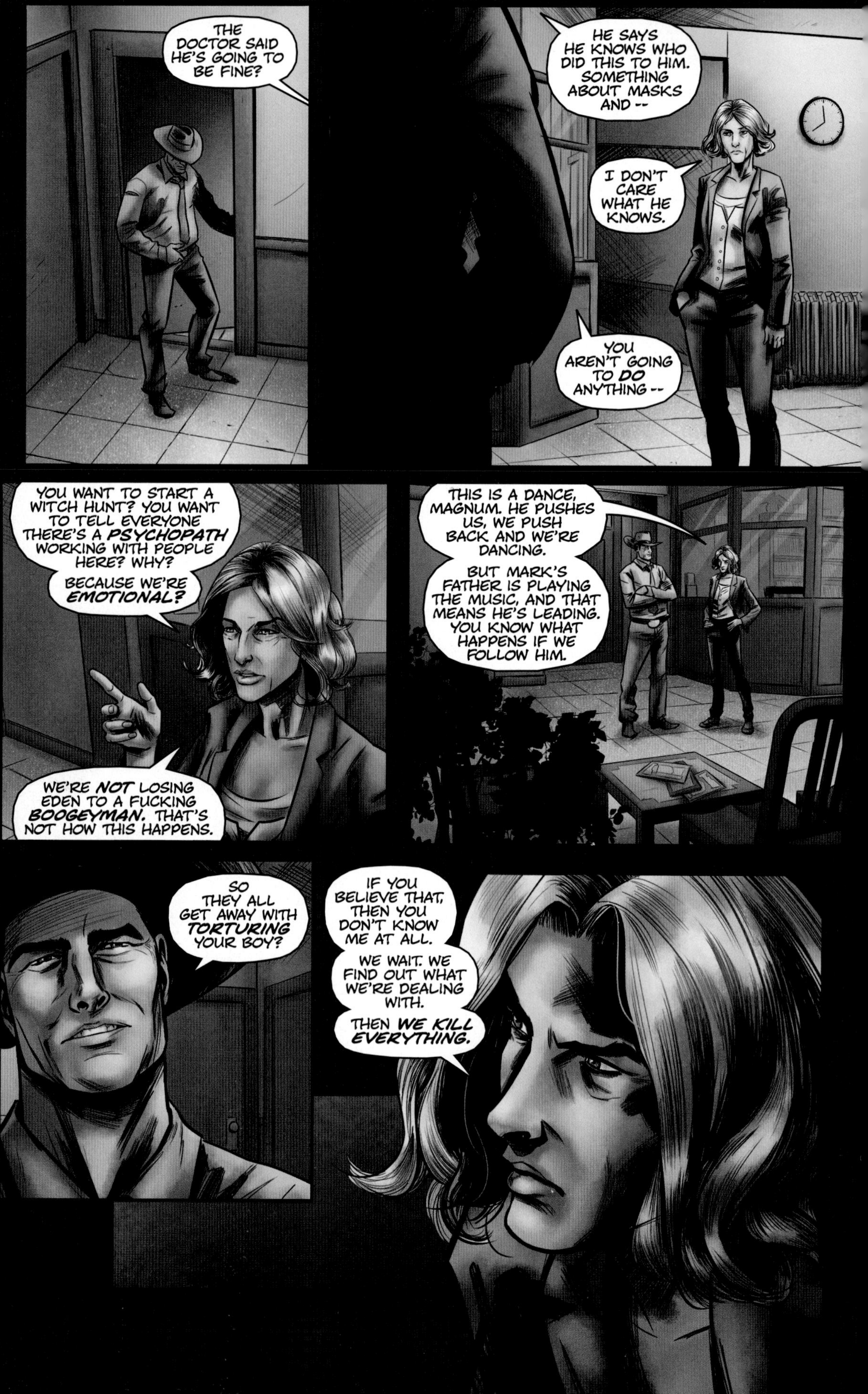
THE DOCTOR SAID HE'S GOING TO BE FINE?
HE SAYS HE KNOWS WHO DID THIS TO HIM. SOMETHING ABOUT MASKS AND --
I DON'T CARE WHAT HE KNOWS.
YOU AREN'T GOING TO *DO* ANYTHING --
YOU WANT TO START A WITCH HUNT? YOU WANT TO TELL EVERYONE THERE'S A *PSYCHOPATH* WORKING WITH PEOPLE HERE? WHY?
BECAUSE WE'RE *EMOTIONAL?*
WE'RE *NOT* LOSING EDEN TO A FUCKING *BOOGEYMAN.* THAT'S NOT HOW THIS HAPPENS.
THIS IS A DANCE, MAGNUM. HE PUSHES US, WE PUSH BACK AND WE'RE DANCING.
BUT MARK'S FATHER IS PLAYING THE MUSIC, AND THAT MEANS HE'S LEADING. YOU KNOW WHAT HAPPENS IF WE FOLLOW HIM.
SO THEY ALL GET AWAY WITH *TORTURING* YOUR BOY?
IF YOU BELIEVE THAT, THEN YOU DON'T KNOW ME AT ALL.
WE WAIT. WE FIND OUT WHAT WE'RE DEALING WITH.
THEN *WE KILL EVERYTHING.*

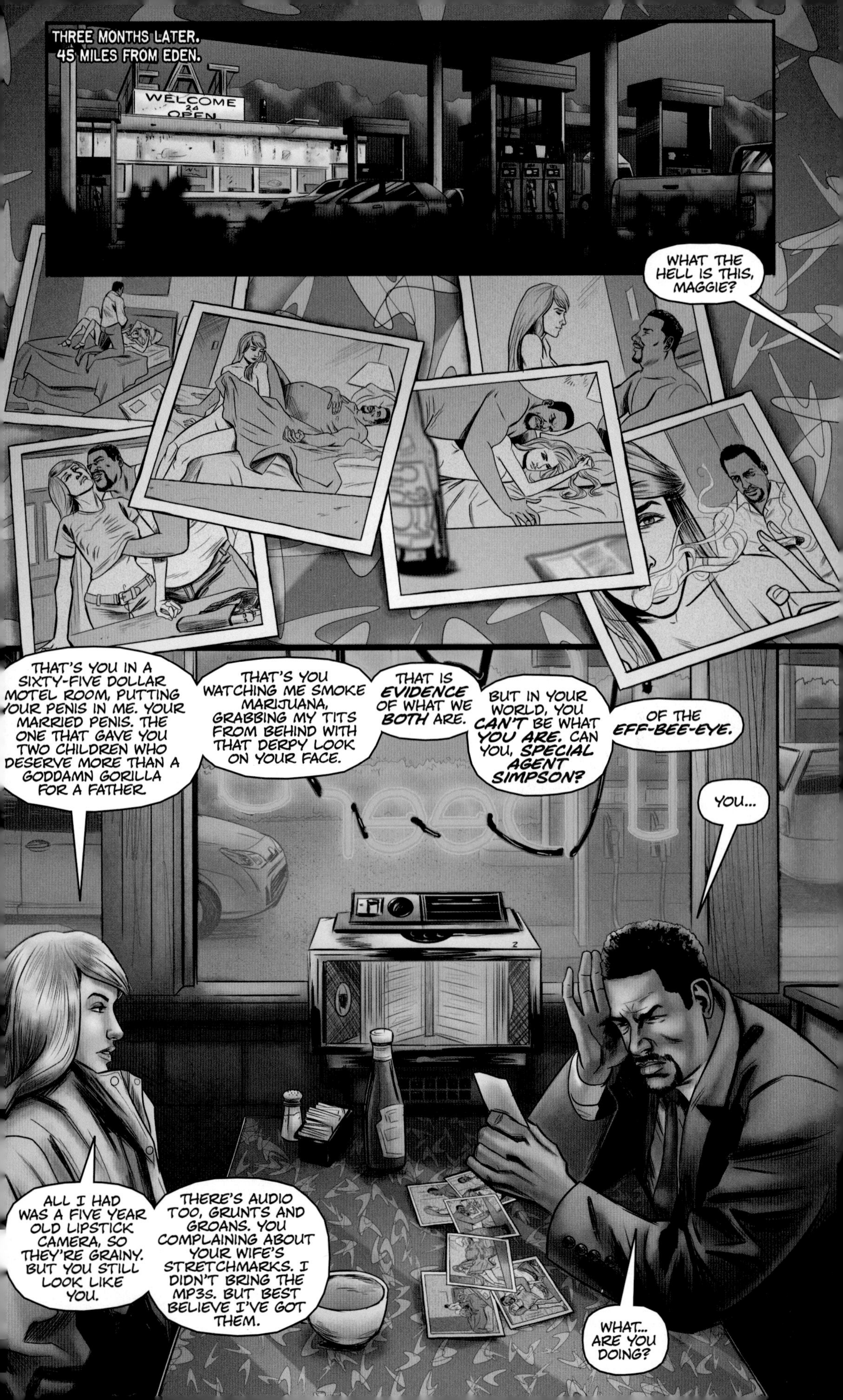
THREE MONTHS LATER. 45 MILES FROM EDEN.
EAT
WELCOME 24 OPEN
WHAT THE HELL IS THIS, MAGGIE?
THAT'S YOU IN A SIXTY-FIVE DOLLAR MOTEL ROOM, PUTTING YOUR PENIS IN ME. YOUR MARRIED PENIS. THE ONE THAT GAVE YOU TWO CHILDREN WHO DESERVE MORE THAN A GODDAMN GORILLA FOR A FATHER.
THAT'S YOU WATCHING ME SMOKE MARIJUANA, GRABBING MY TITS FROM BEHIND WITH THAT DERPY LOOK ON YOUR FACE.
THAT IS *EVIDENCE* OF WHAT WE *BOTH* ARE.
BUT IN YOUR WORLD, YOU *CAN'T* BE WHAT *YOU ARE.* CAN YOU, *SPECIAL AGENT SIMPSON?*
OF THE *EFF-BEE-EYE.*
YOU...
ALL I HAD WAS A FIVE YEAR OLD LIPSTICK CAMERA, SO THEY'RE GRAINY. BUT YOU STILL LOOK LIKE YOU.
THERE'S AUDIO TOO, GRUNTS AND GROANS. YOU COMPLAINING ABOUT YOUR WIFE'S STRETCHMARKS. I DIDN'T BRING THE MP3s. BUT BEST BELIEVE I'VE GOT THEM.
WHAT... ARE YOU DOING?

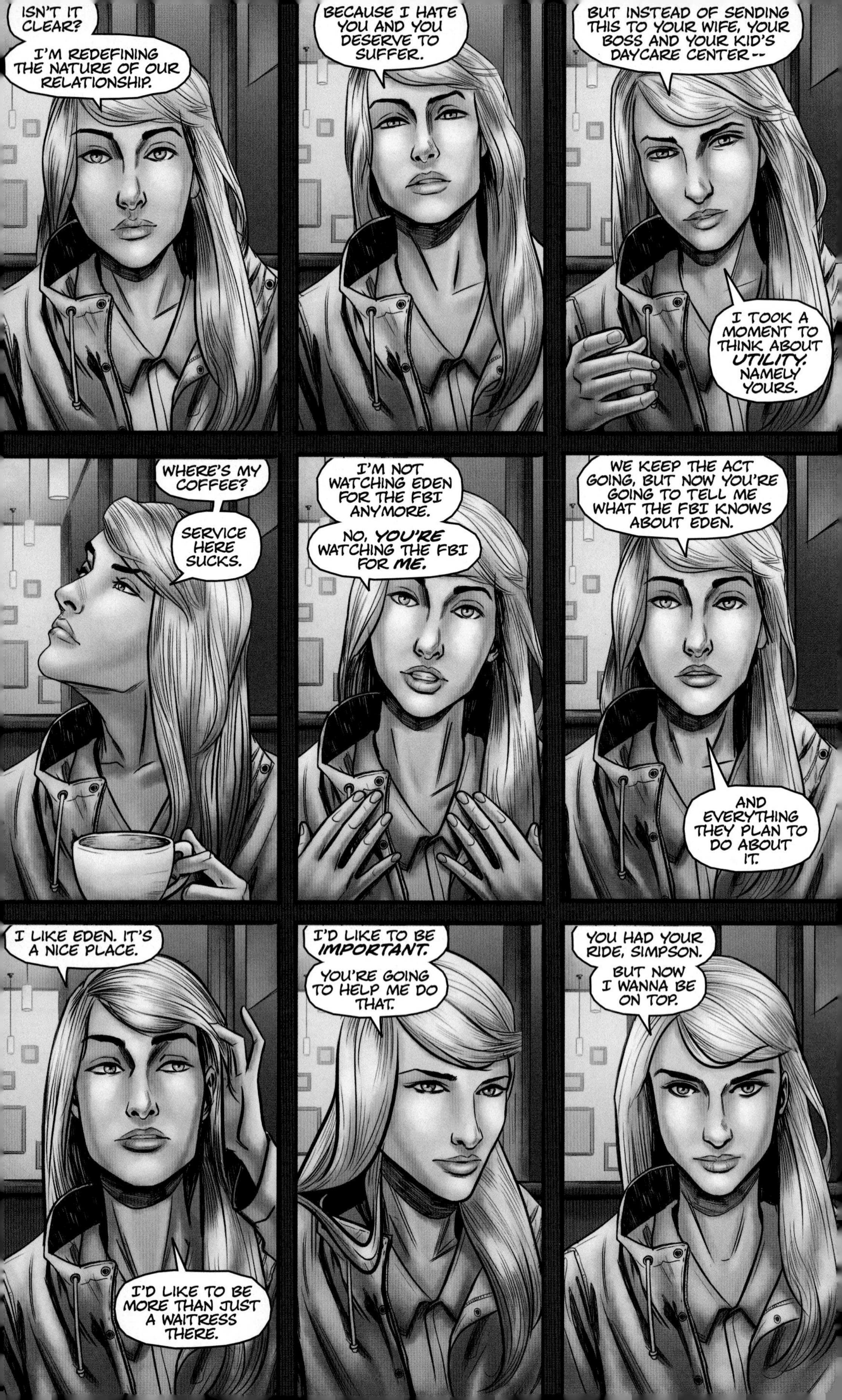
ISN'T IT CLEAR?
I'M REDEFINING THE NATURE OF OUR RELATIONSHIP.
BECAUSE I HATE YOU AND YOU DESERVE TO SUFFER.
BUT INSTEAD OF SENDING THIS TO YOUR WIFE, YOUR BOSS AND YOUR KID'S DAYCARE CENTER --
I TOOK A MOMENT TO THINK ABOUT UTILITY. NAMELY YOURS.
WHERE'S MY COFFEE?
SERVICE HERE SUCKS.
I'M NOT WATCHING EDEN FOR THE FBI ANYMORE.
NO, YOU'RE WATCHING THE FBI FOR ME.
WE KEEP THE ACT GOING, BUT NOW YOU'RE GOING TO TELL ME WHAT THE FBI KNOWS ABOUT EDEN.
AND EVERYTHING THEY PLAN TO DO ABOUT IT.
I LIKE EDEN. IT'S A NICE PLACE.
I'D LIKE TO BE MORE THAN JUST A WAITRESS THERE.
I'D LIKE TO BE IMPORTANT.
YOU'RE GOING TO HELP ME DO THAT.
YOU HAD YOUR RIDE, SIMPSON.
BUT NOW I WANNA BE ON TOP.

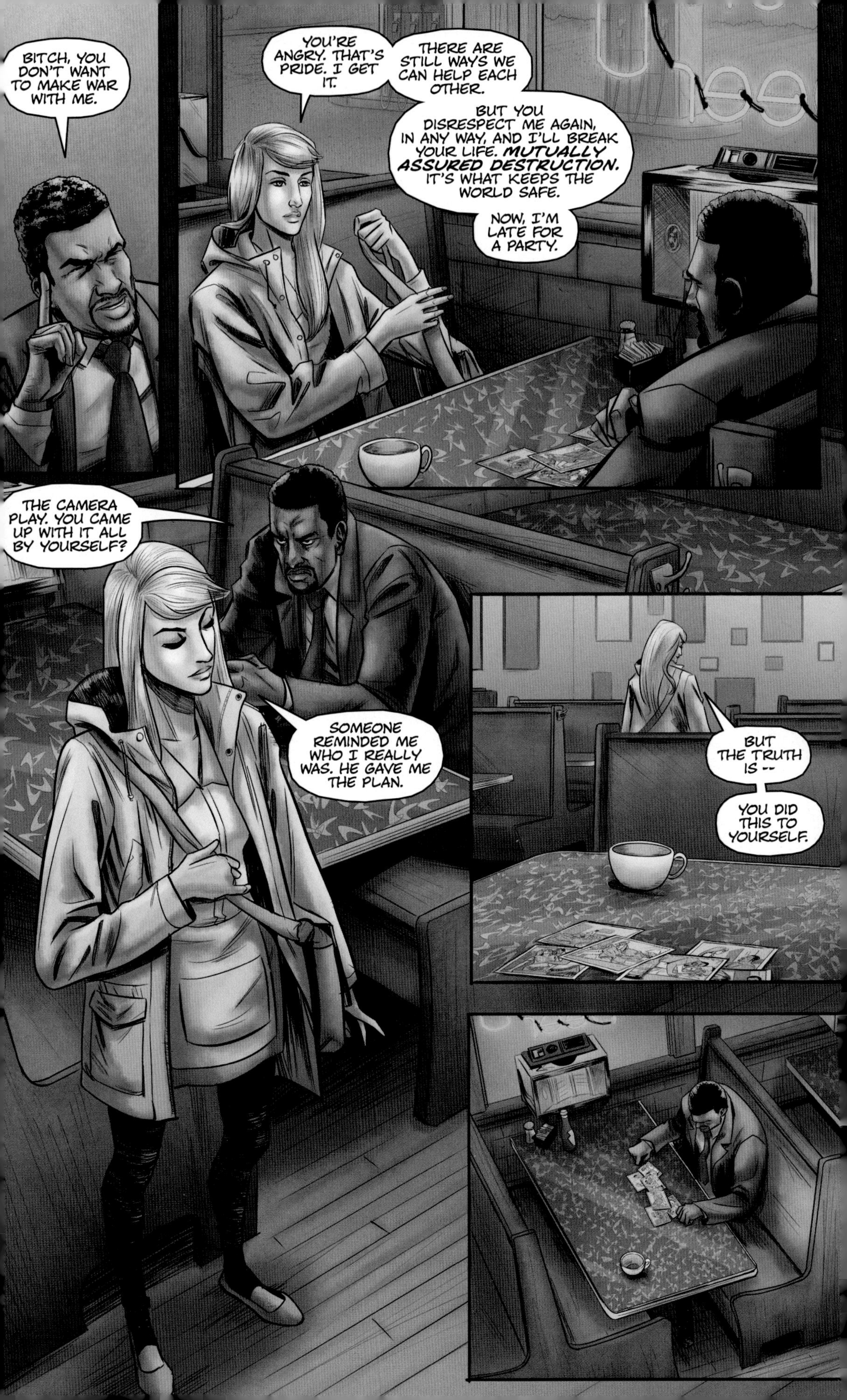
BITCH, YOU DON'T WANT TO MAKE WAR WITH ME.
YOU'RE ANGRY. THAT'S PRIDE. I GET IT.
THERE ARE STILL WAYS WE CAN HELP EACH OTHER.
BUT YOU DISRESPECT ME AGAIN, IN ANY WAY, AND I'LL BREAK YOUR LIFE. MUTUALLY ASSURED DESTRUCTION. IT'S WHAT KEEPS THE WORLD SAFE.
NOW, I'M LATE FOR A PARTY.
THE CAMERA PLAY. YOU CAME UP WITH IT ALL BY YOURSELF?
SOMEONE REMINDED ME WHO I REALLY WAS. HE GAVE ME THE PLAN.
BUT THE TRUTH IS --
YOU DID THIS TO YOURSELF.

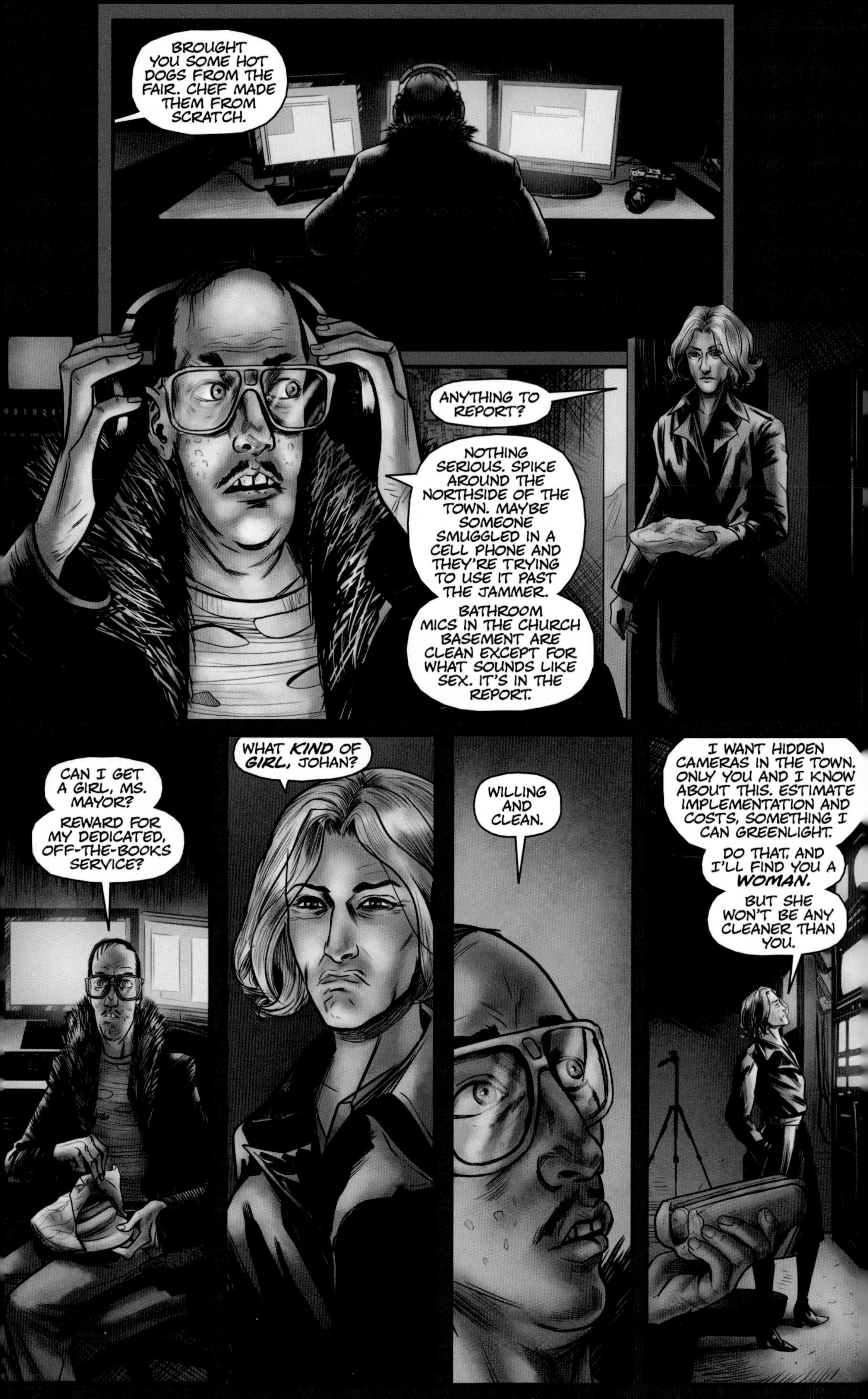
BROUGHT YOU SOME HOT DOGS FROM THE FAIR. CHEF MADE THEM FROM SCRATCH.
ANYTHING TO REPORT?
NOTHING SERIOUS. SPIKE AROUND THE NORTHSIDE OF THE TOWN. MAYBE SOMEONE SMUGGLED IN A CELL PHONE AND THEY'RE TRYING TO USE IT PAST THE JAMMER.
BATHROOM MICS IN THE CHURCH BASEMENT ARE CLEAN EXCEPT FOR WHAT SOUNDS LIKE SEX. IT'S IN THE REPORT.
CAN I GET A GIRL, MS. MAYOR?
REWARD FOR MY DEDICATED, OFF-THE-BOOKS SERVICE?
WHAT ***KIND*** OF ***GIRL,*** JOHAN?
WILLING AND CLEAN.
I WANT HIDDEN CAMERAS IN THE TOWN. ONLY YOU AND I KNOW ABOUT THIS. ESTIMATE IMPLEMENTATION AND COSTS, SOMETHING I CAN GREENLIGHT.
DO THAT, AND I'LL FIND YOU A ***WOMAN.***
BUT SHE WON'T BE ANY CLEANER THAN YOU.

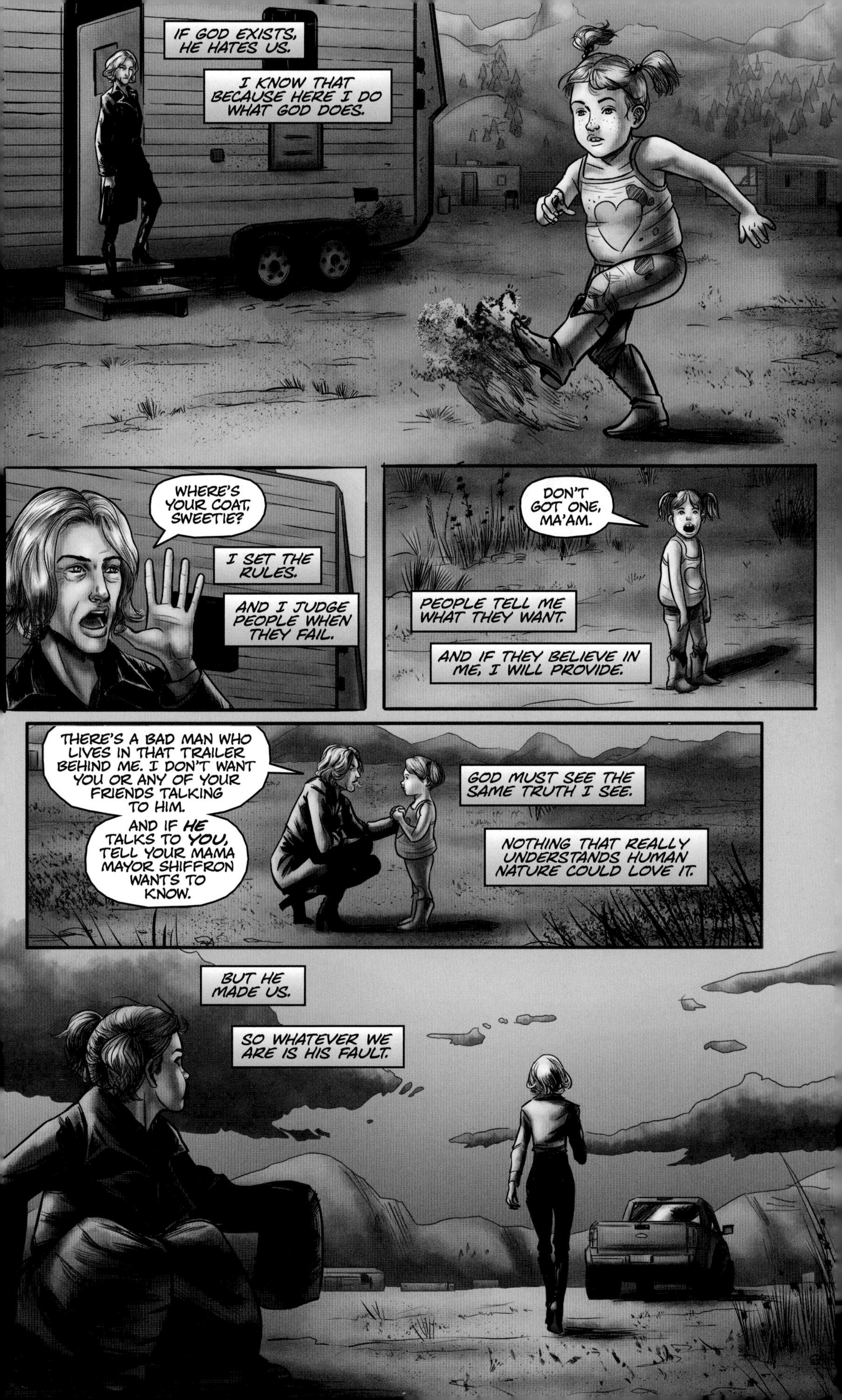
IF GOD EXISTS, HE HATES US.
I KNOW THAT BECAUSE HERE I DO WHAT GOD DOES.
WHERE'S YOUR COAT, SWEETIE?
I SET THE RULES.
AND I JUDGE PEOPLE WHEN THEY FAIL.
DON'T GOT ONE, MA'AM.
PEOPLE TELL ME WHAT THEY WANT.
AND IF THEY BELIEVE IN ME, I WILL PROVIDE.
THERE'S A BAD MAN WHO LIVES IN THAT TRAILER BEHIND ME. I DON'T WANT YOU OR ANY OF YOUR FRIENDS TALKING TO HIM.
AND IF HE TALKS TO YOU, TELL YOUR MAMA MAYOR SHIFFRON WANTS TO KNOW.
GOD MUST SEE THE SAME TRUTH I SEE.
NOTHING THAT REALLY UNDERSTANDS HUMAN NATURE COULD LOVE IT.
BUT HE MADE US.
SO WHATEVER WE ARE IS HIS FAULT.

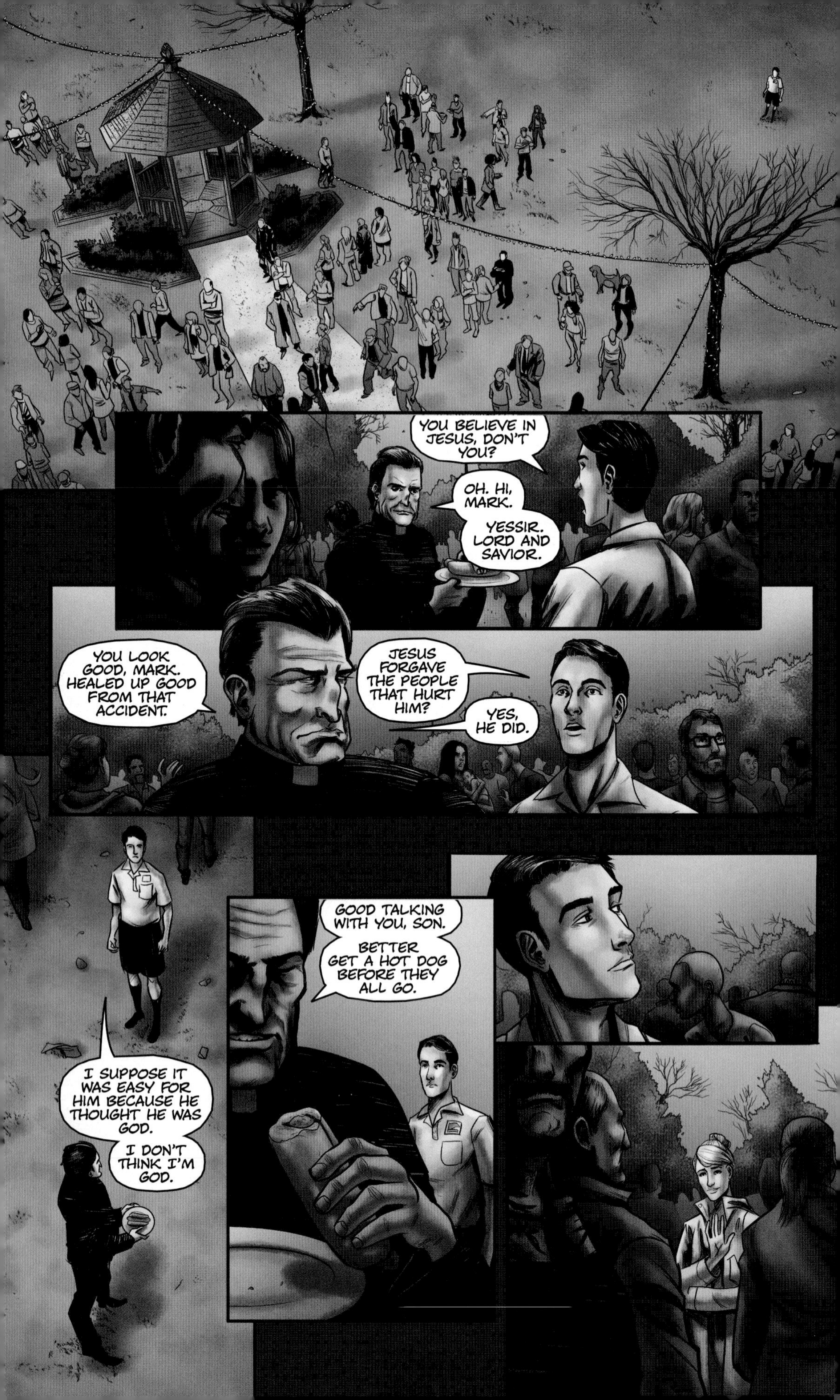

YOU BELIEVE IN JESUS, DON'T YOU?
OH. HI, MARK.
YESSIR. LORD AND SAVIOR.
YOU LOOK GOOD, MARK. HEALED UP GOOD FROM THAT ACCIDENT.
JESUS FORGAVE THE PEOPLE THAT HURT HIM?
YES, HE DID.
GOOD TALKING WITH YOU, SON.
BETTER GET A HOT DOG BEFORE THEY ALL GO.
I SUPPOSE IT WAS EASY FOR HIM BECAUSE HE THOUGHT HE WAS GOD.
I DON'T THINK I'M GOD.

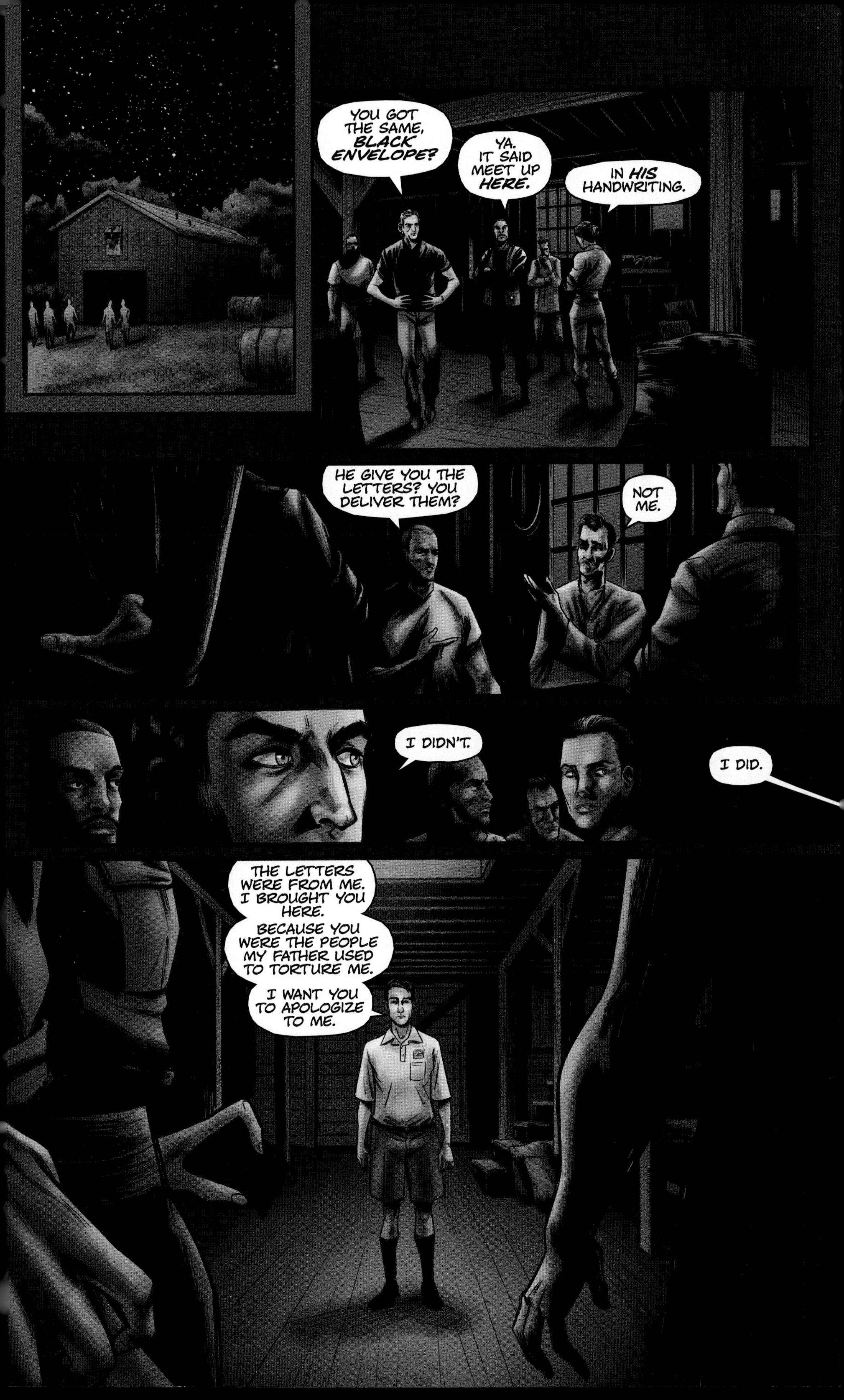
YOU GOT THE SAME, BLACK ENVELOPE?
YA. IT SAID MEET UP HERE.
IN HIS HANDWRITING.
HE GIVE YOU THE LETTERS? YOU DELIVER THEM?
NOT ME.
I DIDN'T.
I DID.
THE LETTERS WERE FROM ME. I BROUGHT YOU HERE.
BECAUSE YOU WERE THE PEOPLE MY FATHER USED TO TORTURE ME.
I WANT YOU TO APOLOGIZE TO ME.

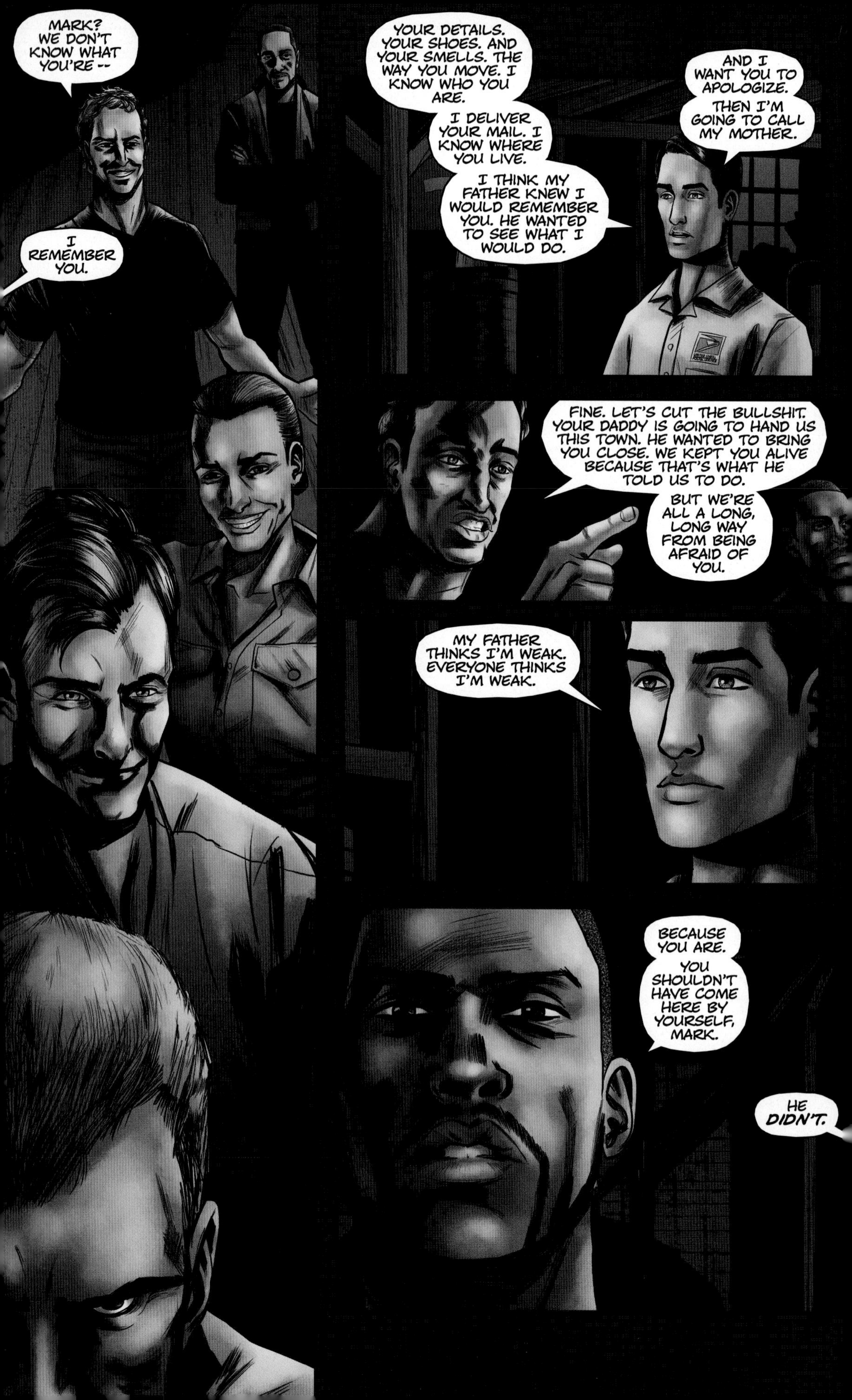
MARK? WE DON'T KNOW WHAT YOU'RE --
I REMEMBER YOU.
YOUR DETAILS. YOUR SHOES. AND YOUR SMELLS. THE WAY YOU MOVE. I KNOW WHO YOU ARE.
I DELIVER YOUR MAIL. I KNOW WHERE YOU LIVE.
I THINK MY FATHER KNEW I WOULD REMEMBER YOU. HE WANTED TO SEE WHAT I WOULD DO.
AND I WANT YOU TO APOLOGIZE.
THEN I'M GOING TO CALL MY MOTHER.
FINE. LET'S CUT THE BULLSHIT. YOUR DADDY IS GOING TO HAND US THIS TOWN. HE WANTED TO BRING YOU CLOSE. WE KEPT YOU ALIVE BECAUSE THAT'S WHAT HE TOLD US TO DO.
BUT WE'RE ALL A LONG, LONG WAY FROM BEING AFRAID OF YOU.
MY FATHER THINKS I'M WEAK. EVERYONE THINKS I'M WEAK.
BECAUSE YOU ARE.
YOU SHOULDN'T HAVE COME HERE BY YOURSELF, MARK.
HE *DIDN'T.*

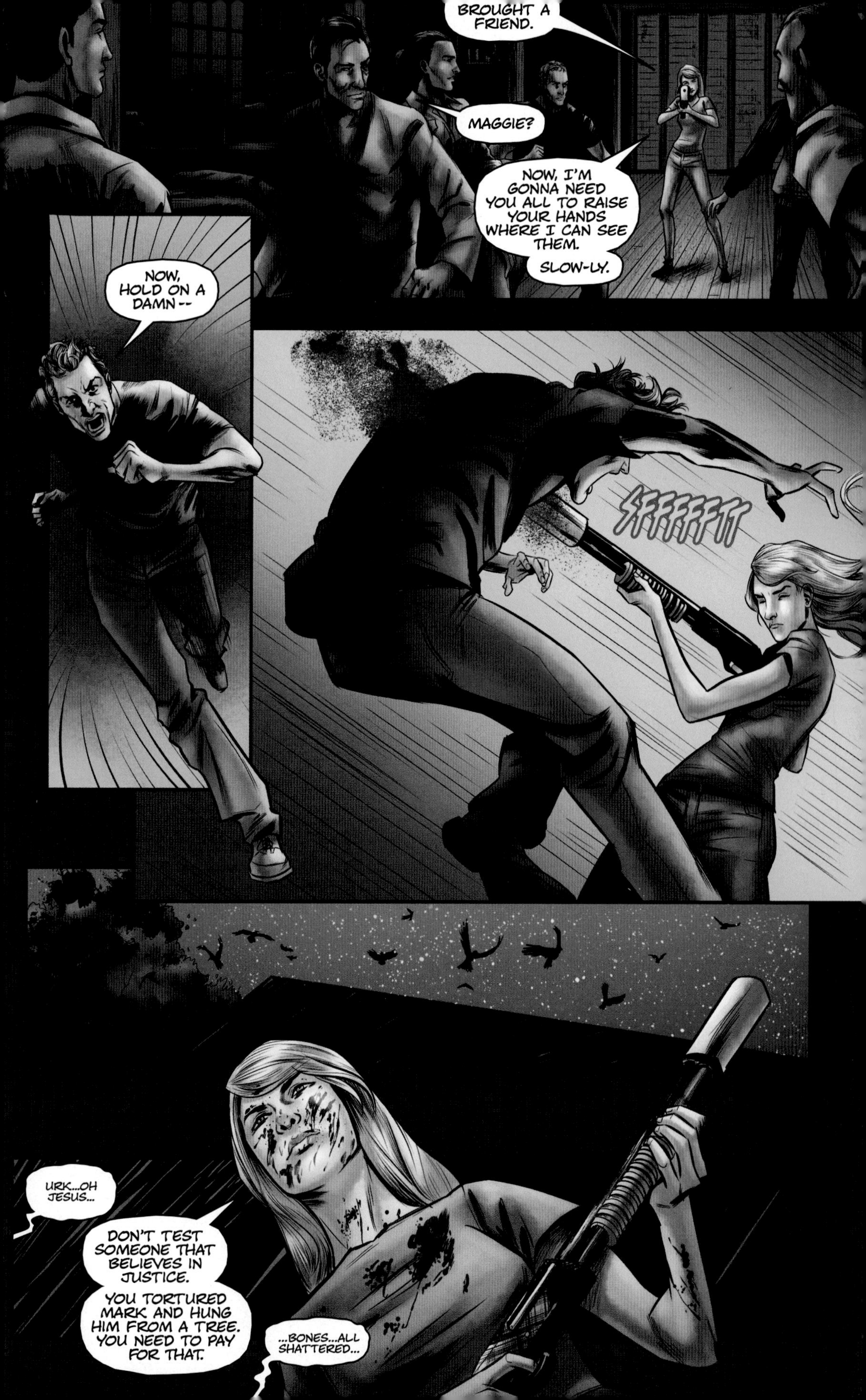
BROUGHT A FRIEND.
MAGGIE?
NOW, I'M GONNA NEED YOU ALL TO RAISE YOUR HANDS WHERE I CAN SEE THEM.
SLOW-LY.
NOW, HOLD ON A DAMN--
SFFFFFTT
URK...OH JESUS...
DON'T TEST SOMEONE THAT BELIEVES IN JUSTICE.
YOU TORTURED MARK AND HUNG HIM FROM A TREE. YOU NEED TO PAY FOR THAT.
...BONES...ALL SHATTERED...

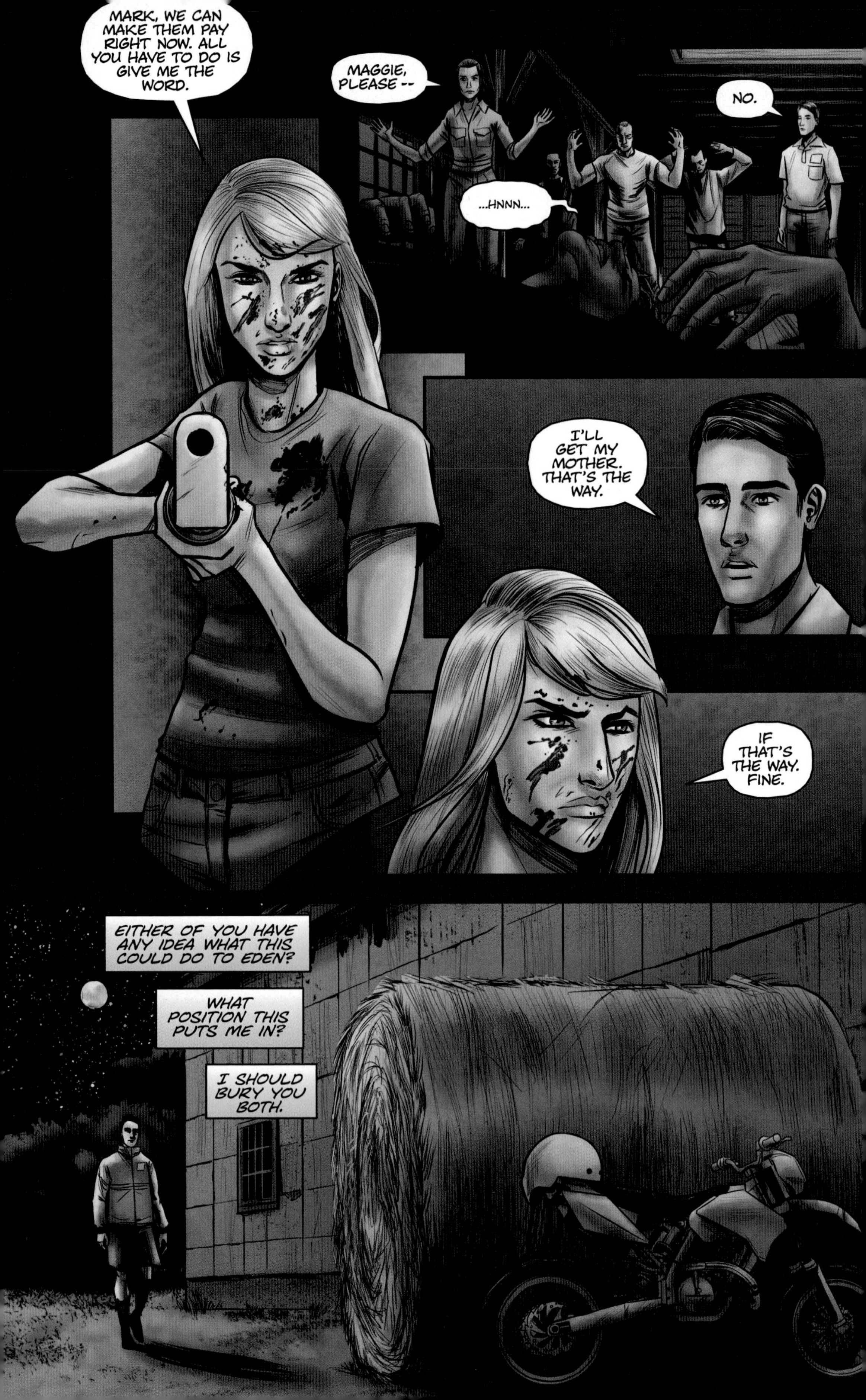
MARK, WE CAN MAKE THEM PAY RIGHT NOW. ALL YOU HAVE TO DO IS GIVE ME THE WORD.
MAGGIE, PLEASE --
NO.
...HNNN...
I'LL GET MY MOTHER. THAT'S THE WAY.
IF THAT'S THE WAY. FINE.
EITHER OF YOU HAVE ANY IDEA WHAT THIS COULD DO TO EDEN?
WHAT POSITION THIS PUTS ME IN?
I SHOULD BURY YOU BOTH.

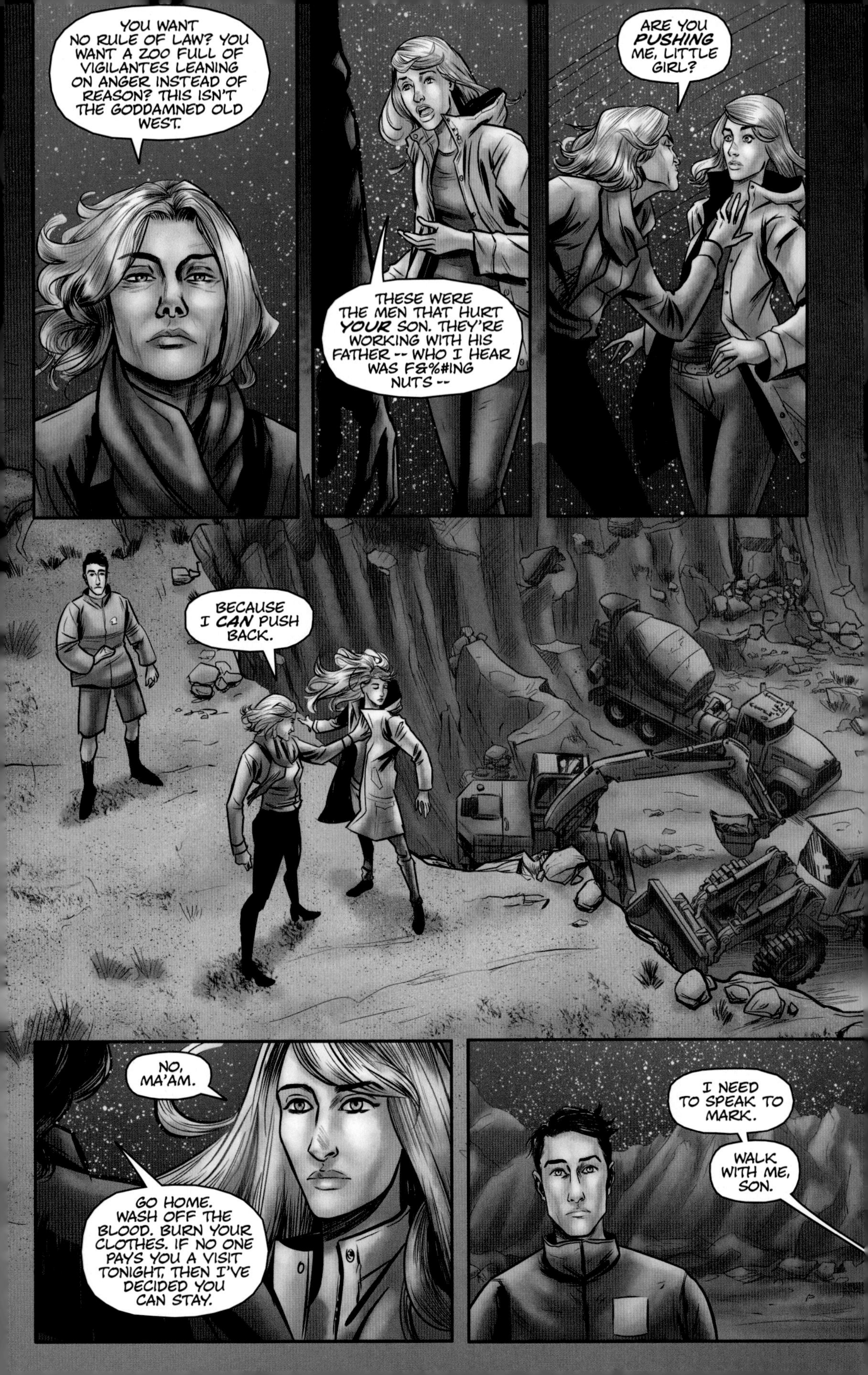
YOU WANT NO RULE OF LAW? YOU WANT A ZOO FULL OF VIGILANTES LEANING ON ANGER INSTEAD OF REASON? THIS ISN'T THE GODDAMNED OLD WEST.
THESE WERE THE MEN THAT HURT YOUR SON. THEY'RE WORKING WITH HIS FATHER -- WHO I HEAR WAS F&%#ING NUTS --
ARE YOU PUSHING ME, LITTLE GIRL?
BECAUSE I CAN PUSH BACK.
NO, MA'AM.
GO HOME. WASH OFF THE BLOOD. BURN YOUR CLOTHES. IF NO ONE PAYS YOU A VISIT TONIGHT, THEN I'VE DECIDED YOU CAN STAY.
I NEED TO SPEAK TO MARK.
WALK WITH ME, SON.

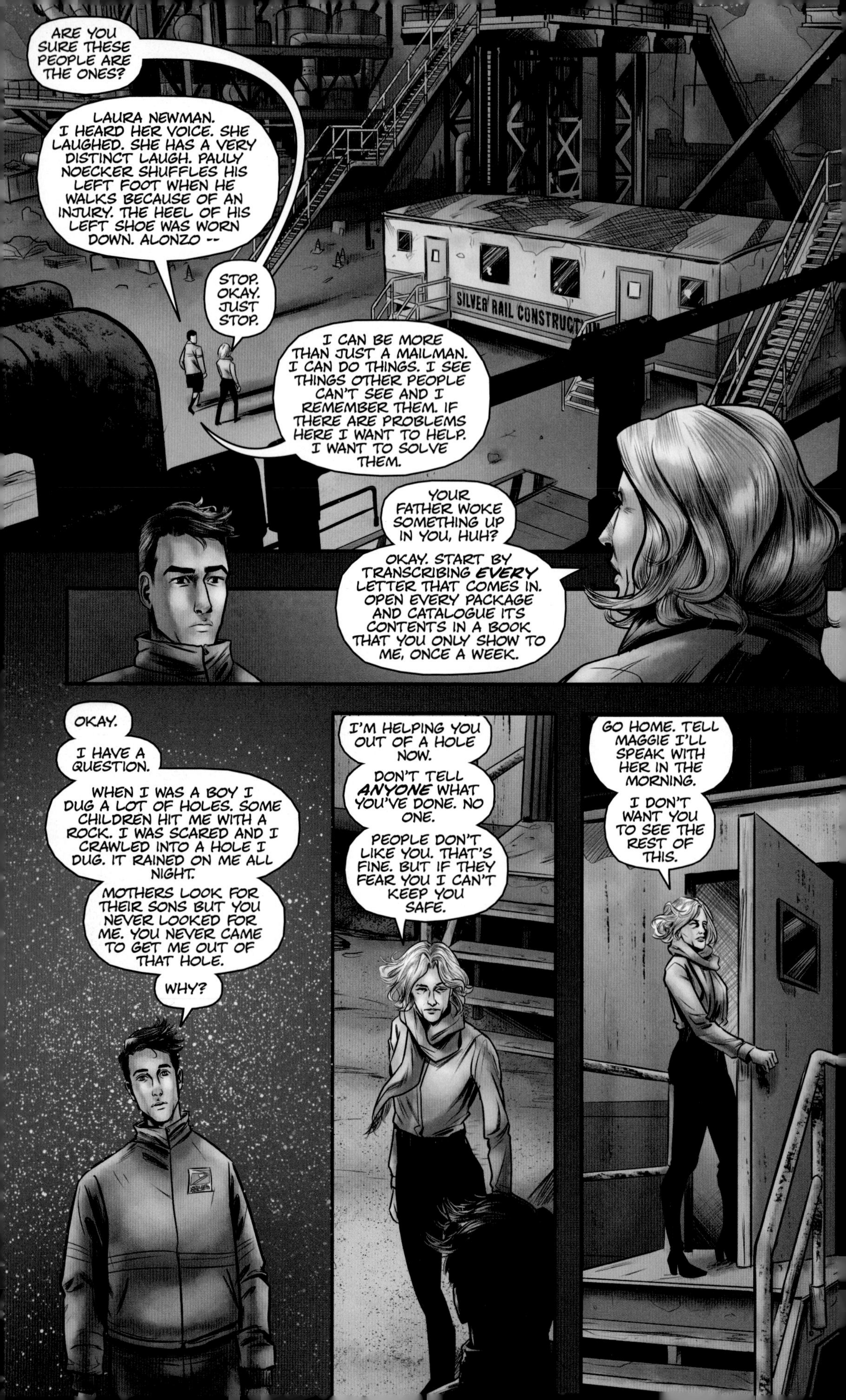
ARE YOU SURE THESE PEOPLE ARE THE ONES?
LAURA NEWMAN. I HEARD HER VOICE. SHE LAUGHED. SHE HAS A VERY DISTINCT LAUGH. PAULY NOECKER SHUFFLES HIS LEFT FOOT WHEN HE WALKS BECAUSE OF AN INJURY. THE HEEL OF HIS LEFT SHOE WAS WORN DOWN. ALONZO --
STOP. OKAY. JUST STOP.
SILVER RAIL CONSTRUC
I CAN BE MORE THAN JUST A MAILMAN. I CAN DO THINGS. I SEE THINGS OTHER PEOPLE CAN'T SEE AND I REMEMBER THEM. IF THERE ARE PROBLEMS HERE I WANT TO HELP. I WANT TO SOLVE THEM.
YOUR FATHER WOKE SOMETHING UP IN YOU, HUH?
OKAY. START BY TRANSCRIBING *EVERY* LETTER THAT COMES IN. OPEN EVERY PACKAGE AND CATALOGUE ITS CONTENTS IN A BOOK THAT YOU ONLY SHOW TO ME, ONCE A WEEK.
OKAY.
I HAVE A QUESTION.
WHEN I WAS A BOY I DUG A LOT OF HOLES. SOME CHILDREN HIT ME WITH A ROCK. I WAS SCARED AND I CRAWLED INTO A HOLE I DUG. IT RAINED ON ME ALL NIGHT.
MOTHERS LOOK FOR THEIR SONS BUT YOU NEVER LOOKED FOR ME. YOU NEVER CAME TO GET ME OUT OF THAT HOLE.
WHY?
I'M HELPING YOU OUT OF A HOLE NOW.
DON'T TELL *ANYONE* WHAT YOU'VE DONE. NO ONE.
PEOPLE DON'T LIKE YOU. THAT'S FINE. BUT IF THEY FEAR YOU I CAN'T KEEP YOU SAFE.
GO HOME. TELL MAGGIE I'LL SPEAK WITH HER IN THE MORNING.
I DON'T WANT YOU TO SEE THE REST OF THIS.

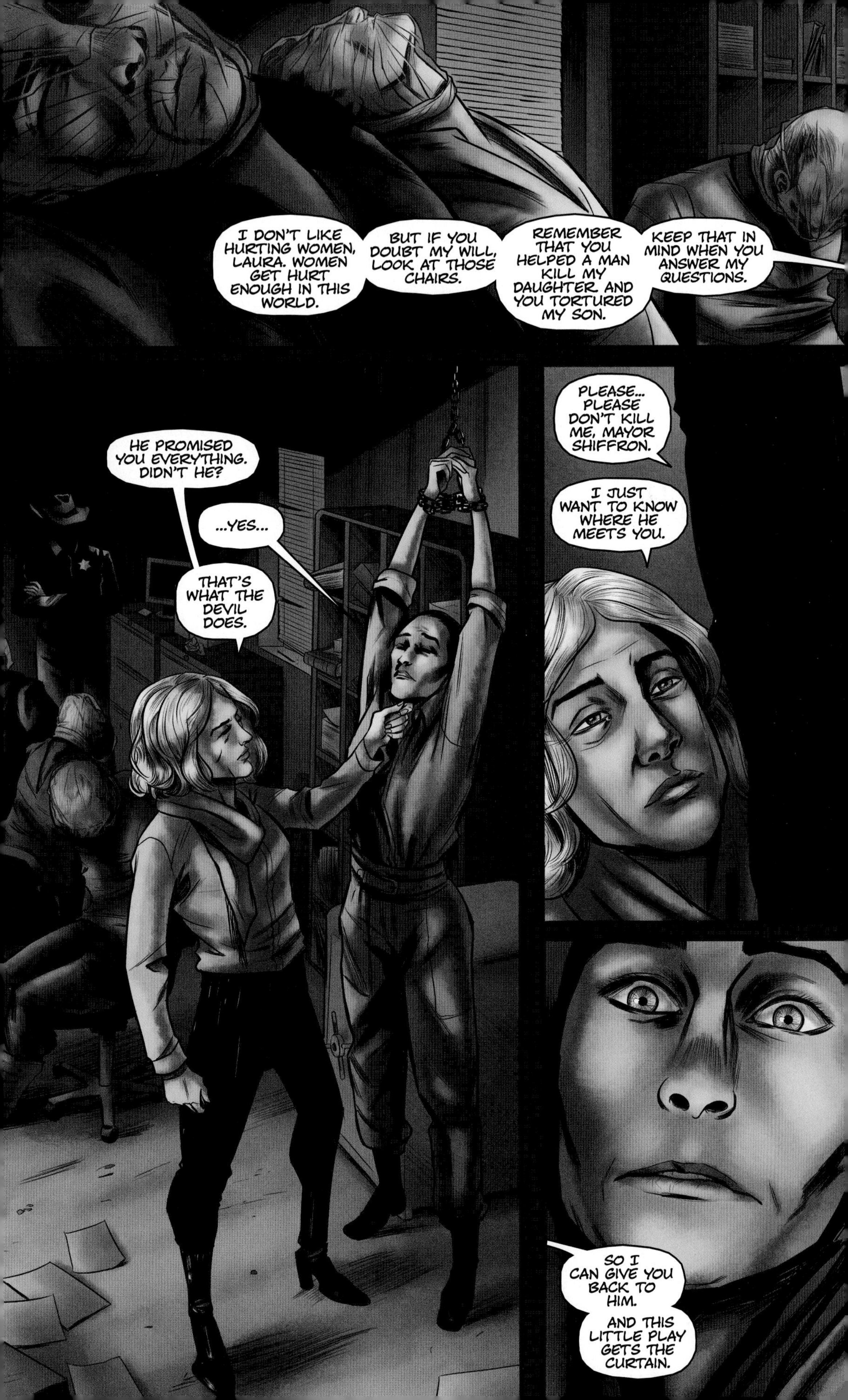
I DON'T LIKE HURTING WOMEN, LAURA. WOMEN GET HURT ENOUGH IN THIS WORLD.
BUT IF YOU DOUBT MY WILL, LOOK AT THOSE CHAIRS.
REMEMBER THAT YOU HELPED A MAN KILL MY DAUGHTER AND YOU TORTURED MY SON.
KEEP THAT IN MIND WHEN YOU ANSWER MY QUESTIONS.
HE PROMISED YOU EVERYTHING. DIDN'T HE?
...YES...
THAT'S WHAT THE DEVIL DOES.
PLEASE... PLEASE DON'T KILL ME, MAYOR SHIFFRON.
I JUST WANT TO KNOW WHERE HE MEETS YOU.
SO I CAN GIVE YOU BACK TO HIM.
AND THIS LITTLE PLAY GETS THE CURTAIN.

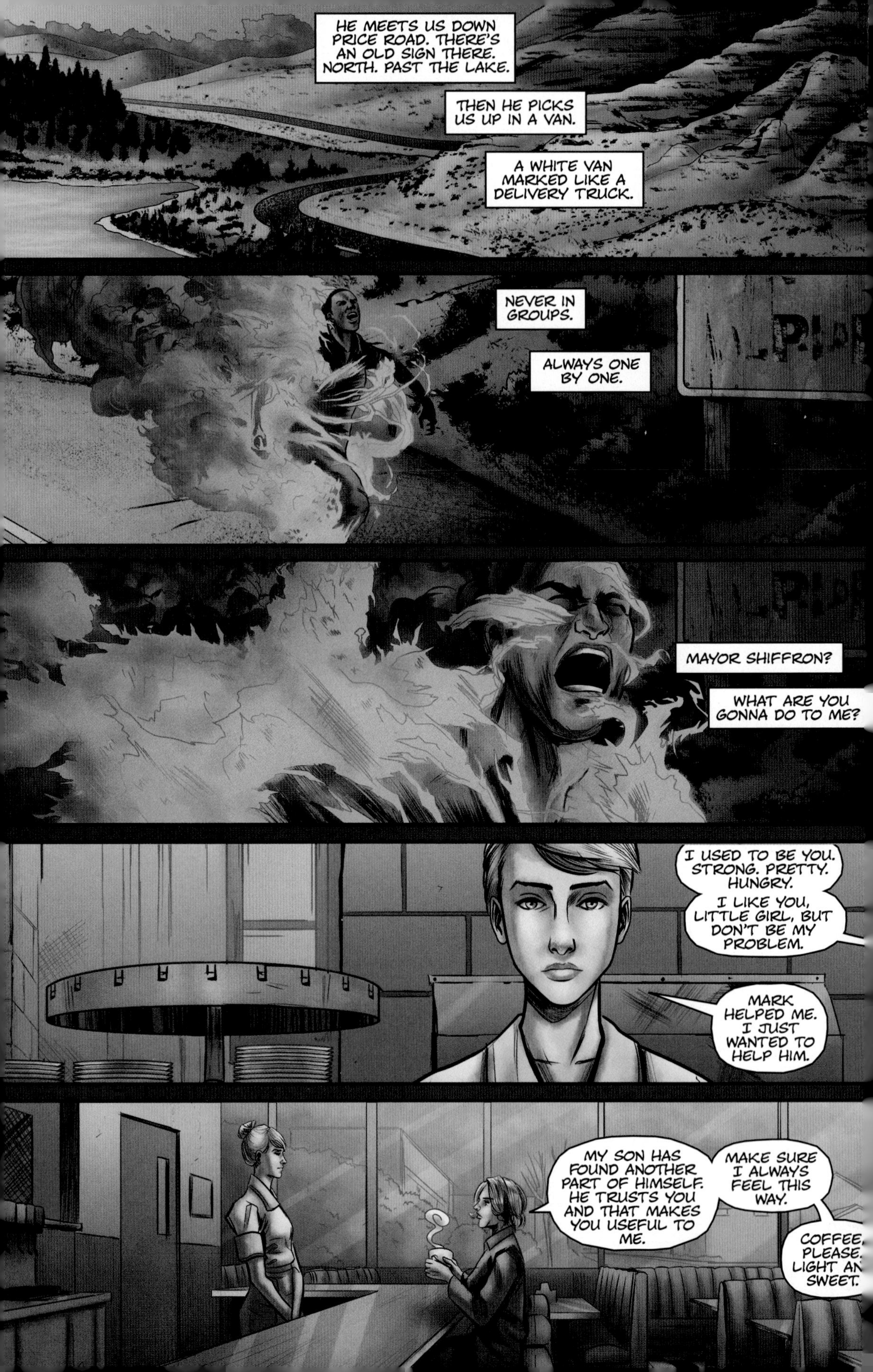
HE MEETS US DOWN PRICE ROAD. THERE'S AN OLD SIGN THERE. NORTH. PAST THE LAKE.
THEN HE PICKS US UP IN A VAN.
A WHITE VAN MARKED LIKE A DELIVERY TRUCK.
NEVER IN GROUPS.
ALWAYS ONE BY ONE.
MAYOR SHIFFRON?
WHAT ARE YOU GONNA DO TO ME?
I USED TO BE YOU. STRONG. PRETTY. HUNGRY.
I LIKE YOU, LITTLE GIRL, BUT DON'T BE MY PROBLEM.
MARK HELPED ME. I JUST WANTED TO HELP HIM.
MY SON HAS FOUND ANOTHER PART OF HIMSELF. HE TRUSTS YOU AND THAT MAKES YOU USEFUL TO ME.
MAKE SURE I ALWAYS FEEL THIS WAY.

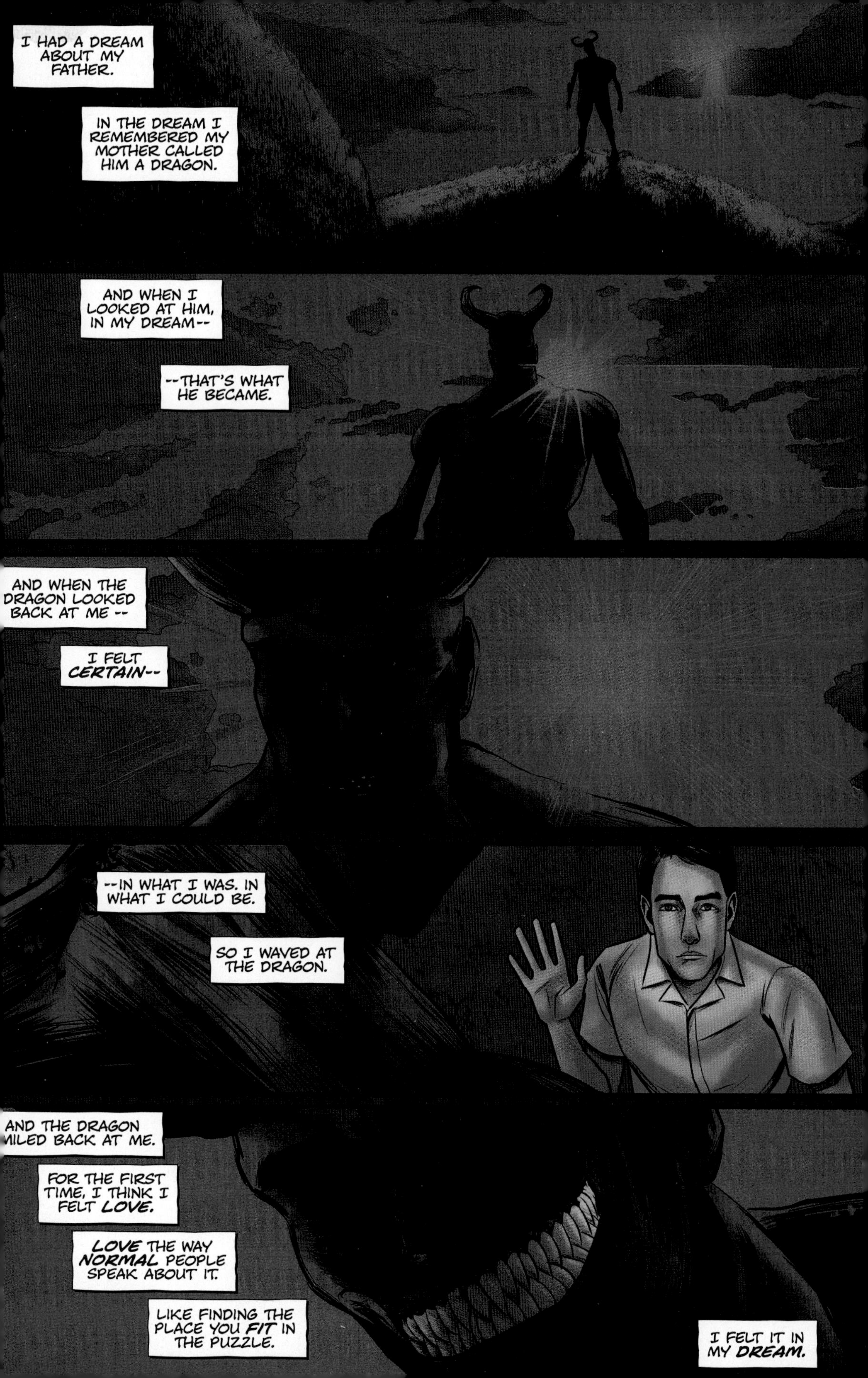
I HAD A DREAM ABOUT MY FATHER.
IN THE DREAM I REMEMBERED MY MOTHER CALLED HIM A DRAGON.
AND WHEN I LOOKED AT HIM, IN MY DREAM--
--THAT'S WHAT HE BECAME.
AND WHEN THE DRAGON LOOKED BACK AT ME --
I FELT *CERTAIN*--
--IN WHAT I WAS. IN WHAT I COULD BE.
SO I WAVED AT THE DRAGON.
AND THE DRAGON MILED BACK AT ME.
FOR THE FIRST TIME, I THINK I FELT *LOVE.*
LOVE THE WAY *NORMAL* PEOPLE SPEAK ABOUT IT.
LIKE FINDING THE PLACE YOU *FIT* IN THE PUZZLE.
I FELT IT IN MY *DREAM.*

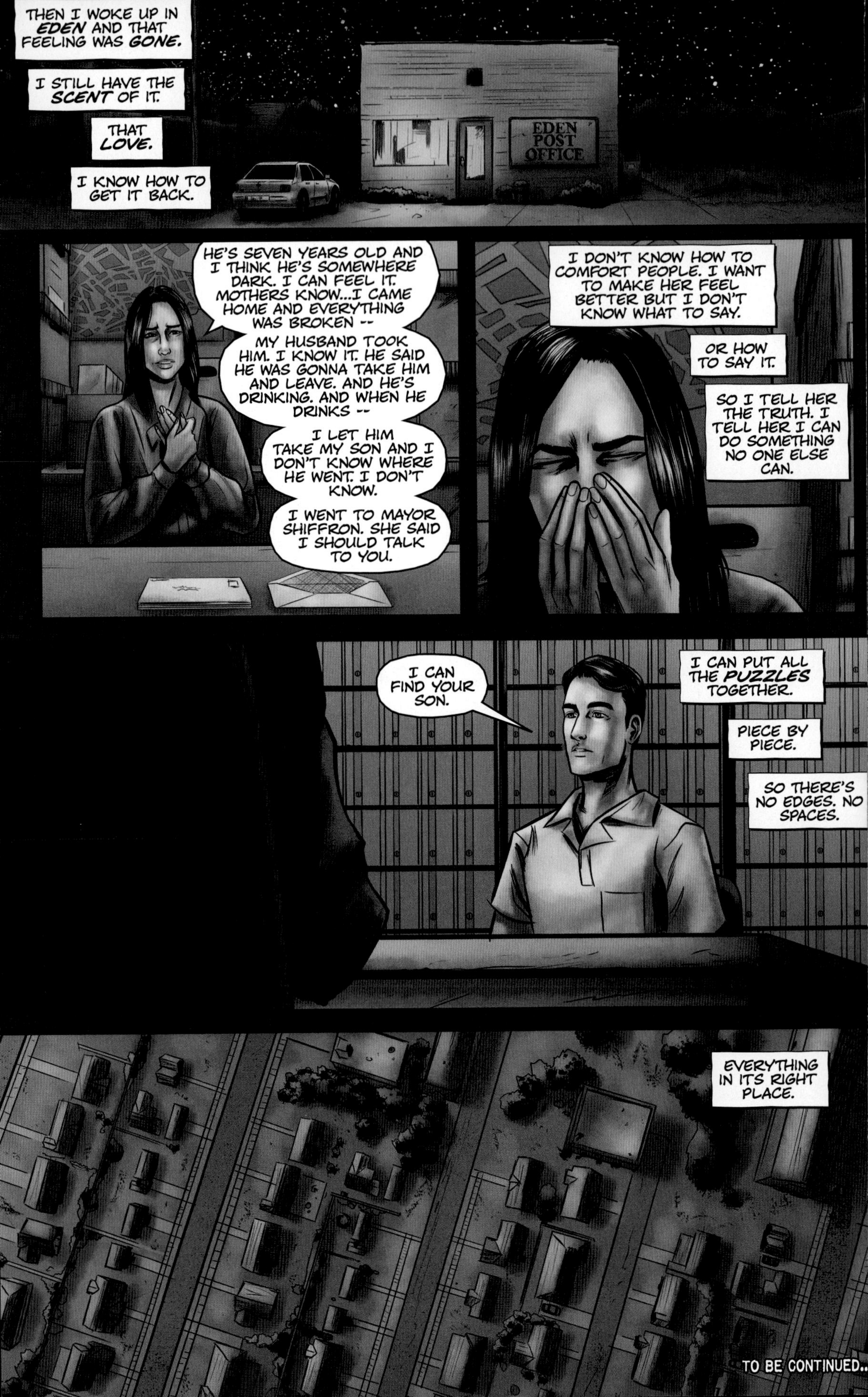
THEN I WOKE UP IN EDEN AND THAT FEELING WAS GONE.
I STILL HAVE THE SCENT OF IT.
THAT LOVE.
I KNOW HOW TO GET IT BACK.
EDEN POST OFFICE
HE'S SEVEN YEARS OLD AND I THINK HE'S SOMEWHERE DARK. I CAN FEEL IT. MOTHERS KNOW...I CAME HOME AND EVERYTHING WAS BROKEN --
MY HUSBAND TOOK HIM. I KNOW IT. HE SAID HE WAS GONNA TAKE HIM AND LEAVE. AND HE'S DRINKING. AND WHEN HE DRINKS --
I LET HIM TAKE MY SON AND I DON'T KNOW WHERE HE WENT. I DON'T KNOW.
I WENT TO MAYOR SHIFFRON. SHE SAID I SHOULD TALK TO YOU.
I DON'T KNOW HOW TO COMFORT PEOPLE. I WANT TO MAKE HER FEEL BETTER BUT I DON'T KNOW WHAT TO SAY.
OR HOW TO SAY IT.
SO I TELL HER THE TRUTH. I TELL HER I CAN DO SOMETHING NO ONE ELSE CAN.
I CAN FIND YOUR SON.
I CAN PUT ALL THE PUZZLES TOGETHER.
PIECE BY PIECE.
SO THERE'S NO EDGES. NO SPACES.
EVERYTHING IN ITS RIGHT PLACE.
TO BE CONTINUED...

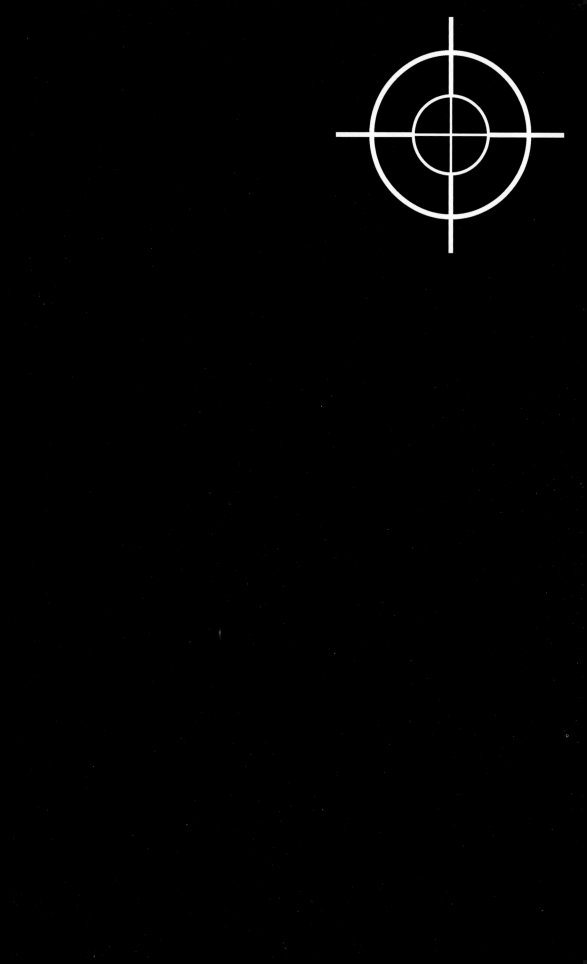

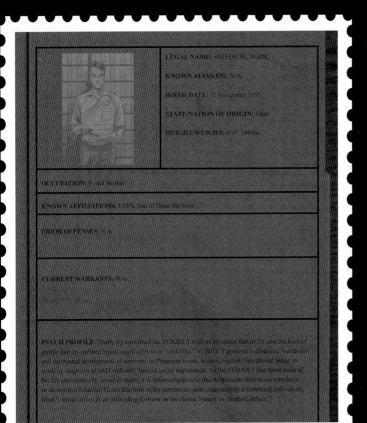

LEGAL NAME: SHIFFRON, MARK

KNOWN ALIAS(ES): N/A

BIRTH DATE: 11 November 1985

STATE/NATION OF ORIGIN: Eden

HEIGHT/WEIGHT: 6'0", 190 lbs.

OCCUPATION: Postal Worker

KNOWN AFFILIATIONS: USPS, Son of Dana Shiffron

PRIOR OFFENSES: N/A

CURRENT WARRANTS: N/A

PSYCH PROFILE: "Early IQ tests found the SUBJECT with an IQ under that of 70, and the kind of profile that an outdated report might refer to as "childlike." SUBJECT presents a simplistic worldview and the mental development of someone, in Piagetian terms, in the Concrete Operational Stage. A working diagnosis of ASD with only limited social impairment. As the SUBJECT has spent most of his life surrounded by moral deviants, it is interesting to note that he presents little to no rebellious or destructive behavior. Given that both of his parents are also considerably disinhibited individuals, Mark's status serves as an interesting footnote in the classic Nature vs. Nurture debate."

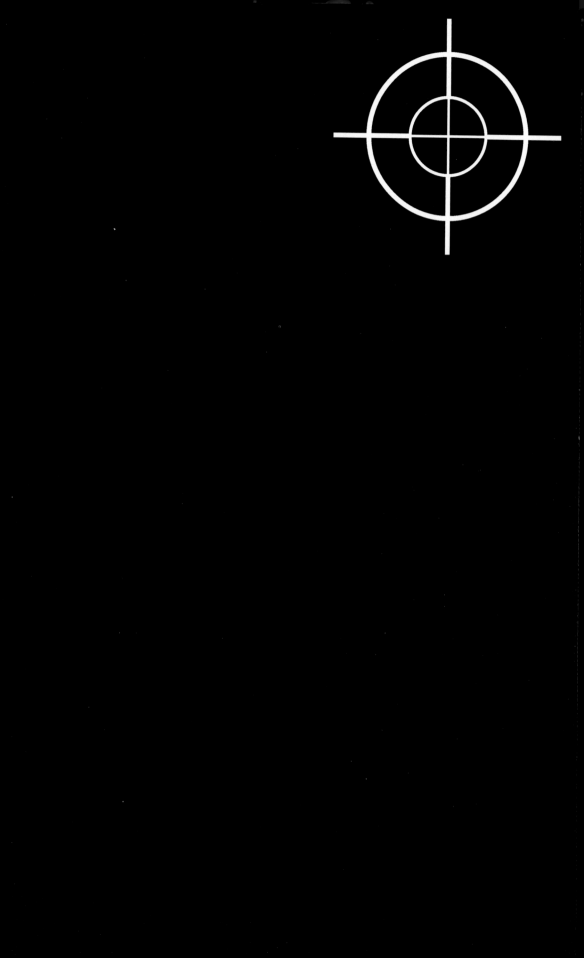

LEGAL NAME: MESSERSMITH, DANIEL P.

KNOWN ALIAS(ES): "MR. PINK"

BIRTH DATE: 12 AUGUST 1981

STATE/NATION OF ORIGIN:
NEW YORK, NEW YORK

HEIGHT/WEIGHT:
5' 8" / 150 LBS.

OCCUPATION: N/A

KNOWN AFFILIATIONS: N/A

PRIOR OFFENSES: Possession and Dispensation of Narcotics, Battery, Possession of an Unregistered Firearm, Burglary, Breaking & Entering, Various Misdemeanors

CURRENT WARRANTS:

WANTED in Cree County, KS for Assault

WANTED in Westin County, NE for Possession

PSYCH PROFILE: "The SUBJECT presents a profile common to those prone to petty thievery. Sinking into a basic cycle of addiction and abuse, followed by criminal offense, SUBJECT shows little potential for reintegration into a law-abiding society.

Text-book addictive personality. Years of stimulant abuse have generated significant physiological and psychological damage. Years of incarceration have engendered a near permanent case of acute paranoia."

STATUS: At this time, Mr. Messersmith should be considered armed and dangerous, but representing an insignificant threat to society at large.

LEGAL NAME: NIXON, ATTICUS F.

KNOWN ALIAS(ES): THE WHITE REVEREND, THE WHITE POWER PREACHER

BIRTH DATE: 9 FEBRUARY 1969

STATE/NATION OF ORIGIN: LOUISIANA (CITY/COUNTY UNKNOWN)

HEIGHT/WEIGHT:
5'10" / 180 LBS.

OCCUPATION: Pastor, First Congregational Church of Eden

KNOWN AFFILIATIONS: The Aryan Brotherhood, Ku Klux Klan

PRIOR OFFENSES: Assault with a Deadly Weapon, Destruction of Public Property, Conspiracy to Commit Murder in the First Degree, Murder in the Third Degree

CURRENT WARRANTS: N/A

PSYCH PROFILE: "SUBJECT incorporates his newfound religious ecstasy into his aforementioned, well-documented Narcissistic Personality Disorder. It is the belief of this profiler that the SUBJECT's previous ethnocentric philosophies were merely an extension of this Narcissism (which presents a fascinating research opportunity about the possible underlying nature of extreme ethnocentrism in certain individuals).
SUBJECT compulsively attends to the presentation and hygiene of his hair with a near-Freudian intensity."

STATUS: All observation following Nixon's most recent release from the state correctional facility seems to suggest that his religious conversion is genuine. There is no evidence to suggest that Nixon is currently involved in any criminal activity.

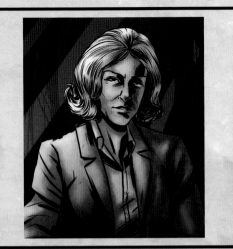

LEGAL NAME: SHIFFRON, DANA

KNOWN ALIAS(ES): N/A

BIRTH DATE: 23 SEPTEMBER 1965

STATE/NATION OF ORIGIN: HARTFORD, CT

HEIGHT/WEIGHT: 5' 6" / 120 LBS.

OCCUPATION: Mayor of Eden

KNOWN AFFILIATIONS: N/A

PRIOR OFFENSES: Fraud, Racketeering, Distribution of Narcotics, Distribution of Firearms, Conspiracy to Commit Murder

CURRENT WARRANTS: N/A

PSYCH PROFILE: "In spite of previous FBI profiles, SUBJECT should not be classified as a clinical sociopath. A cursory examination of incidents surrounding the SUBJECT's childhood suggests a diagnosis of Oppositional Defiance Disorder. Even a passing acquaintance with her criminal record and previous FBI profiles suggest subject is not only able to survive in, but thrives in the exceedingly misogynistic subcultures of organized crime. Again, while previous profiles have suggested sociopathy, this profiler has noted that SUBJECT appears to be capable of certain degrees of guilt, and possesses a strong sense of irony."

STATUS: Maintain round the clock surveillance. Shiffron is the brains behind anything significant going on in Eden. She needs to know that we're keeping an eye on her, and that we're capable of putting a stop to anything she has planned.

LEGAL NAME: LAFLEUR, RORY ASHLEY

KNOWN ALIAS(ES): "ROY MAGNUM"

BIRTH DATE: 14 MARCH 1972

STATE/NATION OF ORIGIN: SAN FRANCISCO, CA

HEIGHT/WEIGHT: 6' 1" / 190 LBS

OCCUPATION: Sheriff of Eden

KNOWN AFFILIATIONS: U.S. Army Rangers (Dishonorable Discharge), Hell's Angels (Note: Never moved further than "Prospect" and ceased any affiliations with the Angels in 1999.)

PRIOR OFFENSES: Fraud, Petty Theft, Vandalism, Breaking and Entering, Assault and Battery, Possession of an Unregistered Firearm.

CURRENT WARRANTS:

WANTED for Solicitation of a Prostitute in Laramie, WY

PSYCH PROFILE: "SUBJECT presents textbook complexes in regards to gender dynamics, fears of emasculation, and projected homophobia. SUBJECT's clear discomfort toward homosexual males, especially in regards to his single conviction for a violent crime (outside of a known gay bar in Downtown Cheyenne), may be representative of internalized bigotry.
SUBJECT's overcompensatory masculine actions (alias, phallic obsession with "manly" firearms and activities, etc.) may be the result of his single-parent upbringing (although most research and literature dismisses this conclusion), but more likely coincides clinical feelings of inadequacy."

STATUS: Likely presents no danger to anyone outside of Eden. A potential weak spot to exploit, given his many insecurities and the comprehensiveness of our profile.

LEGAL NAME: [REDACTED]

KNOWN ALIAS(ES): The Chef

BIRTH DATE: [REDACTED]

STATE/NATION OF ORIGIN:
France (Province Unknown)

HEIGHT/WEIGHT: 6' 3" / 220 lbs

OCCUPATION: Short Order Cook

KNOWN AFFILIATIONS: Situationist International, Alternative libertaire, No Pasaran

PRIOR OFFENSES: A number of charges from French Authorities, including conspiracy to commit terrorist acts and sedition. No discernible criminal record in America, beyond his undocumented status.

CURRENT WARRANTS:

　　　　WANTED for extradition by Parisian Authorities for "questioning"

PSYCH PROFILE: "Given the SUBJECT's lengthy history in the French Anarchist movement, his tame lifestyle since seeking illegal asylum in the United States comes as a complete surprise. Several other profiles have suggested a diagnosis of extreme dissociative identity disorder– especially since, although SUBJECT undoubtedly speaks some English, our recordings and monitoring have only ever captured him speaking French. It is this profiler's opinion that some unrecorded personal event has led the subject into an early, but self-inflicted, retirement."

STATUS: [REDACTED] represents an important bargaining chip as well as a possible source of inspiration on numerous European criminal elements. It would be a shame to lose him to the French before we had a chance at interrogation.

LEGAL NAME: SHIFFRON, MARK

KNOWN ALIAS(ES): N/A

BIRTH DATE: 11 November 1985

STATE/NATION OF ORIGIN: Eden

HEIGHT/WEIGHT: 6' 0" 190 lbs.

OCCUPATION: Postal Worker

KNOWN AFFILIATIONS: USPS, Son of Dana Shiffron

PRIOR OFFENSES: N/A

CURRENT WARRANTS: N/A

PSYCH PROFILE: "Early IQ tests fitted the SUBJECT with an IQ under that of 70, and the kind of profile that an outdated report might refer to as "childlike." SUBJECT presents a simplistic worldview and the mental development of someone, in Piagetian terms, in the Concrete Operational Stage. A working diagnosis of ASD with only limited social impairment. As the SUBJECT has spent most of his life surrounded by social deviants, it is interesting to note that he presents little to no rebellious or destructive behavior. Given that both of his parents are also considerably disinhibited individuals, Mark's status serves as an interesting footnote in the classic Nature vs. Nurture debate."

STATUS: All reports suggest that Mark is utterly harmless, and, per the psychological profile, possessing a childlike innocence. He represents an important asset as well as an opportunity to lean on Mayor Shiffron.

LEGAL NAME: PRENDOWSKI, MARGARET

KNOWN ALIAS(ES): Maggie, "Magazine"

BIRTH DATE: 9 January 1975

STATE/NATION OF ORIGIN: Portland, OR

HEIGHT/WEIGHT: 5' 7" / 120 lbs.

OCCUPATION: Waitress

KNOWN AFFILIATIONS: Several Unconfirmed Mexican Cartel Associations

PRIOR OFFENSES: Possession of Marijuana with Intention to Distribute, Cultivation of Marijuana with Intention to Distribute, Distribution of Marijuana, Tax Fraud

CURRENT WARRANTS:

WANTED for Grand Theft Auto in Eugene, OR

PSYCH PROFILE: "SUBJECT represents an incredible foray into the "foot-in-the-door" effect in regards to criminal activity, especially in instances of exceptionally intelligent individuals. SUBJECT's record shows a chronological descent into deviant, criminal behavior, with offenses increasing at a remarkably steady rate. SUBJECT is incredibly quick-thinking, flexible, and charismatic. SUBJECT presents fascinating arguments of self-rationalization, relieving herself of guilt by justifying each offense, and thereby permitting even further criminal activity, in her own words, with an attitude of "in for a penny, in for a pound."

STATUS: Prendowski, while by no means a sociopath, is likely playing her handler – Agent Simpson's reports seem extremely spotty. We don't suspect violent intent, but you don't start a drug empire without breaking a few fingers.

LEGAL NAME: SAMPSON, ROBERT R.

KNOWN ALIAS(ES): "Big Injun," "The Comanche"

BIRTH DATE: Unknown

STATE/NATION OF ORIGIN: Lawton, OK

HEIGHT/WEIGHT: 6' 8" / 250 lbs.

OCCUPATION: N/A

KNOWN AFFILIATIONS: The Comanche Nation of Oklahoma, The Oklahoma Stage Actors Guild

PRIOR OFFENSES: [REDACTED]

CURRENT WARRANTS:

WANTED for Breaking and Entering from Sherwood, KS
WANTED for questioning in Sexual Assault from Greenton County, KS

PSYCH PROFILE:

"Our data on the SUBJECT is extremely limited. Too limited for a detailed profile."

STATUS: Increase surveillance – we need to figure out what's up with this guy.

RACKETEER INFLUENCED AND CORRUPT ORGANIZATIONS ACT

By 1970, the US Government was done with public corruption. Organized crime, racketeering, the mafia – for decades, it had proven nearly impossible to weed out the brains behind organized crime operations, or pin any real charges on them. In October of that same year, however, President Richard M. Nixon signed into law the Racketeer Influenced and Corrupt Organizations Act, designed specifically to curtail mafia activity by charging organized crime leaders for the actions of their underlings, mainly under conspiracy charges.

While at first untested, RICO proved itself against organized crime families, corrupt city officials, and even the Hell's Angels. The act became the go-to standard case used in a variety of corruption cases – embezzling, bribery, human trafficking, and even terrorism. Its broad language and potential for generalization has made it a favorite tool not only in criminal proceedings but also in several civil cases – most notably against Major League Baseball in 2002.

Of course, a single anti-racketeering act like RICO isn't the government's only tool in their ongoing efforts to combat corruption. According to their website, the FBI considers public corruption their "top priority" among criminal investigation. The FBI runs hotlines, special task forces, and intense undercover operations in order to root out organized criminal activity. A number of these methods are incredibly simple – an anonymous phone number for police officers to report illegal activity on the part of their colleagues or superiors, or algorithms designed to seek out suspicious data.

While RICO tends to work best with high profile, conspiracy cases, and the media focuses on violent crime or mafia indictments, the FBI is just as active and invested in tackling large scale or long-running corruption in smaller arenas. In August 2014, for

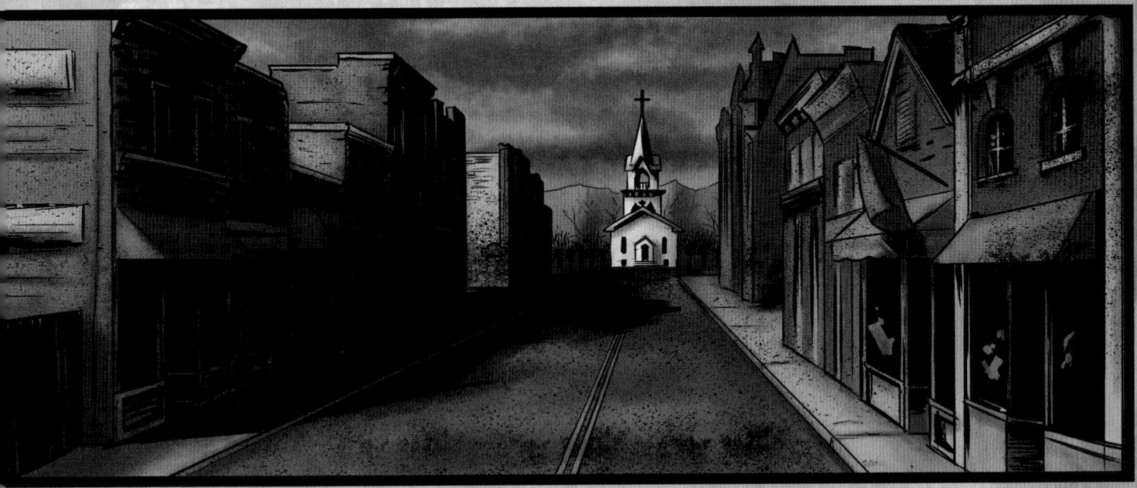

example, the Bureau began investigating a number of public officials and prominent citizens in Progreso, Texas. The small town, located on the Texas-Mexico border, harbored a series of bribery and other corruption violations, the majority of which were conducted by a single family that acted almost like a small town mafia, controlling Progreso's school district contracts and other local government projects. The FBI caught wind of the family's corruption, and on August 11, 2014, several members of the family were sentenced to prison terms.

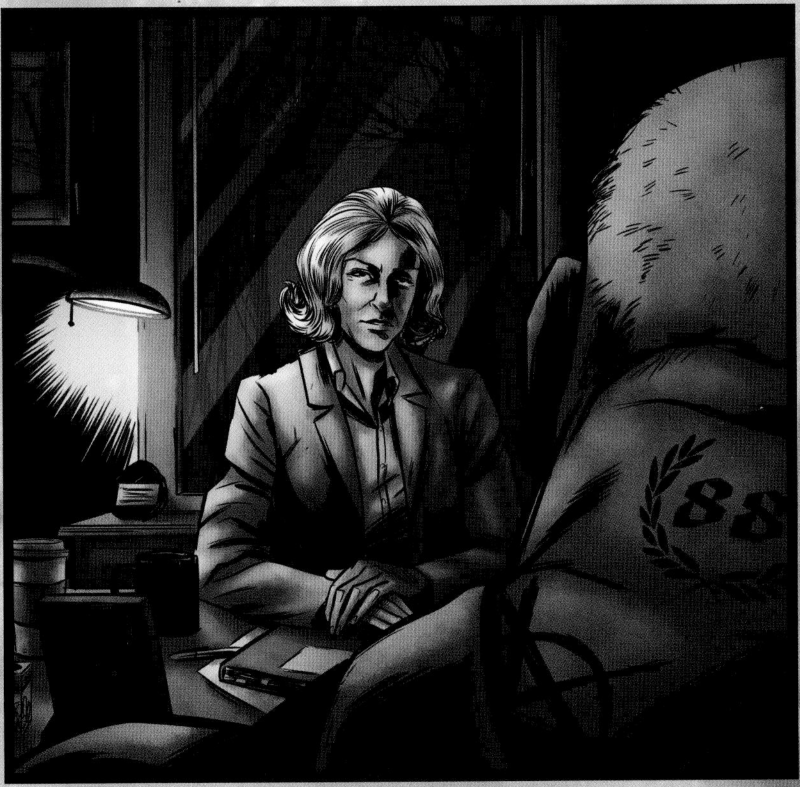
88

The family had, over the course of many years, managed to launder money from federal grants as well as local contracts, and through "confidential sources, undercover scenarios, financial record examinations, and witness interviews" the FBI was able to build an airtight case.

It's not the sort of dramatic Mafioso endeavor that makes the news, but it was still considered a major win for the Bureau. Even though there wasn't much in terms of outright, obvious crime – no violence, burglary, or noticeable lawbreaking – simple cases of following the money toppled what was well on its way to becoming a small-town empire of corruption.

DEFINITION OF ASPERGER SYNDROME

There's a perception in the public eye about mental disorders – an attached stigma – that often only increases as a disorder becomes more common or well-known. Few disorders exemplify this as well as Asperger Syndrome, an autism-spectrum disorder thought to affect as many as 1 in 500 children.

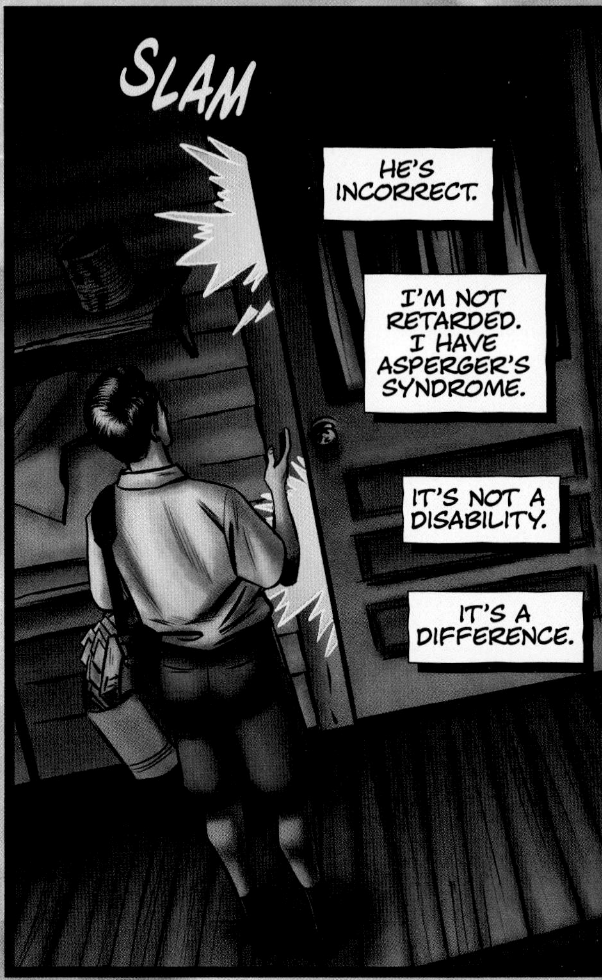
SLAM
HE'S INCORRECT.
I'M NOT RETARDED. I HAVE ASPERGER'S SYNDROME.
IT'S NOT A DISABILITY.
IT'S A DIFFERENCE.

Asperger's is marked by patterns of socially dysfunctional behavior. Asperger's sufferers might appear socially awkward, or even rude. They might obsess over particular behaviors or ways of performing activities. From Wikipedia: "[Asperger Syndrome] is characterized by qualitative impairment in social interaction, by stereotyped and restricted patterns of behavior, activities and interests, and by no clinically significant delay in cognitive development or general delay in language." Patterns of extensive clumsiness seem correlative in many patients, though the relationship between this and other symptoms is less consequential.

While the disorder only relatively recently entered the public eye – many simplified it as "just high-functioning autism," which ironically enough reflects its current status - its roots go as far back as 1944. Hans Asperger, an Austrian pediatrician, began identifying a recurring pattern of behavior in many of his nonverbal patients and designed a series of in-depth communication studies. In the early 1980s, the pattern that he identified and diagnosed was formally standardized as "Asperger Syndrome."

Unfortunately, as the commonness of the diagnosis grew, so did the stigma attached. Whereas before a person might go through their life as "a bit odd" or "socially awkward," the attachment of a mental disorder diagnosis connected with autism introduced a whole new level of social distress and bullying. Look on any forum on the web today – you're guaranteed to find somebody getting called an "aspie," and that's just the cyberbullying aspect.

Still, for many people, Asperger's was a positive diagnosis – it confirmed a manageable social disorder that could be differentiated from autism, and provided an explanation for cognitive differences. Children grew up knowing their diagnosis and compensating for the differences in their neurological function.

Unfortunately, researchers in mental health fields weren't particularly convinced by the notion of Asperger's as a separate diagnosis. Asperger's, they claimed, was just a region of the spectrum that diagnosticians were erroneously lumping together into a single disease. It was incorrect, they claimed, to differentiate it from autism in the first place. In the end, this became the prevailing opinion of most members of the American Psychiatric Association (APA), and in the Fifth Edition of the Diagnostic and Statistical Manual of Mental Disorders, published in 2013, Asperger Syndrome was formally removed as a diagnosis. Autism Spectrum Disorder – "characterized by delays or abnormal functioning before the age of three years in one or more of the following domains: (1) social interaction; (2) communication; and (3) restricted, repetitive, and stereotyped patterns of behavior, interests, and activities" – won out, and former Asperger's patients were re-diagnosed as "high-functioning on the spectrum." Where did that leave them?

Many of those people – diagnosed with Asperger's in the '80s and '90s – are adults with jobs, relationships, and happy, successful lives. There's a scale of stigmatization in our society, and the public's conception of autism is far different from a psychologist's. A lot of people that took comfort in an exceptional label now find themselves lumped in with millions of other people, all of them functioning at drastically different levels.

Of course, that's the pessimistic view – and researchers aren't the only people pleased with a single spectrum disorder diagnosis. The Autism Rights Movement (ARM), for example, maintains the position that people on the spectrum aren't dysfunctional at all – merely functioning differently. After all, the prevailing belief among researchers is that ASD must have a genetic origin, and so, the ARM argues, isn't the spectrum just another aspect of neurodiversity? Former Asperger's patients, now diagnosed with ASD, should simply embrace their new, "more accurate" diagnosis and avoid contributing to a stigma that shouldn't exist in the first place.

THE TITHE

Issue #1 Preview

Matt Hawkins
Co-Creator & Writer

Rahsan Ekedal
Co-Creator & Artist

Bill Farmer
Colorist

Troy Peteri
Letterer

Betsy Gonia
Editor

Published by Image Comics, Inc. Office of Publication. 2001 Center Street, 6th Floor, Berkeley, CA 94704. The Tithe 2015 Matt Hawkins, Rahsan Ekedal, & Top Cow Productions, Inc. All rights reserved. "The Tithe," The Tithe logos, and the likenesses of all featured characters herein are registered trademarks of Matt Hawkins, Rahsan Ekedal, & Top Cow Productions, Inc. Any resemblance to actual persons (living or dead), events, institutions, or locales, without satiric intent is coincidental. No portion of this publication may be reproduced or transmitted. In any form or by any means, without the express written permission of Matt Hawkins, Rahsan Ekedal, & Top Cow Productions, Inc.

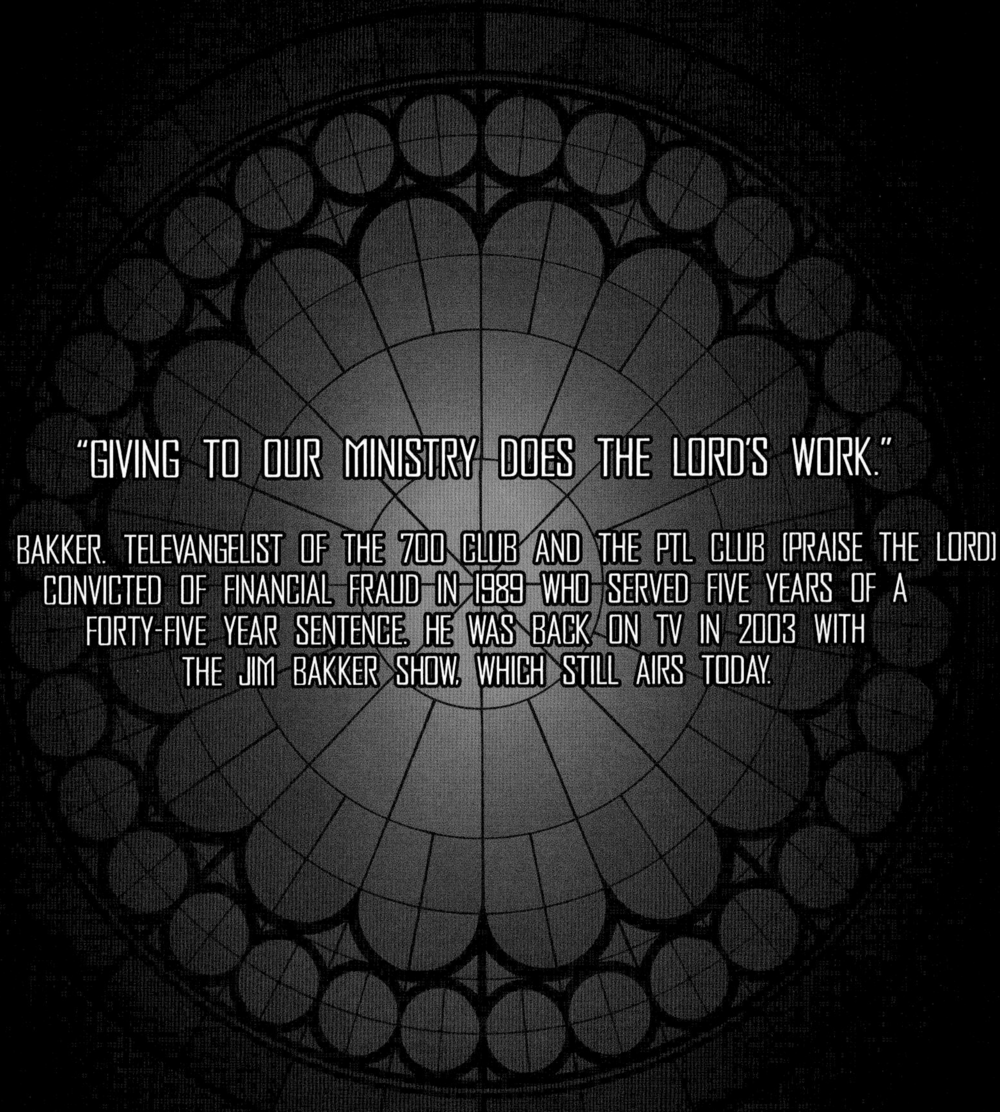

"GIVING TO OUR MINISTRY DOES THE LORD'S WORK."

-JIM BAKKER. TELEVANGELIST OF THE 700 CLUB AND THE PTL CLUB (PRAISE THE LORD) CONVICTED OF FINANCIAL FRAUD IN 1989 WHO SERVED FIVE YEARS OF A FORTY-FIVE YEAR SENTENCE. HE WAS BACK ON TV IN 2003 WITH THE JIM BAKKER SHOW, WHICH STILL AIRS TODAY.

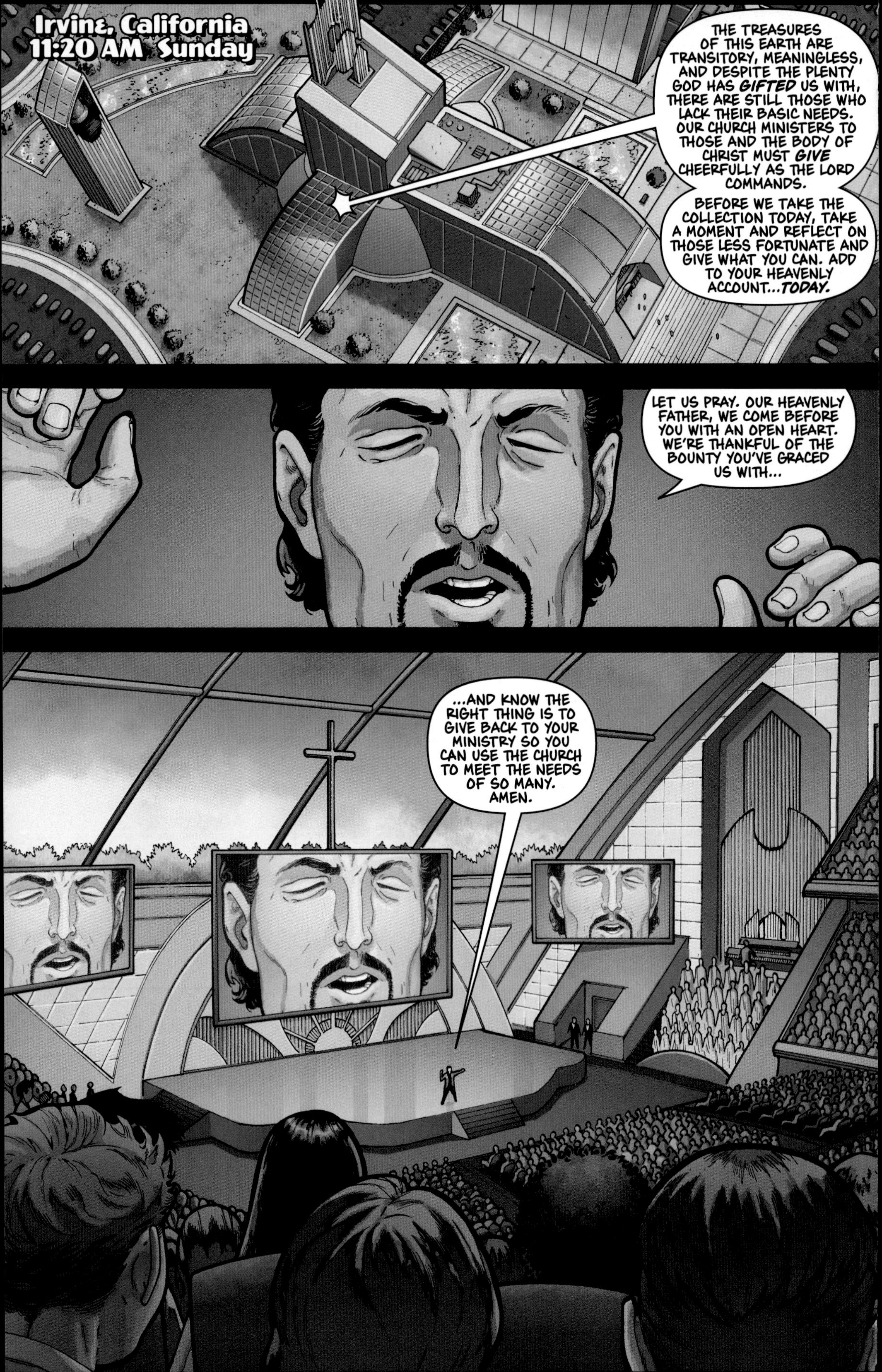
Irvine, California
11:20 AM Sunday
THE TREASURES OF THIS EARTH ARE TRANSITORY, MEANINGLESS, AND DESPITE THE PLENTY GOD HAS *GIFTED* US WITH, THERE ARE STILL THOSE WHO LACK THEIR BASIC NEEDS. OUR CHURCH MINISTERS TO THOSE AND THE BODY OF CHRIST MUST *GIVE* CHEERFULLY AS THE LORD COMMANDS.
BEFORE WE TAKE THE COLLECTION TODAY, TAKE A MOMENT AND REFLECT ON THOSE LESS FORTUNATE AND GIVE WHAT YOU CAN. ADD TO YOUR HEAVENLY ACCOUNT...*TODAY.*
LET US PRAY. OUR HEAVENLY FATHER, WE COME BEFORE YOU WITH AN OPEN HEART. WE'RE THANKFUL OF THE BOUNTY YOU'VE GRACED US WITH...
...AND KNOW THE RIGHT THING IS TO GIVE BACK TO YOUR MINISTRY SO YOU CAN USE THE CHURCH TO MEET THE NEEDS OF SO MANY. AMEN.

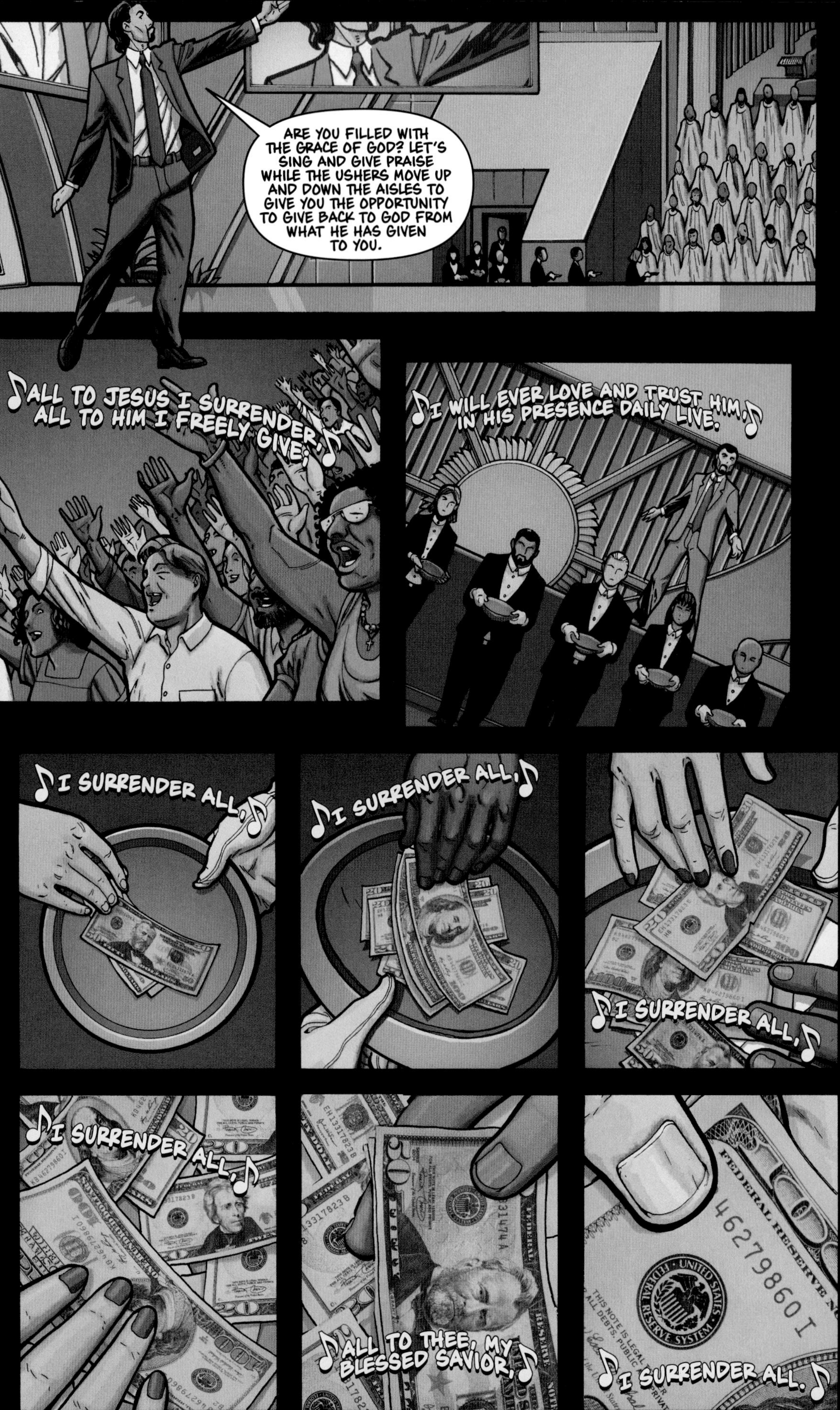

ARE YOU FILLED WITH THE GRACE OF GOD? LET'S SING AND GIVE PRAISE WHILE THE USHERS MOVE UP AND DOWN THE AISLES TO GIVE YOU THE OPPORTUNITY TO GIVE BACK TO GOD FROM WHAT HE HAS GIVEN TO YOU.
♪ALL TO JESUS I SURRENDER, ALL TO HIM I FREELY GIVE;♪
♪I WILL EVER LOVE AND TRUST HIM, IN HIS PRESENCE DAILY LIVE.♪
♪I SURRENDER ALL,♪
♪I SURRENDER ALL,♪
♪I SURRENDER ALL,♪
♪I SURRENDER ALL,♪
♪ALL TO THEE, MY BLESSED SAVIOR,♪
♪I SURRENDER ALL.♪

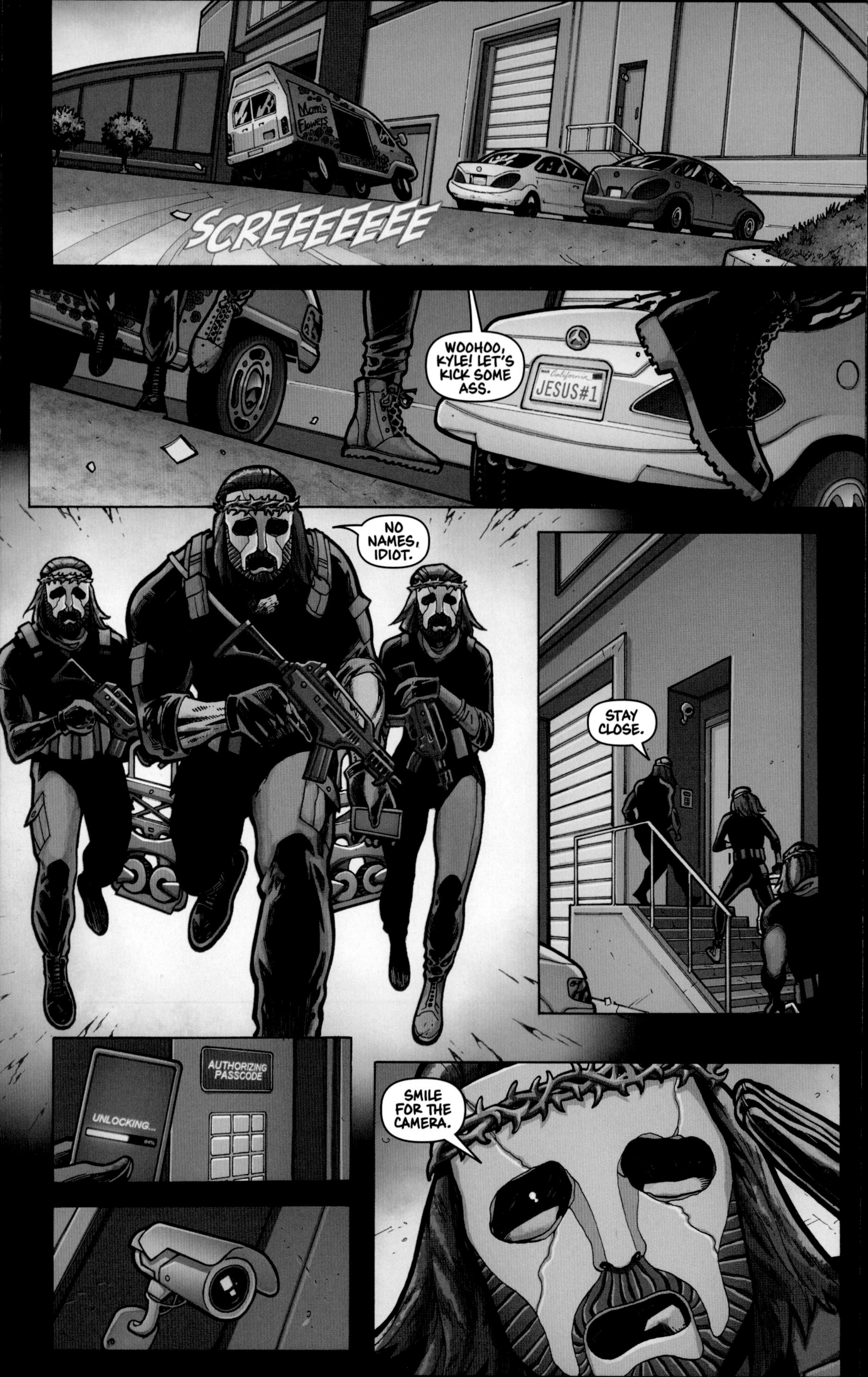

Mom's Flowers
SCREEEEEEEE
WOOHOO, KYLE! LET'S KICK SOME ASS.
California
JESUS#1
NO NAMES, IDIOT.
STAY CLOSE.
UNLOCKING...
AUTHORIZING PASSCODE
SMILE FOR THE CAMERA.

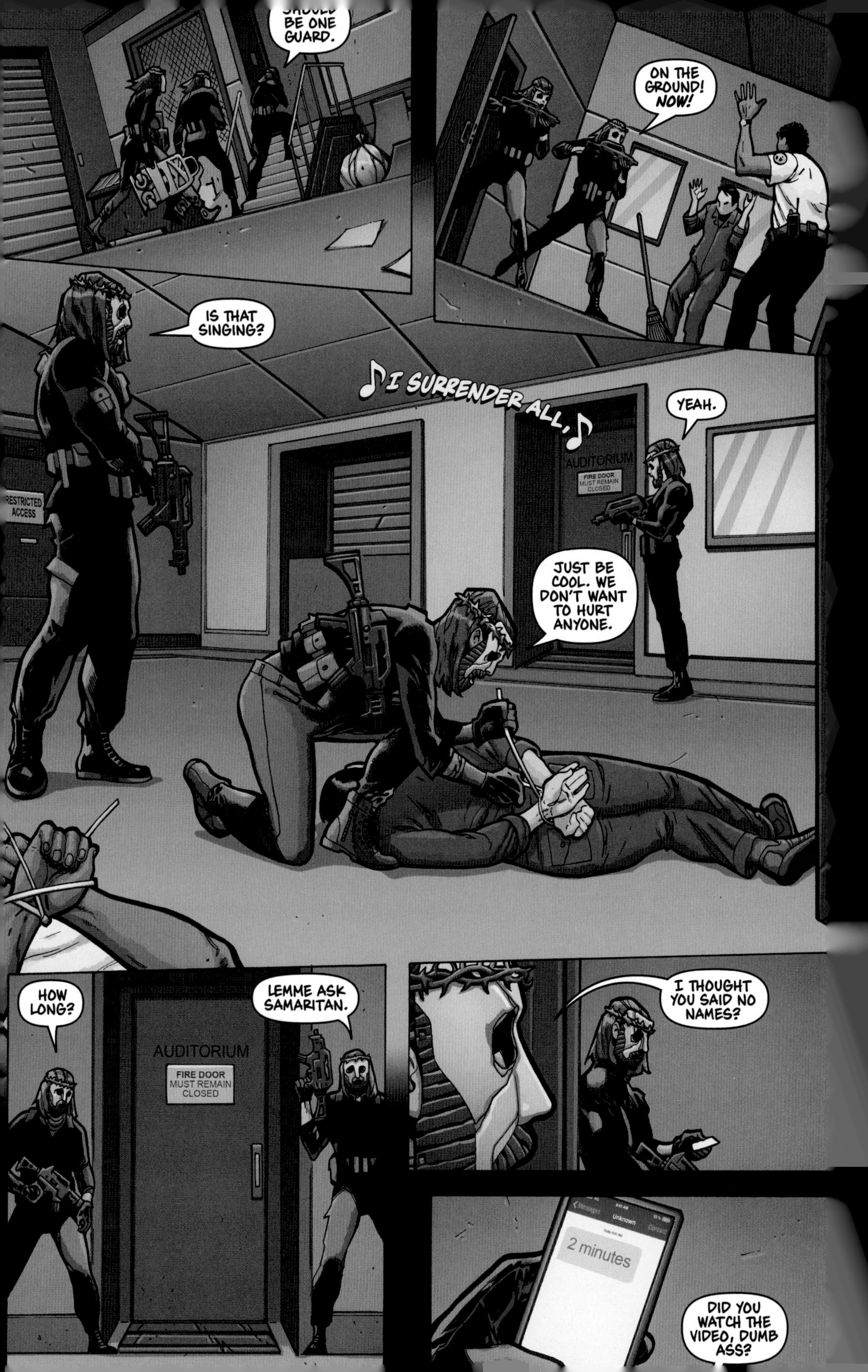
BE ONE GUARD.
ON THE GROUND! NOW!
IS THAT SINGING?
♪I SURRENDER ALL,♪
YEAH.
RESTRICTED ACCESS
AUDITORIUM
FIRE DOOR MUST REMAIN CLOSED
JUST BE COOL. WE DON'T WANT TO HURT ANYONE.
HOW LONG?
AUDITORIUM
FIRE DOOR MUST REMAIN CLOSED
LEMME ASK SAMARITAN.
I THOUGHT YOU SAID NO NAMES?
Unknown
2 minutes
DID YOU WATCH THE VIDEO, DUMB ASS?

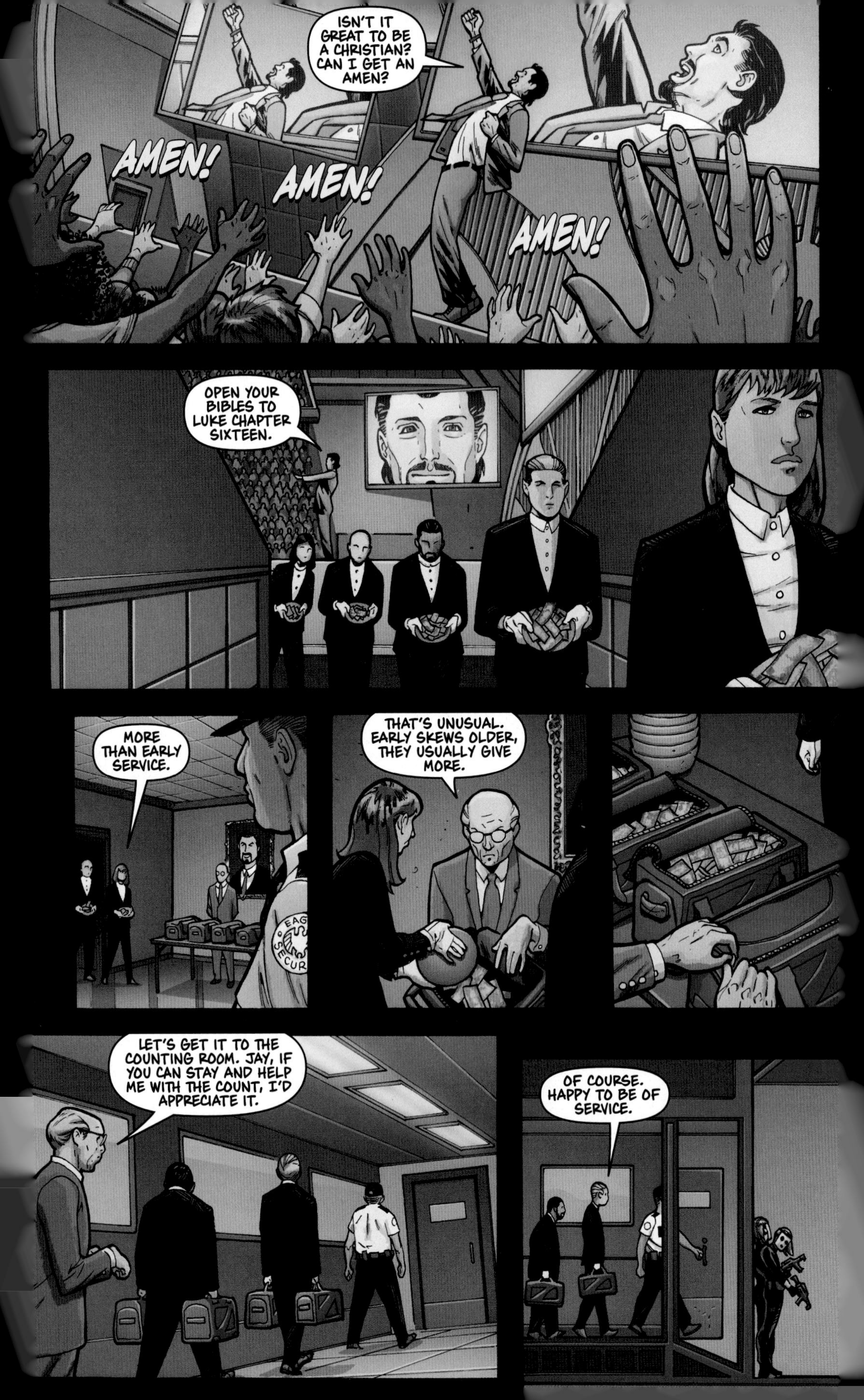
ISN'T IT GREAT TO BE A CHRISTIAN? CAN I GET AN AMEN?
AMEN!
AMEN!
AMEN!
OPEN YOUR BIBLES TO LUKE CHAPTER SIXTEEN.
MORE THAN EARLY SERVICE.
THAT'S UNUSUAL. EARLY SKEWS OLDER, THEY USUALLY GIVE MORE.
LET'S GET IT TO THE COUNTING ROOM. JAY, IF YOU CAN STAY AND HELP ME WITH THE COUNT, I'D APPRECIATE IT.
OF COURSE. HAPPY TO BE OF SERVICE.

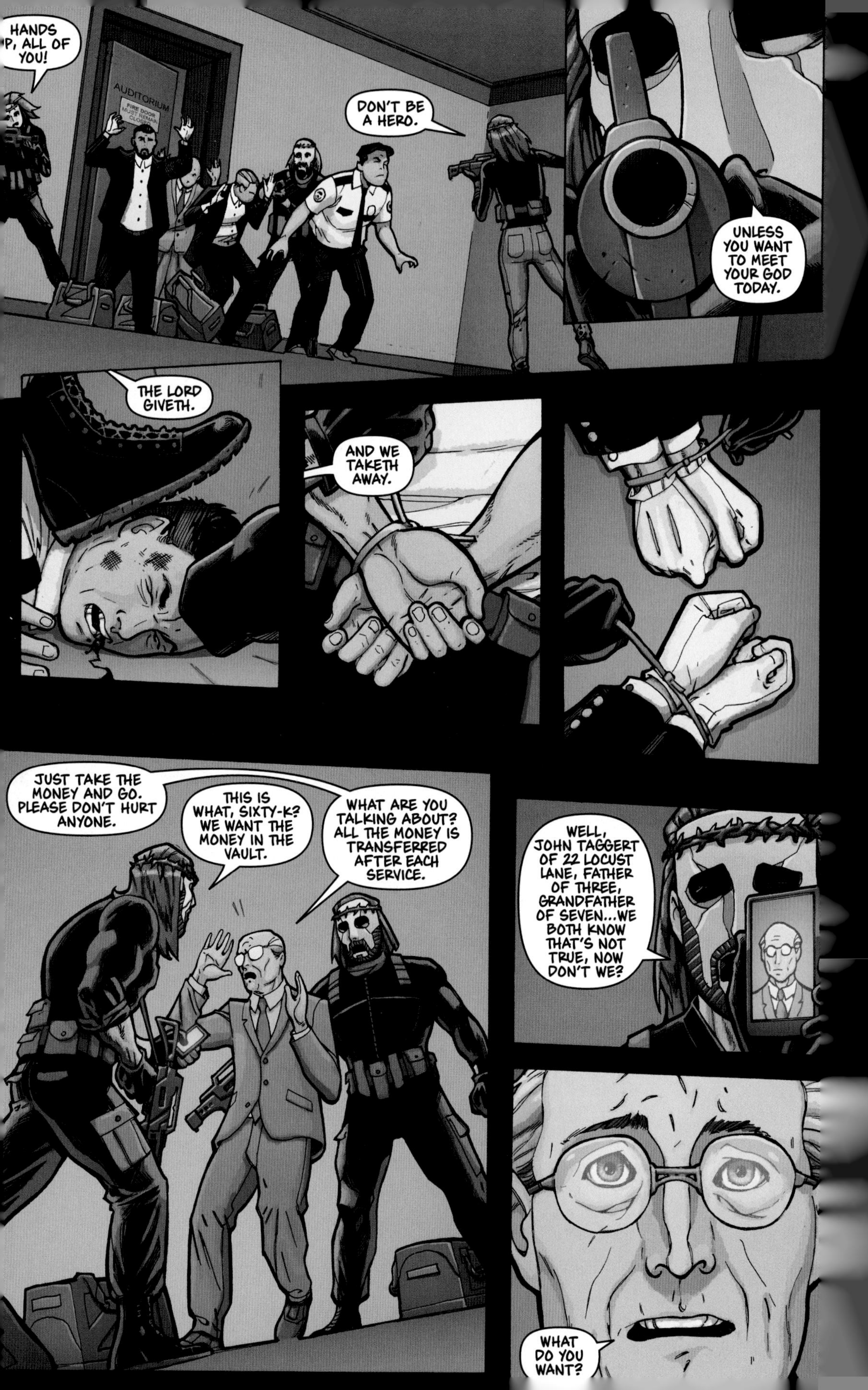
HANDS
P, ALL OF
YOU!
AUDITORIUM
FIRE DOOR MUST REMAIN CLOSED
DON'T BE A HERO.
UNLESS YOU WANT TO MEET YOUR GOD TODAY.
THE LORD GIVETH.
AND WE TAKETH AWAY.
JUST TAKE THE MONEY AND GO. PLEASE DON'T HURT ANYONE.
THIS IS WHAT, SIXTY-K? WE WANT THE MONEY IN THE VAULT.
WHAT ARE YOU TALKING ABOUT? ALL THE MONEY IS TRANSFERRED AFTER EACH SERVICE.
WELL, JOHN TAGGERT OF 22 LOCUST LANE, FATHER OF THREE, GRANDFATHER OF SEVEN...WE BOTH KNOW THAT'S NOT TRUE, NOW DON'T WE?
WHAT DO YOU WANT?

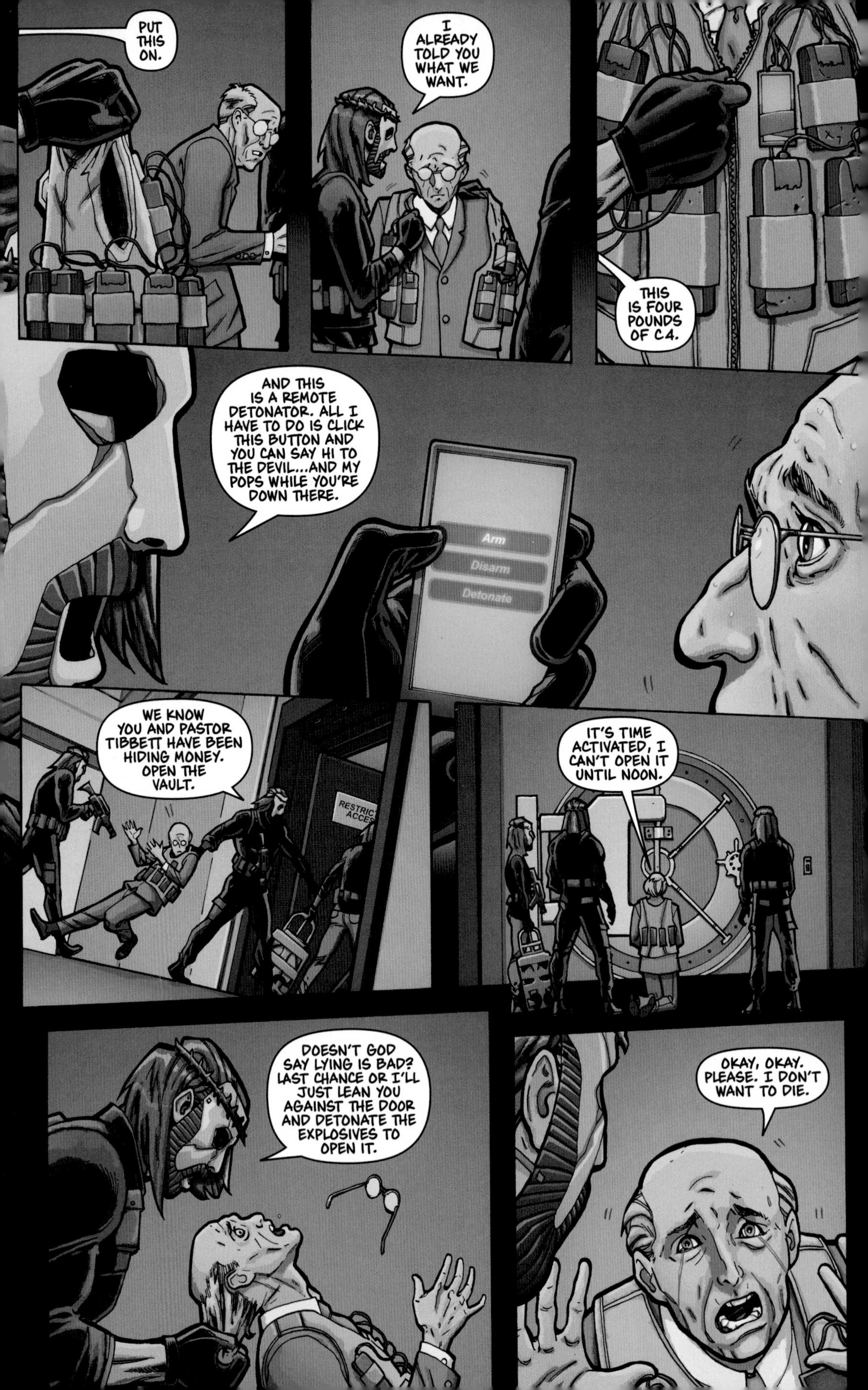
PUT THIS ON.
I ALREADY TOLD YOU WHAT WE WANT.
THIS IS FOUR POUNDS OF C4.
AND THIS IS A REMOTE DETONATOR. ALL I HAVE TO DO IS CLICK THIS BUTTON AND YOU CAN SAY HI TO THE DEVIL...AND MY POPS WHILE YOU'RE DOWN THERE.
Arm
Disarm
Detonate
WE KNOW YOU AND PASTOR TIBBETT HAVE BEEN HIDING MONEY. OPEN THE VAULT.
IT'S TIME ACTIVATED, I CAN'T OPEN IT UNTIL NOON.
DOESN'T GOD SAY LYING IS BAD? LAST CHANCE OR I'LL JUST LEAN YOU AGAINST THE DOOR AND DETONATE THE EXPLOSIVES TO OPEN IT.
OKAY, OKAY. PLEASE. I DON'T WANT TO DIE.

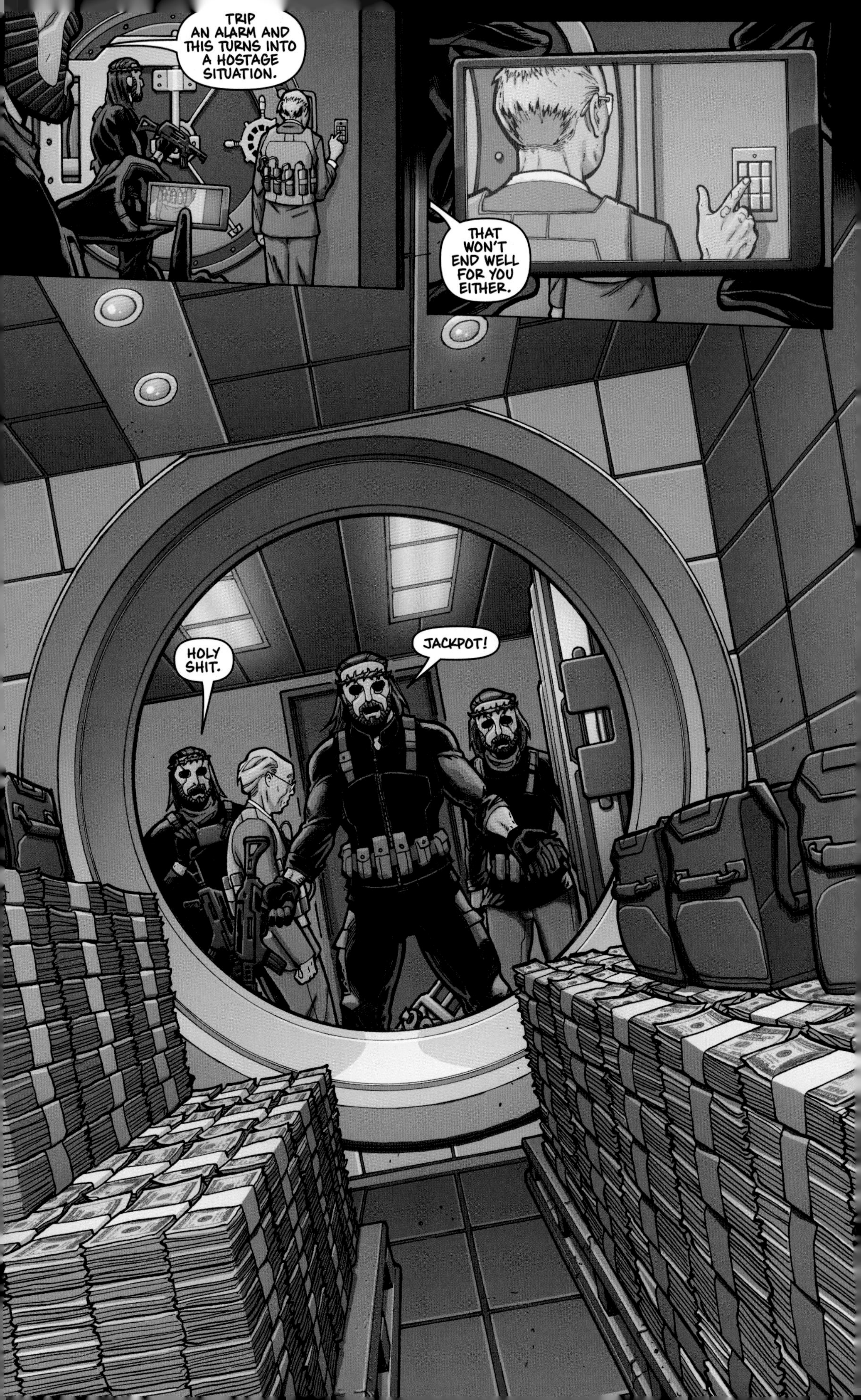
TRIP AN ALARM AND THIS TURNS INTO A HOSTAGE SITUATION.
THAT WON'T END WELL FOR YOU EITHER.
HOLY SHIT.
JACKPOT!

EDEN
POST
OFFICE

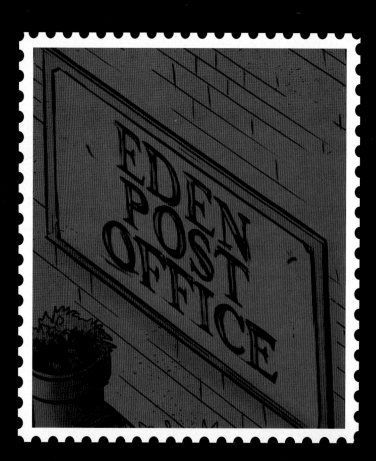

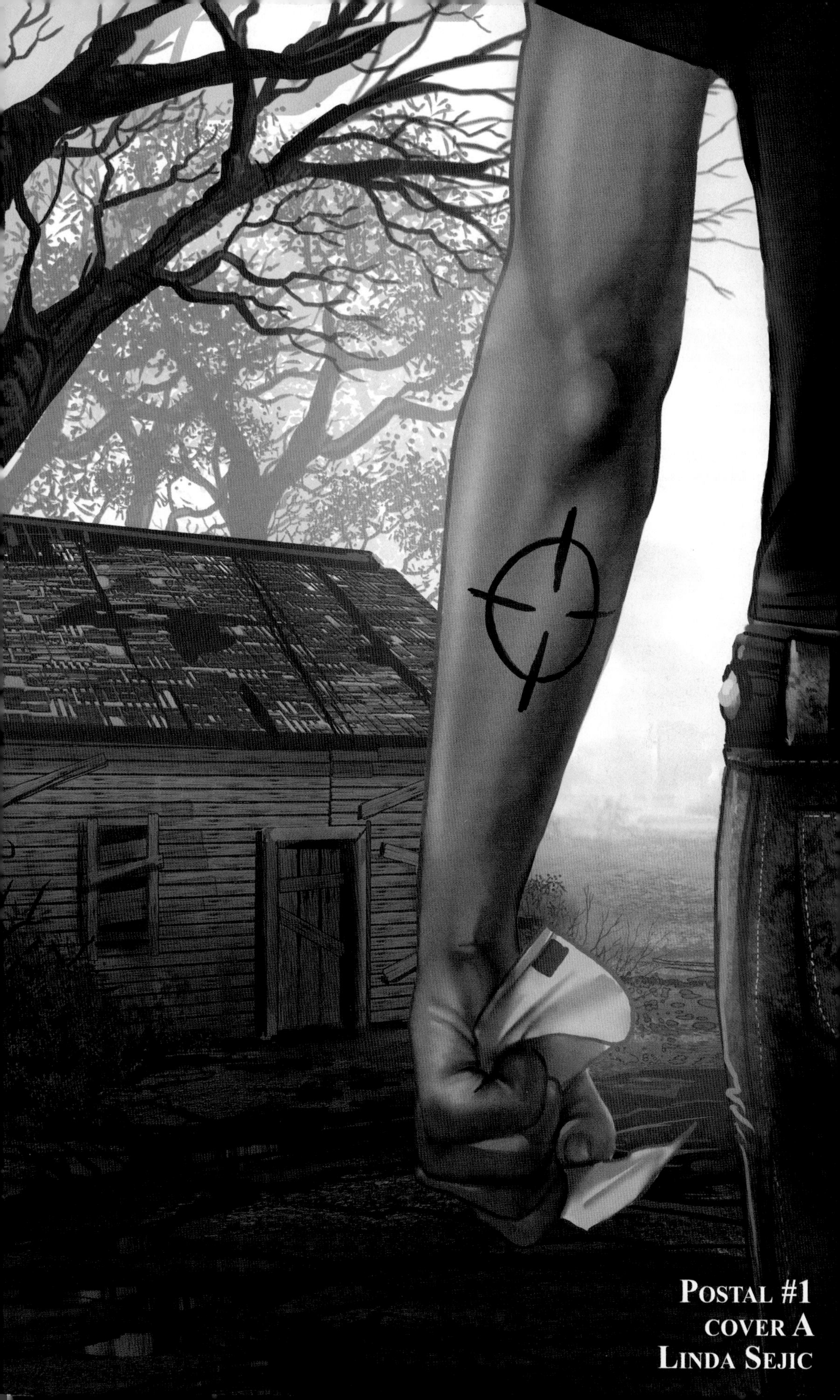

POSTAL #1
COVER A
LINDA SEJIC

Postal #1
Cover B
Isaac Goodhart & Betsy gonia

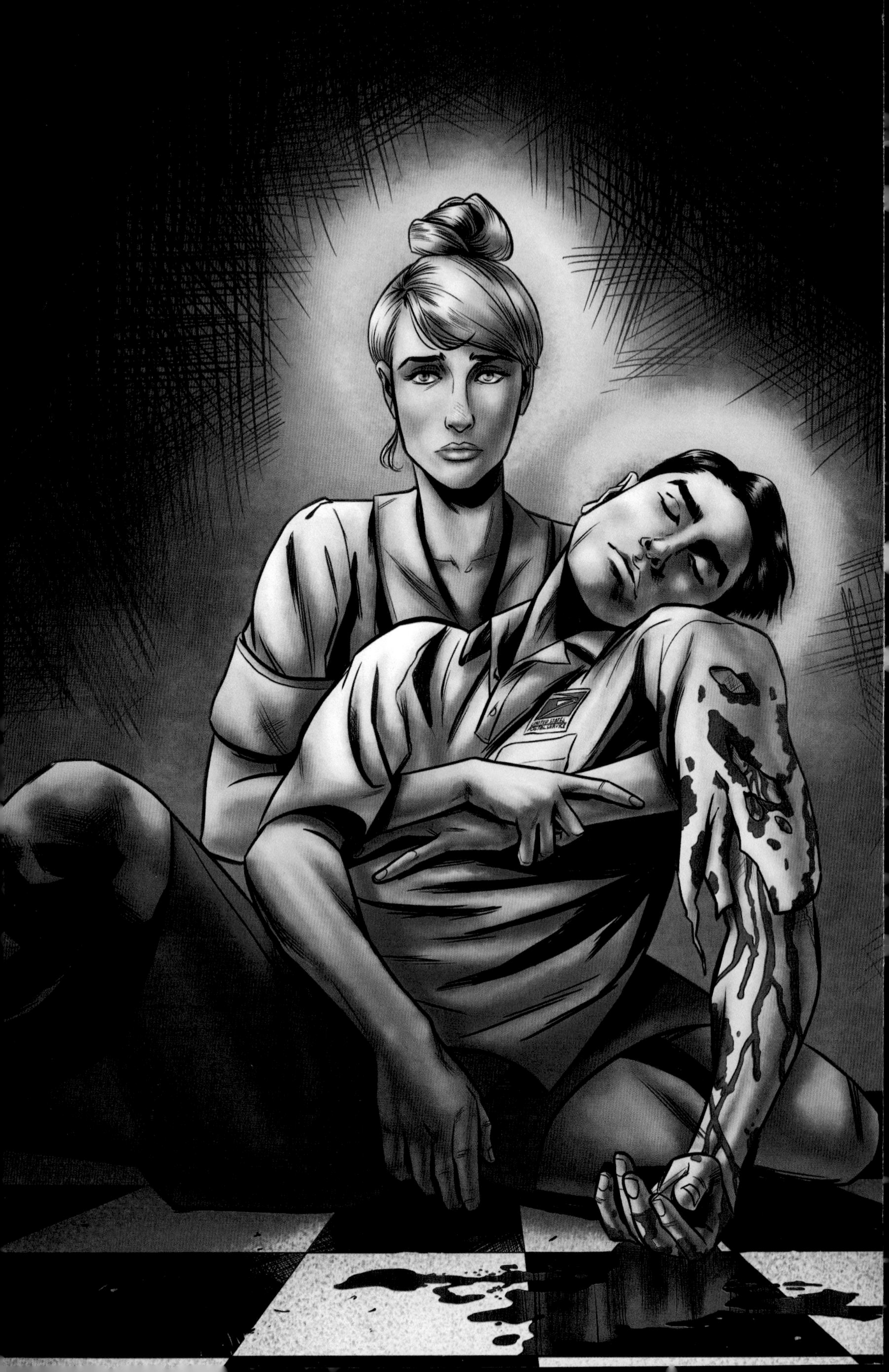

POSTAL #1
COVER C - RETAILER INCENTIVE
LINDA SEJIC

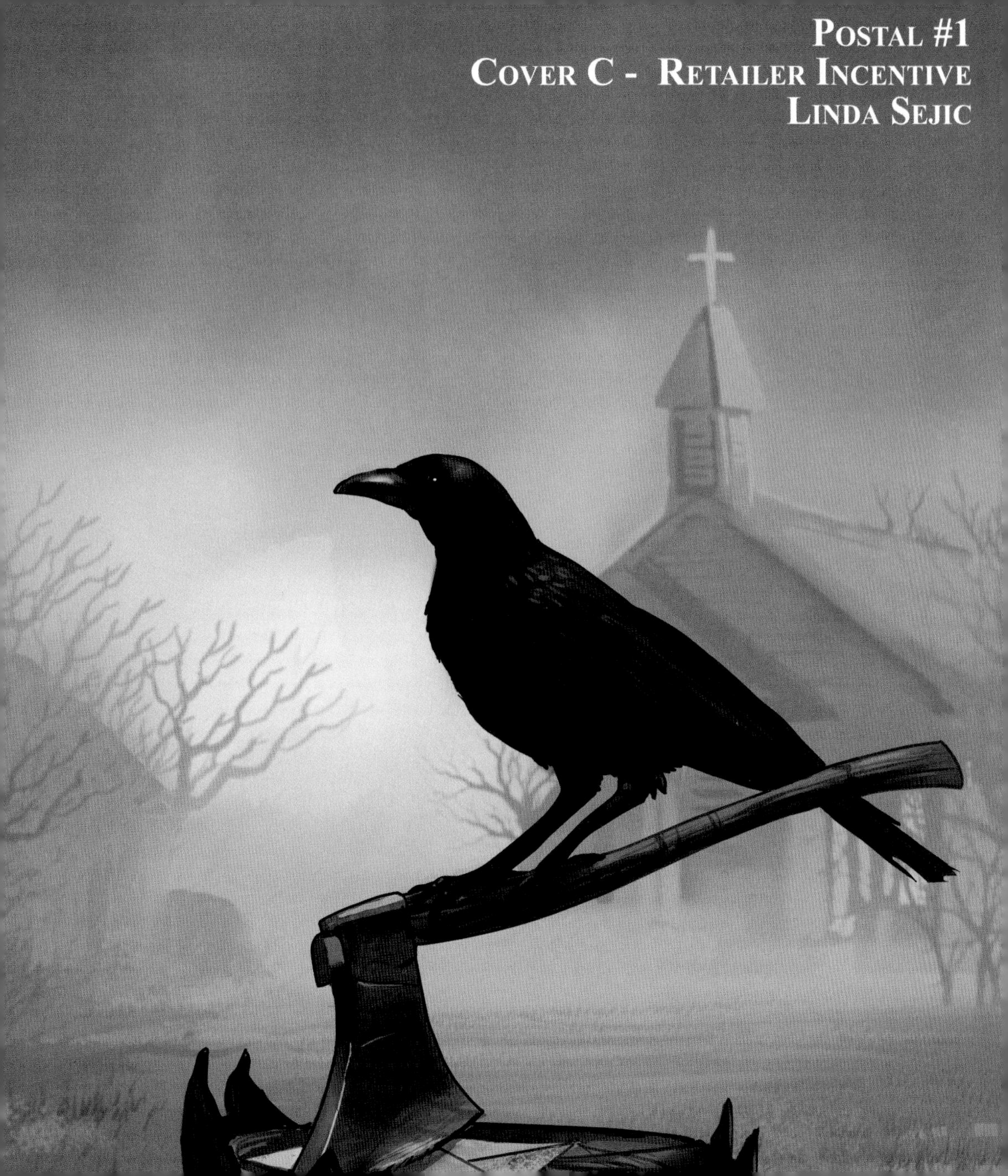

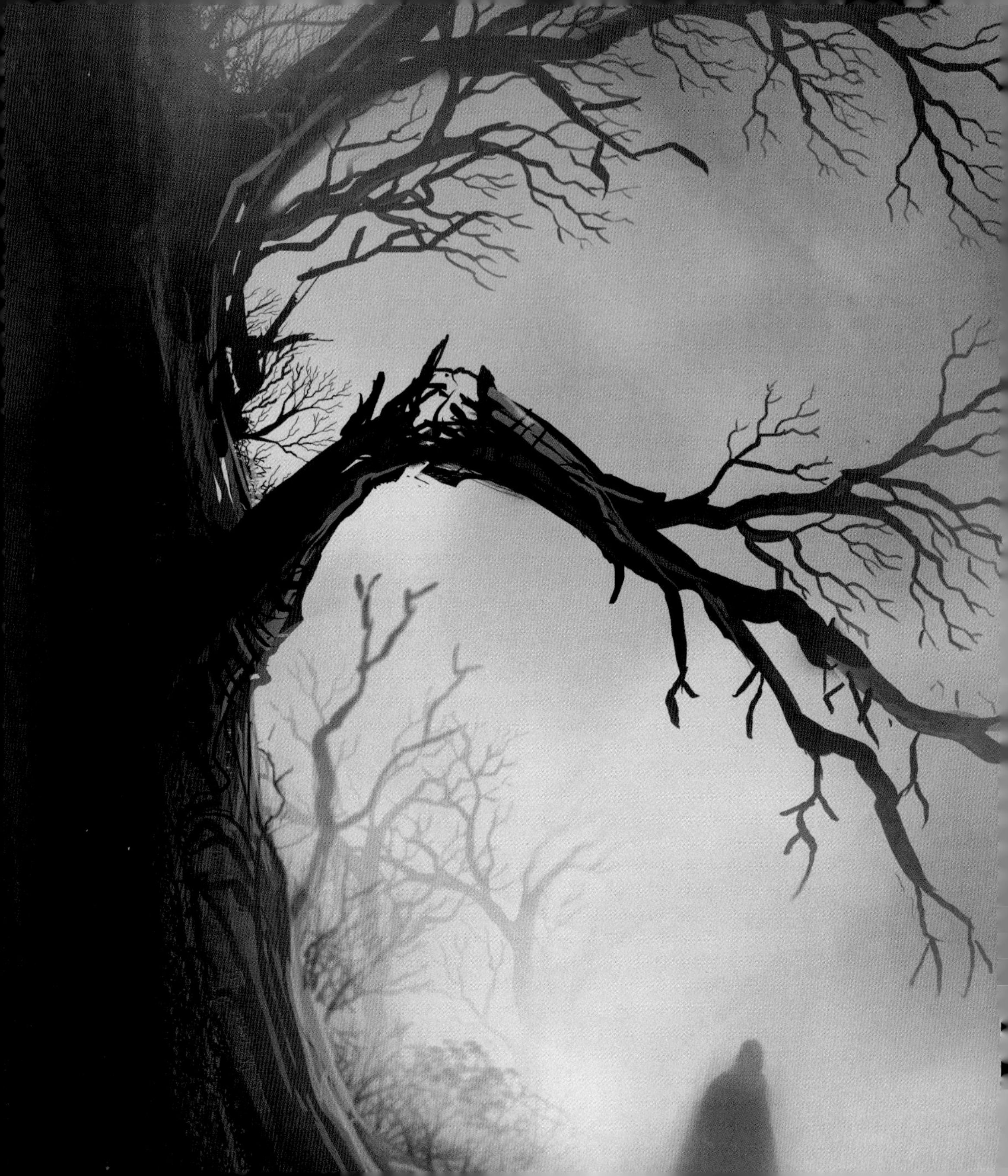

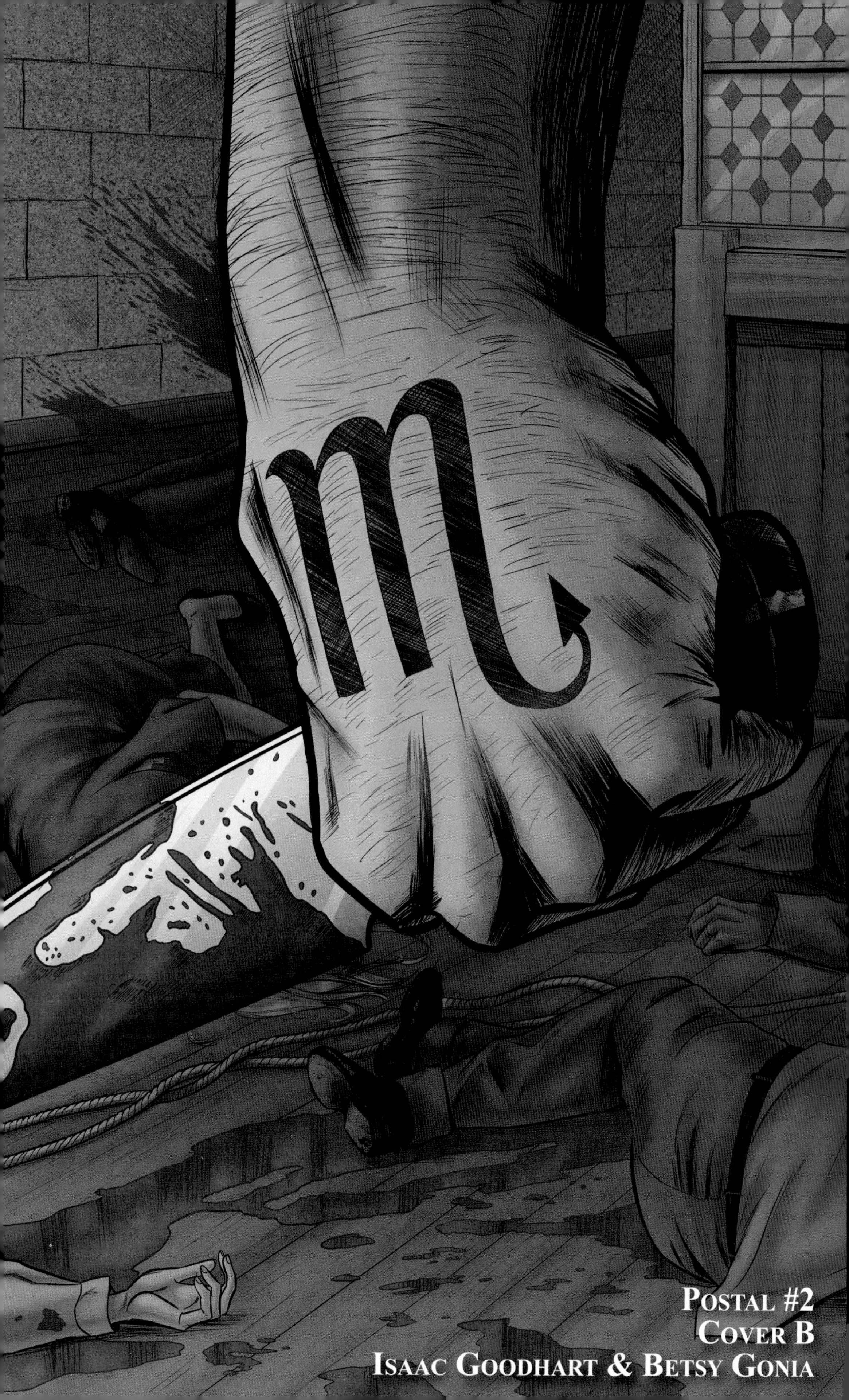

Postal #2
Cover B
Isaac Goodhart & Betsy Gonia

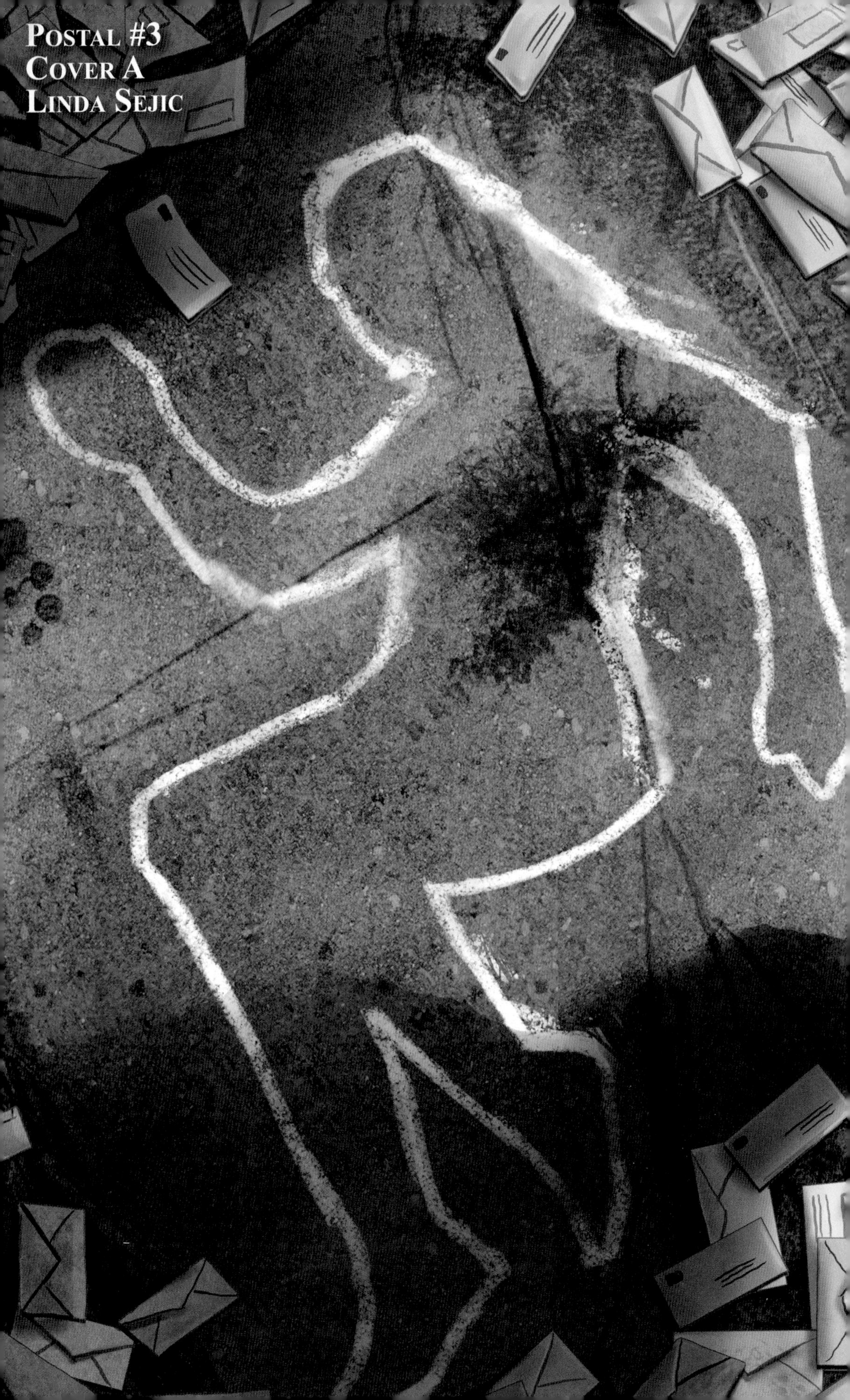

Postal #3
Cover A
Linda Sejic

Postal #3
Cover B
Isaac Goodhart & Betsy Gonia

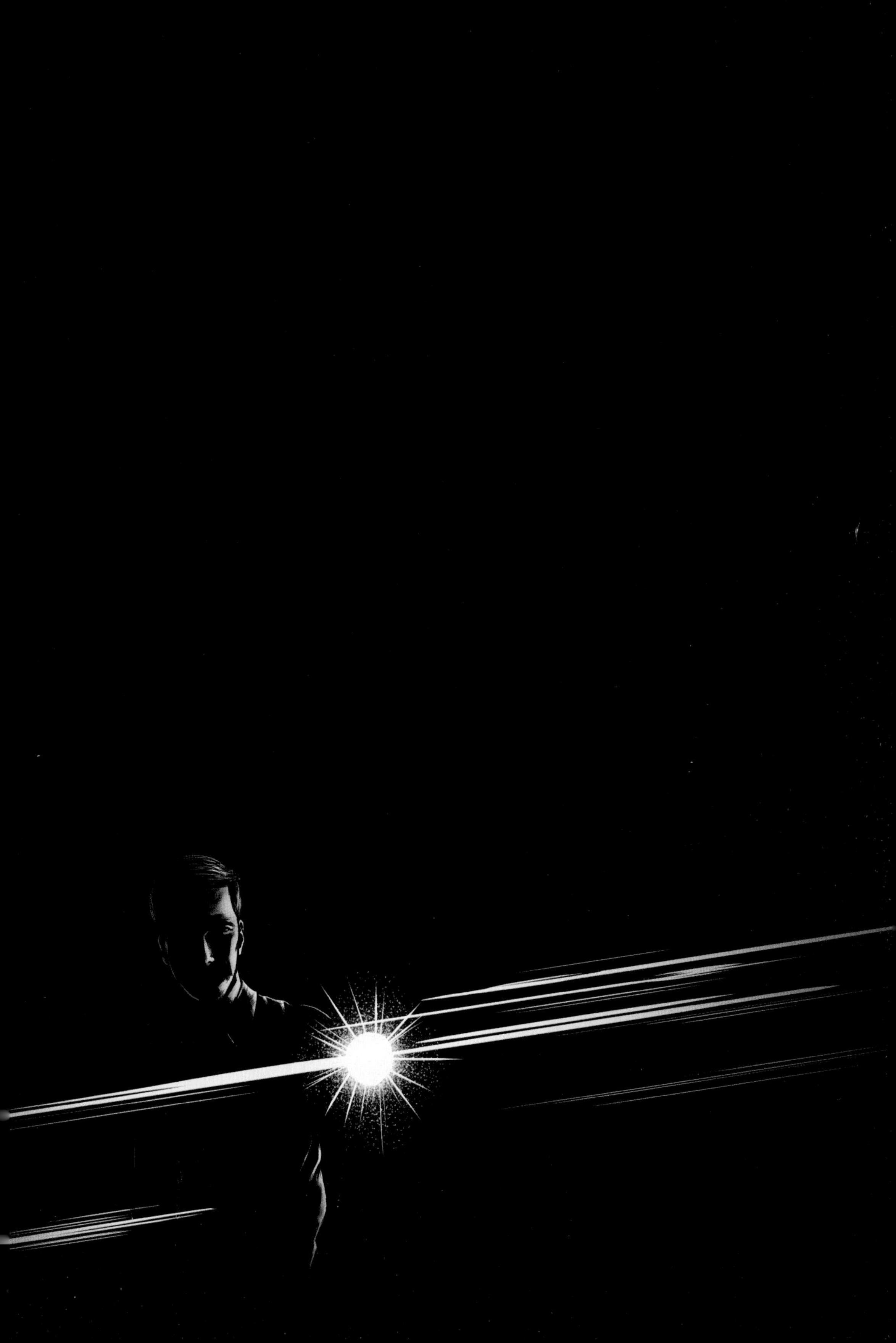

POSTAL #4
COVER A
LINDA SEJIC

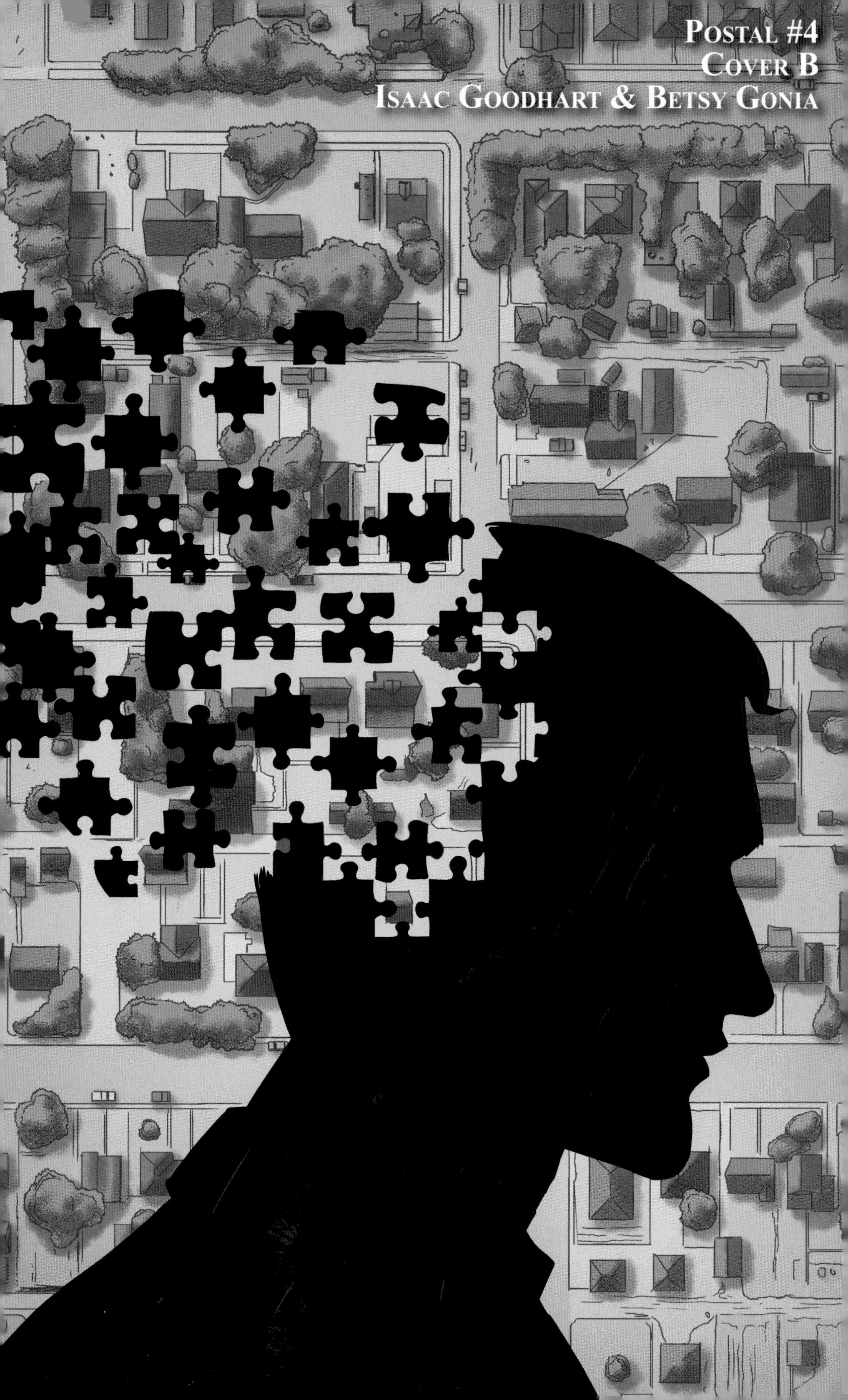
POSTAL #4
COVER B
ISAAC GOODHART & BETSY GONIA

Cover C - Comicpalooza Exclusive
Isaac Goodhart & Betsy Gonia

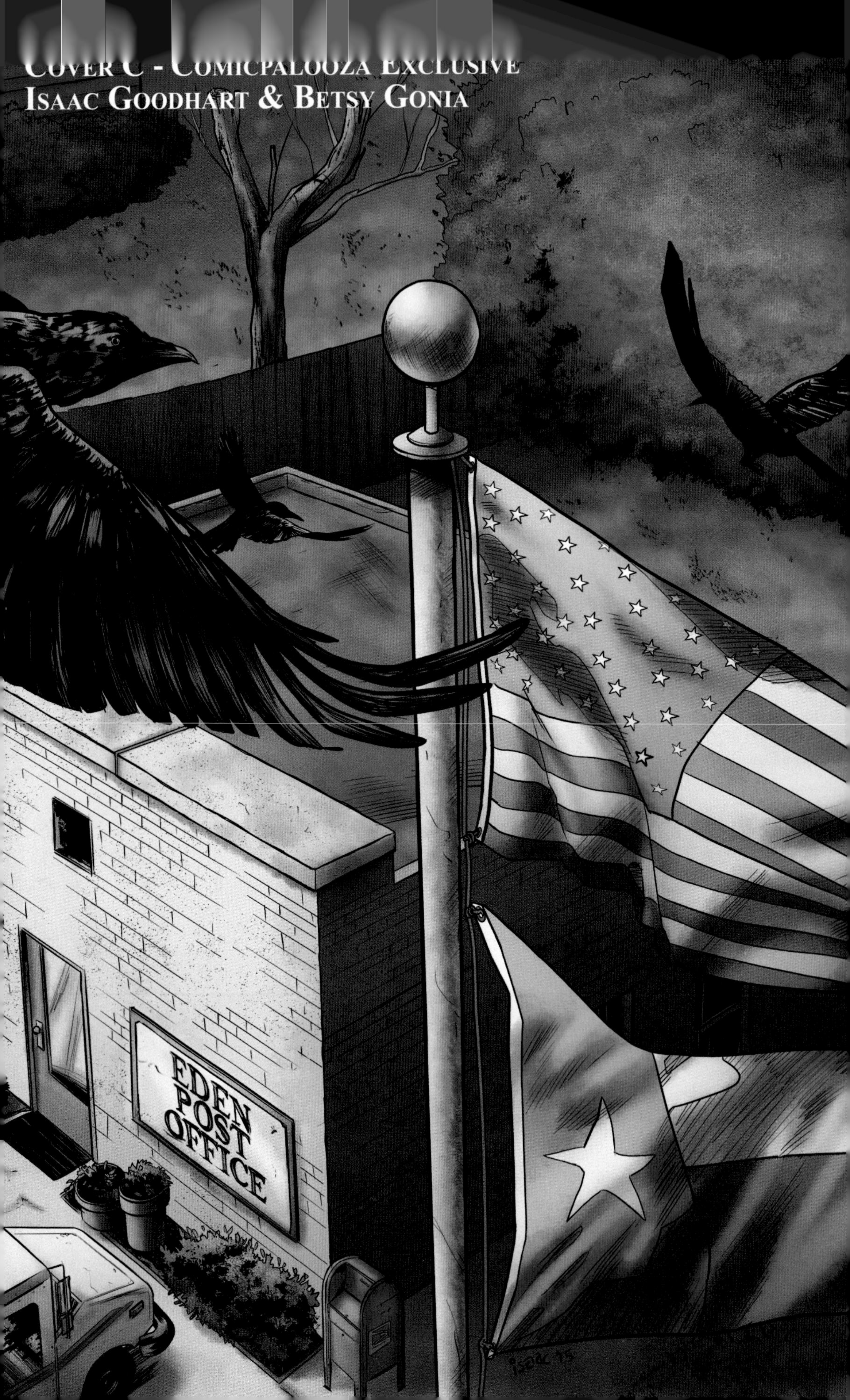
EDEN
POST
OFFICE

Meet the Creators

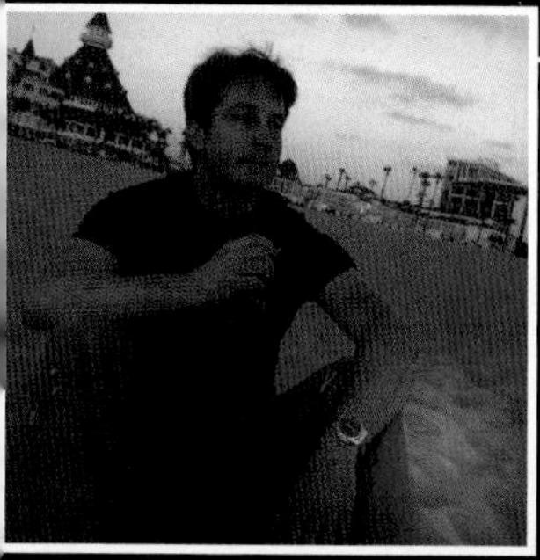

MATT HAWKINS

A veteran of the initial Image Comics launch, Matt started his career in comic book publishing in 1993 and has been working with Image as a creator, writer and executive for over 20 years. President/ COO of Top Cow since 1998, Matt has created and written over 30 new franchises for Top Cow and Image including Think Tank, Necromancer, VICE, Lady Pendragon, Aphrodite IX as well as handling the company's business affairs.

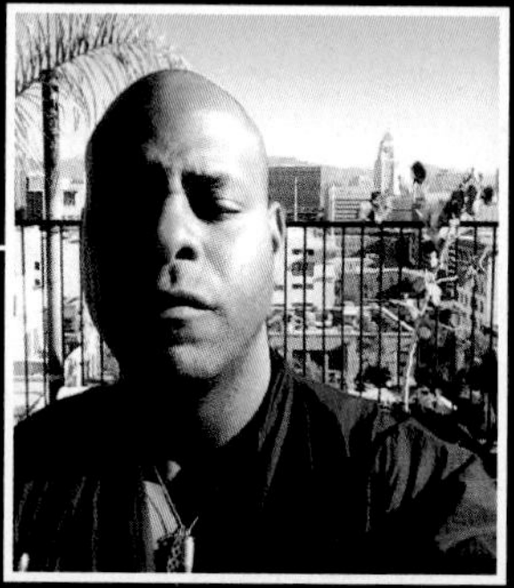

BRYAN HILL

Writes comics, writes movies and makes films. He lives and works in Los Angeles. @bryanedwardhill | Instagram/bryanehill

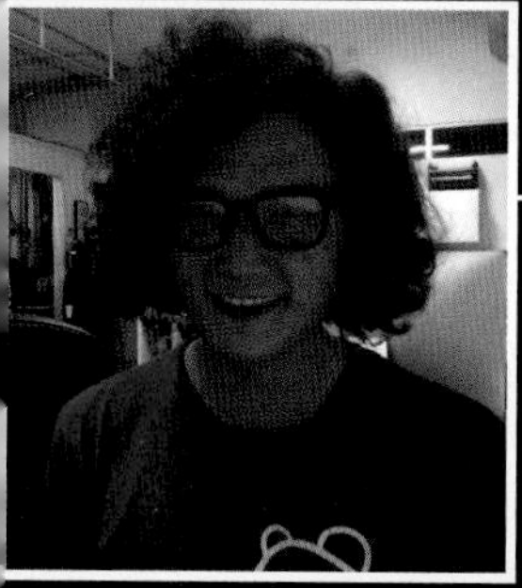

ISAAC GOODHART

A life-long comics fan, Isaac graduated from the School of Visual Arts in New York in 2010. In 2014, he was one of the winners for Top Cow's annual talent hunt. He currently lives in Los Angeles where he storyboards and draws comics.

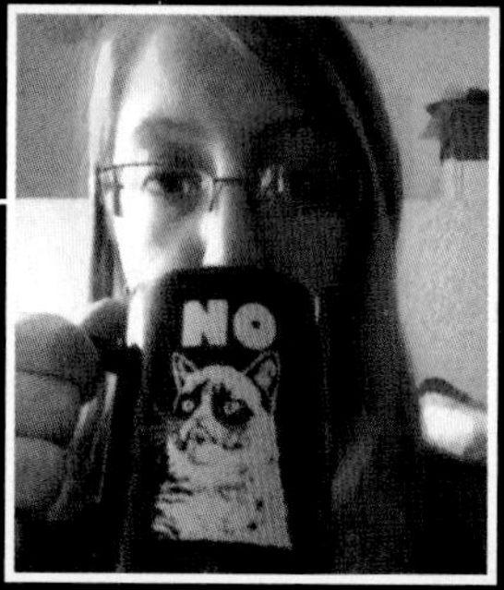
NO

BETSY GONIA

After graduating from the Savannah College of Art & Design in 2012, Betsy began working at Top Cow Productions. Now editing for the company, she also colors a few of their titles to actively partake in her favorite part of comic book creation.

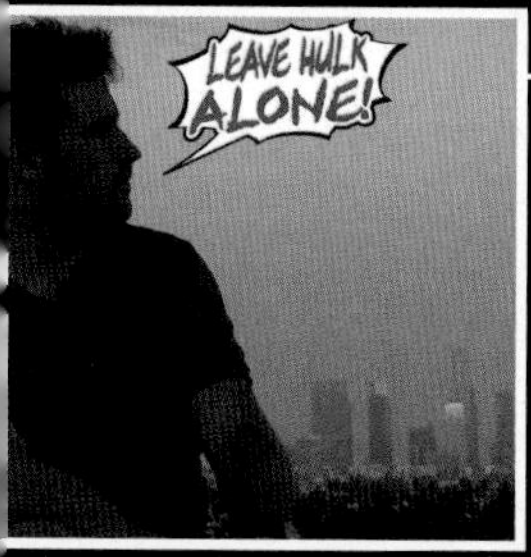
LEAVE HULK ALONE!

TROY PETERI

Starting his career at Comicraft, Troy Peteri lettered titles such as *Iron Man*, *Wolverine*, and *Amazing Spider-Man*, among many others. He's been lettering roughly 97% of all Top Cow titles since 2005. In addition to Top Cow, he currently letters comics from multiple publishers and websites, such as Image Comics, Dynamite, and Archaia. He (along with co-writer Tom Martin and artist Dave Lanphear) is currently writing (and lettering) *Tales of Equinox*, a webcomic of his own creation for www.Thrillbent.com. (Once again, www.Thrillbent.com.) He's still bitter about no longer lettering *The Darkness* and wants it back on stands immediately.

The Top Cow essentials checklist:

Aphrodite IX: Complete Series
(ISBN: 978-1-63215-368-5)

Artifacts Origins: First Born
(ISBN: 978-1-60706-585-2)

Broken Trinity Volume 1
(ISBN: 978-1-60706-051-2)

Cyber Force: Rebirth Volume 1
(ISBN: 978-1-60706-671-2)

The Darkness: Accursed Volume 1
(ISBN: 978-1-58240-958-0)

The Darkness: Rebirth Volume 1
(ISBN: 978-1-60706-958-0)

Impaler Volume 1
(ISBN: 978-1-58240-757-9)

Rising Stars Compendium
(ISBN: 978-1-63215-246-6)

Sunstone Volume 1
(ISBN: 978-1-63215-212-1)

Think Tank Volume 1
(ISBN: 978-1-60706-660-6)

Wanted
(ISBN: 978-1-58240-497-4)

Wildfire Volume 1
(ISBN: 978-1-63215-024-0)

Witchblade: Redemption Volume 1
(ISBN: 978-1-60706-193-9)

Witchblade: Rebirth Volume 1
(ISBN: 978-1-60706-532-6)

Witchblade: Borne Again Volume 1
(ISBN: 978-1-63215-025-7)

For more info , ISBN and ordering information on our latest collections go to:
www.topcow.com
Ask your retailer about our catalogue of our collected editions,
digests and hard covers or check the listings at:
Barnes and Noble, Amazon.com
and other fine retailers.

To find your nearest comic shop go to:
www.comicshoplocator.com